The
Philosopher's Kiss

The
Philosopher's Kiss

A NOVEL

PETER PRANGE

Translated by Steve Murray

ATRIA BOOKS

New York   London   Toronto   Sydney

ATRIA BOOKS
A Division of Simon & Schuster, Inc.
1230 Avenue of the Americas
New York, NY 10020

Originally published in Germany in 2003 by Droemersche Verlagsanstalt Th. Knaur Nachf. GmbH & Co. KG as *Die Philosophin*.

Published by arrangement with Droemersche Verlagsanstalt Th. Knaur Nachf. GmbH & Co. KG.

This book has been negotiated through AVA International GmbH, Germany (www.ava-international.de).

First Atria Books edition April 2011

ATRIA BOOKS and colophon are trademarks of Simon & Schuster, Inc.

For information about special discounts for bulk purchases, please contact Simon & Schuster Special Sales at 1-866-506-1949 or business@simonandschuster.com.

The Simon & Schuster Speakers Bureau can bring authors to your live event. For more information or to book an event, contact the Simon & Schuster Speakers Bureau at 1-866-248-3049 or visit our website at www.simonspeakers.com.

Designed by Akasha Archer

Manufactured in the United States of America

10   9   8   7   6   5   4   3   2   1

Library of Congress Cataloging-in-Publication Data

   Prange, Peter, date.
   [Philosophin. English]
     The philosopher's kiss : a novel / Peter Prange ; [translated from the German by Steven T. Murray]. —1st Atria Books ed.
     p. cm.
   Originally published in German as Die Philosophin in 2003.
    1. Philosophers—France—Fiction. 2. Diderot, Denis, 1713–1784—Fiction. 3. Volland, Sophie, 1716–1784—Fiction. 4. France—Intellectual life—18th century—Fiction. 5. Paris (France)—History—18th century—Fiction. 6. Paris (France)—Social life and customs—18th century—Fiction. I. Murray, Steven T. II. Title.

PT2676.R27P5513 2011
843'.92—dc22   2010035521

ISBN 978-1-4391-6748-9
ISBN 978-1-4391-6749-6 (ebook)

For Roman Hocke

first, because he invented me
second, because he never gives up
third, because it doesn't always have to be Rome

"All people are in agreement in the desire for happiness. Nature has given us all a law for our own happiness. Everything that is not happiness is foreign to us; only happiness has an unmistakable power over our hearts."

—Encyclopedia, article on "Happiness"

CONTENTS

The
Philosopher's Kiss

PROLOGUE

The Bonfire

1740

1

"Credo in unum Deum. Patrem omnipotentem, factorem coeli et terrae . . ."

Sophie closed her eyes as she knelt barefoot on the tamped clay floor of her bedroom to pray with all the fervor of her eleven-year-old heart. And this heart of hers was giving her no rest—it was pounding so fiercely, as if it wanted to jump out of her chest. The Apostles' Creed in Latin was one of the tests that the priest was going to require today of the village children studying for Communion, before they were allowed to approach the Altar of the Lord for the first time in their lives. Although Sophie had already prayed the Credo a dozen times this morning, she said it one more time aloud. The sacrament of Holy Communion, after the sacraments of baptism and confession, was the third door on the long, long journey to the Kingdom of Heaven, and this profession of faith within the Catholic Church was the key to opening this door in her heart.

". . . visibilium omnium et invisibilium. Et in unum Dominum Jesum Christum . . ."

Of course Sophie understood not a word of the prayer, but she knew for certain that the Lord God in Heaven loved her. As she murmured her way through the maze of Latin verses, she felt as if she were running through the boxwood labyrinth that Baron de Laterre had planted in the castle park. She felt utterly lost inside it, without hope, about to reach the end, but if she simply kept rushing along she would manage it somehow. Each verse was a new passageway, the end of each verse a turn in the labyrinth, and suddenly she would be standing free in a sun-drenched clearing. As if she had passed through the gates of Heaven into Paradise.

". . . Et exspecto resurrectionem mortuorum. Et vitam ventura saeculi. Amen."

"Don't you think you've practiced enough? It's time for you to get dressed."

Sophie opened her eyes. Before her stood her mother, Madeleine. Over her arm she carried a white, billowing cloud—Sophie's Communion dress.

"I'm so scared," said Sophie, pulling off her coarse linen shift. "I feel terrible."

"That's only because you've got nothing in your stomach," said Madeleine, slipping the dress over Sophie's naked body. She had sewn it out of a curtain remnant that the baron had given to Sophie. "You haven't eaten a thing since confession yesterday."

"What if I've forgotten one of my sins?" Sophie hesitated before going on. "Then will I be able to let the Savior into my soul at all? It has to be completely pure."

"What sort of sins have you committed?" Her mother laughed and shook her head. "No, I think your soul is as shining clean as the sky outside."

Sophie could feel the curtain material scratching the tips of her breasts, which had been strangely taut for the past few weeks. "People say," she replied softly, "that I'm a testament to sinful love. Shouldn't I confess that too?"

"Who said that?" asked Madeleine, and from the vigorous way she was doing up the buttons Sophie could sense that her mother was of an entirely different opinion.

"The priest, Abbé Morel."

"So, he says that, does he? Even though you relieve him of so much burdensome work? Without you he wouldn't be able to teach the other children at all."

"And he also says that Papa is in Hell. Because he never married you. If men and women have children without being married, then they're no better than cats, Monsieur l'Abbé says."

"Nonsense," declared Madeleine, fastening the last button on Sophie's dress. "The only thing that matters is that parents love each other, like your papa and I. Love is the only thing that counts."

"Except for reading!" Sophie protested.

"Except for reading." Madeleine laughed. "And everything else is foolish talk—pay no attention to it." She kissed Sophie's forehead and gave her a tender look. "How lovely you are. Here, see for yourself."

She gave her a little shove, and Sophie stepped in front of the shard of mirror that hung next to the small altar to the Virgin Mary on the whitewashed wall. When she saw herself she had a delightful shock. Looking back at her from the mirror was a girl with red hair falling in thick tresses over a beautiful dress, like the ones that only princesses and fairies wore in the pictures in fairy-tale books.

"If your papa in Heaven can see you now," said her mother, "he won't be able to tell you from the angels."

Could he really see her? Sophie wished so fervently for it to be true that she bit her lip. Her father had died three years before in a foreign land from a violent fever raging in the south of that country. She remembered him so vividly that all she had to do was close her eyes to see him: a big, bearded man with a slouch hat on his head and a pack on his back. He could imitate all the sounds of animals in his bright voice, from horses whinnying to the twittering of strange birds that were found only in Africa. His name was Dorval, and people called him a peddler, but for Sophie he had been a harbinger from another world, a world full of secrets and wonders.

Each year he had come to the church fair in their village, loaded down with knives and shears, pots and pans, notions and brushes—but above all with books. For three weeks, from Ascension Day to Corpus Christi, they would then live together like a real family in their tiny thatched-roof house at the edge of the village. Then Dorval would move on with his treasures. Those three weeks had always been the best time of the year for Sophie. She spent every moment in his company, listening to his stories of faraway places and dangerous adventures, about the fair Melusine or Ogier the Danish giant. With her father she would leaf through the thick, magnificently illustrated books from among the new ones he kept producing out of his pack. Handbooks, herbals, and treatises that apparently had an answer to every question in life: how to cure warts or the hiccups, how to banish the terror of Judgment Day, or how to overcome the evil powers in dreams. From Dorval Sophie had inherited her red hair and the freckles that were sprinkled across her snub nose and cheeks by the thousands, making her green eyes seem to shine even more brightly than her mother's. Even more important, she had gotten something from Dorval that set her apart from all the other children in the village—an ability that her mother said was worth more than all the treasures in the world: the ability to read and write.

Suddenly something occurred to Sophie, and in an instant her festive mood vanished.

"That man last night," she said softly.

"What man?" asked her mother, startled.

"The man with the feather in his hat. I heard what he told you."

"You were eavesdropping on us?" Madeleine had the same expression as Sophie did whenever she was caught doing something forbidden.

"I couldn't sleep," Sophie stammered. "Is he going to be—my new papa?"

"No, no, my dear heart, most assuredly not!" Madeleine knelt down and looked her straight in the eye. "How could you believe anything so foolish?"

"Then what did the man want from you? He tried to kiss you!"

"Don't worry about that. That's just how men are sometimes."

"So he's really not going to be my father?" Sophie asked. Her whole body was trembling because she was so upset.

"Cross my heart! I told him to go to the Devil," Madeleine said. "But what's wrong? You look all flustered. I think I'd better give you something to help you relax, or else you'll feel ill in church." From the shelf she took one of the many little bottles that stood next to the thick herbal tome, and poured a few drops of a black liquid into a wooden spoon.

"There now, take this," she said, holding out the spoon. "This will calm you down."

Sophie hesitated. "Isn't it a sin? Before Communion?"

"No, no, my heart, it's not a sin," said Madeleine as she carefully stuck the spoon into Sophie's mouth so that not a drop would fall on her white dress. "Medicine is allowed before Communion. You want to pass the test, don't you?"

2

The bells were already tolling in the distance when Madeleine and Sophie walked hand in hand along the path to Beaulieu, a village of three hundred souls. The blue sky arched over the vineyards and meadows that seemed to spread out beneath a green veil, and the warm dirt under Sophie's wooden clogs exuded once more that sweet, familiar scent that already gave a hint of spring. Glittering in the sunshine, the waters of the Loire rolled through the valley. Bushes of lilac and broom lined the banks of the river, and the towers and battlements of Baron de Laterre's castle, where Sophie's mother worked as a seamstress, rose up in front of the hills. Its presence over the land was mighty, as if the castle wanted to take all life under its protection.

"Now isn't this a day to be happy?" Madeleine asked, squeezing her daughter's hand.

"Do you think so?" Sophie could still feel a slight rumbling in her stomach in spite of the medicine. Besides, there was one more question on her mind that she simply had to ask her mother before they reached the church. Yet she didn't know how to broach the topic, so she said simply, "Monsieur l'Abbé said that people are not put on this earth to be happy."

"Who would believe that from the abbé?" Madeleine laughed. "On a day like this?"

Sophie stopped and looked at her mother. Although Madeleine was wearing the ugly shift of shame that she always had to don to go to church, her green eyes were radiant, as if nothing on earth could distress her; around her neck fluttered the colorful silk scarf that Dorval had given her on his last visit. So Sophie mustered her courage.

"Mama . . ." she said hesitantly.

"Yes, my treasure?"

"Will you take me to Communion today if I pass the test? The way the other parents take their children?"

Her mother stroked her hair. Suddenly the joy had vanished from her face. "Ah, Sophie, you know that's impossible. Abbé Morel has banned me from the sacraments."

"Please, I want you to come with me. I don't want to be the only one who goes to the Communion bench alone."

"The priest would just chase me away, and that would be much worse."

"Père Jaubert wasn't allowed to go to Communion either, yet Abbé Morel gave him the Host on Easter anyway."

"Père Jaubert is the sexton, so the priest turns a blind eye."

"Père Jaubert peed in the cemetery, and that's much worse than not being married."

"Oh, Sophie, I'll be with you in the church. Imagine me standing behind you and watching everything you do."

"That's not the same." Sophie had to fight back the rising tears. "Please, Mama. If you won't come with me, then I don't want to take Communion either."

Madeleine stared into her daughter's eyes. Then she shrugged and said, "You think we should give it a try, at least?"

Sophie nodded vigorously. With a smile Madeleine took her hand again.

"All right. Then we'll take a lesson from Père Jaubert."

When they entered the church a few minutes later, the small house of God was already filled almost to bursting. Everywhere excited children were fidgeting, holding hands with their parents. With a hint of pride Sophie ascertained that she was the only girl wearing a white dress. She truly looked like an angel next to the other children, wearing their brown and gray smocks, which made them look like miniature peasants.

She dipped her fingers into the holy water font and made the sign of the cross. But as she walked with her mother up the nave toward the altar, a whispering arose as if someone had released a nest of vipers beneath the pews.

"To think that she dares show her face here!"

"Look at that gaudy scarf! What a vain person!"

"And see how she's decked out her daughter!"

There were still some seats in the third pew. As Madeleine and

Sophie paused before the altar to give a little curtsey, the other parishioners moved to the far end of the pew, as if afraid they might catch something. Sophie suddenly felt quite weak.

"*Dominus vobiscum!*"

"*Et cum spirito tuo!*"

Luckily at that moment the mass began. The congregation stood, and followed by four acolytes Abbé Morel took his place, dressed in his old, threadbare vestments. As he sang the Kyrie in his high falsetto, someone behind Sophie whispered:

"Red hair and freckles . . ."

She looked around in fury. Joseph Mercier, the son of a day laborer, grinned at her with his impudent face, so round that it looked like it would explode. He was the stupidest boy in the whole village, and nobody knew that better than Sophie. At the behest of the priest, who could hardly write anything but his own name anymore, she gave lessons to the children of the village three times a week. She tried to teach them to read prayers and other sacred writings with the help of the Virgin Mary Almanac. But Joseph couldn't tell *A* from *O*. Abbé Morel's voice called her back to the present.

"Recite the Lord's Prayer. Marie Poignard!"

The testing of the communicant children had begun. A red-cheeked girl stumbled to her feet and faltered her way through the Lord's Prayer. In the choir stalls Sophie noticed Baron de Laterre, who was following Marie's stammering with an amused expression on his face. When the baron noticed Sophie, he gave her a friendly nod. She returned his greeting; then for a moment a fluffy red feather appeared behind the baron. Was that the young man who had visited her mother the night before? Sophie craned her neck to see his face.

"Sophie Volland, I asked you something!"

Sophie gave a start. Abbé Morel was giving her a stern look, staring at her with his small gray eyes. His face was as wrinkled and spotty as a salamander's.

"*Credo in unum Deum . . .*"

As if on command she rattled off the Apostles' Creed, but she hadn't reached the third article when Abbé Morel interrupted her.

"You're supposed to answer my question. In what respect does the Body of Our Lord differ from normal food?"

Sophie bit her lip. She had prepared for every question except this one. Abbé Morel's gaze grew even sterner. Sophie began to panic. If she couldn't answer, she would fail. Good Lord, what did the priest want to know?

Sophie's stomach began growling so loudly that it could be heard several rows back. Then the answer came to her.

"Ordinary food is nourishment for the body, but the bread of the Lord is food for the soul—the bread of eternal life."

"Bravo, Sophie!" shouted the baron, nodding to her once again.

With a sour smile Abbé Morel showed his yellow teeth and moved on to query another child. Sophie heaved a sigh of relief. Although a huge stone had been lifted from her heart, yet another hurdle lay before her, a second test that might be more difficult than the first. She was so nervous about the holy transubstantiation that her stomach almost turned over as the acolytes swung their censers and the sweet smell of incense filled her nostrils.

"Lamb of God, Thou takest away the sins of the world, have mercy upon us!"

The moment had arrived. Abbé Morel announced one by one the names of the children who on this day would receive the Body of Christ for the first time, and he asked their parents to guide them to the altar of the Lord. Sophie reached for her mother's hand. It was as damp as hers.

"May this food strengthen you when God and the Devil wrestle for your souls."

Now it was Sophie's turn. She had to clench her teeth so that they wouldn't chatter as she made her way out of the pew with her mother; her heart was pounding so hard that she could hear her blood rushing in her ears like the Loire during spring flood. Side by side mother and daughter approached the altar, exactly the way Sophie had wished. Abbé Morel took the Host from the chalice and Madeleine knelt down.

"What? The whore dares?"

These murmured words spread through the church. The priest looked up in annoyance. Sophie saw his face: his bushy eyebrows rose, his jaw dropped—only now did Abbé Morel realize who was beseeching him for the bread of the Lord. He instantly took a step back as if seeing the very Devil before him.

Sophie said a quick prayer: "Please, dear God, help us!"

The whole church seemed to be holding its breath. Not a sound, not a movement, only the fluttering of a sparrow that had slipped inside the house of God. Suddenly a slight cough broke the silence, coming from the choir stalls. Abbé Morel spun around. The baron had stood up. With a grave expression he nodded to the priest, who failed to understand and responded with a quizzical glance.

"By the Devil, what are you waiting for?"

Finally the priest understood, and the miracle occurred: Abbé Morel turned to Madeleine and, holding the Host high in the air, he growled:

"The Body of Christ!"

"Amen!"

As Sophie saw her mother receiving the Host, tears welled up in her eyes. God had heard her prayer! Overjoyed, she sank to her knees.

"The Body of Christ!"

"Amen!"

Sophie's heart rejoiced, her soul exulted, a heavenly giddiness seized hold of her as she closed her eyes and opened her mouth. Everything inside her was prepared in ardent anticipation to receive the Body of the Lord.

But then the inconceivable happened. The Host had barely touched her tongue when Sophie's stomach convulsed; a violent, uncontrollable reflex that gripped her intestines and squeezed her gullet. Then her stomach emptied in a dreadful torrent.

An outcry filled the sanctuary.

As Sophie came to her senses, she looked down at her white dress. A gigantic stain covered her lap, as black as diseased gall.

3

"The seamstress Madeleine Volland, born and residing in the parish of Beaulieu, is accused of having acted against the faith and the common good of the state, in that she practiced the black arts on her daughter, Sophie, and administered to her a pernicious potion which caused her on the day of her first Holy Communion to vomit up the Body of the Lord, in the presence of the incumbent priest and the assembled congregation."

The hall was filled when the royal judge read the charge. His aged face, furrowed by the years, remained as indifferent as the law itself while he read the indictment, although the wig on his pate slipped now and then. Each time he adjusted it with the same movement of his left hand, repeated already a thousand times, without interrupting the flow of his words. All eyes were directed at the accused, who with her head held high but with her hands in chains stood before him, flanked by two bailiffs.

In the audience sat a young man who differed strikingly from the other viewers in the hall by virtue of his distinguished attire, a *gentilhomme* of eighteen years, the scion of one of the most illustrious families in France and a member of several academies. With bitter satisfaction he listened to the speech of the judge, taking in each word the way a sick man imbibes the drops of medicine he needs to relieve an overwhelming pain. He was attentively searching for some change in the face of the accused, but in vain. This woman, who did not show the slightest sign of remorse, had inflicted on him the worst crime that a woman could ever commit against a man. He was so distraught that he kept turning his hat on his lap—a black, broad-brimmed hat adorned with a red plume.

He was the one who had reported Madeleine Volland to the court in Roanne on the very day the unheard-of incident had occurred in the village church of Beaulieu, in order to repay her for the injustice that he had suffered at her hands. He had even broken with his host, Baron de Laterre, who had implored him to retract his complaint. But as a jurist who had studied with the most prominent scholars in the land, the young man knew that the law was on his side. In the year 1682 a royal edict had made "all deeds of magic or superstition" a punishable offense, likewise "saying and doing things that cannot be naturally explained," and imposed the death penalty for blasphemies committed in connection with "similar imagined magical effects or deceptions." These laws were still valid.

The judge adjusted his wig again and turned to the accused.

"Madeleine Volland, do you confess to having committed the afore-mentioned crimes as here reported?"

"I confess to being guilty of living. Otherwise I have committed no crime."

A loud murmur arose in the courtroom; a couple of spectators laughed. The judge pounded his gavel on the bench to restore quiet.

"Where is my daughter?" asked Madeleine in the ensuing silence.

She turned around and looked at the assembled onlookers. Calmly, without batting an eyelash, she fixed the spectators with her gaze, one after the other, as if hoping to discover Sophie among them. The young man could feel his mouth going dry as the eyes of the accused moved steadily toward him, but he was determined not to flinch.

Suddenly their eyes met. In that instant Madeleine's eyes narrowed to two slits, and from these slits flashed such hatred as though a serpent had hurled its venom into his face.

He uttered a quiet moan. How he had longed for Madeleine to look at him with her green eyes, and what a torment it was now that she had done so. He had loved this witch, had yearned for her as for no other woman before. Ever since he'd last seen her, in Baron de Laterre's castle, he no longer seemed to possess any will of his own. When he woke up in the morning, his first thought was of her; when he went to sleep, he saw her face before him. He had been ready to sacrifice everything for her: his fortune, his title, his honor. But she had spurned him, scorned his love, and when he had implored her to yield to him, as he laid his heart at her feet, she had told him to go to Hell. Yet later that same night, as he lay in the arms of a whore in Roanne, he realized with horror that her words were no empty threat: She had cast a spell on him, poisoned him, just as she'd done with her daughter, Sophie.

Although it now cost him a superhuman effort, he did not avert his eyes from hers. The time had come when she would pay for her crime. At the formal complaint hearing he had offered personally to prove her guilt to the court, present himself for the punishment of retaliation in the event that he failed to do so. But he was confident of his cause. In Madeleine's dwelling he had found a book that left no doubt about her guilt. A thick volume bound in pigskin from which she had drawn her evil knowledge: a herbarium. In addition to the descriptions of herbs and other plants, it contained hundreds of recipes: to counter urgent urination and seeing ghosts, to counter worm damage and the evil eye. This book, which she had used in an attempt to elevate herself above other human beings, would now, as it lay next to the Bible on the judge's table, seal her fate.

As if she could guess his thoughts, Madeleine turned her gaze away.

"I call the plaintiff to the witness stand!"

The young *gentilhomme* stood up and stepped before the judge.

"For personal reasons the witness has requested that his name be kept confidential. As he is known to the court to be a man of high rank and lineage, this wish will be granted."

The bailiff fetched the Bible. With his back to the accused, the plaintiff raised his hand and repeated the oath, though he could feel her icy gaze on the back of his neck.

Then justice took its course.

4

Fat raindrops smacked against the windowpanes and ran down like tears before Sophie's face. The whole world seemed hidden behind an impenetrable gray veil of water and fog.

In the castle, no one was stirring yet. Ever since Sophie awoke she had been sitting at the window of the small chamber where she had been taken, at the end of the servants' corridor. From there she watched the new day breaking. Dripping with moisture, the trees and bushes of the park gradually emerged from the nighttime gloom. Beyond the black labyrinth of boxwood in which Sophie had so often played, she began to discern in the milky fog at the edge of the meadows the solitary willow trees that stood there in the water, their branches drooping limply as if they were dead.

Where was her mother? Baron de Laterre, who had taken Sophie in, had evaded all her questions, as had Louise, the eldest lady-in-waiting at the castle, in whose care the unmarried baron had left Sophie. Then in all haste he had set out for Paris to make inquiries, intending to ensure that Madeleine would soon be set free.

How many hours, how many days had passed since then? With no real sense of time Sophie sat at the window, gazing out into the park and trying to follow the dark, winding paths of the labyrinth. She was living better at the castle than ever before in her life; she had her own feather bed and meals were served three times a day, with as much food as she liked, and yet she had never suffered so much. She would much rather wake up on her straw-filled bedding than among these soft pillows, and she would much rather be eating her daily millet gruel instead of roast meat and stewed compote! As far back as she could remember, she had never been separated from her mother for more than a few hours. Madeleine had always put her to bed at night and wakened her in the morning, and they had eaten each meal of the day together. When the bailiff from Roanne had arrested Madeleine, Sophie felt as though she were walking across a bridge at a dizzying height above a chasm, and suddenly the hand she was holding had let go.

What bad thing had her mother done? Was she having to atone for the fact that she had gone to Communion, even though Abbé Morel had banned her from taking the sacrament?

Uncertainty weighed on Sophie's soul like an oppressive and inconceivable sense of guilt. At first she had been furious and protested loudly, asking everyone in the castle where they had taken her mother. But just like the baron and Louise, the servants and lackeys also held their tongues about what had happened to Madeleine; if anyone tried to explain, Louise would hasten over and forbid all speech.

The longer the silence went on, shielding Sophie from the truth as if from an evil enemy, the more her rage gave way to a vague and unsettling fear. She could feel that something terrible was in the offing; she sensed an ominous danger lurking. Her foreboding grew as she noticed the embarrassed looks and the words whispered behind her back. She began to pray for her mother, lighting candles in the chapel, and almost every night she dreamed that she and Madeleine and her father would all live together at the castle as a happy family. When she awoke in the morning, reality was scarcely to be endured.

Sophie sighed. Before her, on the other side of the windowpane, a sparrow alighted on the sill and scolded loudly as it tried to dry its wet feathers. The rain had let up, and the sky had brightened so much that the dark paths of the boxwood labyrinth in the park had now emerged clear and distinct. How easy it was to see the way to freedom from up here, and how difficult when she was caught inside the labyrinth.

"Come, put on your clogs."

Sophie hadn't heard anyone come into the room. Louise was standing in the doorway, nodding to her.

"Abbé Morel is coming soon to fetch you. He's taking you to the village."

At those words from the lady-in-waiting, hope stirred in Sophie's heart.

"Are we going to see my mother?"

Louise nodded, but she did so with lowered eyes.

5

Damp gray smoke rose over the village square of Beaulieu, where six laborers under the supervision of the sexton, Père Jaubert, were cursing as they attempted to light a bonfire. All night long the rain had been pouring down. A wet wind, much too cold for the season, had driven dark clouds down the valley, and now the wood would not catch fire: five armloads of beechwood, forty pounds each, and a hundred bundles of brushwood and three sacks of coal.

"Such wastefulness!" complained Jacqueline Poignard, the mother of little Marie. "That's wood we won't have in the bake house next winter."

"Punishment is necessary," replied the day laborer Mercier. "That wench simply went too far."

Although there was no work to be done on this day, everyone in the village was on their feet. They all streamed to the church to fortify their souls before the great spectacle began. The custom of punishing blasphemers in this way was as old as humanity, but it had not been used anywhere in the province for decades. Only the oldest citizens could even remember the ritual, just as they did the celebrations for the birth or wedding of a high noble. For three days people had been streaming in from the whole valley, eager to witness a spectacle that had been denied them for far too long.

A new gusty rain shower drenched the vineyards and meadows as Abbé Morel took to the road after the early mass. His galoshes squeaked in the mire, the rain dripped from his hat and ran down his neck, and yet he put one foot in front of the other so slowly that he seemed not to want to reach his destination at all.

Had Madeleine Volland deserved such a punishment? The old priest didn't know. How often had he admonished the woman to live in sin no longer? All she had to do was to marry Dorval the peddler, or abstain from carnal knowledge of him, in order to be granted absolution, but she had always refused. Not even after the death of her husband, who had made her pregnant outside of wedlock, had she been ready to repent. She seemed to detest the thought of casting off her linen shift of shame and reconciling with the church.

To delay his arrival at the castle, Abbé Morel made a detour past the village green. Never before in his long life had a walk made him so depressed, and he would have given his right thumb to spare himself and the child from this. But that decision had not been left to his discretion. The court had ordered that Sophie must attend the administering of judgment as a necessary example for her endangered soul. It was Morel's task to accompany her.

When should he tell the child where this path was taking her? Or was it better to leave her in the grace of ignorance until the very last moment?

With his cassock completely drenched, Abbé Morel knocked at the gate of the castle. Baron de Laterre had set off for Paris on the same day that his guest, the young *gentilhomme,* had hastened to Roanne to lodge his complaint. The baron had wanted to intercede with the parliament, within whose jurisdiction the trial against Madeleine Volland fell, and to speak on behalf of the accused.

A ray of hope still glimmered in the heart of the old abbé, and as long as it was God's will, he would keep that hope alive.

6

A crowd, larger than any Sophie had ever seen, filled the village square as she arrived in Beaulieu with Abbé Morel. The rain had almost stopped; only a few drops fell, yet a damp wind was still gusting across the valley. The smell of burning wood hung in the air.

Involuntarily, Sophie grasped the priest's hand.

"What are all these people doing here? Why aren't they at work?"

Abbé Morel cleared his throat. Had the time come to tell the child the truth? He cleared his throat again, but when he saw Sophie's inquiring look, the truth died on his tongue.

"Who knows? Maybe there will be another miracle, and the baron will return from Paris in time, before it's too late." Sophie didn't know what the priest was talking about. But the quiet confidence she had felt on the way here faded at his words, and again she had a premonition of lurking danger—the same feeling that had plagued her ever since she had been taken from her mother. Uncertain now, as if somewhere an evil monster lay in wait, she looked all around. When people caught sight of her they fell silent and stepped aside to make way.

Suddenly Sophie spied her mother only a stone's throw away, at the end of a passageway now opened through the crowd.

"Mama . . ."

The word stuck in her throat. What had they done to her mother? In the middle of the square, surrounded by hundreds of people who were howling and jeering as if it were Carnival time, a scaffold had been erected. On it stood Madeleine, her hands and feet chained like a criminal, dressed in her shift of shame. Her shaved head was bowed, and she seemed so lost and forlorn in the midst of all those people that it made Sophie's heart bleed.

Behind the scaffold a gigantic bonfire blazed, the flames shooting up into the rainy gray sky, as if the fires of Hell were licking at the firmament.

"Mama!"

The cry that finally escaped from Sophie's throat was louder than all the noise in the square. Madeleine raised her head, and a faint light passed over her face.

"Sophie!"

She sensed rather than heard Madeleine's reply. She wanted to go to her mother, but the priest's hand held her back. The colorful scarf around Madeleine's neck, Dorval's gift, fluttered in the wind as if mocking her. All at once Sophie felt only fear—utter, horrifying fear.

"Let me go!" she screamed. "I want to go to my mother!"

She pulled and tugged with all her might to get away from Abbé Morel, kicking his shin again and again, tearing at his cassock, spitting at him and biting his hand. But the old priest held her arm as tight as a vise, while the district judge in his black robe and gray wig climbed onto the wet wooden scaffold.

At his appearance the crowd fell silent. Suddenly it was so quiet that the raindrops could be heard striking the planks. Even Sophie instinctively stopped struggling as the judge unrolled a parchment and raised his voice to read the sentence that had been pronounced on her mother.

". . . the seamstress Volland endeavored with contemptible and evil intent to do her own child harm, inasmuch as she administered to her a pernicious potion . . ."

What could this mean? All sorts of thoughts were tumbling through Sophie's mind. In her confusion she grasped only scraps of the speech, though certain words stood out like thorny branches from a dark, impenetrable thicket: *lust, black magic, concocting poisons . . .*

". . . for this reason the court has arrived at the verdict that the evildoer shall suffer the pain of death as punishment for her grievous guilt . . ."

What was this man talking about? Incapable of understanding the meaning of his speech, Sophie saw the judge stick the parchment roll in the depths of his robe and then nod to a huge man standing off to the side of the scaffold, his chest bare and his arms folded. Only now did she realize the scaffold was a gallows looming over her mother.

"She will die before the flames reach her," said Abbé Morel. "She must not suffer more than necessary."

Sophie wanted to turn her eyes away, but she could not. As if under a spell she stood there watching helplessly as the half-naked giant stepped over to her mother and placed the noose around her neck. When he tightened the noose, Sophie once again caught her eye; Madeleine's lips moved and again she called out something to her daughter. Sophie understood only a single word:

". . . happiness . . ."

At that moment the floor dropped away under Madeleine's feet. A cry swept across the square, and she was instantly yanked up by the rope. For a second she dangled in the air; then there was a sudden jolt, and the beam from which the body hung swiveled over the bonfire.

"Aaaaahhhhh . . ."

The tension of the crowd was suddenly released, and a moan issued from countless throats as the flames caught the clothes of the hanged woman. Sophie screamed like an animal, screamed and screamed and screamed, as if she would never be able to stop screaming. She screamed out her love and her pain and her despair. But steady and unwavering, the fire greedily devoured first the limbs and then the torso, the flames licked and danced until soon her mother's entire body was engulfed, but all life had already vanished. With her head wrenched to the side, her arms and legs dangling in the air, Madeleine Volland had given up her resistance forever.

All at once Sophie felt paralyzed. She no longer smelled the stench of the fire, nor did she feel the rain on her face; all she saw before her were things that transcended her understanding. Was this really happening, what she saw here before her eyes? A gray cat fled from the scaffold, taking long leaps, as if chased by invisible demons. And as the cat disappeared among the crowd, a black, evil thought rose up inside Sophie: It was her fault, what was happening here.

"Come," said Abbé Morel, "let's go home."

But Sophie refused to budge from the spot. She wanted to stay; she had to stay until the bitter end and see with her own eyes how her mother's remains burned up in the flames. That was the only way she would ever comprehend the incomprehensible thing that had taken place here. Tears poured from her eyes, forming hot, salty streams down her cheeks, mixed with the falling rain. She reached for the priest, from whom she had fought so hard to free herself. Now she took his hand, clasping it as if it were her last refuge on earth.

"May God bless her poor soul!" whispered Abbé Morel.

As the priest said this, the heavens split open somewhere high above, and through a rift in the cloud cover that they could not yet see, a long, oblique beam of sunlight spilled onto the place of execution. A little later the eternal blue of the sky revealed itself between two mountains of clouds; the rift grew rapidly, as if a great curtain were parting on high, and as the crowd in the square gradually dispersed, a magnificent rainbow arched over the countryside. Like a sigh escaping from the earth, a fresh breeze moved through the valley. The spectacle was over, the sin of the seamstress Volland atoned for, and her daughter, Sophie, could finally leave the site, her heart broken and her limbs heavy as lead.

Later, as twilight descended over the village, exhausted from a day that had been much too long, a rider approached the execution site at great speed. It was Baron de Laterre, coming directly from Paris. He raised his arm in the air, waving a decree signed by the president of the parliament, stating that the verdict of the district court of Roanne, whatever it might be, was not to be carried out.

But at this late hour the village square of Beaulieu was as deserted as the world on the eve of Judgment Day. Only a couple of dark figures were searching through the ashes for the charred bones of the woman who had been executed. It was said that such relics would bring good luck, and perhaps they could even be sold.

7

❧ ☙

"Freckles and red hair lead straight to the Devil's lair!"

"Come along, don't listen to them."

Abbé Morel took Sophie's hand and pulled her away. How grateful she was that he was protecting her from the other children, who shouted after her at the edge of the village. She had always thought that the priest didn't like her because she knew full well that he couldn't read. But she was wrong. Abbé Morel wasn't angry at her, he was simply strict. Before she was allowed to take First Communion he had also required of her the Apostle's Creed in Latin, while in all other parishes the Lord's Prayer in French sufficed. Now this stern man was like a father to her, her protector and friend, the only person besides Baron de Laterre who still believed in her. She squeezed his big, heavy hand as hard as she could and looked up at him. His salamander face took on a few more wrinkles as he returned her smile, and his lips bared his yellow teeth.

Without looking back she left Beaulieu behind. Walking along the Loire, above which a cloudless summer sky once again spread out its clear, deep blue, Sophie moved farther and farther away from the village where she had been born and raised. She could no longer live at the castle. She had woken up two days ago with blood between her thighs, and Louise, the lady-in-waiting, had told her that now she was a woman, and they would have to find other lodgings for her. On that same morning the baron and the priest had decided to take her to the convent. There she would remain until she could fend for herself.

"Who was the man with the plumed hat?" Sophie asked.

They had reached the village green. Abbé Morel stopped and pulled a handkerchief out of the sleeve of his cassock. Big drops of sweat covered his brow.

"It's better if you don't know his name."

"The man was a guest at the castle—where is he now?"

"Strive for the Kingdom of God and His righteousness, and then everything will be given to you," replied the abbé. With a sigh he wiped off the sweat. "What an unbearable heat!"

"Why don't you want to tell me?" Sophie gazed at him, but not one wrinkle moved in the abbé's face as he stuffed the handkerchief back in his cassock.

"People say that if it weren't for him my mother would still be alive. Is that true?"

"All people are the instruments of God. His will be done!" The priest stroked her hair. "You shouldn't ask so many questions," he added softly. "It would be better if you cried and prayed for your mother's soul. Or is your heart so hardened?"

Sophie didn't answer. In silence she kept walking up the little hill. The road was dusty, as if no drop of rain had ever touched it. Sophie saw the landscape as a reflection of her soul: a parched wasteland in which all her tears had dried up. Did that mean her heart was hardened too? Whenever she thought about the execution, she saw only the gray cat fleeing the fire in great bounds. She could no longer remember the sight of her mother on the scaffold. That image seemed to have been forever wiped from her memory.

"It's all my fault," she said softly. "The Savior didn't want to abide in my soul."

"No, Sophie," Abbé Morel countered sternly. "Your mother was destroyed by her own sins. She had turned against God and become involved with the powers of the Evil One. For that she had to die."

"But it was my fault that she went with me to the altar. She didn't want to go."

"You mustn't talk that way! Or do you believe that God made a mistake?"

"No, Abbé Morel," she said quietly. "But what did my mother do that was so wicked?"

"Your mother lived in sin, year after year. Because she preferred the love of the flesh to the love of God, and she practiced arts that are denied to a woman, in accordance with the will of Heaven. That was why everything turned out this way, and no power on earth could have changed any of it."

Sophie was silent. Everything within her wanted to deny the words of the priest, and she didn't know how to reply. She tried to think of her mother, of the colorful scarf that she wore around her neck only on special occasions, the scarf that fluttered so gaily in the wind. But again Sophie saw only the cat in her mind. The people at the castle had said that the cat was a sign—a sign that her mother was in league with the Devil. Could they be right?

At last she said, "If the baron had only returned a couple of hours earlier, my mother would still be alive."

"That too is proof, Sophie. If Providence had willed another outcome than decided by the court, the baron would have come back earlier. No, the will of God is stronger than any earthly power." Abbé Morel let go of her hand and looked her in the eye. "So I say to you, beware of walking in the footsteps of your mother! And stay far away from everything she taught you. But look, we're almost there."

They had reached the top of the hill, and in the distance they could see the thick walls of the cloister.

"Please, don't leave me there alone!" said Sophie, reaching for the priest's hand.

"Don't worry, you'll get along fine in the convent. The nuns will do everything to make you a woman who is pleasing in the sight of God." He took her hand and pressed it. "I will hold you in my prayers, and in that way I will be with you, even when you don't see me."

Sophie swallowed hard. "Do you promise?"

"Of course I do." The priest patted her cheek with his heavy hand. "But only if you promise me something in return."

"What's that, Monsieur l'Abbé?"

"That you won't be like your mother, either in word or deed. Are you ready to make that vow?"

Abbé Morel lifted the girl's chin and gazed at her as seriously and sternly as if the dear Lord Himself were looking at her through the gray eyes of the priest. In that instant Sophie understood that the love of God was a gift that one constantly had to earn anew. And suddenly she felt so cold that she shivered in the bright sunshine, as if it were the depths of winter.

"Yes," she whispered, and as she said this one word to seal her promise, she knew that it would change her life forever.

BOOK I

The Thorn in the Flesh
1747

8

To anyone who looked out over Paris from the bell tower of the cathedral of Notre-Dame, the city might have appeared to be a well-formed plaster landscape, a calm, gray sea of houses, from which the churches and government buildings rose up as majestic memorials, immovable rocks in the surf of time.

But this appearance was deceptive, for in reality Paris was a kraken, a gigantic octopus, spreading its arms over the entire French kingdom. Day by day this kraken grew, undulating and unrestrained, as if it knew no boundaries. Greedily it devoured whatever food was harvested or wine was pressed within a hundred leagues, draining towns and cities, incorporating into its inexhaustible organism all offerings and goods, all riches and bounties of the countryside, in order to feed the untold numbers of people born in the bowels of the streets and alleys of Paris, propagating and dying in the eternal cycle of life: a gaping maw into which all of France was fused together, a restless, thrashing labyrinth of passions and desires.

The city was already awake at one in the morning. Like bleary-eyed legions the farmers came driving their carts in from the outlying areas, laden with vast quantities of meat, vegetables and fruits, eggs, butter, and cheese to stuff into the stomach of the ravenous kraken. But not until dawn when the bakers opened their shops did the streets gradually fill up. Craftsmen and laborers, wives and maids, office clerks and shopgirls bustled forth, each in more of a hurry than the one before, through the ever denser traffic of wagons and carriages rolling in every direction. When the early mass concluded and emptied the churches, the priests and devout ladies encountered the professors and students of the Sorbonne, who hastened to their lectures with fluttering gowns and books under their arms, while the waiters at the lemonade stands balanced hot and cold drinks on their trays and threaded their way through the throng. Around nine o'clock the barbers and wig-makers, powdered from head to toe and clutching their curling irons in their hands, set off to make their house calls. By then the alleyways and squares were already overflowing with the masses, and an hour later the city was threatening to suffocate on its own flurry of activity when the civil servants, judges, and notaries rushed in black swarms to the Châtelet and the Palais de Justice, and finally the bankers, brokers, and speculators streamed to the stock exchange, and the idlers headed for the Palais Royal.

When the sun reached its zenith the perpetual smoke that hung over the city, billowing in yellow clouds from the chimneys and hiding the church steeples from view, was joined by a babel of voices, a cacophony of words and responses, curses and cries, shouts and laughter, uttered by the six times one hundred thousand citizens as they fought for their place in the metropolis or simply tried to obtain air for their souls. They all wanted to live, love, and be happy! Not until evening, when they ceased their labors, did the hum and hubbub sink with the twilight onto the houses again and move from the streets and squares into the bars, cabarets, and restaurants, and above all into the coffeehouses. These establishments had appeared in the city only a few decades earlier, but they were growing ever more popular; there news and opinions were traded like goods and securities at the stock exchange.

The first Parisian establishment of this type—where no beer or wine or other intoxicating drinks were served, but instead refreshments that sharpened the senses and stimulated the mind—was located at 13 Rue des Fossés Saint-Germain, directly across from the old Comédie. A Sicilian from Palermo, Francesco Procopio, had opened it in 1686, after he had failed at selling coffee on the streets. Heavy chairs with leather upholstery and thick ceiling beams above low, pastel yellow walls lent atmosphere to the place; at the heavy oak tables the patrons read newspapers, played chess, or got into heated discussions. Here everyone was welcome as long as he could pay his bill. No one was deemed more worthy than anyone else, no one was allowed to assume a more elevated status than another; rather, each new customer simply took the next best place. With the tricorn on his head and a pipe in his mouth, he would claim a chair, stretch out his legs, and grab a periodical or join in the conversation of his tablemates. Outside in the narrow streets the lanterns were lighted. The streetlights had become the national emblem of the king, in whose radiance the city must be aglitter by night, and at the same time the symbol of an enlightened mind, an intellect at work in this very city, probing and questioning the authority of power. It was here that all the diffuse opinions and caprices that had hovered in the air by day became distilled into clear thoughts. Conflicting hopes, smoldering fears, and burgeoning demands were put into words and given voice.

In this place, Café Procope, which was known to the police of Paris as a meeting place for dangerous freethinkers and rabble-rousers, Sophie Volland, having reached the age of eighteen, had found employment as a waitress.

9

"As usual, a cup of hot chocolate, Monsieur Diderot?"

"Yes, with lots of vanilla and cinnamon."

"Will that be all, or do you wish something else?"

"As long as you ask me so nicely—yes, Mirzoza, I do."

"Monsieur Diderot, I've told you a dozen times that my name is Sophie."

"That could be, Mirzoza. But I know better. You're a princess from a fairy tale."

"So why am I working here?"

"Because they baptized you under a false name, Mirzoza."

Sophie didn't know whether to laugh or get mad. This Diderot, a man in his early thirties who came to the Procope almost every day, was one of those so-called philosophers, the house regulars who regarded this as their second home and carried on such ardent discussions both day and night, as if they ruled all of France. As a simple waitress she had no idea what sort of men the philosophers were or what they actually did—they didn't seem to have any regular profession—and yet whenever she served at their tables she felt even younger than she was, and the back of her neck would tingle as if from a swarm of midges. Just as it did now, when Diderot looked at her with those astonishingly blue eyes of his and an impudent grin on his lips; his small head with the blond shock of hair above those broad porter's shoulders moved like a weather vane on a church tower.

"You said that you wished for something else?" she asked, as sternly as she could.

"Correct!" he shouted, and his grin grew even more impertinent. "Are you doing anything this evening?"

Without a word Sophie turned away from him and went back to the counter.

What was it with these men? Even at her previous job in the tobacco tavern, a smoke-filled dump in Faubourg Saint-Marceau, they had pestered her, but there the customers were coachmen, soldiers, or sewer workers stinking of brandy, and Sophie knew how to handle them. But here? If the learned gentlemen in the Procope talked that way, it was probably due to the stimulating drinks that they downed in such enormous quantities—above all coffee, which could cause a person's heart to race wildly. It certainly couldn't be her looks, thought Sophie. She considered herself anything but pretty with her thick red hair, a thousand freckles, and green eyes.

She arranged the crockery on the counter, ready to fill the orders. From here she could look out over the whole café as she poured tea, coffee, or hot chocolate into the cups. The evening show in the theater across the street had just begun, so only half the tables were occupied, and yet there was as much chatter as at the weekly marketplace. Sophie had been in Paris for two years now, but she was still amazed at how fast the people here talked, twice as fast as back home in her village, and they all talked at once, as if they were afraid they wouldn't be able to complete their sentences before someone interrupted them. Would she really ever find the happiness she dreamed of here? A simple, honest man who would love her a little and pilot her into the harbor of marriage?

Sophie set down the pot of hot chocolate and carried her tray to the table.

"There you are, Monsieur Diderot. With lots of vanilla and cinnamon."

"Thank you, Mirzoza." He took the steaming cup and raised it to his lips. "Meanwhile, have you been thinking where the two of us might amuse ourselves? They're playing *Tartuffe* at the Ambigu-Comique. Or would you rather go dancing?"

He drank his chocolate fervently, as if he were savoring nectar, and peered at her over the edge of his cup. All of a sudden Sophie again felt a swarm of midges at the back of her neck, and for a second that strange sensation raced through her young body—the feeling that had sometimes disturbed her in the convent during long nights of lonely yearning.

"Well?" Diderot put down his cup, and his upper lip was now adorned with a thin mustache. "When shall I come to fetch you?"

Sophie lifted the hem of her apron to wipe off the traces of chocolate from his face.

"Instead of going to the theater or to a ball, you ought to pay a visit to the barber, Monsieur Diderot. Or don't people shave in your fairy-tale world?"

Amid laughter from the other philosophers she picked up her tray and left.

This Diderot was the last person she needed!

10

Joining the flood of theatergoers that crowded into the Procope a bit later was Antoine Sartine, a meticulously dressed young man with a friendly, ordinary face and sophisticated manners who gave the impression that he had just been splendidly amused. With his tricorn in hand, he surveyed the crowd and then, as he did almost every evening, he took a seat at a single table near the door. He was so pleasant and unobtrusive in appearance that his arrival was hardly noticed by any of the patrons.

This was entirely as he intended. Antoine Sartine did not frequent Café Procope for the sake of his own amusement; he came here as part of his work. In his position immediately under the lieutenant general of the Paris police, his assignment was to watch the philosophers and authors in the coffeehouses of the city, to take notes on their conversations, and to follow their political development. Concealed behind a newspaper, he seemed utterly engrossed in his reading. Yet he was actually listening with both ears so that not a word escaped his attention, no matter what people at tables to his left and right were engrossed in at the moment: the translation of Homer, the principle of separation of powers, or the Jansenist teaching of predestination.

Yes, Antoine Sartine was a police officer, and he enjoyed his work. Gathering facts was both his profession and his calling. He categorized, labeled, and classified the inexhaustible flow of information according to a strict system, so as to put order into the confused world of garret scribblers who called themselves philosophers and sought to immortalize themselves by writing novels and dramas, treatises and pamphlets of every description. Whether nobleman or cleric, doctor or lawyer, journalist, independent scholar, or librarian—no author in Paris who ever set word to paper escaped Sartine's system. On great folio pages he drew up his reports, noting with painstaking exactitude the name of every person under his observation, also adding the individual's age and place of birth as well as his address and description. Sartine described their habits and thoughts and replicated their often tangled journeys through life. In a manner of speaking he too was an author, and he definitely harbored sympathy for some writers, appreciating intellect, wit, and talent wherever he encountered them. Nevertheless his loyalty never wavered: if an author questioned the orthodox teachings of church and state, Sartine would begin to investigate.

The purpose and goal of his work was to protect the kingdom of France from its enemies. He had not only sworn an oath to this effect, but this sense of duty also corresponded to an ingrained resolve. Sartine had the state to thank for everything he possessed: his education, his suit, his apartment. He took the silver pocket watch out of the breast pocket of his jacket; only a few days ago he had purchased it on the Quai de l'Horloge. He made the case pop open and gazed at the clock face—not to check the time but simply to have another look at the costly timepiece. Yes, if he continued to serve the state in the future with the same zeal he had shown to date, he would go far, possibly even very far.

So he had few complaints about his fate. The only thing he was lacking for happiness on earth was a woman with whom he could share life. Thinking about this, he let himself be guided less by his emotions than by his reason. Personally he could tolerate not being married without feeling deprived; secretly he even shied away from some of the duties that marriage would inevitably entail. Like many other men of middle age and average means he had thought about taking on a housekeeper who would restrict herself to housework and see to cooking the meals, without making any additional demands. But unlike the philosophers, who avoided marriage at all costs because they seldom had money but almost always had children, Sartine regarded marriage as an important step in his professional career. In his orderly world, a wife was as essential at the side of a civil servant as one bell tower of Notre-Dame was beside the other.

Was Sophie the right one?

Just then she emerged from the kitchen, her cheeks flushed from work, making her green eyes gleam more brightly than usual. The sight of her affected him as pleasantly as a fresh sea breeze. With no time to waste, she dried her hands on her apron and hurried to the counter, where two barmaids, under the watchful eye of the owner, were busy filling orders from the customers who came streaming in after the theater.

Sartine lowered his paper and watched Sophie work, filled with admiration. He was well aware that the new waitress of the Procope differed from the other waitresses in a gratifying way. She neither flirted with the patrons nor tolerated their attempts at familiarity. That pleased him almost more than her green eyes, and for a moment he abandoned himself to the happy prospect that she might one day bustle about as efficiently for him alone as she did here and now for these customers. Who knows, maybe she would even be content with the modest comforts that Antoine Sartine could offer to a wife—a secure livelihood and a home—without demanding those secondary obligations that ordinary women so often confused with bliss. Would he find an opportunity today to speak with her in peace and quiet?

At the next table voices were being raised. Although reluctant to do so, Sartine turned his gaze away from Sophie in order to devote his attention to official duties. Unobtrusively he cast a glance at his neighbors. The publisher Le Bréton, a man like a walrus, sat there in the company of three scribblers whom Sartine till now knew only by appearance and by name. His trained hearing filtered out their conversation so clearly and distinctly from the babble of voices that he understood almost every syllable. They were discussing God and the world, and Denis Diderot was speaking.

"Confess, why should I confess?" he shouted. "In order to eat a piece of bread that they call the Body of the Lord?"

"A witty fellow," the lieutenant noted down in his neat hand, deciding to keep an eye on this Diderot in the future. "Renowned for his impiety. Speaks contemptuously of the holy mysteries."

"Now now now," replied the publisher at the next table. "If I were in your place, Diderot, I would already know one reason to confess. An extraordinarily pretty reason. Starts with *P*, just like the pretty posterior of the lady in question."

Sartine knit his brows. After uttering blasphemies they now turned to speaking of worldly things. The philosophers preferred to focus on their womanizing exploits rather than the disparagement of church and state. Anyone who heard them would think that the path to immortality led inevitably through the sins of the flesh. But who were they referring to as "P"? The answer was not long in coming.

"Has Madame de Puisieux as his mistress," Sartine added to his dossier when he heard the name, shaking his head. He knew the woman. Puisieux was a translator who changed her lovers more often than her quill pens. Sartine now had scarcely any doubt that Diderot's career would follow a trajectory leading him from the garret room straight into the gutter, with a stopover in the Bastille. He expressed his preliminary judgment in two words: "Extremely dangerous!"

Then Antoine Sartine disappeared once again behind his newspaper and pricked up his ears.

11

"I want to touch people's souls, make them laugh and cry, enlighten them and shake them awake—everything you can do with books!"

Diderot was speaking with such enthusiasm that he noticed neither the pinch of his tight gray jacket or the scratching of his black woolen stockings. In his life he had two passions: women and literature. Whenever he was preoccupied with either of them, nothing else in the world existed for him—neither the lack of money, which followed him like his own shadow so that he often didn't know how he could pay for the next bottle of ink or the next cup of hot chocolate, nor the police informer who had nested in Café Procope like a flea in an old wig.

"I want to show people how they love and suffer, how they risk their lives for the adventure of their souls. I want to depict their greatness and dignity, the power of their feelings and the surge of their thoughts, the tempest of their inventions and the purity of their ideas. I want to chase away the fog that still fills their heads, all the prejudices and delusions— everything that always enslaves the free spirit who dares to think for himself and accepts only what is attested to by experience and reason."

"And you expect to make your living off *that*?" asked Le Bréton almost sympathetically, placing his fat white hand on Diderot's arm.

"Off it and above all *for* it!"

There was a pause. The publisher squinted so that his eyes almost disappeared among the bulges in his face, as he fixed his gaze on Diderot.

"Then I think," he said at last, "that I have something for you. An English dictionary, the *Cyclopaedia* of Chambers. A reference work that unifies all knowledge from widely divergent fields—a fabulous thing. Would you like to translate it into French? Possibly working with the rest of the gentlemen at this table?"

"I know the *Cyclopaedia*," replied the man sitting next to Diderot. His name was d'Alembert, a man of thirty who with his slight stature seemed as inconspicuous as an office clerk, yet he was actually a famous mathematician. "A highly interesting work, and a very useful one at that—" D'Alembert was still speaking, but then the man across the table from him jumped up and interrupted him.

"Are you out of your mind? I, Jean-Jacques Rousseau, should translate a book? Make myself the slave of a foreign author? And an Englishman at that, who pays homage to a half-witted king?" His suit was covered with stains, his wig sat loosely on his head, and yet his eyes sparkled as he pointed at the publisher, waving his finger as imperiously as a general cutting a recruit down to size. "How dare you insult me this way?"

"Calm down, Rousseau. It was only a suggestion, and it was directed at your friend Diderot."

"That makes no difference whatsoever."

"Besides, you wouldn't be working for nothing. I'm offering a tidy sum for the translation."

"What does money matter?" Rousseau scoffed, making a face as if he'd bitten into a piece of rotten meat. "Only the money in one's possession is a means to freedom. But the money one seeks to acquire is merely a means to bondage. Therefore I c-c-call upon you to t-t-take your m-m-money and . . ."

Like a street preacher he began by spewing forth the words, but when he started to stutter his speech stopped at once. Now he was the mute manifestation of affronted accusation. Full of contempt, he cast one last chastising look at the publisher, then he left the table and stomped off toward the door.

"P-p . . . pay the bill for me!" Rousseau shouted over his shoulder.

"What an unpleasant patron," muttered Le Bréton. "He claims he loves all humanity, but he can't spend more than five minutes with anyone without getting into an argument. But back to you, Diderot. What do you say to my proposal? Would the Chambers book be something for you?"

Diderot hesitated. He knew Le Bréton and he knew about this project—two reasons to watch his step. The publisher had been trying to bring out the *Cyclopaedia* in France for years; he had high hopes of selling many copies. He had already run through one editor, several business partners, and half a dozen translators. To their demands for payment he often responded with his walking stick. Everyone at the Procope knew this.

Diderot shook his head. "No, doing a translation doesn't interest me."

"Nonsense! You're the best translator in all of Paris. The *Medical Dictionary* was a masterpiece, not to mention your Shaftesbury . . ."

"I want to write my own books at last."

"Really?" Le Bréton asked. "I'll offer you eight thousand *livres* for the manuscript."

Diderot gave a start. "Eight thousand?" he repeated like an idiot. He had never even seen, never mind earned, such a sum in all his life.

"Eight thousand," the publisher confirmed. "The first half on signing, the second on delivery." He reached out his hand. "So, come on, let's shake on it."

Diderot crossed his arms in front of his chest. "Money doesn't interest me," he replied, but the lie stuck in his craw so badly that he had to clear his throat.

"Then think of the fame! All of France will kiss your feet because of your translation of the Chambers."

Although it was an effort, Diderot kept his arms crossed. Through the window he saw his friend disappear around the corner. Rousseau didn't even look back; once he was convinced of the correctness of his decision, no power on earth could change his mind. Diderot admired him for this single-mindedness, which precluded any form of adaptation or entanglement.

"I'm a writer, Monsieur Le Bréton."

"I'm convinced of that. And for that very reason I beg you to lend your pen to Mister Chambers. It's only for a short time."

"I have lent my pen to foreign authors far too often and for far too long."

"And if I raise my offer to ten thousand? Living is expensive, and you have obligations. Think about next month's rent."

"Even if you offered me twenty thousand—no!"

Now the publisher let his hand drop. The expression on his face changed like the weather in April. The goodwill that had just flowed from every pore of his pale skin like his interminable sweat suddenly gave way to anger, and his tiny eyes flashed perilously.

"Your final answer?"

Diderot nodded.

"Too bad, I had taken you for more intelligent than that. Apparently I overestimated you."

Le Bréton propped his hands on the table to help push his huge body to a standing position. The delicate d'Alembert moved aside as if fearing he might be crushed by the mountain of flesh.

"Just a moment!"

The publisher gave Diderot a surprised look.

"I would like to propose something else. Something better than the Chambers."

"Indeed? I'm all ears." Le Bréton stopped for a moment, undecided, then dropped back down onto his chair. "But I warn you, don't waste my time."

Suddenly Diderot felt the tightness of his jacket under his arms, and the rough stockings itching his skin from his feet to the back of his knees. He had to clear his throat once again.

"Let's write our own encyclopedia, Monsieur Le Bréton."

"To what purpose?" The publisher looked at Diderot as if he doubted his sanity. "Mister Chambers has already written an excellent one. Even *I* have read some of it, and that's saying quite a lot. Besides, the rights cost me a fortune."

"Nevertheless—the book is worthless."

"And why, if I may ask? All of Europe envies England because of that book."

"Then all of Europe is wrong."

"Except you . . ."

"Yes, except me. And common sense!"

"Could it be that somebody mixed something into your chocolate?"

Diderot shook his head. "No, monsieur, even if you strike me dead, I must repeat: the *Cyclopaedia* is worthless. And I'm also going to tell you why: because an encyclopedia can never be the work of a single individual."

"But almost every book is the work of a single individual."

"An encyclopedia is much more than a book, as indicated by the concept of an 'integration of the sciences.' But how can a single author manage to research the entire system of nature and of the mind, and then describe all the subsequently derived knowledge? Or do you believe that Mister Chambers was granted the ability to learn everything that can ever be learned, to make use of everything that was ever created, and to understand whatever there is to understand?"

"The *Cyclopaedia* may well be imperfect," replied Le Bréton with a shrug of his shoulders. "But, my God, *c'est la vie!*"

"So should we be content with something imperfect?" shouted

Diderot. "If life is imperfect, we have to improve it. No, instead of translating the Chambers, we should venture something completely new. Collecting the knowledge of a single individual in a book isn't enough—we have to compile the knowledge of all humankind in a truly complete encyclopedia of the sciences, arts, and handicrafts, a work that encompasses all branches of knowledge."

"Who in heaven's name would want to do that?" asked d'Alembert. "It took the Crusca Academy in Italy forty years merely to define the vocabulary for such a work. The undertaking is beyond all reason."

Le Bréton raised his hand to object: "Keep talking, Diderot!"

Diderot moved his chair closer to the table so that he was sitting directly across from the publisher. "Let's establish a society of learned men and philosophers who work separately, each on his own and in his own field, so that they don't waste time in discussions, but who all share the same great plan—dozens, hundreds of authors, the best minds in all of France, in order to deal with every topic that applies to human beings: human needs, desires, longings, and pleasures. Together these men will write a book that will turn the world upside down, sweeping away the superstitions and prejudices that have brought so much misery to humanity. A book that not only portrays life as it is, but shows how it could and should be. A book like the book of books, a book like the Bible, a truly new testament for a new era!"

"Aha," Le Bréton wondered, "are we suddenly going to get pious?"

"Yes, a book like the Bible," Diderot repeated, "and at the same time the exact opposite. A holy scripture of earthly life, a compendium of human bliss." He clenched his fists as he spoke. "According to the teachings of the old Bible, humanity has been vegetating for eighteen hundred and forty-seven years in an earthly vale of tears, while people consoled themselves with the prospect of a better life after death. It's time to write a new Bible, a book that will present people with a new world in which they can seek and find their happiness, here on this side of death, a paradise on earth."

"Shhhh," said d'Alembert, looking around anxiously. "It would be wise to change the subject." A bitter smile played over his fleshy lips, while his brown eyes, which had been wandering restlessly about the room during Diderot's speech, now gave the publisher an imploring look.

But Le Bréton paid no attention to him. "Do you seriously mean this, Diderot? A book containing all human knowledge?"

"Yes," replied Diderot. "An encyclopedia that unites all the disparate branches of knowledge on this earth, in order to hand down the wisdom to all posterity. So that the work of the past centuries and millennia has not been in vain. So that our children and grandchildren will be not only more educated but also happier. And so that we don't die without having earned a worthy place in the annals of humanity."

He fell silent. All over his body Diderot could feel his clothing binding and itching as Le Bréton returned his gaze. What was going on inside that walrus of a man? The whole mountain of flesh seemed to be in labor, as if it were costing Le Bréton a superhuman effort to give birth to an answer. He stroked the ends of his mustache over and over, while his face contracted into a thousand wrinkles, and he wheezed and panted with every fiber of his enormous body.

"Do you realize that this would be the biggest task that any writer has ever taken on?" he asked at last.

Diderot nodded.

Le Bréton closed his eyes and sighed. "Then I have no choice but to accept my fate, in spite of the risk that you may ruin me, Diderot—but great success comes only from great ideas." A light passed over his face, as if the sun had come up over a mountain range. "If you're right, I will allow myself forevermore to be carried in a sedan chair through Paris. If not—pistols!" He raised his hand, snapped his fingers, and cried, "Waiter—bring us champagne!"

12

❧ ☙

From the tower of the old abbey church of Saint-Germain-des-Prés
the bells tolled the midnight hour, but Sophie could still find no rest.
Through the open window of her room she heard the yowling of a
tomcat on the prowl over the rooftops and smelled the constant stench
of the rain gutters; for the sake of convenience many residents of the
mansard misused the gutters as a toilet. Sitting in front of a candle that
had almost burned out, the flame emitting only the dimmest of light,
she leaned over her treasure: a little box full of words, written pieces of
paper that Sophie had found somewhere, collected, smoothed out, and
restored, saving them in this little box, which she guarded as carefully as
the money pouch that held her savings. After work she would take the
box out of its hiding place and read what it contained: notes, recipes, old
bills and inventories, theater tickets and handbills, yellowed newspaper
clippings and placards, a prayer book, but most important, handwritten manuscript pages from novels, dramatic scenes, and poems that her
guests had left behind at the coffeehouse like abandoned children, some
of them crumpled up and some even torn to bits. That's why she always
locked the door, out of fear that someone might discover this secret
activity of hers. Nobody must know that she was able to read—that
frightened her as much as the Last Judgment.

Sophie opened the little box with a pounding heart and a guilty conscience, as if she were about to commit a sin. She despised herself for her
lack of will, just as she had previously felt contempt for the day laborers
who came into the tobacconist's shop in Faubourg Saint-Marceau and
crept up to her with shaking hands to beg for a glass of brandy. And yet
she couldn't stop herself; it was an internal, irresistible compulsion to
which she surrendered night after night. Reading these written materials
was her addiction. From the letters of the alphabet, from the words and

sentences, from every scrap and shred of thought no matter how small, new worlds emerged before her, like genies rising out of a bottle in fairy tales; different, more beautiful, better worlds in which she could escape after the toil of the day, worlds full of secrets, in which she could sometimes even find her father, Dorval, and together they went looking for her mother.

But on this particular evening the magic was missing. Instead of causing a colorful world to unfold, the writing remained nothing but dead black letters on old paper, adamantly refusing to divulge their secrets. Yet that was not the fault of the words or sentences written there, but because of Sophie herself. She was utterly confused, incapable of assimilating a single line. Only a few hours earlier, during a calm minute between two theater performances, as the café patrons granted her a breather, Antoine Sartine, the affable regular at the Procope, had offered her a proposal, asking her to be his wife forever.

Sophie placed the papers back in the little box, closed the lid, and stowed her treasure in a niche in the wall behind a loose brick. Although she had to get up at dawn the next morning in order to build a fire in the kitchen hearth, she still wanted to go down to the street and take a short walk along the river. She simply could not sleep in this state of turmoil.

A dark silence enveloped her outside. She encountered only an occasional idler on the street, some accompanied by lantern bearers who for a couple of coppers would light the way home for the night roamers. Here, far from the hustle and bustle of the cafés and theaters, it was so quiet that Sophie soon could hear the rippling of the Seine. A fresh breeze gusted over the river, its surface reflecting the lights of the city and the sky, and drove away the putrid smells of the slaughterhouses and fish markets, the cesspools and graveyards that by day accumulated in the narrow alleys between the tall buildings, creating a sickeningly sweet stench that would make anyone gag.

She breathed deeply of the mild night air. Should she accept Sartine's proposal? The idea aroused a gentle sense of well-being in her. Marriage would change everything about her life in this gigantic, alienating city—for the first time since her mother's death, the image of which she had tried to extinguish from her memory, there would be another person who cared deeply about her, someone who knew all her habits and preferences, who knew which side of the bed she slept on, and which foot she set on the floor first in the morning. How she longed for such closeness! In Faubourg Saint-Marceau she had been living in squalor for over a year, together with the poorest of the poor in Paris, in a building where entire families lived in a single room with bare walls, where the constantly damp, dirty beds had no curtains, where kitchen implements were stacked up next to the chamber pots. Now the young detective was offering her a home and a secure livelihood; as his wife she would always have a decent roof over her head, as well as respectable clothes and plenty to eat. And she would be able to go to Communion. In the cloister she'd been forced to promise, as penance for vomiting up the Body of Christ, not to show herself before the Altar of the Lord until she had found someone who wanted to marry her.

Was Antoine Sartine the man she had been waiting for? Sophie liked him; he always treated her kindly and with respect, although as a civil servant his social standing was far above her own. But he'd had an eye on her for some time now—that fact had not escaped her—and she was pleased. So why was she hesitating now that he'd mustered his courage enough to propose to her? Why had she asked him for time to think it over, instead of giving her assent at once? Was it because she couldn't imagine ever coming to love him one day?

Love—the thought wrenched a sigh from her breast. What sort of word was that? Why did it hold such magic, unmatched by any other word? A night watchman raised his lantern in Sophie's direction. Involuntarily she quickened her steps. Looming before her on Île de la Cité was the huge, dark silhouette of Notre-Dame, a mighty ship of God on the glittering swells of the Seine, seeming asleep in the moonlight, with the water flowing around it. The noise of humanity was completely muted here on the riverbank; only those creatures who were nocturnal filled the silence of the night with secretive, noiseless life. Huge birds flew up, soundless dark patches, and vanished like shadows in the air; somewhere a toad raised its lonely call to the moon.

Love! Ever since Sophie left the cloister, she'd felt anxious at the approach of this sinister power. Her mother had paid the penalty for it, and the abbess had never dared say the word above a whisper, as if fearing that merely by mentioning it she might summon a plague, an evil demon of the underworld. Yet despite all the fear engendered by the sound of this mysterious word, Sophie felt a longing that she otherwise experienced only during the holy mass, when the other faithful stepped forward for Communion, to receive the Body of the Lord. She had to remain in her pew, shut off from the congregation, in order to fulfill the penance she had brought upon herself.

At the Pont Neuf Sophie turned around. She couldn't wander through the streets all night long—it was only a few hours until she had to get up, and then another long day lay before her, during which she would serve hundreds of guests at the café. Who cared that Antoine Sartine had asked her to be his wife?

She chose the route along the broad Rue Mazarine, which was quite lively even at this late hour. She turned back in the glow of the street-lights, which were small artificial moons in the darkness, hanging every thirty paces from cords above the street and protecting with their dim oil-fed light the nighttime passersby from attack. She had just reached the intersection where Rue des Fossés Saint-Germain began, and she could already see the tall building that housed her meager bedroom in its mansard, when she suddenly heard footsteps. The next moment a man stood in front of her, a stranger wearing a hat. She involuntarily took a step back, but when the stranger doffed his hat and bowed before her, she recognized him: Before her stood the broad-shouldered porter, the man with the small head, the chocolate drinker—Monsieur Diderot.

"What's the meaning of lying in wait for me?" she cried when she had recovered from the initial shock.

"I lie in wait for Beauty wherever I hope to encounter her."

"Then why don't you visit Madame de Puisieux? I'm sure she's waiting for you."

"Like the great monarch Mongagul waits for his Princess Mirzoza?"

"Mongagul?" asked Sophie, curious in spite of herself. "What sort of monarch is that? I've never heard of him."

"What, you don't recognize your most ardent admirer?"

Before she could say another word, he began telling her a story. About Sultan Mongagul, whose palace loomed up from the Desert of Sadness, where instead of sweet water the fountains had their source in salty tears, and the sultan suffered an ever greater tormenting thirst the more often he drank from them. Only a smile would free him from this curse. But in vain did the court jesters try to cheer him up; not even the most entic-ing maidens in all the realm, whom the noted sorcerer had summoned to beguile their lord and master, were capable of releasing Mongagul from his terrible grief.

"Weren't any of them beautiful enough?" asked Sophie with a laugh. "Poor Madame de Puisieux."

"Poor Mongagul," Diderot countered, pulling a face as if he were suffering the torments of the sultan. "But one day," he went on, "a young princess knocked on the door of the palace. Mirzoza was her name, and she came from the most distant province in the kingdom, the smallest and also the loveliest province, the province of bliss. Her hair blazed like flames of fire, and she carried a steaming bowl of sweet hot chocolate. That was the medicine of her homeland which she wanted to bring to the monarch. And truly, as soon as his lips touched the rim of the bowl, all sadness fell away from him, and his weary eyes began to gleam. For even sweeter than the drink was the charm exuded by the princess herself."

"That is simply amazing," said Sophie. "The bowl was steaming hot? Even though she had come from such a distant province? How did the princess manage to keep the chocolate from getting cold along the way?"

"I probably forgot to say that she carried the bowl on her head like all the women in the East do. So the flames of her hair took care of heating the chocolate on the long journey."

Sophie laughed. What nonsense! Nothing in his story was true—yet it was so lovely that she could have listened to him for hours. And maybe the reason for that was because it was all make-believe.

"I don't believe a word of it," she cried.

"Try it yourself and you'll see. Or do you think I would make up something impossible? No, Mirzoza, everything you can imagine will happen someday, even if it may take a while."

He lifted her chin so that she had to look at him. His expression was now quite serious. Suddenly all thoughts vanished from her head; she thought neither of the next day nor of Madame de Puisieux, nor even of Antoine Sartine. She didn't even notice when the lights went out in the barroom of the Procope, next to which they were standing—she saw only his unbelievably bright eyes, which seemed to gleam like two stars in the darkness.

"Do you know what I like about you?" he asked softly.

She returned his gaze mutely as the midges at the back of her neck buzzed louder than ever.

"You're able to forget yourself. When you're working, when you're laughing, when you're listening. I envy you that. Would you help me learn that from you?"

"Please," she whispered without taking her eyes off him, "don't speak to me like that, Monsieur Mongagul!"

"What did you call me, Sophie?"

He looked at her as if waking from a dream. His smile, with which he had embraced her, gave way to a distressed look, as if he only now became truly aware of her presence. All at once his eyes seemed much darker. And infinitely sad.

"Don't you feel well, Monsieur Diderot?"

Abruptly he hurried off and left her standing there without uttering a word in parting. She could still feel the touch of his hand on her chin. But before he vanished into the dark night, from which he had materialized like a ghost, he turned around and blew her a kiss.

Sophie felt as though she'd drunk a glass of wine on an empty stomach. The street was deserted, and from the rooftops she heard a meow. Had the whole encounter been only a dream?

A tomcat landed next to her with claws spread and ran off with a hiss.

13

The events in Café Procope did not go unnoticed by the authorities. The very next morning Antoine Sartine gave a report to a man whose simple priest's habit belied the immense responsibility resting on his shoulders. Father Radominsky, as he was called, a man of almost forty, was a Jesuit born in Poland, who took his religious vows at the local ecclesiastical province of the order and had been sent to France as confidant of the general of the Church of Rome. He was to serve as the father confessor of Queen Maria Leszczynska, also born in Poland. Endowed with extensive powers by the Curia, he was enjoined to use his influence at the court of Versailles for one sole purpose: to ensure that in the capital of the kingdom of France God's will might be done . . . or at least the will of the pope.

"What is being hatched in this coffeehouse?" he asked the lieutenant.

"The publisher Le Bréton," Sartine reported, "is preparing a new reference work, a dictionary of considerable scope. It appears that he intends to realize this undertaking by using all the means at his disposal. Allegedly he has put all his money into the project and his debts have brought him to the brink of ruin. They say to the tune of eighty thousand *livres*."

"Eighty thousand?" Radominsky said, astonished. "So much money for a dictionary?"

"They're calling it an encyclopedia. All the knowledge in the world, from *A* to *Z*, organized according to philosophical principles. Naturally, I didn't understand every word of the discussion—"

"Who else is involved in this undertaking?"

Sartine pulled out his notebook. "Primarily the two editors, Jean Le Rond d'Alembert, an illegitimate scion of Madame de Tencin—"

"Madame de Tencin, the former canoness who ripped the veil to bits in order to make herself the whore of half of France?"

"If you'll pardon me for saying so," confirmed Sartine. "She abandoned her son immediately after his birth; he was standing in the way of her career at court. Monsieur d'Alembert suffers from this even today, although he enjoys an excellent reputation in the realm of science."

"What sort of man is he?"

"An armchair scholar with minor human weaknesses. His primary goal is to recruit noted authors for the dictionary, colleagues and professors of the Sorbonne. The second editor, Denis Diderot, seems to be more important," the lieutenant added. "He's the actual brains of the enterprise."

"Diderot? I've never heard that name."

"An extremely mercurial spirit. He has hundreds of different physiognomies, all according to where his enthusiasms happen to take him at the moment. Man of letters, philosopher, demagogue. He knows a lot but has never really studied anything properly; nor does he have any academic title, which is why d'Alembert secretly holds him in contempt. A man who believes in very dubious things—the future, progress, and the like."

"Does he believe in God, or at least in the church?"

Sartine shook his head. "He says that when he dies he wants to receive the sacraments only out of consideration to his relatives, so that they won't think that he died without religion. In addition, last year he published a defamatory pamphlet, *Philosophical Thoughts*, in which he declares the Christian belief in miracles to be religious delusion."

"What else do you know about him?"

"He comes from a decent family; his father owned a cutlery workshop in Langres, where Diderot was originally supposed to become a cleric like his uncle, a canon in the local cathedral. He already had the tonsure and wanted to enter the order, in the Society of Jesus," Sartine added cautiously, "but instead he came to Paris to study."

"An apostate Jesuit?" Radominsky raised his eyebrows, impressed. "What did he study?"

"Law, theology, medicine, mathematics, philosophy—almost every subject offered at the university. Nevertheless, he has never made anything of himself. He has written sermons for future missionaries and articles for dubious newspapers, including theater critiques and translations. A man who makes his living exclusively from what he writes—a so-called professional writer, a new, as yet unknown species among the philosophers."

Radominsky nodded. "Obviously a man who must be taken seriously. Another Voltaire?"

Sartine hesitated before answering. "I fear that this Diderot is even more dangerous. Would you like to hear what he calls this dictionary?" The lieutenant turned to a page marked in his notebook and quoted: "'A book like the Bible. A true new testament for a new era. A holy scripture of earthly life.'"

"He really said that?" Radominsky gave Sartine a searching look. Among the lower ranks of the police there were many individuals who, in order to make themselves look important, would grossly exaggerate their reports or even invent stories in the hope of praise or promotion. But this young officer did not seem to be that sort. Sartine was clearly as ambitious as he was intelligent, two qualities that did not exactly instill trust in an experienced father confessor; but he did have an honest, open face, with alert eyes. It was because of his eyes that Radominsky had asked the lieutenant general of the Paris police to assign Sartine to him.

"What are your orders?" asked the lieutenant.

"I'll have to think about that. But first, please continue with your observations."

After Sartine left, Radominsky cleared his schedule for the rest of the morning. The report by the lieutenant had triggered his interest. Certainly, the scribblers in the coffeehouses were largely parasites from whom, taken individually, little danger could be expected: impoverished nobles who cursed their forebears, lusty abbés who wanted to abolish celibacy, shady lawyers who opposed the law, as well as a horde of journalists and learned men from all fields—a terribly disparate bunch, in agreement on two or three issues, at odds on two or three thousand. But a project such as this encyclopedia might change things abruptly. Nothing united and strengthened people as much as the power of an idea that ignited their belief. The Disciples of Jesus had been only simple fishermen, and yet they had conquered the world because they were imbued with a message. Was it possible then that another belief might release similar forces in other people? No, whoever gave credence to that notion was either a fanatic or a fool. And Father Radominsky was neither.

"A holy scripture of earthly life," he murmured. "What a bold plan."

Fascinated by the idea, he had to make an effort to suppress his admiration. What this Diderot was preaching was a paradise on earth—truly a belief that could move mountains! A shudder ran down his spine. It was as if he'd caught a glimpse of a beautiful woman who was in the process of undressing in front of him. Radominsky closed his eyes and clutched the crucifix on his chest in order to kiss the Savior as the blood shot into his loins and the flesh pulsated and rose between his thighs.

This feeling lasted only a few seconds. By then the father had gotten hold of himself. Although he had been born in Kraków, the Kingdom of God was his true and only home, and he saw it as his calling to defend this home. As a Jesuit he knew very well that the weapons of the spirit were more dangerous than all the guns and cannons in this world. With a sure instinct he understood that if the encyclopedia could unite all the disparate spirits in Paris who were sowing discord and doubt into one closed fighting troop against the faith, it also might plunge church and state into a crisis as grave as the one sparked by that devil Martin Luther two hundred years earlier with his damned Reformation. Knowledge was power, and whoever offered knowledge gave people power over their own lives. With that the law of God was annulled along with everything that bore witness to His heavenly omnipotence on earth: the hegemony of the Catholic Church, the divine right of the king, the eternal order of things.

Keeping the commandments of God on earth was the task of the state, the purpose and goal of the monarchy. But was the French state prepared to fulfill this task? Father Radominsky was skeptical. King Louis XV, known to the people as the "Much Loved Monarch," was a debauched man reeking of sweet perfume and acrid bodily fluids who, instead of attending to government business, had only two pleasures: lovemaking and the hunt. Maria Leszczynska, his wife, complained about this every day in confession, and she was not exaggerating. The court of Versailles had been turned into a huge park for dissolution and depravity, where each revelry was more bawdy than the last.

No, the church could not rely on this king. Radominsky sat down at his desk, took out a sheet of paper, and dipped his quill into the inkwell. In clear, concise sentences he warned Monseigneur Beaumont, the archbishop of Paris, of the impending danger, seeking to ensure the chief representative of the French spiritual leaders the full support of the church in the battle against this threat. Radominsky ended his letter with his unadorned signature and sprinkled sand over the ink; even before it had dried he rang for his servant and ordered him to hitch up the coach.

"To Versailles!"

Shortly after noon the equipage reached the seat of the monarchy. But instead of heading for the main palace as usual, in order first to visit the queen, Radominsky had the coachman turn off toward La Celle, a small village located about a league away. A canal lined the road there, and among gold-colored gondolas a sloop lay at anchor, ready for a pleasure outing along the colonnades of delicate rosebushes that bloomed pink and yellow along the banks and were reflected in the smooth surface of the water. Beyond, framed by artfully designed arcades and arbors, a castle loomed in meerschaum white atop several terraces; with its numerous turrets and oriels it resembled a magnificently decorated cream gâteau. Radominsky's face contorted in disgust. With its charming frothiness, the scene affected him as if it were a reproduction of the mythical isle of Kythera—even nature seemed not created by God's hand, but arranged instead by an artist or dealer in fashion accessories, as fantastic as it was tasteless. Only reluctantly did Radominsky leave the coach. But then he mustered his resolve and headed for the flight of stairs. In this castle, to which only a small circle of select guests were ever granted access, resided Madame de Pompadour, the mistress of the king and the most powerful woman in the entire kingdom. She was the one whom the father now wished to visit.

14

The Marquise de Pompadour was only twenty-six years old, and yet she was already regarded as the perfect symbol of her sex. All talents and all charms seemed united in her. With her white complexion, pale pink lips, and eyes of an indeterminate hue, in which black yearning and blue promise were combined, she possessed all the gifts needed to fulfill her self-appointed goal in life: to please her sovereign lord, in order to control him by means of her favor.

At the tender age of nine it was prophesied that she would one day be the mistress of the king of France. Ever since, she had cultivated this dream and put all her energy into making it come true. Even her marriage to Monsieur d'Étiolles served this single purpose. Without inhibition she used her husband's fortune to perfect herself: She learned to sing and play the cembalo, took dancing lessons, and studied elocution and horseback riding. In so doing all her thoughts were focused solely on attracting the attention of Louis. Whenever the opportunity arose she could be seen among the horses, the dogs, and the followers of the king, and at a masked ball she finally succeeded in approaching Louis. Wearing a Domino disguise, she courted him with a smile that her husband would have given his life to receive, and as she raised the half-mask at the urging of the monarch, she let her handkerchief fall to the floor. At that moment she won the heart of the king, never to relinquish it—she would sooner have sacrificed her own heart.

The masked ball had taken place a year and a half ago, and since then scarcely a day had passed in which the monarch had not bestowed on her his favor. As the latest sign of his affection, after he'd had her divorce from Monsieur d'Étiolles decreed, Louis had given her the pleasure palace of La Celle. Here she was at the moment twining a flower wreath with her three-year-old daughter, Alexandrine, when a lackey announced a visitor.

"Father Radominsky?" she said in amazement.

She set the wreath atop Alexandrine's blond locks and sent her away with a nursemaid. What could Radominsky want from her? Had he come on behalf of the queen to take her to task? Maria Leszczynska did not want to admit that her husband preferred the delights he found in the arms of his mistress over the edifying prayer sessions with his wife.

Madame de Pompadour was on her guard. Although Louis had elevated her to the rank of marquise, her position at court had not yet been solidified because a flaw clung to her character and could not be corrected: the stigma of her birth. She had the misfortune to be the daughter of a Monsieur Poisson, who because of shady transactions had been sentenced to death by hanging and therefore preferred to live abroad. With a knack for malice the courtiers had penetrated to the depths of her soul, ransacked her background like a pile of refuse, studied her speech and manners, and at last found her to be lacking the refinement that could be neither purchased nor learned, but had to be passed down through generations.

United by this discovery, a league was formed at court whose goal it was to turn Louis against her. The most diverse parties treated her with hostility. Not merely the queen and her devoted retinue, but also the chancellor and the president of parliament made every effort to curtail her influence on the king. And only one thing, the love of the king, protected her from all these attacks and intrigues; yet this love was as transitory as her beauty, and on that score Madame de Pompadour had no illusions.

"I have come here," Radominsky began as soon as he had kissed her hand, "to ask a favor of you. A bagatelle that will cost you very little effort."

"A favor?" asked La Pompadour, a bit irritated. As father confessor to the queen, Radominsky was her natural enemy.

"It's about naming a new director of the court's Royal Library. Her Majesty is very concerned with putting some order into the collection of books." He paused, then added significantly, "I thought perhaps this might be an occasion to deepen the friendship between you and Her Majesty."

"Pleasing the queen is my most sincere desire," replied La Pompadour. "But I'm at a loss as to how I can serve her in this matter. Until now I didn't even know that there was such a position. What did you call it? Director of the court library?" She motioned for the priest to take a seat.

"A very important position. The director of the court library is also the supreme censor of France. Dozens of new books appear daily, and it's a matter of separating the wheat from the chaff." He waited until his hostess sat down before he took a seat and continued with his speech. "The queen is worried about the state of the church in this country. It's not enough that some bishops and priests are negligent in their display of obedience toward Rome, but they are also spreading their critique among the people through defamatory writings in order to fan the flames of dissent."

"Is our church in such a poor condition?" Madame de Pompadour asked. "That surprises me. Its power continues to be adequate for excommunicating the female favorites of the king."

"Let me answer that in general, madame," said Radominsky evasively. "The church is like a magnificent edifice, a building that over the course of time has acquired cracks. Criticism is to blame for this, eating away like dry rot at the joins and gaps in order to erode the masonry. If we wish to maintain the edifice, we must put an end to this creeping decay."

"And this decay is caused by harmless books?"

"Books are never harmless, madame," he declared sternly. "They either strengthen us or they weaken us in our faith. Some of them do this even as they entertain us, others as they teach us. In an invisible way their teaching penetrates into our hearts and souls, to continue its work inside, and we inhale the spirit of these books as healing or poisonous vapors. They can bring the greatest benefits and the greatest ruin, for from the ideas that they spread come the deeds of the future. This is why the church has the greatest interest in supporting only those books that serve to benefit the faith, and in stopping those that may cause harm. Would you help the queen in this endeavor?"

Madame de Pompadour looked at Radominsky. What kind of offer was this that the queen's father confessor was making to her rival? Was he reaching out his hand to her or luring her into a trap? She had great respect for this man. The Polish Jesuit was not one of the many conceited abbés at court who thoughtlessly shed their cassocks at the sight of a pretty woman as easily as they once had sworn their oath of chastity at their ordination. He took his priesthood seriously—La Pompadour had never heard of a single transgression committed by Radominsky, although with his tall stature and his intelligent features he was a strikingly handsome man who certainly did not lack for opportunities. Yet he had the strength to renounce passion. It was this fact, probably more than his official position, which gave him the air of authority he radiated.

This man, she felt, possessed power over others because he had power over himself. She felt a kinship with him.

"What can I do, Reverend Father, to support the queen in her efforts?"

A satisfied smile passed over Radominsky's face. "You have the ear of King Louis," he replied. "If you could mention a name to His Majesty at a propitious moment, you would be doing the church a great favor."

"And what name did you have in mind?"

"Perhaps René-Nicolas de Maupeou? A man whose resolute faith is above reproach."

The smile on her face died. She knew the young *gentilhomme*—he was one of her worst adversaries at court. If the position in question was so important, she ought not suggest his name to the king. But what would happen if she refused the priest's request? Then she would be turning down the peace offering he was now making, but she would also be severing any possible bond between herself and the queen even before it was initiated. Madame de Pompadour could tell that this was a moment that would decide her entire future. She had to say something—but what? "Monsieur de Maupeou," she repeated hesitantly, "is surely a man of the highest qualities. But what would you say," she asked, following a sudden impulse, "of Chrétien de Malesherbes?"

"Malesherbes de Lamoignon? The son of the chancellor?" asked Radominsky, his eyebrows raised. His face showed surprise and deep respect at the same time. "A brilliant idea, madame."

"I'm pleased at your approval, Reverend Father. Then you also think that Monsieur de Malesherbes is a candidate that I could recommend to the king in good conscience?"

"Most certainly," said the father. "Only . . . would you please speak with him soon? The matter is urgent. Some of those so-called philosophers are already banding together to write an encyclopedia, which could jeopardize the welfare of the church and the state in the extreme."

"It would be my pleasure to attend to this matter," said Madame de Pompadour, her confidence restored. She reached out her hand so he could take his leave. "Please give the queen my most humble regards."

15

Sophie had seldom been so distracted at work as she was today. She had hardly closed her eyes all night, and by afternoon she had dropped an expensive pitcher of milk out of sheer clumsiness, and now she would have to pay for a replacement out of her own savings. What was the matter with her? Was it because there was a full moon? To make things worse, she had hardly eaten a thing—the cook had given her only moldy scraps. But no matter how hard she tried to find a logical explanation for the state she was in, she knew that something quite different was the actual cause. In reality she found herself constantly thinking about Monsieur Diderot. Would he be coming back to the Procope today?

"Mademoiselle Sophie!"

At a small table not far from the entrance sat Antoine Sartine, craning his neck to see her, as always with a friendly smile on his face. Seeing his expression, Sophie was overcome by a guilt that felt like a flash of heat. She had completely forgotten about his proposal! She wiped her hands on her apron and hurried to his table.

"As always, a cup of coffee, Monsieur Sartine?"

"As always, a cup of tea," he corrected her, still smiling. Then his expression turned serious. "Have you had a chance to think about my question?" An embarrassed twitch tugged at the corner of his mouth, and his face flushed bright pink.

"Yes, certainly," she stammered, "I mean . . ."

A customer coming in shoved his way between them. Before Sartine could say another word, Sophie took the opportunity to flee to the counter. As she attended to his order she wondered feverishly what to tell him. Of course she couldn't decide here and now—this would determine the future of her whole life!

"Chocolate?" Sartine asked, bewildered, when she returned with her tray to his table.

She looked at his cup with annoyance—the foam was sprinkled with cinnamon and vanilla. She hurried to go back and correct her mistake. Then she caught sight of Diderot, only an arm's length away from her. With an impudent grin he looked at her as if he'd surprised her in her bath. The tray, the cup, the saucer, all fell out of her hands. To the laughter of the guests she rushed past Sartine and Diderot and through the kitchen door.

There she sank down onto a stool. What a day! Along with the milk pitcher, the broken crockery would cost her a whole week's wages, more money than she possessed. She knew that she had to hurry back to the counter—if Monsieur Procope threw her out, she would have no choice but to return to Faubourg Saint-Marceau, frequented by the day laborers and sewer cleaners. She shut her eyes at the thought. But back out to Diderot and Sartine? She asked a woman washing dishes to gather up the shards and then trade jobs with her. Ten horses couldn't drag her back to the main room of the café. She would rather work in a tobacconist's shop to the end of her days than spend another minute in the presence of those two men.

At seven o'clock she had an hour free. Happy for the break, she took off her apron and left the café. She wandered aimlessly through the narrow streets, where twilight was gradually descending. While most Parisians were at dinner, a deep, tenuous peace returned to the city. In the squares the hackney cabs awaited, the horses eating oats from their feed bags and stamping their hooves on the cobblestones. Preparations for the opera performance had not yet begun, and the night roamers were busy with their toilette. For this one hour the great city rested, as if the hustle and bustle were tied to an invisible chain.

"Why did you run away?"

She was on Rue Mouffetard, and Diderot suddenly stood before her.

"Did you follow me?" she asked, as much bewildered as angry. "Haven't you done enough damage already?"

"Naturally I followed you, Mirzoza," he replied with his brazen grin. "How could I not? Everyone at the palace is on their feet searching for you. Look there," he said, pointing with his thumb to two whores standing in an entryway, freshly made up with bosoms half exposed and looking at them curiously. "Even the ladies of the harem have come to bring you home."

"Ladies of the harem?" Against her will Sophie had to laugh. "So in the East they must not look much different than they do in Paris."

"Don't worry," he said, "you have no need to be jealous. Mongagul has eyes for the princess alone. Do you happen to know what the first words were that the sultan said to her?"

"Let me guess. Perhaps 'a cup of hot chocolate'?"

"Totally wrong," he protested. "'With plenty of vanilla and cinnamon'!"

As matter-of-factly as if she'd been expecting it, he took her hand, and as he urged her along, he continued spinning his tale: How Sultan Mongagul was so in love with Princess Mirzoza that he commanded his sorcerer to make him grow a dozen arms so he could embrace her to his heart's content, a dozen hands to caress her, a dozen mouths to kiss her.

"Is that all he wanted?" asked Sophie.

"No," Diderot replied, "he needed a dozen ears too. Because nothing made the sultan happier than the sound of her voice, and when she laughed he thought he would perish from sweet bliss."

For Sophie his words felt like tender caresses. Could life be as beautiful as it was in his stories? Forgotten were the broken dishes, the café owner, the tobacconist in Faubourg Saint-Marceau. A couple of plasterers crossed their path to talk to the whores—stragglers of the great army of day laborers and craftsmen who streamed back to the outlying towns around Paris each evening. The lime on their shoes colored the cobblestones white, and as Sophie followed their tracks with her gaze, she listened to Diderot's words, which were as surely conveyed by his dark, warm voice as boats on a calm, broad river. Living in his fairy tales must be like living in paradise.

All at once he stopped and said, "Tell me a story. Why did you come to Paris?"

"How do you know that I'm not a Parisian?"

"Perhaps it's your accent?" He laughed. "No, you come from a region where the good wine grows."

"You can hear that from the way I talk?" she asked, astonished.

"Language reveals more than words can say. I would wager that you have lived in Langres, which is where I'm from. Or in Dijon? Or perhaps farther to the south"—he paused—"for example, in Roanne?"

As he so unexpectedly pronounced the name of the town that had brought her so much misfortune, the past rose up in her like a tidal wave. Suddenly she saw her mother before her, wearing her shift of shame, her face a blank white spot in which a mouth, a ghostly pair of lips, formed the word *happiness,* as if to warn her, and below that a colorful fluttering scarf.

"I needed work," she said softly. "That's why I came to Paris."

"Wasn't there anyone in your hometown who cared about you?"

Sophie hesitated. Should she tell him her story? She saw Baron de Laterre before her, saying farewell at the castle—he bent down to kiss her hair—then Abbé Morel, who delivered her to the cloister gate, entrusting her to the nuns. She had reached Paris as if through a labyrinth. After she left the convent, she first returned to Beaulieu to work at the baron's castle. But after only a few days she had secretly fled at dawn—she couldn't live in that place, where every house, every street, every tree reminded her of her mother, whose image she had tried to banish from her memory forever. After that she had been in all the towns that Diderot had named, first in Roanne, then in Dijon, and also in Langres, where she worked for two weeks as a washerwoman. But she had stayed nowhere for more than a month; she kept moving north, toward the capital, as if Paris were the clearing in the center of the labyrinth through which she was wandering. Deep inside she knew what she was seeking in this city. But could she speak of it to a stranger?

Suddenly she was aware that Diderot was still holding her hand. She pulled it away, and instead of answering him she asked a question that had been on her mind all day long. The question had come to her the night before, in her room, as she rummaged through her secret little treasure chest.

"Is it true that you write books?"

"Certainly," he replied with a hint of pride. "That's my profession."

"That's a profession?" she said, amazed.

"Of course! The best there is. Because if you make up a story, you can experience anything you want. Without leaving the house you can travel to foreign lands and get to know foreign peoples. You can talk with kings and wise men, meet women almost as beautiful as those here on Rue Mouffetard; and if you want, you can drink the most expensive wines without paying a *sou* for them. When you write, the whole world changes; all you need to do is give in to your wishes and imagination."

"Doesn't that frighten you?" asked Sophie. "It's so dangerous!"

"Dangerous? Why?"

"Because you act as though something exists when it doesn't. If people who aren't really alive, kings and wise men and beautiful women, suddenly pop up like genies from a bottle, that's like . . ." She searched for a comparison. "Like magic, like sorcery."

"And that's exactly how it must be!" he exclaimed, his eyes gleaming.

"Like magic and sorcery. But tell me, how did you come to think of this? Do you mean to say that you can read?"

"No!" She shook her head as vigorously as if he'd asked her to marry him. "Women who can read and write will never find happiness in life."

"Pardon me? Why is that?"

"Because that's just how it is," she said defiantly. "Besides," she added as he was about to contradict her, "Abbé Morel said so, the priest in my village, and he knows the whole Bible by heart."

"Probably because he can't read it himself."

"Why would you say that?" she asked angrily.

"Most village priests don't know how to read. It goes with the profession."

"I don't care what you say," she retorted. "God doesn't want women to read or write. Nor does He want them to love strange men . . ."

She fell silent. Those last words had tumbled out of her mouth all on their own. Why had she said that? All at once she felt terribly stupid and hardly dared look at Diderot. But when she raised her eyes he was smiling at her, and his smile seemed to envelop her in a cloak of silk.

"You shouldn't believe such things," he whispered, stroking her cheek. "God has nothing against love, only the Devil does."

His face was now quite close, and she was almost drowning in his luminous blue eyes. But strangely enough, that didn't scare her in the least; on the contrary, it was such a wonderful feeling that she no longer knew where she was at all. Was she in the mystic East? In the realm of Sultan Mongagul?

Then from somewhere came a woman's voice, loud and shrill like that of a fishwife: "Denis? What are you doing there?"

Diderot gave a start, and the smile vanished from his face. Like a thief he looked around, suddenly nervous. Sophie woke up. The wonderful feeling was gone, and she was once again on Rue Mouffetard. The two whores minced past, clinging to the arms of the two plasterers and grinning at her spitefully.

"Was that Madame de Puisieux?" asked Sophie.

"Why do you say that?" he stammered. "No, that . . . that was . . ." He didn't finish his sentence and tried in vain to smile.

"I don't believe a word you've said," she told Diderot and then left him standing there.

16

A new day was dawning at La Celle, a day like one on Kythera, the isle of love. Weightless, fleecy clouds floated in the pastel blue sky, which arched over the meerschaum-white pleasure palace like the ceiling of a theater; in the conical pollarded treetops the birds twittered as if a mechanical music box were producing their song; and above the canal lined with colonnades of roses hung the Chinese lanterns for the next evening gondola outing. But the Marquise de Pompadour could enjoy neither the new day nor the silky air streaming through the open window, caressing her young body that was clad only in a lilac négligée. Her lovely face wore a grave expression as she looked back at herself in the mirror, while a lady's maid fastened the tall wig on her head with golden clasps in order to prepare her for the *lever*, the morning audience held in her bedchamber; on this day La Pompadour was awaiting an important visitor.

What could be worrying the king's favorite so much that her smile, which usually revealed two of the loveliest dimples, had vanished so completely? It was concern for Louis's welfare and moody state of mind—a reflection of the plight of the entire court. Viewed from outside, Versailles seemed like a place of light and constant merriment, but in its depths lurked a terrible boredom. Like a deadly miasma it wafted through the palace to poison the spirit of the people living inside. The same men and women who attended balls and dinners like carefree butterflies, as if wanting to surpass one another in shamelessness and frivolity, fell as soon as they were alone into an emptiness and futility; only the prospect of further dissipation promised them any sort of escape. No one suffered more from this melancholy than did the king, and it was the task of his favorite to make him forget his satiation, to fill the unbearable surfeit of time with ceaseless activity, in order to protect his mind from the never-ending boredom that settled over Versailles during the daytime hours.

In the past La Pompadour had been more successful at this than any other favorite of Louis before her. She possessed the monarch with her body and with her spirit, without ever allowing him even for a moment to think about himself. She invented new distractions and amusements daily, kept every dark cloud and every shadow far away, eased and relaxed him with her charms in an enchanting whirl of sensual bewilderments, making the king yearn for her all the more, as she spoiled him with increasing extravagance. But in this incessant spiral of artificial desire, in which thrill replaced ecstasy, her powers threatened to wane. No matter how willing her spirit was to snatch Louis from apathy, her flesh was simply too weak to kindle anew the fire that he needed each time. The furrows on his brow had not escaped her notice last night, and to drive them away she'd had to resort to the most daring devices of the art of love. Was her time about to run out? For the sake of her daughter's future she was prepared to do anything to counteract such an outcome.

Perhaps Father Radominsky's suggestions would give her an opportunity to do just that. During his visit, the queen's father confessor had made her realize something new. In order to exert influence over people, there were other things that could be used besides love. Knowledge, as La Pompadour had gathered from his speech, seemed to be an equally strong force, perhaps even stronger. Whoever possessed knowledge not only had power over the changeable passions of people, but also power over their thinking, over their minds, hearts, and souls.

There came her guest already—in the mirror she saw him approaching: a young, rather stocky, red-faced man in a chestnut-colored coat with huge pockets, the lace ruffles strewn with snuff residue.

"Monsieur de Malesherbes," she cried, rising from her dressing table. "Such conduct! One may betray a woman, but one should never surprise her."

"To what do I owe the distinction of your invitation, Marquise?" he asked, without entering into her little coquetry.

La Pompadour reached out her hand to him with a smile, cautiously making sure that her negligée did not reveal too much of her charms. Was this the right man to consolidate her position at court? An ally against the many jealous individuals who strove to disparage her in the eyes of the king? How awkward he was as he bowed over her hand without wasting even a glance on her shapely body. No one would ever think that Malesherbes was the son of the chancellor and scion of one of the most powerful families in France; no older than thirty, he had already acceded to the posts of parliamentary councillor and public prosecutor. But La Pompadour was too experienced in the art of creating false impressions to let herself be misled by his behavior. Malesherbes was merely feigning modesty, just as he feigned indifference; actually he was an intelligent careerist who never let anyone see the cards he held. She decided to subject him to a little examination.

"Why have I summoned you here? Ah yes, I wanted to ask you about your dancing lessons. Have they brought the desired progress?"

Malesherbes grimaced. "My dance instructor told me yesterday that I am hopelessly without talent for the dance floor."

"That's why you move with so much more confidence on the much slipperier ground of politics. Ah," she sighed, "if only someone would explain to me how to place my feet in that venue. I'm afraid of stumbling at every step."

"An accomplished dancer such as yourself, madame? Politics is really not much different from dancing. In both instances it's a matter of leading other people. Admittedly not where they want to go, but where they ought to go."

"That might seem easy to a man; he is born to lead. But what do you advise for a woman?"

"That depends. Politics is the only field in which the character of a person does not stand in the way of his career. I would advise a stupid woman always to follow her husband—however, a smart woman should rely on her own instincts. After all, politics is nothing more than the art of being able to tell friend from foe."

"If only it were that easy," said La Pompadour. "How is one to distinguish all the factions at court and in the city? They seem to me a minuet gone wild. The parliament opposes the will of the king; in the church the Jesuits and the Jansenists are fighting like foxes and wolves; some support the state councillor, some the parliament—it's enough to make one dizzy."

"That too is like dancing. You get dizzy only if you concentrate too much on the steps and forget the overall objective. And it's the same in politics: to achieve the least for the many and the most for the few, but when in doubt, everything for oneself."

"So what distinguishes one party from another?"

"Their relationship to the truth," replied Malesherbes. "There are parties that actually believe what they say. Others, and they are in the majority, do not. Only the former are dangerous."

La Pompadour motioned for him to take a cup of coffee from the tray that a servant was proffering. As Malesherbes with lips pursed took a sip of the hot, black brew, she sat back down in front of the mirror, for a second displaying the pink calf of one leg.

"And to which party would you count the philosophers? From what I hear, they are planning an encyclopedia, a dictionary of heretofore unavailable erudition."

Malesherbes set down his cup as if he had burned his tongue. "The philosophers," he replied, "belong indubitably to the party of those who proclaim to possess the truth. Whether they actually possess it is another matter."

"You mean you consider the encyclopedia a dangerous undertaking?"

"Allow me to answer with an illustration, madame. The encyclopedia, if indeed it should come into being, is like a knife—one can use it either to slice bread or to kill a human being. What matters is what one chooses to do with it."

She liked his answer, but she held back her smile. "What would you do, Monsieur de Malesherbes, if you possessed such power?"

She gave him a searching look as she allowed her slipper, as if by accident, to glide off her pretty foot.

He returned her gaze without making the slightest move to pick up the slipper, and with an ironic smile he said, "I would place it at the feet of a beautiful woman—I am a Frenchman, after all."

Now she no longer needed to restrain her smile. "Monsieur de Malesherbes," she said, trusting in the effect of her two dimples, "I would very much like to recommend that His Majesty appoint you to an important position. The Royal Library needs a new director. It seems to me that you would be the proper man for the job."

"I am honored by your confidence in me," he replied. "But what service would you expect in return?"

His directness bordered on impertinence, and she almost regretted the favor that she had shown him. Reluctantly she pulled the slipper onto her naked foot. Should she, because of his impudent behavior, give up the idea of filling the position of censor with a man of her choice?

"Simply carry out your duties to the best of your ability," she said at last. "Ensure that I receive a copy of all dangerous printed material circulating in Paris, fresh from the press—and so on," she added, recalling the worried frown on the sovereign's brow. Her expression was so innocent that Malesherbes could not fail to interpret what she meant by such an ambiguity.

17

At the start of every third month Paris was gripped by an anxious foreboding, as if before an impending disaster or plague. The usually packed coffeehouses seemed to empty out, grown men blanched at the sight of the calendar, and housewives sold kitchen utensils and furniture. For on the eighth of the month the rent was due, and this payment tolerated no postponement. Anyone who didn't pay the rent would be out on the street.

But none of this agitation reached Diderot's ear. What did he care for the worries of everyday life? He was concerned with the happiness of the whole world! Unaffected by the comings and goings in the stairwell, or by the quarreling of the primary tenants and the subtenants, or by the threats of the building owner and the bailiff, he sat in his writing room under the roof beams and worked, all his senses immersed in the world that flowed from his pen.

It had been less than a month since he had seized upon the plan for the greatest and most important book of his life, perhaps even of the entire century: a book that would contain all human knowledge. With this book he, Denis Diderot, would move humanity forward into a state that would create a paradise on earth!

The work was going well. While his publisher, Le Bréton, was making a great effort to obtain the royal privilege to print the work, his co-editor, d'Alembert, was corresponding with the most important minds in France to acquire them as contributors. The famed natural scientist Buffon had already agreed to work with them, as well as the well-known legal scholar Montesquieu—even the great Voltaire, who tirelessly lent his voice to the forces of reason, in order to storm all the bastions of superstition and despotism, was prepared to put himself at the service of the cause.

It was Diderot's task to gather themes and ideas for the articles. And he did so with the greatest pleasure. Whatever there was to discover under the sun and in the human mind aroused his curiosity; for him, discussing the boundaries of knowledge was not work but enjoyment. He gave his spirit free rein, pursuing at random the first idea that occurred to him, like an idler at the Palais Royal running after a courtesan only to abandon her the next moment for another beauty. His thoughts wandered from one subject to another, from politics to philosophy to justice; from happiness to good taste to love.

Yes, love—that would have to be given a special place in the encyclopedia. Wasn't it the most beautiful promise of paradise, at once the presentiment and the fulfillment of earthly happiness? Diderot put down his pen and leaned back. Yesterday evening Sophie had spoken the word for the first time in his presence. How she had gazed at him with her green eyes. . . . He had feared that the time for love had already passed him by, that he had used up all the glorious emotions this condition could release in the soul and body of a man. But now, at the age of thirty-four, he had looked into these green eyes, and ever since that moment he had felt the wondrous desire that could elevate any gray, ordinary life to a celebration.

What sort of woman was Sophie? Twice she had evaded his questions about her background and her relatives, but her silence only enhanced the spell that she had cast over him—the secret of her past enveloped her like a gown of fine, delicate lace. What was she hiding from him? Did it have to do with her fear of books? How could she be afraid of books when she spoke so wisely and sensitively about them? He wanted to take away her fear of the magic of words and initiate her into it as if into a religion. Or was there another reason for her fear? Was she afraid of him? Or of Madame de Puisieux? Sophie had turned away from him so abruptly that he hadn't been able to disperse the doubt that had suddenly sprouted between them.

Madame de Puisieux . . . Thinking about his mistress, his mood darkened. How weary he'd grown of that woman! He had wanted to flee the confines of daily life with her, but how much more confining were the fetters in which he now found himself. She kept demanding money, money, and more money. Before him lay a manuscript that he had begun just for her, the beginning of an erotic novel for which Le Bréton had promised him fifty *louis d'or*—twelve hundred *livres*. But the assignment inspired him as little as did Madame de Puisieux herself—the surest sign that his love for her had come to an end. As soon as he looked at those damned pages, his inspiration flagged like an old, tired horse hitched to a cab.

Did Sophie reciprocate his feelings? Ah, if she only knew how things stood with him! Everything was quite different from what she imagined. Much simpler and at the same time much more complicated. Would he tell her the truth? Who knew, maybe there was a young man somewhere in Paris to whom she was promised, a worthy, industrious craftsman or laborer. If that was true, should he continue to court her? The notion that she might be giving another man her glances, her smile, and her laughter burned like acid in his soul. He shoved the manuscript for Le Bréton aside, took up his pen, and wrote on a fresh sheet of paper the title "Princess Mirzoza and Sultan Mongagul."

He had scarcely begun to write when the acid in his soul dissipated. If Diderot loved a woman, she inspired him—and no other woman had inspired him as much as Sophie. No, surely she was not promised to some unknown, nameless craftsman, but rather to Diderot himself, and he was free to pursue his love without regard for false realities that were merely inadvertent. He would make the most of all the tender emotions, all the wonderful sensations that she inspired in him—feelings that he had thought were lost to him. Ideas poured out of him so fast that his pen could hardly keep up and capture them. The story seemed to be inventing itself; he didn't need to stop to consider how it should proceed. All he had to do was listen to himself, follow the stirrings of his heart, as it covered one page after another.

When he had finished the first chapter, he made a decision. First, he wasn't going to visit Sophie again until he was done with this story. What he was writing here was no novel that he could sell for fifty *louis d'or*, but their own inescapable destiny, which now seemed to have conquered all doubt.

He wanted to give the story to Sophie so that they could experience it together.

18

The sense of relief was palpable at the Café Procope, like a sudden change in the weather. The newspaper readers kept rustling their papers; at the heavy oak tables the philosophers kept shouting their opinions at one another as if they'd spent weeks in a cloister under a vow of silence; and the chess players laughed, even when their own king fell. After long days of privation when everyone was busy scraping together every *sou,* they could finally come to the coffeehouse again. For the rent had been paid, wherever the money had come from, and with that their credit had risen with Monsieur Procope, and new credit could be chalked up.

Only one customer in the premises was unable to share the high spirits of springtime: Antoine Sartine. The prime minister, Malesherbes, the new favorite of the Marquise de Pompadour, had given him a tricky assignment: Sartine was supposed to track down "interesting" literature. The lieutenant had no doubt as to what that meant. The pornographic scribblings with which most of the so-called writers earned their living were circulating everywhere. Thank God somebody had finally decided to muck out the pigsty!

Antoine Sartine dearly wanted to help with this. But the fact that he was serving two masters had already caused him some concern: Father Radominsky was a man of the church, while Malesherbes was a man of the state. With an intuitive feeling for the play of powers, Sartine feared that such double loyalties would not go well in the long run. Whenever the big wheels turned in the mill of power, the smaller wheels usually got broken. And there was a second worry weighing on his soul; although it was of a private nature, it weighed no less heavily than the first: Sophie still had not given him an answer. She evaded him, avoided being alone with him for even a second. Did she sense his powerlessness? Had he given himself away by his hesitant behavior? And was she just like all other women?

"Where's Diderot? I have to speak to him urgently! At once! This very minute!"

A patron had grabbed Sophie by the arm and was haranguing her: Jean-Jacques Rousseau, the Swiss composer and libretto writer. His eyes were like those of a street preacher; as always, he was beside himself. About him Sartine knew only that the man suffered from two chronic illnesses, headaches and urinary problems, and that he had already had a big flop with an opera entitled *Les Muses galantes*.

"I'm sorry," replied Sophie. "But Monsieur Diderot hasn't been here all week. He seems to have vanished from the face of the earth."

"Vanished from the face of the earth? Nonsense! Don't think you can hide him from me!"

"Who, me? Hide Monsieur Diderot? What makes you say that?"

As she spoke her gaze fell on Sartine. At that instant the blood rushed to her face, and she quickly vanished into the kitchen, as if the milk were burning on the stove. Stammering a couple of unintelligible sounds, Rousseau flopped down on a chair with such a grim expression on his face that the other patrons at the table turned away or disappeared behind their newspapers.

Sartine didn't pay him any more attention. His one exchange of glances with Sophie had been enough to confirm his fears. Diderot! All she had to do was hear his name, and she became flustered. A week ago she had dropped a tray full of crockery when Diderot entered the café, and she confused the orders from her customers—yesterday she had even brought Sartine a scrambled egg sprinkled with cinnamon and vanilla. She kept looking toward the door as if expecting someone. Could all these things be coincidences?

Sartine counted out six *sous* to pay for his tea, and then he saw Rousseau leap to his feet.

"Have you also sold your soul? To that bloodsucker Le Bréton?"

In the doorway stood Diderot, a manuscript under his arm. He seemed far from happy to see his friend in the café.

"My soul is sitting precisely where it belongs, in the pineal gland," he replied, laying the manuscript on Rousseau's table. "Sit down, I'm buying. What would you like to drink?"

"Are you trying to bribe me?" Rousseau looked at him as though overcome by distaste. "How low you have sunk! You wanted to write novels, dramas, pamphlets—and now a dictionary? What a betrayal! You will regret it for the rest of your life!"

He was causing such a commotion that everyone in the café was staring at him. Diderot grabbed Rousseau by the arm and dragged him to the door. Sartine couldn't hold back a small gleeful smile.

When the two men stepped outside onto the street, Sartine stood up hastily. As he picked up his walking stick his eyes fell on the manuscript that Diderot had left lying on the table. As if issuing a mute challenge, the stack of pages looked back at him. Was this an opportunity? A sign? At the thought that the packet of paper might contain the smut that Malesherbes was searching for, Sartine felt something like excitement course through his humble body. Of its own accord his hand reached for the manuscript.

"Doesn't that belong to Monsieur Diderot?"

Sophie was looking at him as if he were a pickpocket who had just stolen a money purse.

"I . . . I just wanted to put it in safekeeping. But please, if you would rather . . ."

Without finishing his sentence, Sartine handed her the manuscript as if it were her property. Then he put the six *sous* for his tea on the table and turned to leave the café.

By the time he reached the door he had regained his composure. Gripping the door handle, he turned back and said, "With regard to my question, Mademoiselle Sophie—please give me your answer by the end of the month. I . . . I can't wait any longer."

19

"You wanted to touch the souls of men, to make them laugh and cry, to enlighten them and shake them up—everything that one can do with books. And with what? With an article about a boiled chicken? A treatise on the pocket watch? Don't make me laugh!"

Diderot would have gladly responded, but it was pointless. Once Rousseau flew into a rage, there was no stopping him. In the meantime they had walked through half the city, but Rousseau refused to calm down, even in the gardens of the Tuileries, where behind the yew hedges, scarcely hidden from the eyes of marquises and duchesses, the strollers for lack of public toilets answered the call of nature. Rousseau did what he always did: He talked, preached, challenged.

"Friendship, love—don't our ideals count anymore? Virtue, freedom, progress—all superfluous, just because Monsieur Le Bréton wants to get rich on a dictionary? That's why you're sacrificing your books? And you call yourself an author!"

Rousseau's whole body was shaking with agitation. He was shorter than Diderot, reaching barely to his shoulder, and by comparison he seemed almost a youth. They had known each other for several years, and both of them came from the provinces; they were almost the same age, and both sons of craftsmen, yet Diderot always thought of his friend as older and more experienced, and above all as far superior. He admired the incongruity with which Rousseau demanded change and renunciation from everyone, and how nothing could shake his belief in himself and his ideas. He would rather see the world end than give up his ideas. He remained unaffected by the putrid stench that hovered over the terraces of the Tuileries as if the royal pleasure garden were an absolute toilet.

"I don't know," said Diderot uncertainly, "whether I'm really an author. An author is someone who creates his destiny solely from within himself, in order to solve the riddle of existence. If I were that sort of man—wouldn't I have written my novels and dramas long ago?"

"What's the point of this feminine twaddle? You have all the gifts you need to do great work. Feeling, reason, anger!"

"Anger? At whom?"

"You can't be serious. At the legal system, at the royal court, at the clerics—at the whole corrupt society. You've always criticized the belief in miracles and exposed the corruption of morals."

"And I'm pursuing nothing less with the *Encyclopedia*."

"Shall I tell you what you're pursuing with the book? An annual income—that's your real interest. Damn it, man!"

Rousseau stopped and shook his head like a teacher disappointed by a misguided pupil. And Diderot did feel like an errant pupil under the reproachful gaze of his friend. For a moment all his courage dwindled away. Could Rousseau be right? Was his decision to undertake the *Encyclopedia* actually a betrayal of his own as-yet-unwritten works?

"It's not the money," Diderot said tentatively. "The *Encyclopedia* is the advance artillery of reason, an armada of philosophy, a war machine of enlightenment—"

"You can't fool me," Rousseau interrupted him. "You have your Nanette, I have my Thérèse, and I know what I'm talking about. Every year she gets pregnant, and I have to take the brats to the foundling home." He turned away and walked on. "A man of your talent! A genius who can make history with his pen! Selling yourself for a few pieces of silver! What an appalling thought!"

"So what do you think I should do?"

"Why are you asking me? Go ask your beloved d'Alembert."

As he spoke the name Rousseau's face contorted as if only now did he notice the stench issuing from the yew hedge. Diderot stopped short: Was this the real reason for Rousseau's agitation? Because Le Bréton had not offered him, but Diderot and d'Alembert, the editorship of the *Encyclopedia*?

"How would it be if you were to write the article on music?" Diderot ventured. "You could present your new system of music notation, and that way the whole world would learn about it."

Rousseau waved aside the offer. "Le Bréton is a publisher, and publishers hate me. They're too stupid to understand me. My ideas overtax those moneybags."

"The *Encyclopedia* offers asylum for all great ideas. Voltaire has already agreed, as well as Buffon and Montesquieu."

"Voltaire?" Rousseau snorted. "Ten years from now nobody will remember that old windbag."

Without further comment he disappeared behind a hedge so abruptly that Diderot could do nothing but follow him.

"Good Lord, what have I done to deserve this?" Rousseau stood softly cursing in a corner as he tried to empty his constantly irritated bladder. "Ah—finally . . ." Diderot heard a faint splashing. "Does she have big breasts, at least?" Rousseau asked over his shoulder.

"Big breasts? Who do you mean?" Diderot asked in return.

"The woman for whom you're selling your soul. Big breasts are important. One time in Venice a whore plied all the arts of her trade to enchant me, but when I saw her naked I clapped my hands to my face and cried. Not what you think," he explained gruffly, as Diderot grinned. "I was holding a deformed woman in my arms! She had the chest of a boy. Incapable of suckling a baby. Against *that* my body revolted!"

There was one last splash.

As Rousseau buttoned up his fly, he said suddenly, "If I were to agree to take part in this encyclopedia, it would be under one condition . . ."

Diderot pricked up his ears. "Namely?"

"That you ask me to do it as a favor to you, as my friend. I wouldn't be capable of leaving you in the lurch."

"Then I hereby solemnly beg this favor of you," said Diderot. "And if you like, I'll even get on my knees."

He made as if to follow his words with action, but Rousseau magnanimously restrained him.

"It would be best if I wrote the foreword to the whole thing. So that readers will grasp what the *Encyclopedia* is all about. That society has to change, radically, in all ways and from the ground up. . . ." Instead of finishing his thought, he changed the subject once again. "Could you possibly lend me ten *sous*? As an advance against my fee? Thérèse told me to bring home some bread."

"Here's a *livre*," said Diderot happily, pressing the coin into Rousseau's hand.

"Don't think I owe you any thanks for this," said Rousseau as the coin disappeared into his pocket. "I'm merely giving you the opportunity to do a good deed. But tell me, what was that manuscript you had under your arm at the Procope?"

20

The echo of millions of words still hovered between the black ceiling beams of Café Procope. The low, pastel yellow walls were saturated with the thoughts and conversations of the day. Sophie heaved the heavy red-leather chairs onto the massive oak tables. The lamps had burned down as the last patrons left the café. Then Sophie was alone in the huge, dark room, in which the shadows gradually devoured the rest of the light.

How long she had waited for this moment! Instead of bolting the oaken door as she should, she dashed to the counter almost before the last customer had reached the street. There on the shelf lay the stack of paper that had drawn her attention all day like flypaper drew flies in the room. She kept checking on it to make sure that it was still in its place, panicked that someone might have taken it; at the same time she had hoped that it would dissolve into nothingness.

Should she or shouldn't she? As if she'd touched the top of a hot stove, the paper burned her skin as she reached for the manuscript. Several hundred handwritten pages, the greatest treasure that had ever fallen into her hands. What story might it contain? What spirits lived in the curves and lines of the letters, in the sentences and words?

She had the same feeling as when she was a child and had reached for one of the books that her father, Dorval, had taken out of his pack. The memory filled her with such joy that she grew anxious and afraid. No, she would resist the temptation. Instead of taking the manuscript to her room, she put it back in the drawer, deciding to give it to Monsieur Procope early the next morning for safekeeping. After all, she knew who had written all those pages. She would never read a single line of that manuscript.

She ran her hand over the stack once more—then the cover page slipped aside, and before she could look away, the title jumped out at her: "Princess Mirzoza and Sultan Mongagul." At the sight of those words the most contradictory feelings seized hold of her; she felt a sweet and simultaneously painful dwindling of her willpower, a sensation that had sometimes confused her mind back at the cloister through long nights of wistful loneliness. And without realizing what she was doing, she began to read.

> *The palace of the sultan loomed up in the desert of sadness, where instead of sweet water the springs fed on salty tears, so that the ruler Mongagul suffered a greater torment of thirst the more often he drank of them. Only a smile would free him from this curse. Yet in vain did the jesters at court attempt to cheer him up; not even the realm's loveliest maidens, whom the famed sorcerer Cucufa had commanded with his magic ring to beguile their master, could release Mongagul from his great sorrow. But one day a young princess knocked at the gate of his palace. Mirzoza was her name, and she came from the farthest province of the kingdom, the smallest and yet most beautiful province, the province of happiness. Her hair blazed like flames of fire, and with her she carried a steaming bowl of sweet chocolate. That was the medicine of her homeland, and she wanted to bring it to her master. . . .*

With pounding heart Sophie read on, page after page, immersing herself in the story, as she forgot everything around her, enchanted by a world that was her own and yet as foreign to her as the world in a fairy tale. She didn't notice as the lamps in the café burned out one by one, she didn't feel the cold of the night that slowly crept in through the gaps in the windows, nor did she hear the creaking of the door or the approaching footsteps. While her lips whispered the words and sentences as if she were reciting a prayer, Sophie was aware only of her own body, her heart and soul, and what was happening in the story, all the events and the emotions. She shared the hopes and fears of the princess as if Mirzoza were none other than herself; she shared her tears and laughter, her sorrows and desire, but above all her love.

"You can read!"

Sophie gave a start as though encountering someone in a dark cellar. Before her stood Diderot, a look of joyous amazement on his face.

"R-read?" she stammered, his manuscript in her hand. "I? How do you mean? Yes . . . no . . . I mean . . ."

She was so confused that she was nodding and shaking her head at the same time. Diderot looked at her with his blue eyes. Without a word he stuffed the manuscript into the big pocket of his coat, took her by the hand, and led her outside.

The night was bright with moonlight. The stars shone so clear and close in the sky above that it almost seemed possible to reach out and touch them. Silently the two walked side by side in the direction of the Seine. The streets were practically deserted. As they neared the river Sophie waited for Diderot to speak, but he did not. He simply held on to her hand, a warm, strong grip, as if their hands already belonged together; he held her hand in his and walked beside her through the night. And the farther they walked, the calmer they both became.

As they saw the Seine before them shimmering in the moonlight, Sophie asked, "Have you written many stories like this before?"

"No," he said. "This story is for you alone. Because you gave it to me."

"I did? In my entire life I've never made up a story!"

"That's the magic of it. A smile, a wink from you, and already a whole story has come into being." He stopped and looked at her. "Why did you claim that you couldn't read?"

She lowered her eyes and said nothing.

"Out of fear of books? Or fear of me?"

"Both," she said softly.

"But you don't have to do that! Anyone who's afraid of books is really afraid of life!"

Sophie hesitated. Was this the moment to tell him the truth? "I once knew a man," she said at last, "I don't know his name, and I remember only that he wore a plumed hat. He reported a woman to the police because she owned books. And because of that the woman—"

"Do I look like I'm wearing a plumed hat?" Diderot interrupted her with a laugh. "I don't even wear a wig. So there's no reason to be afraid of me." He took her hands and gave them a squeeze. "Do you know why I write books? Because I believe that nobody should be afraid of any other person. Because I believe that life can be much more beautiful than it is for most people. And because I believe that every person has the right to find happiness in this world, and not wait until the hereafter."

"Don't you want to know who the woman was?" Sophie asked. "And what happened to her?"

He shook his head, then stroked her cheek so tenderly that he scarcely touched her. "Forget about the past. Forget your fear of books. Forget what this abbé told you. Priests warn people away from books because of their own fears. Because books might unmask their lies."

"But it wasn't lies, it was God's will! I saw myself how the woman—"

"Shhhh," he said, placing his finger to her lips. "Do you really believe that everything that happens is God's will? Like the time you dropped the tray at the Procope? Or when a customer lights a pipe?"

"But God is the Almighty," she protested. "So nothing could happen against His will."

"That's what people claim who want everything to remain exactly the same." Diderot shook his head again. "We have no idea who God is or what He wants. If we could see or hear Him or at least touch Him—I would fall to my knees before Him and say, 'Thy will be done!' But as things stand? We don't know a thing about Him, we know only our own ideas, the images that we make of Him. Does He really have a long white beard like in the pictures in church? Or could it be that He shaves every morning?"

"Like Sultan Mongagul with his hot chocolate mustache?"

"You see?" said Diderot when he saw her smile. "It doesn't matter how we imagine God, it always seems a bit comical. The pictures that we draw of Him are no more true or false than any made-up novels or stories. And that's why I believe that God, if He does exist, leaves the choices to us. We have to decide for ourselves how we want to live. We just need the courage to take responsibility for our own lives."

He pulled his manuscript out of his coat pocket and handed it to her.

"I want you to take it."

"B-but . . ." Sophie stammered, surprised at the sudden gift, "I . . . I just can't—"

"Of course you can!" he replied. "It's our story. It belongs to you. I want you to read it."

As she held the manuscript in her hands she felt as though it repre-sented her own life. Suddenly she saw her mother before her, her figure and the contours of her face blurred but unmistakable, her eyes, her mouth, the last word on her lips: *happiness.* Had she misunderstood her mother's message all these years? Did her mother want to warn her away from happiness, or embolden her to seize happiness? Was she telling her not to be afraid? Either of books or of love?

As if he were guessing her thoughts, Diderot said, "Life is more beau-tiful than any heaven. Shall I prove it to you?"

Then his face came so close that she thought she could feel the warmth of his skin. The midges at the back of her neck buzzed as she looked into his bright eyes.

"How?" she asked softly, although her body already knew the answer.

Instead of replying he kissed her. Then she was no longer in control of the situation. As his lips touched hers, she closed her eyes, and all at once a thousand arms seemed to enfold her, a thousand hands to caress her, a thousand mouths to kiss her. The world vanished along with her senses, and she lived only in this single kiss: She was in paradise.

"What's the meaning of this?"

A shrill, sharp voice yanked her back to reality. Sophie opened her eyes. Before her stood a blond woman, as pretty as a cherub with a trumpet, but furious as a fishwife. In her arms she carried a sleeping child.

"Madame de . . . Puisieux?" asked Sophie when she regained her voice.

Diderot shook his head. His broad shoulders, sturdy enough to carry a heavy load, had caved in; his small head twitched like that of a bird before a thunderstorm. He didn't dare return her gaze.

"Madame de Puisieux? His mistress?" screeched the stranger. "How? What?" She kicked Diderot in the shin and beat him with her fist. "Go on, tell the little strumpet who I am, so she knows! Or shall I tell her?"

"This is . . ." he stammered at last, "this is . . . my wife."

Although the streetlamps were still burning, all at once it seemed to be darkest night. The ground beneath Sophie's feet pitched, the stars in the sky seemed to dance, and suddenly Diderot was wearing a hat from which a big plume sprouted into the air.

Without a word she tossed his manuscript at his feet.

21

"So this is where you hang around! With strange women! I've been looking all over town for you."

The reproaches that Nanette heaped on him struck Diderot like a bucket of cold water.

"I waited for you until midnight, then went looking for you at the coffeehouse, but the place was dark. The landlord came by and he wants his rent. He's threatening to call the bailiff!"

"Why is that? We paid the rent."

"Only the first installment. And only because I sold my morning coat, while you crept up to your garret. We'd be on the street if I didn't take care of everything. What a contemptible man you are!"

Her voice broke into a sob. Diderot wanted to put his arm around her, but as soon as he touched Nanette's shoulder her wrath flared up again. His guilty conscience seemed to give her new energy.

"Ever since we got married you've betrayed me. All the promises you've broken! Your own father would curse you if he saw the misery that you've brought upon us."

The baby in her arms was awakened by all the shouting and began to cry. As Nanette tried to calm her son, Diderot bent down to gather up the pages of his manuscript. His story threatened to blow away in the night wind—the only true story in his life. Was he supposed to sacrifice this work for the trashy novel of his marriage?

As he rearranged the loose pages, all the misery he had suffered with Nanette broke open inside him. How he had fought to win this woman! He had met her in the shop owned by her mother, a seamstress, and that same day he had bought three shirts from her, although he'd had to borrow the money from a pawnshop. Because of her lovely milliner's face he had quarreled with his father, whom he revered more than any other man in the world; he had gone behind his father's back and married

Nanette in all secrecy. For the sake of her caresses he had entered service as a chancellery scribe, selling his pen to missionaries and newspaper hacks so that she would no longer have to prick her fingers for strangers. And for what? Her stupidity repelled him as much as her physical charms attracted him; their love was spent in breathless nightly embraces for which he cursed himself in the morning—although he did wish that nature had not endowed her quite so generously.

"I'm not even allowed to take your name," she bickered. "And yet I've borne you three children. What a disgrace! Am I not good enough for you? After all that I've given up for you? My profession! My mother's trade! Because of your jealousy I was forced to close the shop, since you couldn't stand to see a customer smile at me!"

"You threw yourself at the customers," replied Diderot, still picking up the loose pages. "You flirted with them and made me look like a fool . . ."

"You locked me in! Like a nun! I was hardly allowed out on the street—it was always work, work, work. Look at these hands, nothing but calluses and blisters. Hands like a washerwoman."

"I don't keep a *sou* for myself. All the money I make I give to you."

"You give it to your other women, and I don't know how I'm supposed to feed our children. Two of them have already died for lack of food to eat. In the meantime Monsieur drinks hot chocolate at the café like a refined gentleman." Her voice broke again. Sobbing, she went on: "You promise other people a paradise on earth, but for us you make life a hell. I'm going to write to your father and ask him to take us in."

Finally Diderot had gathered up all the pages of his manuscript. When he straightened up he saw his son: His face smeared with tears, the boy reached out his little hand to his father. Diderot suddenly recalled a moment from his own childhood. The incident had happened more than twenty years ago, but he remembered it as if it were yesterday. He had come home from school, loaded with prizes, and over his shoulder he carried a laurel wreath that was much too big. His father was already working at the open window, and when he saw his son from afar he put down his tools and cried with joy. Diderot had to swallow hard. Wasn't that all he wanted in life? To be a good son, a good father? No longer listening to the accusations that Nanette was flinging at him, he opened his arms wide to give his son a hug—then he caught sight of Madame de Puisieux. Lifting her skirts, she came hurrying from the direction of the Procope.

Diderot knew what was going to happen now, but he was unable to move; he couldn't stop the drama. Like two furies the women fell upon each other, yanking at their clothes and hair, as they berated each other with the foulest language, paying no attention to the child, who shrieked with fear.

Suddenly Diderot flew into a rage. Why did he always try to make things right for everyone except himself?

22

❦

"Credo in unum Deum. Patrem omnipotentem, factorem coeli et terrae . . ."

With great fervor Sophie recited the prayers of her childhood, the Lord's Prayer and the Credo, the testament of her Catholic faith, but she couldn't find the way out of the labyrinth. Every new passageway merely led deeper into the maze, this inescapable jumble of tangled paths that was her life, without a single clearing opening up anywhere.

As she knelt on the floor barefoot, the way she had always done as a child when praying, the sounds of cats penetrated into her room from outside. This wasn't the meowing of a tomcat in love, but the cries of pain uttered by a dying animal. Almost every night the printer's apprentices in the neighborhood tormented the stray cats because the beasts kept them awake with their yowling. They would knock the cats off the rooftops or kill them.

". . . visibilium omnium et invisibilium. Et in unum Dominum Jesum Christum . . ."

Sophie didn't stop whispering the foreign words, which were nevertheless such familiar sounds; she poured all her despair into her prayers. How could this happen? What was happening now? She did know, and had always known, what happened to women who fell in love with such men. Diderot was dangerous, as dangerous as her father, Dorval, a married man who made up stories and even wrote his own books. And then all this talk about God and Heaven, about Paradise and love and being happy . . . Hadn't her mother warned her about such men?

Outside, the cats were shrieking for the last time. Then everything was quiet. Sophie looked up but saw only her own face in the shard of mirror she had fastened to the wall: red hair and freckles . . . Was she going to turn out like her mother? A woman who rebelled against every law in her attempts to attain a forbidden happiness? In the end only to be punished twice and three times over?

"*. . . Et in unum Dominum Jesum Christum, Filium Dei unigenitum. Et ex Patre natum ante omnia saecula.*"

Sophie was overcome by desperation. She had come to Paris to find justice, because this was the city from which the official pardon had once come for her mother. Here she had hoped to find answers to all the questions that had haunted her since childhood, that had pursued her first in the cloister and then later in Dijon and in Langres and in Roanne, through all the events of her life. Was this the answer? The justice she was searching for? That she was doomed to be as cursed and damned as her mother?

On the staircase were footsteps, loud, hurrying, stamping footsteps. Then there was a knock at her door.

"Mirzoza!"

Sophie gave a start. She clasped her hands again and closed her eyes.

"*Deum de Deo, lumen de lumine, Deum verum de Deo vero . . .*"

"Mirzoza! Open the door! I have to talk to you! Please—Sophie!"

Again and again he called her name, called and knocked and called again. Sophie covered her ears with her hands and blocked out everything with the power of her prayer. No, she was not her mother, she understood the example that had been made of her. She spoke the words of faith so loudly that she could no longer hear him calling. And yet she couldn't banish the images that she saw in her mind's eye—images of his face, of his head, of his hat, from which a big plume seemed to grow. . . .

"*. . . Et in Spiritum Sanctum . . . et unam, sanctam, catholicam et Apostolicam Ecclesiam. Confiteor unum baptisma in remissionem peccatorum. Et exspecto resurrectionem mortuorum. Et vitam ventura saeculi . . .*"

Again and again she repeated the prayer. But while her lips confessed the faith, she was filled with fear; she felt only fear, was nothing but fear.

How could she free herself from the fear?

23

Champagne corks popped. The champagne foamed white into the glasses that were held out to Le Bréton from all sides. Half of the customers in the Procope were crowded around the publisher, who was pouring from two bottles simultaneously as he spoke. "With the birth of Moses began the reckoning of time by the Jews, with the birth of Jesus the chronology of the Christians, and with the birth of the Prophet the age of the Mohammedans. These birthdays have now become history. Because today begins a new reckoning of time—the chronology of the philosophers!" He put down the bottles and held a document in the air triumphantly, like a trophy. "Here is the endorsement of the king, the permission to print the *Encyclopedia!*" He smacked a kiss on the parchment and then solemnly read the text aloud. "'For a universal lexicon of the sciences, arts and handicrafts, based on the principles of reason, translated from the dictionaries of Chambers, Harris, and Dyche, augmented by additional contributions edited by an association of learned men . . .'"

His words were drowned out by calls for more champagne. It was as if all the garret scribblers of Paris had streamed out of their dens and into the Procope to pay homage to Le Bréton. Like a king the publisher held court, flanked by his partners and investors, who in celebration of the day had deigned to put in an appearance at the coffeehouse.

"I admit," said d'Alembert with an embarrassed smile, "that until today I never really believed it would succeed. But if the king gives you his consent"—childlike amazement filled his russet eyes—"it means that not only is he granting permission for the *Encyclopedia,* he is giving it his official stamp of approval, thus recommending it to all Frenchmen to read—"

"To buy, you mean!" the publisher corrected him with a look of rapture on his walrus face.

"And how did you manage that?"

"You just have to know how to talk to people—the king's chancellor is only human, after all." Le Bréton's wrinkled visage was flooded with self-satisfied bliss. "The chancellor was worried about only one thing: as little theology as possible! Otherwise the priests would make things hot as hell. But I was able to reassure him. I talked to him for half an hour about farming and raising livestock, about how useful the *Encyclopedia* would be for French agriculture, until he started to yawn with boredom. Farming and raising livestock—the noble ladies and gentlemen will be amazed!"

"And do we actually have the freedom," asked d'Alembert, "to modify the English edition?"

"The more the better; then I won't have to pay the Englishmen a royalty," Le Bréton replied with a chortle. He raised his glass and toasted his guests. "But where in hell is Diderot? Wasn't he just here?" He stood on tiptoe to look for his editor. At last he discovered him standing at the counter in conversation with the proprietor. "Hey, what are you waiting for? Come over and join us. We're drinking a toast."

Diderot raised his hand. "Just a moment." As he answered he turned back to the owner. "Yes, it's Sophie I mean, the waitress with the red hair. I have to speak to her at once. Is she in the kitchen?"

Monsieur Procope shook his head morosely. "She's off today, of all days."

"Off? Why is that?"

When Diderot heard the answer, he blanched.

"She got married this morning, to one of the regulars. He usually sits over there by the entrance. I think his name is Sartine—you might know him."

24

Sophie had climbed into bed before her husband. She had pulled the covers up to her chin in order to hide her nakedness—underneath she was wearing only a shift. What would happen when Sartine came to her? Her heart pounding, she waited for him to lie down beside her.

What a day! Everything had happened so quickly that Sophie could hardly take it all in. A young curate had married them after morning mass in Saint-Germain-des-Prés, and now she lay in a soft, expensive feather bed instead of on her straw mattress in the garret above the Procope. Sartine's apartment had two rooms, a kitchen and a bedroom, and even its own privy on the landing; they had to share with only three other families. What luxury! The bed linens, the sheets—everything was new. Sophie had thought she would have to purchase her trousseau at the Marché Saint-Esprit, the flea market on the Place de Grève, where the executions were held. But Sartine didn't want any used items and had insisted on buying everything needed in the household at respectable shops, from towels to washcloths.

His whole face beamed when she finally told him her answer was yes. For Sophie his joy was still a mystery. Why had he chosen her for his wife? She was poor, no prettier than thousands of other girls, and she brought no dowry to the marriage. Sartine had a chiming pocket watch, a framed mirror, and silk stockings; above all, he earned a steady income. On every street, in every building, there were dozens of women who would have married him on the spot. What price would he demand of her?

Noises were coming from the kitchen; it sounded like water being poured into a basin. She thought of the whispering of the maidens in the convent, dark hints of what awaited a woman on her wedding night, and she felt a vague longing in her body. But for what? The nuns had kept talking about pain; how she would hurt and bleed, and the best thing would be to shut her eyes tight and pray softly until it was done with. Suddenly she got goose pimples all over. She really knew nothing about Sartine, only that he was a civil servant and preferred tea. Now she was going to spend the rest of her life with this man. She wondered if he had bad breath. Nothing could be more disgusting. The coachmen and sewer workers at the tobacco shop in Faubourg Saint-Marceau had stunk so abominably that she often felt sick to her stomach when she waited on them.

She gave a little sigh. No, she really didn't know a thing about her husband. But what woman did when she married?

When Sartine came into the room, she imagined at first that it was Diderot. But it was only a fleeting image that vanished as soon as her husband sat down next to her on the edge of the bed. He was wearing a white nightshirt that reached all the way to the floor. It was strange, but wearing that garment, he looked just as proper as he did by day in his suit, and his expression was as friendly as it was in Café Procope when she brought him his tea. Relieved, Sophie noticed how good he smelled—clean and fresh, as if he had just had a bath.

"Are you frightened?" he asked.

She nodded without looking at him.

Gently he touched her shoulder. "You don't have to be. I won't hurt you. We don't have to . . . today—I mean, if that's what you're afraid of."

She could feel by his touch that he was as nervous as she was, and his face almost showed gratitude as she returned his smile.

"I would never force you to do anything that you didn't want to do. I promise. You . . . you can decide for yourself when you're ready." He pulled open the drawer of the bedside table and took out a small silver ring.

"May I?" he asked, taking her hand. And as he slipped the ring on her finger, he said, "I have only one request: that we respect each other as is proper for a married couple, and that neither of us does anything to offend the other."

"Then you don't want to do what love demands?" Sophie asked, unsure whether she had actually understood him.

Sartine shook his head. "Love is not the best guide. I've seen too many people who have followed love, only to end up in misery. No, I'm more richly rewarded simply by having you as my wife."

He leaned over to blow out the candle on the nightstand. Then he lay down beside her.

Sophie scarcely dared breathe when she felt his body at her side. Sartine hardly moved either; his breathing was regular, and yet she knew that he was not asleep. Why hadn't he touched her? That was the least he could demand from her. Outside, a coach rattled past from time to time, full of late-night theatergoers and gamblers just now making their way home. Night after night the clatter of the coach wheels woke sleeping citizens, and Sophie knew that some Parisians had this noise to thank for their own conception. The sound reminded quite a few couples of the consummation of their marriage, an act from which she had been spared tonight.

"Are you still awake?" he asked so softly that she sensed rather than heard the words.

"Yes," she whispered.

"I can't tell you how happy I am."

With that he took her hand, and although it was the first time he had done so, his touch seemed familiar to her, as if they had belonged to each other for years. A warm feeling spread inside her, a feeling of safety and security, a feeling that she had thought lost for all time. With a sigh she responded to the tender pressure of his hand. He was not a stranger, after all; he was her husband, and she felt closer to him than to any other person since her mother died.

Suddenly Sophie needed to talk, to tell him her story and who she was, and before she knew what she was doing she began to speak, whispering softly as if to herself, while outside the night watchman sang his weary song. She spoke of the day of her First Communion, of the trial they had made her mother endure because she had vomited up the Body of Christ, about the man with the plumed hat . . . And later, deep in the night, when the streetlamps had long since burned out and the last cabs had rolled by, she told him about the worst day of her life, the day they executed her mother. She told him about the great loneliness that had enveloped Madeleine as she stood on the scaffold wearing the shift of shame, with both hands chained and forever separated from Sophie. She told him about the multicolored scarf around her mother's neck that fluttered defiantly in the wind, about the cat that had fled from the scaffold, taking long leaps as if chased by a thousand demons as the flames shot up into the air.

Sartine did not interrupt her even once; quietly attentive, he listened to her story until she finished speaking.

"Is that why you came to Paris?" he asked her then.

"I don't know," said Sophie, surprised by his question. "But perhaps, yes, I think so. You're right. It was like a compulsion; I simply had to come to Paris after I left home. But how could you know that?"

"Maybe I can help you," he said.

"Help me? How? It was all so long ago, and my mother . . ." She faltered, then added, "It was God's will, what happened back then."

"Could be," he replied. "But isn't it also a question of justice?" He sat up next to her, and although she couldn't see him in the dark, she knew that he was looking at her. "Justice is not subject to the limitations of time. I could help you find the man who testified against your mother, the man with the plumed hat. There must be documents, reports, protocols . . ."

"You would do that for me?" she asked, using as always the formal *vous*. "Really? But what have I done to deserve this?"

"You don't have to address me with *vous* any longer, Sophie! You're my wife now, so call me *tu*."

Without a word she squeezed his hand. Then she felt his lips on her cheek—a soft, tender kiss in the dark.

"Which side do you prefer to lie on when you sleep?" he asked.

"On the left," she whispered happily and turned on her side.

Yes, she thought as she finally closed her eyes, she had found the right man, a simple, honest man who loved her and was ready to share his life with her. Feeling as warm and cozy as if angels had tucked her in, she fell asleep, back to back with Antoine Sartine, lieutenant in the Paris criminal police, who was still holding her hand in his.

Only once, for a second, did she see Diderot's face. But by then she was already dreaming.

25

❦

That night Diderot could not sleep. While the great kraken of Paris sluggishly greeted the new day, insensible of the irritations and flatulence in its bowels, Diderot sat in his scarlet robe at his writing desk, the goose quill in his hand, his eyes shining with tears. It was neither the clatter of the coaches nor the shouts of the night watchmen that were keeping him awake at this late hour, but the bitter realization that love was the most common, the most treacherous, the most malicious of all illusions, a deception from heaven or from the bestial bodily fluids in human beings, invented solely to lead astray whoever succumbed to it. There was no such thing as love, there was only passion or surfeit of desire—the liaison with Madame de Puisieux or his marriage to Nanette. Anyone who claimed otherwise was telling fairy tales.

With a mixture of fury and disappointment Diderot took out a manuscript that was soiled with dirt from the street: "Princess Mirzoza and Sultan Mongagul." It contained so many stories that all conspired to shape a reality, and he had squandered his spirit, his energy, his entire life force on this falsehood, under the delusion that here he had found his true story, the one great novel that his destiny had reserved for him alone, a love that had never before been described in any book. But Sophie was not Mirzoza, nor was he an Oriental sultan—she had betrayed him!

How could he have been so wrong about this woman? Sophie—a princess? She was a little strumpet who threw herself at the first available man! There were thousands of her type in the coffeehouses of Paris. On the very day that his great dream had been fulfilled, when the *Encyclopedia* had been approved for printing by the king's chancellor, on the day when this book, with which he would change the world, actually took on concrete form, she had married a police officer, an informer and spy.

He slapped his forehead so hard that it hurt. What an idiot he'd been! He had made a fool of himself. He had even refused fifty *louis d'or* because like a lovesick tomcat he had wanted to believe in the chimera called love, against all reason and philosophy. What was love, really? Nothing more than the exchange of moods and the touch of skin between two people.

Suddenly he had an idea. He now knew the truth of this woman and decided to rewrite the novel from scratch. He would unmask Sophie for all the world to see, reveal her soul, tell the entire loathsome story the way it deserved to be told. And with the help of the only organ by which women could be cured. He tore up the pages of his novel and wrote a new title on a cover sheet: "The Indiscreet Jewels." He would divide up the fee fairly: twenty *louis d'or* for the rent and his wife, thirty for his mistress and his amusement.

With the feeling of finally becoming a man again, he began to write.

26

"It is the malady of our time that Faith is dragged before the Bench of Reason. But anyone who wants to enter into the Kingdom of Heaven must put Reason in the service of Faith. Faith alone will show us the way and the goal. . . ."

But would everything come to a good end? As great and sublime as the Kingdom of Heaven, so heralded by Father Radominsky in his mighty voice, was the cathedral of Notre-Dame, in which Sophie was attending holy mass on this Sunday morning. Near the pulpit she sat in the pew, her eyes fixed on the preacher, whose gaze and words struck her like lightning and thunder. Through his sermon he seemed to be looking straight into her heart, seeing all the doubts that had pursued her in recent weeks and nearly brought her down.

"Do all of you not hear the hiss of the serpent when you vacillate between following the Lord and giving in to your desires? Do not forget that the desires of the flesh are directed against the spirit. The two confront each other as enemies and make you incapable of doing God's will. . . ."

Sophie opened her ears and her heart in order to let the words find their way inside her and stifle the last doubt in her soul. Today, on the first Sunday after her marriage to Antoine Sartine, she would finally approach the Altar of the Lord. She put her hand on the back of her neck to drive off the swarm of midges that she seemed to feel at the words of the priest. Had she been granted a small measure of happiness at the side of her husband?

"If you live by the flesh, you must die. But if you kill the sin through the spirit, you shall live. Desire is the thorn in the flesh. Everything in the flesh nourishes it and tries to lead you astray into sin. That is why you must despise lust as much as sin itself. . . ."

The voice of the priest filled the mighty house of God. Clearly and distinctly he delivered his sermon; each word seemed chiseled from the rock of eternal truth. How pleasantly this speech differed from the jabber and prattle that Sophie usually had to listen to, all the frenzied, incensed verbal exchanges on the street and at the café. The priest rolled his *R*s the way she did. He too was no Parisian, and his dialect would sound as foreign and false in the Procope as hers did. But wasn't that a sign? That this was the speech of truth, the speech of eternal God?

"He who wishes to please a woman is concerned with worldly matters; he who wishes to please God is concerned with the divine matters of the Lord. Yet everyone is given the grace of God, each receiving it in his own way. Therefore, because of the danger of fornication, each man must have his wife and each woman her husband. But do not believe that marriage allows one to give in to carnal desire. On the contrary! Marriage is a cure for evil, a means to counter lust, and through marriage the two of you are together washed free of sin. . . ."

Sophie was beginning to understand. Was this why Sartine had left her untouched on their wedding night? Was he leading the way with his example in order to conquer the thorn in the flesh? How thankful she was that Heaven had sent her such a man. As the priest descended from the pulpit to proceed to the holy transubstantiation, she whispered to God her promise to follow Sartine on the path of salvation. Full of reverence, she waited for communion.

"Lamb of God, Thou who taketh away the sins of the world, have mercy upon us!"

Finally the moment had come for which she had waited for so many years. She heard the sound of bells tinkling, and with her hands clasped Sophie left the pew to approach the Altar of the Lord for the first time since her First Communion.

As she knelt down before the altar, Radominsky raised the Host into the air.

"The Body of Christ!"

"Amen!" said Sophie, returning the stern gaze of the priest without flinching.

Then she closed her eyes, and as she received the Host she prayed to God that she would never set eyes on Denis Diderot again.

BOOK II

From the Tree of Knowledge
1749

27

From the loins of an angel, it is said, sprang the great river that flowed through Paris like time itself. Up to three hundred yards across, it divided the capital of the country and at the same time connected it to the rest of the kingdom. Every day it transported thousands of boats and barges that provided the city with a never-ending influx of food and goods, which contributed so significantly to the welfare of the capital and its inhabitants.

On many days, however, when the wind suddenly ceased and the temperature sank below the dew point, a dangerous exchange would take place between the water flow and the layers of air hovering above. It would start with a harmless overcast sky because of the condensation of moisture forming fine droplets, but this mist would soon thicken to an impenetrable fog that would accumulate between the chain of hills on both sides of the river. As the boat traffic gradually came to a standstill, the patches of fog would creep to the riverbanks and roll in across the land, there to propagate a white dimness and finally take possession of the entire city. In ever-growing masses the fog would drift down the streets and alleys, spread across the squares, and envelop the buildings, the churches, and the palaces as well as the simple homes of the citizens, so that it sometimes seemed as though the cloudy sky had sunk to earth.

Then the kraken that was Paris would lie there under a gigantic shroud, motionless, the life in its bowels threatening to suffocate. Because the fog mixed with the eternal smoke emitted from chimneys all over the city—myriad particles of dust and soot that hovered between the tall rows of buildings—and together formed such a thick vapor, even the torches burning to mark the streets at intersections were invisible. The otherwise unbearable noise of the city seemed to be swallowed up by the maw of an enormous ghost; sounds reached the ears, but muted and as if from a great distance. People ran right into one another on open squares because they couldn't see through the impenetrable haze, they walked up to the door of their neighbor's house instead of their own, and the coachmen climbed down from their boxes and felt for the curbs with their hands when they needed to move their carriages forward or back.

Whenever the fog reached such ghostly proportions, the magistrate would call on the Hospice des Quinze-Vingts for assistance from the blind, who squatted there with their collection plates, crying out in their nasal monotone for alms while examining the legs of the passersby with their canes. Familiar with eternal darkness as they were because of the loss of their eyesight, they could find their way through the maze of streets even better than the topographers who had drawn the plan of Paris. As long as the fog reigned, they were each given five *livres* daily. Their assignment for this fee was to guide citizens safely through the fogbound city.

Without complaint, Parisians accepted this disruption of their lives and businesses. Anyone who had an errand to run would grab on to the coattail of a blind person and follow this guide through the streets and intersections. The baker delivering bread, the doctor hurrying to a patient, the housewife shopping for groceries, the judge searching for the Palais de Justice, even the priest on the way to his church—they all relied on the guidance of the blind. Like ants moving through the underground tunnels and passages of their mounded domicile, they were incapable of recognizing the relationships between individual locales. And why should they? Wasn't every perception in the drifting shreds of fog merely a deceptive ghost?

Yes, it was astonishing with what equanimity the Parisians accepted their fate. They took the fog as an unalterable vicissitude of the weather, like rain, snow, or sunshine. Only a few grumbled about it or demanded that measures be taken by the magistrate and the government. In the strange and menacing events triggered by the fog on such days in their city, they saw a reflection of the state of mind of the entire kingdom of France.

The concern they voiced was this: How had a country ended up in such a predicament that only the blind could see?

28

"What have you brought for us today, Monsieur de Malesherbes?"

Madame de Pompadour scrutinized the director of the Royal Library, who was paying his customary visit of every Wednesday morning during her *lever*, in order to bring her the latest publications from Paris. Two years had passed since she had appointed the young member of parliament to his sensitive position. She knew that whoever held this office ran the risk of quarreling with all the factions at court simultaneously—or else he would manage to make commitments to all of them at once. From what she could see, Malesherbes was determined to exploit his position in the latter sense.

"Something very interesting," he replied as he took a pinch of snuff. "'A Letter Concerning the Blind, for the Use of the Sighted.'"

"Pardon me?"

"That's how the title reads, Madame. It comes from an anonymous writer and is directed at a certain Madame de Puisieux."

"A medical treatise?"

"If you like. The author describes the case of an English mathematician who lost his eyesight as a child but later became a professor, teaching optics, of all things."

"That is certainly most remarkable. But why was such a book issued anonymously?"

"The medical aspect serves only as a ruse. In reality the author does not refer to actual blind people; rather, he is speaking of a whole different type of blindness: the inability of people to recognize the truth. With this the author is venturing into dangerous territory. For example, he asks what ideas about God a person could possibly have."

"And what answer does he give?" La Pompadour wanted to know, suddenly keen to hear the response.

"That we are like blind people groping in the dark. According to the thesis of this book, in order to make statements about God we have to be able to touch Him."

"Oh, I see. One of these deists who claim to believe in God without going to mass on Sunday. Please leave the book for me. I'll pass it on to Father Radominsky today. I'm sure that my friend the queen will thank you for it. By the way," she added, as he placed the volume on her dressing table, "you cut quite an excellent figure dancing at the masked ball."

"Fortunately one makes progress even in dancing." He sighed. "Even if one only turns in a circle. But my poor display of artistry is nothing in comparison with the advances that you have made on the floor of politics. I have heard that your greatest wish for Alexandrine is that she marry the Duc de Picquigny."

The daughter of La Pompadour, who was playing softly by herself in a corner of the dressing room, raised her curly blond head and beamed when she heard her name mentioned. Although she was not yet five years old, with her pretty doll-like face she was the perfect image of her mother.

"Not until after she turns thirteen," replied the marquise. "Before the family of the duke will consent to the marriage, the king still has to appoint the father of the groom as tutor to the dauphin."

"Haven't I said that politics is the continuation of the dance by other means?" Malesherbes asked. "In both instances it's a matter of linking contradictory movements into one harmonious whole."

"You're right about that." She sighed. "And in both cases it's a question of explaining to an ass that he isn't one. But I see that you have brought us something else."

"Didn't you instruct me," he asked with a suggestive smile as he handed her a small octavo volume, "not only to track down subversive books for you, but also *this kind*?"

"Most certainly," she replied sternly. "His Majesty places great value on learning everything that goes on in this country."

"Happy are the subjects whose king deals personally with the secret reports of the police," said Malesherbes. "And happy is the king who is granted the opportunity to stave off boredom in this manner."

Determined to ignore his remark, she accepted the book. "*The Indiscreet Jewels*?" she asked, ruffling through its pages. "I must say, the titles that you are presenting to me today grow more and more peculiar."

"An atrocious story," said Malesherbes. "Seldom has it been so hard for me to finish reading a book. The plot, if one can speak of it as such, takes place at the court of an Oriental ruler and concerns his favorite concubine."

"A tale from *The Thousand and One Nights*?"

"More of a wild tale in the style of the *Decameron*."

"Books of that sort are unknown to me," replied La Pompadour, although a copy of the notorious story collection was always under her pillow. "Please free me from my ignorance."

"At the risk of offending your delicacy of feeling," said Malesherbes with a bow. "This novel deals with a most sensitive wager. The sultan claims that not a single woman at his court is capable of remaining faithful to her husband. Perhaps you may think: What sort of argument is this?"

With that he gave her a stare as if they were talking about her.

"Why would you say such a thing? I fear I won't be able to avoid the torment of your story. Alexandrine!" she cried, clapping her hands. "It's time for your lessons. Your dancing teacher is waiting for you."

As her daughter left the room with a perfect formal curtsey, Malesherbes took another pinch from his snuffbox before he began to summarize the content of the novel. La Pompadour listened attentively, interrupting only occasionally to express her abhorrence. But actually, the longer she listened, the more she felt a tingling excitement in her young body. What a delightful little novel! Jewels that could speak! She had seldom heard such an enchanting caprice. . . . The author must be a genius.

"Yes? What is it? Why don't you continue?" she asked impatiently when Malesherbes abruptly stopped.

"I don't know whether I should trouble you with any more," said the state councillor with an anxious expression. "Even though I'm only relating what a stranger has invented, I'm afraid of offending the mistress of the king."

"You have already related enough outrageous things that I can't imagine anything worse. So, what are you waiting for?"

As if to conquer his reluctance, he blew his nose before he bent to whisper the rest in her ear. When she heard his words, she rolled her eyes in astonishment.

"The favorite concubine of the sultan? Like a matron in one of these houses? You see me blush, monsieur," she cried as Malesherbes finished speaking.

"Didn't I warn you?"

"Certainly, certainly. But I must fulfill my duty, after all. As always, for the sake of the country's welfare I have gladly taken the torment upon myself."

La Pompadour spoke nothing but the truth. What her guest had just whispered in her ear inspired her to do something that had never occurred to any other mistress of the king. This delightful little novel, an inner voice was telling her, might perhaps offer the solution to all her problems. This very day, she decided, she would give orders to translate her idea into action.

Aloud she said, "Please see to making the necessary inquiries. We cannot possibly tolerate such books. Apropos," she interrupted herself to change the subject, "what have our Encyclopedists been up to lately?"

29

At this hour, like every morning, Denis Diderot was sitting at his desk without wasting a thought on the little novel in question, which on a whim he had put down on paper so many months before. Surrounded by twenty big cardboard cartons filled to the brim with notes, copies, and excerpts, he was writing a new article for the *Encyclopedia*. He was so engrossed in the work that he hadn't even thought to change out of his scarlet robe covered with ink spots and put on a proper suit.

With each passing day the great work took on a more distinct form. If everything went according to plan, the first volume would appear next year; he had already written the pamphlet with the advance notice. Meanwhile, Le Bréton was drumming up printers and typesetters all over France and was stockpiling vast quantities of paper in his publishing house on Rue de la Harpe. Splendid sales were on the horizon. The subscription drive that the publisher had advertised in the newspapers of Paris had been so successful that he'd had to increase the originally calculated print run of 1,625 copies by several hundred even before printing. Since then Le Bréton had moved his massive body through the city only by means of a sedan chair.

He paid his editors, Diderot and d'Alembert, 144 *livres* each per month, enough to secure their livelihoods, and yet not so much that it would put a brake on their enthusiasm. The two were working around the clock. Like the recruiters at the Pont Neuf who enlisted troops for the king's army, they gathered their combatants for the battle from among the philosophers and writers. While Diderot was recruiting for his armada in the coffeehouses, d'Alembert frequented the literary salons and kowtowed to government ministers and judges of the courts. In order to strengthen the reputation of the *Encyclopedia*, they had to win over as many learned men as possible in official positions: royal advisors, members of the Sorbonne and the academies. Fortunately, an impressive number of famous men had confirmed their participation; besides Voltaire, Buffon, and Montesquieu there were also Marmontel and Turgot—even the ancient Fontenelle, who was already approaching a hundred years of age, wanted to write an article. In their wake a whole army of nameless authors sprouted up: experts in medicine and theology; in chemistry, surgery, and grammar; in geography, rhetoric, and architecture; in horticulture and military science. Only the topic of music had already been exhaustively covered. Jean-Jacques Rousseau, Diderot's old friend, had blazed through 390 articles in an incredible show of endurance, putting them down on paper in less than three months. However, the question of who should write the preface to the complete work had not yet been decided by the editors.

Diderot dipped his goose quill one last time into the inkwell and signed his name to the manuscript. Another article was done. What subject should he take up next? As he eyed the material in the cartons, he felt like a climber at the foot of an enormous mountain range. Thousands of questions were awaiting answers. Yet as huge as the effort that still lay before him might be, he had the peak firmly in sight. Knowledge was power—how could he acquire it? The field of human knowledge was boundless—which area of knowledge from which spheres should he take up next?

He was determined to grant space in the *Encyclopedia* not only to noble book-learning. Equally important were the mechanical arts, the new techniques and processes that were being introduced into more and more operations and manufacturing methods. Diderot knew that a revolution was in progress, one that would change the world from the ground up. He wanted to enlist draftsmen who were capable of rendering mechanical processes precisely, and to speak with master craftsmen in order to learn from them the technical terminology of their trades. The readers of the *Encyclopedia* should not merely comprehend how the solar system functioned, but also how a shoe or a tool was made. He was already looking forward to the day when he could show his father the volume with the article about the craft of making cutlery. The old man would be as proud of him as he was earlier, when his son had come home from school with a laurel wreath around his shoulders.

Voices were raised in the street. What was all that noise, as if two fishwives were arguing? Sensing something amiss, Diderot got up from his desk and went to the window. Not again! Down below were his wife and his mistress going at it: Xanthippe and Messalina—one as stupid as the other was beautiful. They were surrounded by street vendors and passersby who were following their squabble attentively.

"You? His wife? He told me himself that he had no desire to see you anymore."

"So how did I get pregnant again? From the Holy Ghost?"

Suddenly a water carrier leaped out of the crowd and dumped a bucket of water over the two women. As the spectators doubled over with laughter, Diderot shut the window. They could do what they liked—it didn't matter to him. Thanks to Le Bréton's regular allowance, Nanette could pay the rent punctually on the eighth, and Madame de Puisieux got whatever was left over at the end of each month. With that his obligations were fulfilled.

"So what's this? An article about chocolate? All we need now is one about chicken in the soup."

Diderot turned around. At his desk stood Rousseau, holding the article that he had just finished. His friend made a face as if he were in urgent need of the nearest toilet, as he began to read from the page.

"Once the sugar is mixed with the cacao mass, a fine powder of ground and sifted vanilla beans and cinnamon sticks is added . . ." Shaking his head, he put down the manuscript and looked at Diderot. "Can you tell me why you're wasting your time on this?"

"It's not a waste of time," Diderot countered. "I simply want to tell my readers what gives me pleasure every day. Besides, chocolate is valuable nutrition. A cup costs six *sous*—the most pleasant and least expensive way of keeping one's strength up until evening."

"What colossal wisdom," Rousseau mocked him. "Where did you get this? From Plato? From Aristotle? Or from your pretty shopkeeper on the corner?"

"It all belongs together, Jean-Jacques, the philosophical mucking-out of the mind along with such bagatelles to make life easier."

"And your own work? Your genius? How many pounds of chocolate is it worth?"

The sudden reminder of the novels and dramas he was not writing because of the *Encyclopedia* ruined Diderot's mood for a moment. But he had a proper answer ready.

"Have you forgotten 'A Letter Concerning the Blind'? Voltaire has already read it and written to me. He's showered me with praise and invited me to a philosophers' dinner."

"Who sent the book to that old chatterbox? D'Alembert?" Rousseau squinted at him as suspiciously as a jealous wife. "If you accept the invitation, I'll terminate our friendship."

"Is that why you came to visit me?"

"Of course not! I wanted to go to the Procope with you and discuss the preface. Yesterday I wrote a draft; you're going to love it. But why are you looking at me like that?"

The question was justified. Diderot looked as annoyed as if someone had poured sour milk in his chocolate.

"To the Procope?" he asked. "No, certainly not. Let's go to the Régence, or the Gradot, but not to the Procope."

"And why not? Before it always had to be the Procope, as if there were no other café in Paris." Rousseau angrily knitted his brow. But then a light went on for him. "Ah, I see—is it still because of the little waitress?"

30

"Another slice of roast?" asked Sophie.

Her Sunday guest, Monsieur Cocheron, a paying boarder, shook his head and wiped the grease from his lips with his coat sleeve. Sophie felt the greatest loathing for the man, who joined them at her table every Sunday evening. His very presence almost made her hold her breath, so strongly did he reek—like a boar in rut.

"But you can't possibly be full yet!" cried Sartine. "Come, have another portion. Otherwise my wife will think you don't like her cooking."

"Impossible." Cocheron emitted a belch and stood up. Sophie cleared off the table. Her husband had come up with the idea of inviting a boarder to dinner on Sundays who would pay them ten *livres* a month. Earning a little money this way was nothing unusual; many people did it. Yet it bothered Sophie: Where had Sartine's generosity gone, especially since he'd been promoted to detective inspector? But above all it bothered her that a stranger was present at their table on her only evening off.

"Until next week," said Cocheron at the door.

"Until next week," said Sartine. "And bring a bit more of an appetite with you!"

Finally they were alone. Sophie took off her apron and opened the window to air out the flat. The street outside was full of people returning from excursions as they did every Sunday evening: families with grandparents, servants, and children, as well as crowds of young people, workers and craftsmen holding their girlfriends by the arm, tired from dancing and celebrating, but with flushed, laughing faces. As Sophie inhaled the fresh air that seemed to flow into Paris with the holidaymakers, she looked over at her husband.

How would they spend the rest of the evening? Would Sartine overcome his shyness for once? She had even washed her hair especially for him at dawn that morning, before he woke up. Maybe she should ask him to help roll up the yarn so that he would notice. They had several hours left before bedtime.

"Would you please close the window?"

As always when they were alone, Sartine suddenly seemed to feel uncomfortable. When he talked to her his gaze wandered and he would grab the newspaper lying on the table, unfold it carefully, and start to read, as if he wanted to hide from her.

"Would you like a cup of tea?" she asked, closing the window.

"Yes, please."

He glanced briefly over the top of his paper, his expression so friendly, and at the same time guilty, that it gave her a pain in the side. As he vanished behind his newspaper again, she set the kettle on the stove and put a spoonful of leaves in the teapot that the owner of the Procope had given her to take home as part of her wages.

What sort of man had she married, anyway?

Sophie had no reason to complain. Sartine was a good provider: at the start of each week he gave her household money, and he even gave her little presents from time to time—a few bonbons, a hair ribbon, or a colorful bow. In two years of marriage he had never once raised his hand to her. And yet with each day it was harder for Sophie to feel any affection for him. She was now twenty years old—the perfect age for child-bearing——but nothing happened. Her colleagues at the Procope were already teasing her because she was not yet pregnant. But how could she be? In all those months Sartine hadn't touched her once, although she had long since given him to understand that she was ready to do the things with him that married couples normally did. But she was still a virgin, like the Holy Mother.

Did he intend to go through life keeping the promise that he had made to her on their wedding day?

In the evening he sometimes read a book that he locked away in a drawer before he joined her in bed. Then he would kiss and caress her and take her hand. They would lie there like that, without moving, her hand in his, as he stared mutely into the darkness, only giving a soft sigh now and then. If she tenderly pressed him with small gestures and caresses to indicate what she was longing for, he would start talking about his time as a young sublieutenant when he had been assigned to pursue sexual offenses, about the terrible things he had seen among the prostitutes and their customers. As if with these accounts he sought to cure her longing as he might with bitter medicine.

"Here you are, your tea."

"Thank you, that's very sweet of you." He put the newspaper aside and touched her bare arm with his hand.

Sophie felt a powerful tingling on her skin. If only he would truly touch her for once! How she hoped that his hand would move; every inch, every pore of her skin was longing for it, crying out, whimpering, pleading for him to stroke her arm, her shoulder, her throat, her neck, her breasts. This yearning in her body, which spread out in warm waves from her womb, was almost unbearable.

"Have I ever told you that I'm so happy to have you as my wife?"

Sartine pulled his hand back. The contact had not even lasted a second.

"Yes." She nodded. "And I'm very happy that you're pleased."

How often he had told her that before, almost every day since their wedding. But how much better it would have been if he made her feel his happiness! If he would simply take hold of her and kiss her, hug her, and press her to him until she could hardly breathe! Instead he raised his newspaper in front of his face once again. The silence in the room wrapped around her neck like a gigantic hand. While the street noise outside bounced off the closed window like the faint echo of a distant joy, here inside only the rustling of the paper was heard, and occasionally a slight clattering and slurping when Sartine took a sip of tea.

In resignation Sophie turned away to wash the dishes. No, she was not angry at her husband, but she was sad. And this sadness had settled so deep inside her that she couldn't imagine ever being released from it.

"Could we go out to the country next Sunday for a change? What do you think?"

"To the country? Yes, why not? I'll think about it." Sartine pulled out his pocket watch with the bell that chimed the hour and looked at the face. "What, so late already?" he said then, suddenly in a hurry. He took one last gulp of tea, folded up the paper, and stood up. "I have to go at once."

"Today? On Sunday evening? I thought we might perhaps—"

"An important operation, I'm afraid." He stroked her cheek, so fleetingly that she hardly felt his touch. "By the way, they've promised me that if I continue to prove myself, I may get a week's vacation this year. Then I could go to Beaulieu and make some inquiries for you."

He gave her a kiss on the cheek. She wanted to fling her arms around him to kiss him back, with a real kiss, but he fended her off, gently but firmly.

"Not now!" And with a weary shake of his head he said, "I'm sorry."

A little later she heard him going down the stairs; she heard every one of his retreating footsteps so clearly that she could picture how he looked, his posture, his face.

She wondered if he was relieved to escape her presence.

No, it was not greed that had given Sartine the idea of inviting a boarder to Sunday dinner. He merely wanted to avoid being alone with her. That was the simple truth, and Sophie had realized it long ago. But why? What did he have against her? She didn't know how much longer she'd be able to stand it without going crazy.

As she turned around her gaze fell on the chest of drawers in which her husband hid the book that he sometimes read before they went to bed.

What sort of book was he hiding from her?

The question had scarcely entered her mind before she was overcome by an urgent feeling, impossible to dismiss. It was the same feeling she'd had when she still lived alone; it came over her on so many nights like a temptation in her room above the Procope, when she sat before her little treasure chest full of writings, not sure whether she should open it.

31

It was almost impossible to make any progress through the throng of revelers. What a slovenly company, thought Antoine Sartine as he made a great effort to push his way forward. Everywhere he looked were the faces of couples in love; in the afternoon sun they glowed, besotted from the brutish amusements in the village saloons, where men and women drank themselves senseless and danced barefoot in circles, kicking up so much dust that he couldn't see his hand in front of his face. His wife longed for such amusements. . . . Recalling Sophie's sad expression, Sartine felt the pain of a guilty conscience, as if he were sick at heart, and once more he cursed his wretched body.

But was there anything more important that a man could do for his wife than take her out to the countryside on a Sunday afternoon? He hoped he would eventually get a vacation—he would do everything he could to shed some light on Sophie's past. Then she would no longer have to suffer under the frightful events of her childhood, which she was dragging through life like a big heavy sack fastened to her back.

If only she would help him! After their wedding he had asked her to keep her eyes and ears open in the Procope and report everything to him that seemed suspicious. But she had never told him a thing, although there were always so many rabble-rousers in the café. Why not? Because she didn't want to spy on her customers? He was unable to see anything wrong with such inquiries; after all, they were made in the service of the welfare of the church and the state. He acquired his information from many different sources; he inquired of landlords and father confessors, questioned the neighbors of suspects, talked to spurned lovers, angry sons, and neglected wives. Nevertheless he respected the conduct of his wife. Because he loved her.

Sartine crossed the Place Royale. Before him loomed the imposing

three-story façade of the Saint-Paul-Saint-Louis church, under whose
cupola the Jesuits of Paris gathered. It was here he had been summoned
to participate in the discussion of the situation. He hurried up the few
steps to the church and was met by two monks who checked his identi-
fication. After he had told them his name and his mission, they stepped
aside and opened the portal.

Like a call from the Almighty a voice resounded as he entered the
house of God. In the pulpit not far from the shimmering white marble
altar stood Father Radominsky, preaching to a small audience that had
already assembled below him. Sartine made the sign of the cross and
took a seat in a pew.

"The philosophers are mobilizing," intoned the Jesuit priest, raising a
bound prospectus in the air. "With this booklet, of which eight thousand
copies have been printed, they are calling for subscriptions to their encyclopedia. Eight volumes of text and six hundred illustrated plates is what
they have announced, published in sequence without interruption."

Sartine looked around. The words of the father apparently made no
great impression on his colleagues. But was that any wonder? Only a
few of the inspectors and sergeants pursued their work out of any inner
conviction; for most of them serving in the police was a way of earning a living like any other. Whether they were pursuing philosophers or
prostitutes made no difference in their eyes, not to mention in the eyes of
the spies and informers who sat side by side with the royal civil servants,
youths who could be bought cheaply and would betray their own parents
for a few *sous*. Sartine had nothing but contempt for them. They were
hardly better than the riffraff on whom they spied.

"The philosophers," Father Radominsky went on, "promise to give the
readers of their encyclopedia a general picture of the achievements of the
human mind, in all fields and down through the centuries. They boast
of creating a work like none that has gone before, more educational than
all the books in the world put together. They even call it a sacred text
in which they intend to preserve the knowledge of humanity from the
storms of the era. Yet they actually intend nothing more than to kindle
those storms themselves. What the philosophers are planning is a revolution! A repudiation of all values! A new order of things! In Heaven and
on earth!"

Sartine listened to the priest attentively, carefully analyzing each of
his words. Father Radominsky, and here there was no doubt, was a man

utterly immersed in the fulfillment of his duty. He believed what he said, and said what he believed. He was a soldier, stalwart and unwavering, and no personal advantage would move him to betray his cause. This led Sartine to think of Malesherbes. Was the new head censor possessed of an equally unimpeachable character? Sartine didn't know, but if he were ever forced to decide between these two men, he would not hesitate long before making his choice.

He cleared his throat and raised his hand.

"You have a question?" Astonished, Radominsky interrupted his tirade.

Sartine felt how all eyes turned to him. He had to clear his throat again before he spoke.

"On what authority can we proceed against Diderot and his accomplices? The *Encyclopedia* is a legal undertaking. The king has given his consent to have it printed."

"You are right," replied the priest. "But if the king has underestimated the danger, we must be all the more vigilant. You, the soldiers of the police, have been summoned to be vigilant for us father confessors! Listen to everything, but keep it all to yourself. You know these people and their crimes, their temptations and their vices; you know what they are capable of. You should never relinquish your distrust, and your suspicions should never rest."

"What do you expect from us, *mon père*?"

"Tips, evidence, proofs—but above all, arrests! Everyone who delivers an Encyclopedist shall receive a reward from me personally."

Radominsky gave Sartine a penetrating look, as if his words were meant for him alone. Sartine reciprocated with an equally piercing gaze. Was this the chance that he had so long been waiting for? The chance to distinguish himself before his superior? For his wife—for Sophie?

32

Sophie's hands were trembling as she looked at the book as if it were a magnificent treasure. *The Indiscreet Jewels* . . . what an odd title. She wondered what sort of stories were hidden inside. With a pounding heart she opened the cover. She had resisted the temptation for what seemed an endless time and kept putting the book back in the drawer where Sartine had hidden it from her. But as dawn was breaking, her resistance dwindled. As greedily as a brandy drinker who empties the first glass after an abstinence that had lasted much too long, she drank in the words.

> *It was in the earthly year of 150,000,003,200,001 that the rule of Mongagul began. In less than ten years the sultan had gained the reputation of being an important man. He led battles, fortified cities, expanded his realm, and pacified the provinces. And in the seraglio he proved to be no less popular than he was on the throne; he was tender, chivalrous, and full of charm. But I must refrain from listing all the charms and fine qualities of the young Mirzoza, or this work will never come to an end. . . .*

Sophie couldn't believe her eyes: What she was reading was her own story, the novel that Diderot had given her. She looked at the binding—there was no publisher's name, only the place where it had been printed: Kythera. What could that mean? The characters in the stories were the same ones she knew, Sultan Mongagul and Princess Mirzoza, and the palace of the sovereign as well. Everything matched what she remembered, even Cucufa the sorcerer was mentioned. In annoyance she read on.

> *"If it should ever please Heaven, which has placed me on this throne, to make me of humble birth—would you then descend to me in order to hand me the crown?" Mongagul asked his favorite concubine.*

*"If Mirzoza," replied the concubine, "should ever lose the few charms
that she is thought to possess, would Mongagul still love her?"*

Sophie studied the syllables, the words, the sentences without understanding their meaning. Yes, it was the same story that she was reading. And yet how much everything had changed! The love between
Mongagul and Mirzoza had cooled, the fire of the favorite completely
extinguished. She was as reluctant to receive the sultan's caresses as he
seemed inclined to give her any. In the desolation of their togetherness
she summoned the sorcerer, who was to bring the sultan and his favorite concubine some information about the amatory adventures of the
ladies at court, in order to deliver them from their ennui. Cucufa gave
Mongagul a magic ring; if he pointed the gemstone toward a woman's
jewel, it would reveal to him all her love affairs. But what was meant by
a woman's jewel? Sophie had a vague notion of what it must be, but she
would have preferred to spare herself the answer. The novel left no doubt
about what was intended, as did the illustrations, which she now discovered were equally revealing: pictures of naked bodies entwined with each
other. It was as though the jewel could determine the destiny of any sort
of woman.

*The Aloof Woman: She's acting as if she doesn't want to listen to her
jewel. The Amatory One: Her jewel demands much of her, and she
bestows it even more. The Coquette: Her jewel is mute or finds no
audience. Yet she instills in all men who approach her the hope that
her jewel will one day speak, and then she can no longer pretend not
to hear.*

Dark night descended over the city, but Sophie didn't notice. In the
light from the lamp she read on, page after page, completely under the
spell of this story which had once been hers. What a cold, calculating
woman the sensitive Mirzoza had become! In order to bind Mongagul to
her for all time, she set up a harem for him with a thousand playmates.
This way she could remain the sultan's favorite without herself carrying
out the duties of love, which she no longer required: She was a procurer
like the madams of those houses of ill repute that Sophie knew of from
her time in Faubourg Saint-Marceau, houses in the neighborhood of
the tobacco tavern, where old women supplied men with young girls, in
accordance with their tastes and wishes.

Alcine was lively and pretty. The court of the sultan hardly possessed a more charming woman, and certainly none as amatory. Monsieur pointed his ring at her, and instantly he discovered a whispering beneath her skirts. . . . In rapid succession Mongagul pointed his ring at all the women except for Mirzoza, and all the jewels answered, one after another: "I am often visited, I am damaged, abandoned, perfumed, exhausted, badly served, bored . . ."

The words blurred before Sophie's eyes as tears rolled down her cheeks. The stories that the sorcerer's ring elicited from the women's jewels grew ever more dreadful, more offensive. Sophie had never heard of such things: couples that made love under the open sky, in public baths, and before the eyes of strangers, by twos, by fours, by the dozen. . . . Against her will she felt the tingling sensation at the back of her neck, felt desire taking possession of her yearning body more and more, an urgent, irrepressible craving that originated between her thighs, spreading from there throughout her body like a warm stream, as if the monstrous fantasies that rose up out of the words and took shape before her eyes were an answer to all the disappointments and deprivations she had suffered in the two years of her marriage. Or as if her own jewel had begun to speak.

"What are you doing there?"

Sophie hadn't heard her husband come home. Sartine looked at her as if she were a stranger. His normally friendly face was expressionless, his eyes were hard and cold. She had no doubt that he looked like this when he arrested someone.

"This is not for you," he said, taking the book from her hand. "Or are you looking for some sort of vicarious amusement?"

"Vicarious? What do you mean?" Utterly confused, she whispered, "I don't understand all this."

"What don't you understand?" he asked sharply.

"All of it," she stammered. "The whole story has changed; the people, what they do . . . Nothing is the way it used to be. The princess, Mirzoza, how could she be like this? She used to love the sultan . . ."

Without feeling the tears that ran down her cheeks, without hearing the words that she was saying, she stared at Sartine and grabbed for his hands as if seeking support from him.

But her husband didn't move.

"How do you know what the princess was called?" he asked. "How can you know anything about this story? You can't even read!"

"The story belongs to me," she said, caught in the darkness of her feelings. "He gave it to me—"

"*He?* Who is *he?*"

"Diderot . . ." she whispered.

Only now did Sartine lose his composure.

"What are you saying?" he asked, his expression that of astonished disbelief. "Diderot? You mean that *he* wrote this filth?"

33

❧ ❧

"Sometimes I ask myself what it is you really want, Diderot. A reference work or a war machine?"

"Aren't they the same thing? Every word that springs from truth is a weapon, every article a cannon of the soul aimed at superstition."

"That may be." D'Alembert shook his head pensively. "But if that is true, we have twice the reason to be careful. We mustn't stretch the bow too taut. A frown from the censor and we'll land in the Bastille. Everything depends on the boundaries we set, on the hierarchy that we assign to things. It mustn't betray us, in any case."

Surrounded by Diderot's boxes of notes, the co-editor of the *Encyclopedia* was brooding about the most difficult task of the entire work. Infinite was the sea of knowledge through which they were navigating. What principles should they use to divide it up? First, a completely new order of things, the systematic linking of all knowledge, would determine the true value of their work. On that they were both agreed. In comparison with other lexicons, which gave separate definitions for individual concepts, this was intended to be a complete world map of the human spirit; it would not only depict the various fields of knowledge, but would also describe their status and size, their interdependence on and their connections among one another—like the countries on a geographical map. But what about these relationships? How was science related to art? Or art to handicrafts? Or handicrafts to technology? Or technology to philosophy? Or philosophy to theology? For weeks the two wrangled over answers to these questions, arranging, subdividing, discarding, and then starting over from the beginning.

"In the end isn't every attempt to squeeze reality into a system completely arbitrary?" asked Diderot with a hint of despair. "Reality, after all, offers us only an array of individual things, without fixed subdivisions.

Everything is fluid, one thing merges into another imperceptibly, revealing scarcely noticeable nuances. How can we hope to find the true relationships?"

"Viewed scientifically, there is only one way to do it," replied d'Alembert. "We have to create a tabula rasa, then start at the very beginning, with the very first origins. Only then can we record the individual results of the arts and sciences, in a methodical progression, according to the principles of mathematics, clear and distinct."

"That sounds like a primer in geometry! What happened to real life?"

The tone of the conversation suddenly grew heated. Diderot hated the condescending way in which d'Alembert sometimes spoke to him; on the other hand, d'Alembert grew anxious and frightened each time Diderot appealed to "real life." They were like an old married couple: They needed each other without loving each other.

"Life is chaos," declared d'Alembert. "Thinking is order! Even Bacon knew that."

"And what ever came out of it? The whole history of philosophy is nothing but a continual rearranging of mental furniture. Instead of renovating the building itself, people just keep moving around the contents. Human knowledge in the Procrustean bed of logic and metaphysics."

Diderot took a sheet of paper and sketched a tree with a mighty trunk and an even mightier crown with numerous branches and forks, which connected circles of different sizes with one another. Into these he wrote individual concepts: astronomy, surgery, painting, wool production, black magic—one concept in each circle of the tree's crown.

D'Alembert raised his eyebrows. "The tree of knowledge?"

"Yes. As presented by your admirable Francis Bacon. All knowledge as one organic whole, despite the difference in its branches."

"The Jesuits will claim that we're copying Bacon."

"All the better," cried Diderot. "Then they won't notice if we change things! Bacon is a saint; he makes us unassailable. As long as we appeal to him, no one can throw us in the Bastille."

Diderot again took pen in hand and crossed out several of the circles in the crown of the tree.

"What's that supposed to mean?" asked d'Alembert.

"Can't you guess?" Diderot retorted as he crossed out even more circles.

"Oh, now I understand." A shy smile lit up d'Alembert's face. "You mean, instead of changing or enlarging the tree of knowledge, we should first prune it?"

Diderot nodded. "True philosophy is modest. It admits as truth only what can be deduced through reason and experience. All other assertions are dogma or prejudice. They belong in church, not in the *Encyclopedia*."

"So that means we have to reject most of what is considered sacred to humanity." D'Alembert's eyes again showed the same anxious expression. "But from the standpoint of science I cannot contradict you." All of a sudden his soft features hardened, and he took the pen from Diderot's hand. "I think I know now where we have to draw the line."

"Then you're smarter than I am."

"You said it yourself already. Here," declared d'Alembert, drawing a line diagonally across the paper, "between what we know and what we can't know. That is our boundary, the methodically based border between verifiable cognition and metaphysical speculation."

Diderot grinned at him.

"But monsieur," he said with a mixture of derision and admiration, "are you of sound mind? What would Master Bacon say to that?"

D'Alembert was not to be put off. "Bacon must have been born in the dark of night; first he had to break the chains of Scholasticism. For us. If we make use of his tree, it is our duty to draw it anew, according to our best knowledge and conscience." With increasing certainty he drew his corrections on the sketch. "If we call the whole thing the 'system of human knowledge,' then reason supersedes all individual fields. Do you agree with me on that?"

"Gladly. But what comes below reason?"

"From what do we deduce the things we know?" d'Alembert replied. "From the things themselves? From revelation?" He shook his head. "I would say, from our own abilities. They characterize and shape everything that we know."

"I don't understand. Give me an example."

"Take history. It is the result of our ability to remember, our memory. It is quite similar with philosophy—since it is based on our own reasoning. Just as we have our imagination to thank for poetry." He wrote the three concepts under the roots of the tree. "With that, in my opinion, the main sources would be named."

D'Alembert's brown eyes shone as if he could already see everything in his mind's eye—clear and distinct.

In astonishment Diderot could only attempt to follow his ideas.

"So you mean that memory, reason, and imagination are the three great categories?"

"Yes. Together they form the trunk of the tree of knowledge, from which all other branches and twigs evolve."

"But where does theology fit in? If we neglect that topic, we'll be done for!"

"In theology as well, the facts are derived from history and refer to *memory*, even the prophecies. Indeed, they are only history, by which the narration precedes the events. The mysteries, the dogmas, the commandments comprise eternal philosophy and divine *reason*, and the parables of the Bible originate from the power of *imagination*."

A light went on for Diderot. "You are absolutely right—one follows from the other." He took the quill from d'Alembert's hand and continued filling in the drawing from where the other man had left off. "Accordingly, history would be divided into church history, worldly history, natural history, et cetera; philosophy into the science of God, the science of human beings, the science of nature; poetry into narrative works, dramatic works, allegorical works."

"Precisely!" d'Alembert replied. "And then we reach theology, physics, metaphysics, mathematics, and on to meteorology, hydrology, et cetera."

"Not to mention more subjects on the tree: mechanics, astronomy, optics . . ." Diderot filled in.

"Of course. And we can connect the various branches of knowledge to one another, through cross-references between individual articles, from which the whole is put together as in nature from individual phenomena—"

"Through the intertwining of the roots with the branches. In order to show how they mutually affect and explicate one another—"

"Because the individual parts of the whole are impossible to understand without taking into account the higher and more deeply situated parts. . . ."

Their ideas came faster and faster as the new tree of knowledge grew, sketched on the page before them and organized to show the sum of human knowledge in a revolutionary way that had not existed before. Theology and metaphysics, which had so overgrown the old tree of knowledge with their wilting foliage that the other disciplines underneath could hardly develop, now atrophied to a few scraggly branches and twigs, while philosophy and the natural sciences, together with handicrafts and the mechanical arts, kept branching out ever farther, displaying ever new ramifications.

By the time they were finished with the drawing, it was a new day outside. Completely exhausted, yet still in a state akin to intoxication, they regarded their work. Unchanged in position was the knowledge of God, resplendent high above all the other sciences and arts, just as Bacon had decreed before them, portrayed as if God were still the absolute ruler; but actually an army of once nameless subjects and skills had almost entirely conquered the new tree of knowledge.

The two men gazed at each other. Had they succeeded in cutting through the Gordian knot?

"I think we should congratulate ourselves," said Diderot, reaching his hand out to d'Alembert.

"May Francis Bacon protect us!" sighed the other, returning his smile.

As he shook the proffered hand, hurried footsteps echoed loudly in the stairwell.

"What's going on?" d'Alembert asked, annoyed. "Haven't you paid your rent?"

"The Devil knows," Diderot cursed. "The new month hasn't even begun yet."

The door flew open. In the next instant two strangers entered the room.

"Which of you is the writer Denis Diderot?"

"I am," said Diderot, bewildered. "How may I help you?"

"Police," replied one of the strangers, holding up an official seal before his nose. "You're under arrest."

34

Everything happened so fast that, hours later as Diderot waited in the main station of the Paris police to be questioned, he still did not understand. Toward nine o'clock the officers had appeared as if out of nowhere, in order to transport him here in a barred coach. What in the world were they accusing him of? He had told his wife, Nanette, for her protection as well as his own, only that he had to leave on business and would probably eat dinner out—if she didn't hear from him by evening, she should ask his publisher Le Bréton for news.

Fortunately they had let d'Alembert go and given the room only a cursory search. Just imagine if they had rummaged through all the cardboard boxes full of notes and documents! The contents were downright incendiary. Diderot rubbed his arm. He was still in pain from the blow that one of the officers had given him when he was arrested, to stop him from accepting the galley proof that a printer's apprentice had just delivered as they left the house. The officer had confiscated the text—Diderot hoped it wasn't the "Letter Concerning the Blind," which he'd demanded from Le Bréton so he could correct a couple of passages before the second edition went to press. If the bruise on his arm was the only injury he took away from this morning, he would count himself lucky.

Impatiently, Diderot looked around. Good Lord, when would he finally find out what they intended to do with him? In the entry hall of the police station there was already plenty of activity despite the early hour. The soldiers of the night brigade, who frequented streets and alleys with their informers until dawn looking for suspicious individuals, led in the people they had arrested, mostly petty thieves and crooks who made the city unsafe at night. In addition there were a dozen prostitutes who had been picked up in some bordello, yawning and tired. A diminutive inspector with a shrill childlike voice, who kept rocking on the balls of his feet, divided those arrested into two groups: The first he sent off to the clinic for treatment, the other to the Bastille for improvement.

Now and then a door would open, and Diderot caught a glimpse of the secretary to the lieutenant general. This man was the one solely responsible for deciding who would go to prison and for how long. Dozens of people were standing around him to present their complaints and requests. The petitions on his desk were stacked so high that the office staff assigned to gather them up could hardly lug them off, while petitioners addressed him as "Your Grace" out of fear. They pestered him, shoved gifts at him, and whispered in his ear. But he answered curtly or with merely a gesture. Diderot could feel the rage boiling up inside him. How could the freedom of so many people depend on a single man? Apparently without giving the matter any thought, the secretary took only seconds to decide on each case that the prosecutor presented. The Bastille devoured all who were sent there, and most people who ended up in the dreaded prison came back more corrupted than before.

"Come along!"

A guard led Diderot into a small, dark room. In the back wall there was only a tiny hole for a window. In the dim light he could hardly make out a thing.

"Please sit down."

Someone lit a candle. Diderot turned around, surprised at the polite tone of the speaker. Only now did he see the table in the middle of the room, and seated behind it the official who was to interrogate him. As the man turned his head, Diderot gazed into a familiar face.

"Monsieur Sartine?" he asked in disbelief.

"Quite right," the man replied as he indicated a chair with his hand.

"But we . . . we know each other," Diderot stammered.

"That has nothing to do with the matter."

Diderot knew that he had made a completely senseless remark and cursed himself for it. A thousand thoughts raced through his mind as he took a seat. What did it mean that precisely this man should be the one to question him? Had Sartine arranged for his arrest? Did he want to take revenge on him somehow? Because of Sophie?

Before Diderot could ask a question, Sartine showed him the arrest warrant: a couple of hurriedly scribbled lines. Diderot could decipher only the signature. It was by d'Argenson, the vice-chancellor and keeper of the seals.

"It would be best if you confess to your guilt."

"What do you mean? I don't even know what I'm accused of doing!"

"You don't?" Sartine raised his eyebrows in astonishment. "Didn't they tell you? That is naturally an impropriety for which I must apologize. The charge is dissemination of writings dangerous to public morals."

"There must be some mistake. I have done nothing of the sort."

"Please stop. You were positively identified as the author of a pornographic novel." Sartine shoved a document aside and picked up a book. "You did write this, didn't you?"

Diderot at once recognized a copy of *The Indiscreet Jewels*.

"If you admit your guilt, your confession will be given consideration at sentencing. If you lie, you're only hurting yourself."

"I can only repeat what I just said: I have nothing to do with that book."

"Really?"

Diderot shook his head.

"All right then. If you refuse to confess, we'll clear up the matter in our own way."

Sartine picked up a little bell from the table and rang it. Immediately, one of the officers who had arrested Diderot came into the room.

Sartine gave him the book and said, "Please take this to the publisher Le Bréton on Rue de la Harpe and ask him the name of the author. If he refuses to name the writer, inform him that we shall call him to account instead of the author. Printed on the island of Kythera—don't make me laugh! We have sufficient evidence that this book comes from his workshop. All right then, get moving! What are you waiting for?"

"Here is something else that we confiscated at the arrest this morning." The officer held up the galley proof that Le Bréton's apprentice had delivered. "Apparently a philosophical treatise. At least, I didn't understand a word of it."

"What's the title?"

"'Letter to the Blind,' or something like that."

"Interesting. Let me see it."

The officer handed him the unbound pages.

"My compliments, Monsieur Diderot," said Sartine as he leafed through the galleys. "I didn't know what a versatile and productive author you are. —Oh, what do I see here? The 'Letter' is dedicated to Madame de Puisieux?" Sartine gave the galleys back to the officer. "Well done, constable! When you speak to the publisher, check the origin of this text at the same time."

Sartine stood up and left the room with the constable. Diderot heard a key turn in the lock. Alone in the room, he no longer felt compelled to remain seated. What sort of mess had he gotten himself into? He positively felt the noose around his neck tightening. Sartine even seemed to know about his mistress . . . Now everything came down to his publisher. But could he trust the walrus? On the one hand, Le Bréton needed him; on the other hand . . . Diderot closed his eyes. If Sartine could prove that he had written the 'Letter Concerning the Blind,' he would languish in the Bastille for years. D'Alembert would look for another co-editor for the *Encyclopedia,* and others would complete his work, while he moldered away in his cell. And Nanette would have to move out of the apartment with their son and find a room in some outlying town.

Diderot uttered a curse. That miserable little novel . . . he would give his right thumb if he could make it vanish, as if never written.

To distract himself he took out the books that he had stuffed in his coat pockets during the arrest, *The Trial of Socrates* and *Paradise Lost.* But he was much too nervous to concentrate on reading. Who had betrayed to Sartine that he was responsible for *The Indiscreet Jewels?* A jealous scribbler from the Procope? That was rather improbable. In police matters the authors usually closed ranks, even if they were archenemies. Some informer or denouncer? More likely. The cafés were teeming with such creatures—even among the printers and typesetters there were traitors who would sell what they knew for a few *sous.*

Or was it—Diderot hardly dared entertain the thought—Sophie?

In less than an hour the door was opened again and Sartine returned together with two guards whom Diderot had not seen before.

"Just as I suspected," said the inspector. "The publisher Le Bréton has confirmed your authorship of this novel—as well as the galley proofs that were confiscated from you this morning." Shaking his head, he gazed at Diderot. "For such trash you jeopardize a work like the *Encyclopedia?*"

For a second Diderot drew some hope. Was the inspector a secret sympathizer?

But before he could open his mouth, Sartine turned to the two guards in the doorway and commanded: "Take him away!"

35

Sartine's report to his superiors led to a dispute that was played out under the most beautiful eyes in France, the eyes of the Marquise de Pompadour. Without this woman no matter of significance could be decided in Versailles. Ever since she had followed the example of a minor erotic novel to arrange for her monarch a veritable seraglio in which ever-changing, ever-new female playmates competed to please His Majesty, her position at court had become inviolable. Plans and petitions were presented to her and her response was a majestic "We shall see." With this "We," which flowed from her lips as if she had been born to use the royal plural, she seemed to place the entire kingdom under her command. Her daughter, Alexandrine, for whom she had arranged an education befitting a princess, called herself only by her Christian name, as was usual for genuine princesses.

"The novel portrays a dangerous attack on morality. If the people practice the views of love and marriage as depicted in this abominable little book, all of society will collapse."

"Don't you think you're exaggerating a bit? This book called *The Indiscreet Jewels* is a trivial matter. Not to mention the fact that the author has been in a cell since this morning and regrets his deeds. On the highest orders I have had him investigated and locked up."

"Trivial? The novel describes the activities in an Oriental harem! It's not enough that this Diderot is put behind bars for a couple of weeks. You have to get him out of circulation once and for all!"

"Am I supposed to make a fool of myself? If I acted that way with all the authors that at some time in their lives have written a suggestive novel, I'd have to put half of France in prison. Who knows, perhaps I'd end up in the awkward situation of having to arrest myself."

Father Radominsky had to make an effort to suppress his rage. He had hoped that the director of the Royal Library would support him in using the arrest of Diderot for the good of the church and the state; instead the man was making fun of his concern. The father was having more doubts that the son of the chancellor was the right man for the position of head censor of France. This Malesherbes was an intelligent fellow, no question about it, but he had no character; he was an ingenious opportunist who would sacrifice the future of France for a successful bon mot. It was enough to make one sick. With a forced smile Radominsky turned to Madame de Pompadour, whom both of them wished to consult.

"What is your opinion, Marquise? Can the government tolerate such a lack of discipline as this novel seems to propagate?"

La Pompadour hesitated before answering. *"Quod licet Jovi, non licet bovi,"* she then said with an innocent smile, as if she had never heard of the book in question. "If two people do the same thing, it is by no means the same."

"Bravo!" exclaimed Malesherbes. "A truly majestic assessment!"

Radominsky paused for a moment. What was the meaning of the sympathetic look that La Pompadour and Malesherbes had just exchanged? Might it really be true, what was rumored at court? That the Parc-aux-cerfs, the new pleasure palace of the king . . . Before he said anything wrong, the priest decided to change his strategy.

"I admire your Latin, madame, and even more your philosophical spirit. But we should not allow ourselves to take this matter lightly. Diderot is no insignificant hack titillating the lascivious tendencies of his readers for a few *sous*; he is the editor of the *Encyclopedia*, which the philosophers intend to use to declare war on us. We now have a unique opportunity to put a stop to their game before their sorry effort is published."

"Is the *Encyclopedia* so dangerous that we must tremble before it?" asked La Pompadour. "From what I've heard, most of the articles deal with agriculture and raising livestock."

"Ostensibly, yes," said Radominsky. "But appearance is the domain of the Devil."

"In my childhood," said Malesherbes, taking a pinch of snuff, "I was taught that agriculture and raising livestock are exceedingly useful endeavors."

"The Devil prefers two disguises," Radominsky countered, "beauty and utility."

"Indeed? Is it your intent to insult our hostess?" asked Malesherbes in amusement. "Besides, what have we recovered so far? A couple of dozen contributions that our informer at the print shop has copied. Most of it is deadly boring stuff."

"This Diderot knows his business," Radominsky went on, undeterred. "Every article in this dictionary, no matter whether it apparently deals with how to grow vegetables or how to mill grain, is in reality an attack on orthodox teachings."

"One might think that you secretly harbor admiration for these philosophers. My God, what a commotion over a mere book! If I'm not mistaken, even in Jesus' time vegetables were cultivated, and grain was already being milled in the Old Testament."

"What did Madame the Marquise say? If two do the same thing, it is by no means the same. Don't you understand? It's not about vegetables and grain, but about earthly happiness, which the philosophers place above faith and the order of things willed by God. That is the demon which makes the *Encyclopedia* so dangerous."

"And for that reason should we close our eyes to the reality of the situation? The publisher—what's the name of that fat man? Oh yes, Le Bréton—has apparently invested eight thousand *livres* in the undertaking. This dictionary will give hundreds of people jobs to make their daily bread. It could be that the book contains a few heresies, but who knows, perhaps it will serve our purposes more than the editors intend. Don't forget: Hungry subjects are bad subjects. Only when they are well fed do they love the king and his government."

"For every man that the *Encyclopedia* feeds, there will be thousands who are incited by its words. It will fan the flames of revolt and rebellion."

"The *Encyclopedia* will contribute to the reputation of France. I've heard from our envoys in London that the English king is now furious about the imminent competition it will offer to his beloved Chambers."

"The English king is a fool. Education is a blessing for a few, the elect, but for the masses it is poison—the more they know, the greater will be their doubt," replied Radominsky. "If we, the representatives of the church and the state, allow the philosophers to disseminate these teachings condemned by God, we are encouraging our own demise. No, it's a gift from Heaven that Diderot has fallen into the police net. And it would be an unforgivable mistake to let him escape."

He looked at La Pompadour. She was the one who would decide this argument. Her gaze, in which black sinfulness and blue innocence seemed to merge, shifted back and forth between the two adversaries.

"All in all we are of the opinion," she declared at last, "that no evidence exists against the editor of the *Encyclopedia* that would justify a lengthy imprisonment—the economic interests at stake are far too considerable. On the other hand, it seems obvious to us that Monsieur Diderot should be given a reminder."

"What form of 'reminder' do you suggest?" asked Radominsky.

"Talk to Diderot, *mon père*, visit him in his cell. Perhaps with God's help you will succeed in leading him back to the path of virtue."

"And if not, madame?"

"Then we shall see."

36

The respite of early evening had returned to Café Procope. In the borderland between day and night, time seemed to stand still for a while inside the yellow walls below the smoke-infused beams of the ceiling. At the dark oak tables only a few conversations were under way; most of the guests were playing chess, while others leafed through their newspapers. Some had leaned back comfortably in their heavy easy chairs upholstered in red leather to take a nap before the word duels and speech battles of the new night commenced.

Sophie used the interlude to finish up the work that had been set aside during the hectic activity of the afternoon. As she polished glasses at the counter and put them away on the shelves with the freshly washed cups and plates, in her thoughts she was with her husband. Sartine had set off for Beaulieu an hour earlier. At noon he had been surprised to be given leave and had subsequently taken the night coach to Dijon, where he would change to travel farther to the south. If all went well, he would arrive at his destination in two days' time.

The idea that Sartine would be conducting an investigation in her old village filled Sophie with a mixture of nervousness and hope. She wondered which of the people who had witnessed the trial against her mother back then were still living. Abbé Morel was already an old man when she had left home, and Baron de Laterre was not many years younger. If they were indeed still alive, would they be prepared to give Sartine information that would shed light on the darkness? So that Sophie would finally find out the truth about her mother's death, and discover the name of that unknown accuser who had Madeleine on his conscience? At the thought that she might soon know the identity of the man with the plumed hat, Sophie felt quite strange.

Suddenly the door opened and a man came rushing in, excited and out of breath, as if he were being chased by a pack of wild dogs. His clothing looked as though it hadn't been cleaned in months, and his round wig had slipped halfway off his head. Sophie knew him; he was a regular at the Procope, a man with an oddly guttural accent who sometimes fell to stuttering when he spoke: the Swiss writer Rousseau.

"They ha-ha-have arrested Diderot!"

He shouted the news so loudly that everyone turned to look at him. The chess players looked up from their boards, the readers peered over the tops of their newspapers, and those who were napping awoke in their easy chairs. All at once the whole coffeehouse was gripped by a mood of agitation, much like at the beginning of the month when the rent was due.

"Diderot, arrested?"

"Impossible, I just saw him yesterday."

"When did it happen? Where?"

"This morning," Rousseau cried. "In the midst of his work."

Sophie put down her dish towel as the questions and shouts struck Rousseau like hail; he was having a hard time making his answers heard. Sophie could feel her heart pounding. It had been almost two years since she had last seen Diderot.

"They just took him away?"

"Like during the Inquisition?"

"But why? What are they charging him with?"

"They said he wrote some silly novel. Pornographic stuff, an Oriental fairy tale—how do I know!"

"And where is he now?"

"In prison. They took him to Vincennes. In a coach with bars on the windows."

"To Vincennes? That's worse than the Bastille!"

"Yes, it's a catastrophe. But that's not all." Rousseau raised both hands, his eyes flicking around, and waited for the noise to die down. Not until it was completely quiet and all eyes were on him did he continue: "Le Bréton betrayed him—his own publisher!"

An outraged murmur rippled through the coffeehouse.

"No! It can't be true!"

"He would never do such a thing!"

"It's true! The police searched the publishing house that issued the book. And that swine admitted everything."

The news left the listeners speechless. In disbelief they stared at Rousseau, who was now relating the course of events, speaking with the accent of his hometown of Geneva. He began haltingly, then spoke faster and faster, until finally the words came pouring out of him in a flood. As he spoke, a tiny, wicked suspicion stirred inside Sophie, and it grew bigger and bigger with every sentence Rousseau said. Was this the reason Sartine had been given an unexpected leave of absence? As a reward?

All of a sudden Rousseau fell silent and gazed about the room, bewildered and apprehensive, as if someone had offended him.

Without thinking about what she was doing, Sophie stepped out from behind the counter and said, "Excuse me, monsieur . . ."

"What is it?" Rousseau barked at her. "Can't you wait to take my order until I call you?"

"It's not regarding your order, only a question. Please."

"Then make it quick! What do you want to know?"

Sophie had to swallow before she could speak, it was so difficult for her to utter these few words. "What," she asked softly, "was the name of the novel for which Monsieur Diderot was arrested?"

37

The tower of the fortress of Vincennes was wrapped in a milky gray pall of haze, and its battlements seemed to disappear into the sky, as Father Radominsky climbed out of the coach that had brought him to the infamous prison at the gates of the city. It was here that all the lawbreakers were held in custody when the dungeons of the Bastille could no longer take in more prisoners; it was also the jail for those whose offense required particularly severe punishment.

The warden of the fortress, a rosy-faced man with an immaculately powdered wig, received Radominsky at the gate. The father shivered as he followed his host along a cold, damp corridor lit by only one torch. It smelled of rot and decay. Behind the bars of the cells to left and right, living like ghosts, were crowds of filthy, emaciated figures who had on their conscience all the crimes and sins of which the descendants of Adam were capable. The prisoners stretched out their hands to the two gentlemen. At the end of the corridor two prisoners under the supervision of a guard were busy placing a meagerly shrouded corpse in a coffin made of rough-hewn planks: the scum of creation on the way to the grave. "Peace be unto thy soul!"

Radominsky had only a fleeting glance for the dead man, to whom he gave his blessing as he passed by. With all his senses he was feverishly anticipating his meeting with the most dangerous prisoner, who at the moment was locked in the tower. The warden led him up a narrow staircase to a room illuminated by daylight where a jailer guarded a bolted door along with a gigantic black dog; the dog's brawny face bore a grotesque resemblance to that of his master.

"I'll leave you alone with him," said the warden. "But don't worry—the guard will be outside the door."

Radominsky watched impatiently as the jailer removed the heavy bar on the door. Now he would look into the face of the man who had embarked on producing the most devilish and yet most splendid book ever written in France. The Jesuit was as excited about the impending debate with his spiritual opponent as a lover might be before his first night with a beautiful woman. Would he succeed in persuading the other man to surrender? He knew that the task before him was worthy of a Grand Inquisitor.

With a loud creak the door opened. Radominsky closed his eyes for a second to pray to God for assistance. Then he entered the cell.

"Praise be to Jesus Christ!"

"What do you want? I haven't called for anyone."

Radominsky had expected a grim Saul type of person—but now he found himself looking into a pair of incredibly bright blue eyes. So this was the famous Denis Diderot: a man in the prime of life, with broad shoulders and a blond shock of hair, sturdy as a sedan bearer, squeezed into a coarse gray jacket. His heart did not seem to depend on worldly things—his calves were clad in cheap black woolen stockings darned with white thread and must surely have been terribly scratchy. Diderot got up from the plank bed, the only piece of furniture in the cell, and stood before the priest with his arms crossed.

"Who are you, anyway?"

"Father Radominsky, the father confessor of the queen. I have come here to help you."

"Would you like to hear my confession?" replied Diderot. "I'll have to disappoint you on that score. I have done nothing for which I need to ask forgiveness. On the contrary. I strongly object to my arrest. It is an arbitrary act of wrongful deprivation of personal liberty!"

"Only one's immortal soul is free, Monsieur Diderot; the body is but a transitory shell."

"Then even greater haste is required so that this shell can get out of here. There is no reason to hold me any longer in this hole."

"Is that what you think?" Radominsky scrutinized Diderot from head to foot. "And what about your writings?"

"You mean the *Jewels*?" asked Diderot contemptuously. "Don't make me laugh. La Pompadour used the example in the novel to establish a harem for the king; even the sparrows are chirping about it from the rooftops, and in return she even received from His Majesty a new pleasure palace."

Radominsky shook his head. "You know very well why you've been locked up. Not because of this tasteless little novel, but because of your mobilization against the church and the state."

"I am a baptized Catholic and a loyal subject of the king."

"Your 'Letter to the Blind' is heresy, a materialistic manifesto in the demon spirit of Spinoza!"

"My 'Letter Concerning the Blind' is a medical treatise. In it I depict the true case of the English mathematician Saunders."

"Your answer offends my philosophical vanity. Do you really consider me so stupid?" Diderot said nothing, so Radominsky continued. "Then allow me to remind you of your own theories. In the letter you claim that the spirit could neither create matter nor have an effect upon it. So the source of this matter must be eternity, and whatever we call thinking or volition is only a modus, a type and manifestation of its existence. How would you characterize this argument if not by calling it materialism?"

"I'm a good citizen. I deal only with things that affect the welfare of society and the lives of my fellow human beings."

"I recognize this claptrap; it's what you repeat at the start of all your treatises. You may use it to fool a lazy censor, but not me." He took a step toward Diderot and looked him in the eye. "You deny the existence of God, monsieur! In order to believe in God, in your own words, one must be able to touch Him."

Diderot did not flinch from his gaze. "My philosophy," he replied, "is merely a humble attempt to deduce the knowledge of men from their own capacity for knowledge, from the senses and from reason. Everything else is speculation."

"You call the revealed Word of God speculation?"

"I have never claimed anything of the sort."

"You do much worse—you sow doubt in the hearts and minds of your readers, so that you need only look on to see its effects. In this way you undermine the teachings of the church. And if that wasn't enough, you question the very sovereignty of the king."

"That is an untenable misrepresentation!"

"Is it? Then what about this?" Radominsky took a notebook from his pocket: Sartine's notes from Café Procope, together with copies of still unpublished articles for the *Encyclopedia* that an informer inside Le Bréton's publishing house had acquired. It didn't take the priest long to find an appropriate quotation: "Here, under the heading 'Authority,' you write,

'No man has received from Nature the right to command others.... The true and lawful power thus inevitably has its limits.... It seems that only slaves, whose spirit is as limited as their convictions are low, could think otherwise....' And it goes on like this—from blasphemy straight to high treason. All words that originated from your mouth and your pen. Or do you wish to deny it?"

Diderot bent down to scratch his leg. Radominsky smugly registered this action.

"On whose behalf did you come here?" Diderot asked.

"On behalf of God, the supreme authority in Heaven and on earth. And in His name I tell you: Stop before it's too late! Don't make yourself as common as the refuse of humanity gathered here, all the thieves, murderers, and child molesters. Your crimes, as hideous as they are, are not nearly as dangerous as the book that you're planning. For whoever spreads such ideas is lighting the fuse of a powder keg that could blow all of society sky high."

"Nothing could be further from my mind than that. I love France and I love the monarchy. But," Diderot went on in a gentle voice, "can a society persist in the long run if it turns against the law of Nature? Or is it then not condemned to destroy itself?"

"Not Nature—God Himself has rightfully set the king above his subjects!"

"Only as a father over his children! And his power ceases when the children are capable of leading themselves. But the power that is gained through force is usurpation, and it lasts only as long as the strength of those who command exceeds that of those who obey. This is why true and legitimate power has natural limits. As the Holy Scripture states: 'May your subordination be reasonable.'"

"But the Holy Scriptures also say: 'All power that comes from God is well ordered.'"

"Does that mean that all power, no matter what type, comes from God? Is there no unjust rule? Do the usurpers have God on their side? If that were so, wouldn't it follow that even the power of the Antichrist, wherever he attains it, would be legitimate? And wouldn't Enoch and Elias, who resisted such power, then be counted as rabble-rousers who incited unrest? Weren't they instead reasonable, courageous, and above all pious men, who thought as Paul did that all power comes from God only as long as it is just and well ordered?"

Diderot spoke with such fervor, with such enthusiasm, that Radominsky could not withhold his respect. What an overburdened education!
What a squandered imagination! The philosopher accompanied each
of his words with a gesture: He balled his fists to emphasize his arguments, even pointed with outstretched arm at his opponent, so that
his speech seemed transformed into a sword. Here was a man who
believed in what he said! Imbued with his message, nothing could hold
him in one place. He paced up and down in his cell, sat down, and
jumped back up; the words poured out of him in a torrent, as if his
tongue had trouble forming all the words fast enough to express the
ideas that tumbled from his brain. Radominsky understood: Instead of
destroying this man in the name of God, it was his duty to win him
over for God's cause.

"I recognize with joy that you are citing the words of the Lord. Even
if pride and arrogance are perhaps whispering something different, deep
inside you know the truth: You are one of us, but you are fighting on the
wrong side."

"I'm fighting on the only correct side—on the side of reason."

"Perhaps, but why are you then content with its mere reflection,
instead of dipping from the spring itself?"

"You speak in keeping with the guild to which you belong, Reverend
Father—in riddles."

"Then I will express myself more clearly. You are too late, Monsieur
Diderot—your encyclopedia was published long ago, written by an
author whose skills you could never hope to equal."

Diderot blanched. He gazed at the priest with incredulous eyes, like
a man who returns from a journey and learns that during his absence his
house has been robbed.

"Where did this book appear? In England? In Germany?"

"In all countries on earth, in Africa and Asia and America as well as
Europe, yes, even in the new land of Australia. There is no spot or corner
of the world that this book has not already reached."

"And why," Diderot asked crossly, "haven't I heard about this book?"

"Because you, who never tire of extolling the senses as the source of
knowledge, close your eyes to the truth as if covering them with pitch."
He grabbed hold of Diderot's coat and led him to the cell window.
"There, open your eyes. The world itself is the book I'm talking about—
the book of creation. This book is the only valid encyclopedia, written

by the Holy Spirit; it is the eternally true text which the Lord God, the arch-encyclopedist, has given us to read."

Outside they saw the meadows and fields enveloped in haze, as if through a fine gauze veil.

"Then perhaps we are indeed looking at the same book," said Diderot after a while. "There is only one difference: You call it the book of creation, I call it the book of Nature. And I consider it my task to rip away the veil of fog that has settled over the pages of this book down through the centuries, woven from false teachings, dogmas, and prejudices that prevent us from reading the words correctly."

Radominsky shook his head. "You are so close to the truth—and yet you refuse to grasp it. Why this obstinacy, Monsieur Diderot? Do you want to be a blind man leading a blind humanity? If we are unable to read the book of creation, there is only one reason: because we have sullied the text with our sins and the perversion of free will, which prompts us to defy God day after day. That's why we can no longer decipher what is written; we can only guess at the holy words, which seem to be specters in the infinite sea of depravity, like a text written in ink that is washed from the page when water is poured over it." He turned away from the window and placed a hand on Diderot's shoulder. "Instead of writing a new encyclopedia that can never equal the original, it is our task to return the book of creation to its original condition, to cleanse this Holy Scripture of the errors and distortions that we humans have added to it, so that we can again read the revealed truth of God. That is the task, our common task, yours and mine; it is our obligation to God and necessary for the salvation of our souls. In order to enter into the Kingdom of the Lord, of which the creation here on earth is but a pale reflection."

Diderot turned to the priest. Contempt blazed from his eyes.

"You mean the heavenly paradise? On the other side after death?"

"Mors porta vitae," Radominsky replied gravely. "Death is the gateway to life. For true life begins first when our transitory shell falls away from us. Yes, of course I mean the hereafter. Where else would there be a paradise?"

Diderot took a step back, as if to free himself from Radominsky's presence; the contempt in his eyes gave way to growing indignation. "What gives you the right to consign people to waiting for the hereafter? How dare you, with all the misery and poverty that exists in the world?"

"I understand your sympathy for the less fortunate of this earth," said

Radominsky, "and believe me, I share your feelings. But their suffering has a purpose. Our earthly existence is only a probationary interlude. It is meant to purify us for eternal life. 'My kingdom is not of this world,' saith the Lord. Would you doubt these words?"

"No, but God came down to earth in the form of his son. Why did He do that, if not so that we could complete His work together with Him?"

"'The Word is become flesh and abides among us.'" Radominsky nodded. "Yes, you're right. No being has ever displayed such humility as the Lord God, who became a human being for our sake. Even more, He rooted in the muck in order to make Adam from a lump of clay, and He breathed into him with His own mouth the breath of life. Yet should we thank Him for this self-abasement by raising ourselves above His will, by imagining ourselves greater than Him in order to intervene in His eternal plan for creation?"

"It's not my intention to raise myself above God. But hasn't God given human beings a clear task? 'Fill the earth and subdue it.' Instead of hoping for the hereafter, we are called to continue God's creation and turn it into a Garden of Eden. So it is not our right, but our duty, with the help of science and all the experience that other people have accrued before us, to order life on earth so that we might grant ourselves the greatest good."

"And what would this greatest good be?"

"Happiness!" said Diderot without hesitation. "The end of suffering and affliction."

"You call that the greatest good?" Radominsky exclaimed with a laugh. "Do you actually believe that?"

"What else? The desire for happiness is the one thing about which all people agree."

"We are not here on this earth in order to be happy. We are on this earth to obey God."

"But God Himself has given us the yearning for happiness. Why would He do that?"

"To test us."

"Then why does He say: 'My people shall have the fullness of my gifts'? Isn't that the promise of happiness?"

"Possessing everything is a curse much worse than suffering and affliction," Radominsky replied, undeterred. "'But I will leave as a remnant in your midst a people humble and lowly, who shall take refuge in the name of the Lord.' Zephaniah 3:12. According to the law of grace, man is much happier because of what he hopes for than because of what he possesses. The happiness that he enjoys on earth is at best the seed for eternal happiness."

"Only those who possess the most would ever claim such a thing. And for what reason? In order to withhold from other people what they themselves cannot do without."

"Then answer me a simple question," said Radominsky. "Who in this country possesses the most?"

"The king, of course."

"Quite right. Yet do you believe that he wishes the irrevocable continuation of his existence merely because he has everything? No, the king's only happiness is to forget himself. For no one feels as deeply as he does. Whoever possesses everything in actuality has lost the most valuable thing—the hope for redemption."

Radominsky stopped talking and looked at Diderot, who returned his gaze without protesting further. Nervously the younger man fumbled with his coat as if something were pinching him. Had he finally gotten the message?

"Come over to our side, Monsieur Diderot," said Radominsky. "Help us to cleanse the stains of sin from the work of God. Together let's write the book of creation. The two of us, you and I, have the intellect and the grace to write the only encyclopedia that corresponds to God's will, a compendium of eternal truth. Not for the common people, but for the elite, the best of the best, the chosen of the Lord." He held out his hand. "Take my hand, and you're a free man!"

Diderot looked at the priest as though only now did he really see him.

Radominsky nodded encouragement. "What are you waiting for? Build with me the stronghold of the Holy Spirit!"

Nothing in Diderot's face betrayed what he was thinking. After a long while, which seemed like an eternity to the priest, he finally opened his lips to speak.

"Have I understood you correctly? You're offering me release from prison if I shake your hand and accept your proposal?"

"Yes. God has blessed you with too many talents for you to wither away in this tower."

"And all the other prisoners, to whom God was less generous at their births—what about them?"

Radominsky shrugged his shoulders. "It is your decision alone, Monsieur Diderot. But if you come with me—who knows, perhaps I can do something for one or two other prisoners . . ."

The words crumbled on Radominsky's lips like moldy mushrooms. Because as he spoke, Diderot's eyes narrowed to two slits, his bright, clear gaze darkened, as if the Tempter incarnate stood before him. In a voice so low that his words were scarcely audible, he said: "Leave this room at once!"

38

The cell door had hardly closed behind Radominsky before Diderot's energy dissolved. As tired as an old man, he sank down onto his plank bed, and as the footsteps in the corridor faded into the distance, melancholy descended upon his soul as outdoors the twilight settled over the waning day. His whole body was numb, paralyzed, no longer feeling the prickling and scratching of his filthy, stinking clothes.

A noise woke him from his paralysis. The door flap opened, and behind it appeared the bulldog face of his guard.

"There—for you. A candle."

"What do I need a candle for? It's summer; I have enough light."

"I would take it anyway," said the guard, baring his teeth. "The days will soon be growing shorter. It's not long now until winter."

Diderot spent the next few weeks in deep despondency. Only one thought kept circling in his head, a thought that had been gnawing like a rat at his soul ever since his arrest. A hundred times he had driven it off, but now he could no longer deny the truth: He had been arrested because Sophie had betrayed him.

This truth was worse than any lie. For hours he lay on his plank bed, motionless, staring at the ceiling, then he would run back and forth like an animal in a cage, flinging himself at the door of his cell and banging his head against the bars until his forehead began to bleed. But nothing helped him to banish the truth. He cursed the day he had met Sophie, cursed her words, her gaze with which she had seduced him, cursed the kiss into which they had tumbled together. She had destroyed his life: himself, his family, his work. No kiss was worth such a price.

His only distraction was the cockroaches. As he suffered from the thought that each hour he spent in confinement was an hour stolen from his life, the crawling beasts, driven by some mindless instinct, sought refuge in his cell; the damp walls seemed to them a paradise. Since they had taken away his books and writing materials, the lack of any activity soon drove him to mania and he began studying the black roaches. With their flat, egg-shaped, armored bodies they came creeping out of the corners and niches, their heads hidden beneath the big neck plates, their feelers stretching forward, long and brushlike. The sight of them moved him to rage that grew more violent each time. He stamped on the beasts with his feet, smashed them between his fingers, and set out bait—pieces of cloth soaked in brown beer, for which he had to pay his guard horrendous bribes—in the hope that the bugs, compelled by their instincts, would follow the scent during the dark hours. And indeed, when he removed the pieces of cloth at night he discovered in the light of his candle a milling swarm of thousands, which he struck with his palm in paroxysms of uncontrolled glee until the pain made him stop. But no matter how much cunning and energy he devoted to the persecution of this plague, it was in vain. With each cockroach he killed, a dozen more new larvae crept out of their eggs to nest all over the cell.

One morning he heard a rattle of keys, the door of the cell opened, and his wife came in.

"Nanette!" shouted Diderot, jumping up from his bunk as the guard relocked the door. Never since the day he had fallen in love with her pretty face had he been so glad to see her; after the visit of the Jesuit and three weeks alone, she was the first human being to come to see him.

"Look at you!" she exclaimed, clapping her hands to her head. "As filthy as a sewer cleaner. Isn't there any water here?"

"Don't you want to kiss me?"

"What a hole you're living in! Not even a table and chair. If your father could see you now! Aren't you ashamed?"

He dropped his arms. Her gaze, her expression, her voice—everything told him that she was in no mood for tender caresses. Sobered, he decided to change the subject.

"Have you heard what's happening with the *Encyclopedia*?"

"I wish I had your worries. Instead of asking about your child, all you care about are your books. As if this misfortune wasn't bad enough!"

"How is Didier?" he asked, feeling guilty. "What about his cough?"

"I fainted when I heard the news. My husband in prison! Like a common criminal. And you told me you were going out to eat. You lied to me!"

"I didn't want you to worry."

"You should have thought of that when you were writing such filth. I went to see the lieutenant general of the police, I beseeched him on my knees to set you free. But he can do nothing for you."

"Talk to d'Alembert. He knows some important people, maybe they can help."

"More important than the lieutenant general? He told me I should look to see if I could find a white dove among your papers. What do I know about your papers?" Suddenly she stopped her flood of words. "White dove—what did he mean by that, I wonder?"

Diderot shrugged his shoulders.

Full of mistrust, she looked at him. "Is it just about the books that you've written? Or have you broken other laws?" Her gaze was so insistent that she was almost squinting. "Have you stolen something? Or killed somebody? Tell me the truth!"

Diderot did not answer. He saw only her pretty, perfectly stupid face. Was it really possible that only a minute ago he had longed to take her in his arms and kiss her?

"When is your trial?" she asked.

"No idea. Many prisoners have been here for years and are still waiting to be charged."

"Years? Are you mad?" She grabbed her belly, which was swelling under her skirts. "The next child is coming in the winter. Do you want us to starve?"

"No one is going to starve. You do have the allowance from Le Bréton."

"So that's what you think," Nanette snorted. "That filthy pig isn't paying us a *sou*. He canceled the allowance."

"That's not possible. We have a contract."

"Of course it's possible! Monsieur Publisher has been gallivanting all over Paris in his sedan chair, and everywhere he goes he makes a big fuss about your arrest, but he lets us starve. Is it true that he betrayed you?"

"*Betrayed* isn't the right word," said Diderot. "He had no choice. Otherwise they would have taken away his printing permit, and it would all be over. Besides, even without him they knew that I—"

"What? Now you're defending him? I don't believe it!" Nanette's voice cracked from excitement. Suddenly she calmed down and said softly, "Then we have only one option."

"Namely?" he asked, although he knew the answer in advance.

"You have to write to your father. He will help us."

"It wouldn't do any good."

"Why not? He's your father!"

"Because it wouldn't do any good," he repeated impatiently. He hesitated for a moment, but when he saw from her expression that she lacked any understanding, he flew into a rage. "Why should he help you? He doesn't know the slightest thing about you. Not even that you exist!"

"What's that supposed to mean? He doesn't know about me?" asked Nanette, as if he'd been speaking Chinese. "But he's . . . he has . . ." Then, with agonizing slowness, as if her innermost being were resisting it, a desperate comprehension penetrated her cluelessness. "Are you trying to tell me . . . that he still doesn't know . . . *that we're married*?"

She shrieked these last words, then her voice gave out. Tears filled her eyes so that her vision blurred, while her lips, incapable of articulating another word, quivered with fury.

Diderot cast down his eyes. Her stunned silence, which now filled the cell to bursting, was even worse than her previous nagging.

Fortunately, Nanette's speechlessness did not last long.

"You have to write to the chancellor," she said. "You have to beg him for mercy. The chancellor or the king or some other important person."

"No," said Diderot.

"What do you mean, no?"

"No," he repeated, looking at her. "They can keep me here in prison, but I will never admit that they have set themselves up as masters of my life."

Footsteps were approaching outside. Keys rattled, and with a loud creak the door opened. In the doorway stood the guard with his dog.

"Visiting hours are over."

Nanette didn't move. Tears were running down her pretty face. Diderot almost felt sorry for her.

"What sort of man are you?" she whispered.

Suddenly she turned around and without another word dashed off.

On the floor at his feet, two cockroaches were copulating.

Like an idiot Diderot gazed at the two beasts.

The image was as hopeless and intolerable as eternity.

39

How long would the money last that he'd had on him when he was arrested? Although his cell was as cramped and damp as a well shaft and smaller than ten feet square, it was as expensive as a luxury hotel in the middle of Paris. In order to avoid being locked up with murderers and other riffraff, Diderot had requested a private cell, which now cost him sixty *livres* per month. Added to that were his living expenses, which he had to pay out of his own pocket. In prison everything cost twice as much as it did outside, as if a special tax were being levied outside the slot of his cell door. With a mixture of red wine and slate that he rubbed into powder, he had made a sort of ink, and a toothpick served him as a pen, with which he wrote a letter to his father. In it he recounted his entire misfortune, confessing at the same time his marriage to Nanette; in closing he begged for support for his family. In exchange for the weekly wage of a postilion the guard declared himself prepared to mail the letter.

From hearing remarks made by the warden, Diderot concluded that he had been arrested in the wake of a sweeping general action. A whole horde of writers and philosophers was imprisoned along with him at the fortress: doctors of the Sorbonne and journalists, versifiers and brochure writers, jurists and abbés, all of whom were accused of having insulted the king. There was talk of revolt, of the spread of deism, and an assault on good morals. But the real reason, Diderot knew, was something else: The government needed scapegoats for the unrest that was smoldering among the populace because of the ever harsher taxes being imposed by the state simply to finance things that were a thorn in the eye of the subjects—the gigantic army, the luxuries at court, and the extravagances of the reigning favorite, the Marquise de Pompadour. The convenient solution was to take into custody all the freethinkers who could be rounded up. They would be denounced in public as the vermin in the edifice of the state, and they could be eradicated just as Diderot tried to get rid of the roaches in his cell.

How long would he be able to stand this?

He was squatting near the floor, where he was arranging a little piece of wood as a footbridge to a pot, when he had an unexpected visitor.

"What are you doing?" asked Rousseau, staring down at him.

"I'm building a trap. For the cockroaches."

Rousseau poked his foot against the construction.

"Listen, I need your advice," he said after they had embraced each other. His face glowed as if he had run all the way to Vincennes from Paris.

"Did another of your operas flop?" Diderot asked.

"I don't write operas anymore. Here—read it for yourself! It was in today's *Mercure*." Rousseau pulled a newspaper out of his coat pocket and held it up to Diderot's face.

"A contest?"

"From the academy in Dijon. To debate whether the progress of the arts and sciences has contributed to the depravity or the elevation of morals."

"Is that the topic?" Diderot asked without real interest.

"Yes," said Rousseau, taking off his wig. His head was drenched in sweat. "I feel that here Providence is calling me by name."

"And how are you going to answer?"

"In the spirit of progress, of course!"

"So you think that science and art promote morality? Are you so sure?"

"You mean you aren't?" Rousseau asked in turn, completely astonished.

Diderot shrugged. "Every ass who takes part in that wager will be blaring the fanfare of progress. Where's the wit in that? If you want to win the prize, you have to launch a strategy that no one else would dare venture."

"You're advising me to take a stand against progress? You, of all people? I thought your encyclopedia was going to be the Bible of the future."

"Can't you see where progress has led me?" Diderot countered. "Straight into prison! And I'm not its only victim. Everything that men have invented, society has used against them. The sciences, trade, shipping—don't they always end up being the source of misery and devastation? The compass, mining, gunpowder—haven't they increased the wretchedness of humanity rather than fostering its happiness? No," Diderot went on as his friend tried to protest, "what we call progress is merely a result of dangerous errors. True progress is nothing more than the restoration of things to their natural state."

"What are you trying to say? Should I perhaps grow a beard?"

"I'm serious," said Diderot. He paused for a moment to find a suitable comparison, then went on: "Nature lies before us like an open book, with all her laws. But we are incapable of reading this book. And why? Because over the course of time the text has become less and less legible. By now the letters are hardly decipherable, faded and blurred like ink that someone has doused with water."

"You mean," said Rousseau, gradually comprehending, "that progress is the water in which the writing of nature has dissolved? But with that you are turning on its head everything that we previously thought and believed!"

"So what?" replied Diderot. "Take me, look at me! For over a month I've been living in this hole!"

"What does that have to do with progress?"

"Don't you understand? At birth all human beings are free—the first state that they acquire from Nature is the state of freedom. But what becomes of it when they begin to live? Wherever you look, freedom is repressed. I've learned that here. —But what's wrong?"

Even as Diderot spoke, Rousseau began to behave quite oddly, as though all his afflictions were affecting him at once. Stammering incomprehensible sounds, he paced back and forth in the cell, grabbed his head, clenched his fists; his face was full of anxiety and rage, and his eyes flickered as if with fever. At the window he suddenly stopped, his features relaxed, and his eyes widened as he looked into the distance, as if there he might catch sight of a foreign landscape, and he whispered, "Man is born free, but everywhere he lies in chains . . . What a thought! I see wild animals before me, breaking out of the primeval forest; I smell the bonfires on which the old order is burning." He almost seemed delirious. But as suddenly as this transported state had overcome him, it fell away, and the distant expression left his face. With a jolt he turned around. "Call the guard! I want out."

"Why? Do you have to pee? The privy is behind the curtain."

"No. I can't stay any longer. I have to get back to Paris at once!"

"But you just got here."

"Duty calls. Inside me a new universe is coming to life, I can feel it, I know it! I . . . I . . . I'm a new man!"

Without waiting for a reply, he called for the guard himself.

"By the way," he said from the doorway, "I saw Madame de Puisieux yesterday at the Procope."

"Yes, and . . . ?" Diderot asked. "Is she coming to visit me?"

"It's better if you don't expect her. She betrayed you. She has found another."

"Another—what?" Diderot spluttered.

"Another lover," said Rousseau with a grin.

That evening Diderot lit a candle and wrote a long letter. It was the most hypocritical letter he'd ever written, yet he wrote it with a clear conscience—because it was the only chance he had to save his life.

40

As fast as the wind the six-horse diligence raced down the paved *chaussée*. Antoine Sartine, in order to conserve his meager cash, had made do with one of the cheap seats on the roof of the coach. Because of the breathtaking speed the passengers were constantly sent into the air, and it was a wonder that they always landed back in their seats. Nevertheless, the journey to his wife's home region filled him with boundless pride in his country. Apart from the visit to an uncle in Normandy when he was a boy, he had never been farther than a day's journey from Paris. With even greater astonishment he now learned how big the kingdom of France really was. Towns and cities flew by, situated in fruitful valleys and on top of charming hills—gardens and meadows, fields and pastures, forests and vineyards. Wherever Sartine looked, he discerned the diligent labor of people who with the toil of their hands had cultivated nature in order to perfect God's creation.

Most of all he was impressed by the road system—a genius must have devised it. Post roads reinforced with basalt and limestone linked all the important places in the country; the roads were further subdivided and connected through central junctions. At these relay stations the horses were changed, and the passengers could have a meal or spend the night. Exact departure times were displayed at the ticket windows, and punctually coordinated timetables made it possible to plan trips most precisely. What wonderful progress this was!

Not until Roanne did Sartine have to leave the post coach in order to travel the last miles to Beaulieu by oxcart, which rumbled with intolerable slowness through the vineyards, where farmers and their day laborers harvested the grapes in the still warm October sun. Seated in the jolting cart, Sartine painfully felt each pothole with his body sore from traveling, but when after a bend in the road he spied the church tower of Beaulieu jutting into the blue autumn sky, all tribulations fell away. Finally he would have an opportunity to show Sophie his love—a love that was immeasurably more worthwhile than the brutish pleasures that other men shared with their wives. He only hoped that the town priest was still alive.

Even before he went to the inn, Sartine sought out the presbytery. With pounding heart he knocked on the door. Shortly he heard heavy, shuffling footsteps, and then the door opened. Before him stood a tall, big-boned old man in a black habit worn smooth by age.

"Abbé Morel?"

"Who are you?" asked the priest. "I've never seen you in my church."

"I bring greetings from Sophie Volland, who used to live in your parish."

When he mentioned the name a light suffused the leathery, lined face.

"Sophie Volland . . . Yes, I remember, a bright young girl. She could read as well as a scribe, much better than I. But come in, my son. You must tell me about her. Where is she now? How does she make her living? Is everything going well for her?"

The presbytery stank like a pigsty, and in the hallway there was such a clutter that Sartine had to take care not to trip over the objects strewn all over the clay floor. Obviously the abbé lived without female help in this low, dark house; he fetched a bottle and two glasses from a cupboard and poured drinks for them.

"Plum brandy," he said. "Made it myself. Only for honored guests."

Suppressing his disgust, Sartine put the dirty glass to his lips and tossed back the brandy, while Abbé Morel asked more questions about Sophie. He wanted to know everything about her: whether she attended mass regularly, whether she was married, whether she had children.

"What?" he said when Sartine shook his head. "You mean God hasn't blessed your marriage? Perhaps you need to help Him out a bit, don't you think?"

He gave Sartine a conspiratorial wink. Then the priest began to tell him about Sophie, speaking in such elaborate detail that Sartine almost had the impression he was trying to avoid other topics. He described how Sophie had taught the children in the village to read, how she had always been the first in catechism lessons to raise her hand and gave such intelligent answers that even Baron de Laterre took notice of her—yes, Abbé Morel even seemed to remember her baptism. An hour passed in this way, until Sartine finally had a chance to bring up the actual reason for his visit.

Instantly the expression on the abbé's face darkened, and grave sadness filled his old eyes.

"My God! How long ago is it now? Almost ten years. It was the last bonfire that was ever lit here; the whole valley came to see it."

"Are there still records? Documents?"

"Come with me, I'll show them to you."

With weary, shuffling steps, as if the weight of the past were on his shoulders, the priest led Sartine into the sacristy. There he opened a huge cabinet overflowing with yellowed papers. Sartine was astounded at how quickly the old man found the right documents in those untidy piles.

"Here, these must be the ones," said Abbé Morel, placing a thick bundle on the table. "The witchcraft trial against the seamstress Madeleine Volland. A nasty business, but it was God's will."

"What exactly was the charge?"

"Sophie had vomited up the Body of the Lord—the poor child." The priest's voice quavered, and he passed his bony hand over his eyes. "After that her mother was accused of the most heinous crimes. Allegedly she had cast a spell on a young man, a guest of the baron. At the trial he testified against her. Out of revenge, some people later claimed."

"Out of revenge?"

The priest nodded. "They said he'd had an eye for Madeleine, but she'd refused his affections."

Sartine pricked up his ears. That was a plausible motive. If a woman spurned the love of a man, he would be capable of anything. How many times he had encountered this very situation during his career.

In a voice hoarse with agitation he said, "Can you recall, Reverend Father, the name of this man?"

Abbé Morel shook his head. "I don't know his name; he wasn't from here. A nobleman from Paris. Perhaps you can find out yourself; everything that happened here was written down."

He pointed to the documents; then he exited the sacristy and left Sartine alone in the small, cool room.

The inspector blew the dust off the bundle before he untied the cord around it. He looked carefully through the material. Yes, it was all there: the indictment, the transcripts of the examination of the witnesses, the judgment. He separated the documents into several piles on the table, then he began to read.

"The seamstress Madeleine Volland, born and residing in the parish of Beaulieu, is accused of having acted contrary to the faith and to the common weal of the state, in that she practiced the black art on her daughter, Sophie, by administering a magical poisonous potion, causing her on the day of her First Communion to vomit up the Body of the Lord, in the presence of the incumbent priest as well as the congregation there gathered."

What was the real charge: witchcraft or preparing poison? The examination of the accused was as contradictory as the indictment itself.

"Why did you give your daughter, Sophie, the potion before Holy Communion? Did the potion also contain, besides herbs, the blood or entrails of dead animals? Why and to what purpose did you teach her to read?"

Sartine stopped short. Sophie had learned to read and write from her mother? Why had she concealed this ability from him for so long? Because it was connected to Madeleine's death? The questions of the court regarding the relationship of the accused to Sophie's father seemed to corroborate his suspicion.

"Did the peddler Dorval instruct you in reading and writing as well as in black magic? With which parts of the body did he rob you of your virginity? Did you want to kill your daughter in order to indulge in your lust undisturbed?"

The interrogation had lasted three days, according to the documents. Then additional witnesses were questioned, neighbors and members of the congregation, in order to clear up inconsistencies in the statements of the accused. The court had consulted physicians and theologians, a veterinarian had testified to the extraordinary effectiveness of some herbal drinks and salves, and Abbé Morel had been deposed as saying that the seamstress Volland in his opinion was indeed a dangerous rabble-rouser, but not a real witch—after all, she had kept down the Host that was given to her, unlike her daughter, Sophie.

The longer Sartine read through the old documents, the more agitated he grew. What an abyss of ignorance and superstition opened up before him! It was only ten years earlier that the case of Madeleine Volland had been argued, but the court had conducted the trial exactly as in the days of the Inquisition. Sartine was almost ashamed of his country, which had made possible such a process with its antiquated laws. But reflections on morality were not his present assignment. He had promised Sophie to find an answer to one specific question: Who was the man with the plumed hat?

With the sure gaze that he had developed in the practice of his profession, Sartine examined page after page. Then finally, as it was beginning to grow light outside, he discovered the decisive document. There he was, the man who had sent Sophie's mother to her death! He had really stirred up the court. At his instigation the privy of the seamstress Volland had been ransacked, and there in the filth had been found a whitish substance. This discovery had been enough to serve as proof that the accused had excreted the undigested Host. Was she in league with the Devil?

"In addition," he read in the statement of the witness, "she committed the worst crime against me that a woman can inflict on a man. She poured a potion as bitter as gall down my throat and in my presence tied a knot, as she softly intoned a spell, both to one and the same purpose . . ."

Sartine licked his fingertips to turn the page.

". . . namely, in order to make me incapable of copulating. In this she succeeded for a period of several days with the help of the Devil."

Sartine put down the document. If he'd had any doubt about the motive of the witness, it was now dispelled. His hands trembling with fury, he proceeded to the end of the document where the clerk had entered the name of the young man, who apparently had not had to give any personal details before the court.

As Antoine Sartine read the name, he froze. It felt as though two hands were closing around his throat to choke off all air.

41

"Should the king's subjects love the state or fear it?" Madame de Pompadour asked her two advisors, from whom she hoped to glean information as controversial as it was exciting.

"As far as I'm concerned, I plead in favor of love," said Malesherbes. "Love may be blind, as we all know, but it saves the government a lot of trouble."

"That could be," replied Father Radominsky, "but what happens if people awake from their blindness? No, I plead in favor of fear. Only fear can keep a tight rein on the people. It tempers the soul the way cold does iron."

"Then I agree with you, *mon père*." La Pompadour nodded. "But can fear not turn to hate? And is it not possible that a completely new and much greater danger might grow out of it? The danger of revolution?"

"I have the impression, madame," said Malesherbes with a smile, "that you are asking with some ulterior motives. Is there a reason for your concern?"

"How well you know me. As a matter of fact, this morning I received this letter." She picked up an envelope lying on her dressing table and opened it. "From Monsieur Diderot, addressed to the police prefect of Paris as well as to the king's chancellor. Are you gentlemen interested?" When her guests affirmed with a bow that they were, she handed the letter to Radominsky. "If you would perhaps be so kind?"

The priest unfolded the letter, and in a firm, clear voice he read it aloud.

" '*A man of honor who had the misfortune to attract the disfavor of the ministry beseeches your benevolent assistance. From the fortress of Vincennes, in which he is being held and where he is about to succumb to physical pain and torments of the soul, he throws himself at your feet and begs you for his freedom.*

I have suffered all that a human being can suffer; I am exhausted, despondent, consumed by sorrow. Nevertheless I must confess to you that I would rather die here a thousand times than—in the eyes of you, of myself, and of all honorable people—leave here in dishonor. I am also unable to believe that you might hold me in such contempt as to make this attempt with me. But you wish to be satisfied, and so you shall.

To you as my worthy protectors I therefore confess that which neither a long sojourn in prison nor all conceivable sufferings could ever make me confess to the judge about myself: that both The Indiscreet Jewels *and the "Letter Concerning the Blind" represent examples of an intellectual presumptuousness hatched from my own pen. But I can assure you on my honor (and I do possess some honor) that they are the last and the only ones.*

Concerning those individuals who were involved in the dissemination of these works, I will withhold nothing from you. I will verbally communicate their names to you. In addition, I vow, insofar as you demand it, to inform these individuals that their names are known, and henceforth they will behave as well as I am determined to do.

I implore you most fervently to see to my case and to spare my life by restoring my freedom to me. I promise you to make full use of both my life and my freedom and to make good past errors, in that I shall finish the Universal Lexicon of the Sciences and Arts, *of which I am one of the editors, upon which I have worked for a full three years, and for which I have incurred many expenses and have taken on endless trouble.'"*

Radominsky put down the letter.

"What can have induced this Diderot to write such a plea?" asked Madame de Pompadour.

"Certainly not love for the state," Malesherbes declared. "Rather the fear of an outraged wife."

"Do you share that opinion, *mon père*?" said La Pompadour.

Radominsky shook his head. "Absolutely not," he replied. "I'm more inclined to believe that love probably guided the pen of the writer of this letter."

"Pardon me?" said Malesherbes, raising his eyebrows. "I must confess, you surprise me, Monseigneur. What sort of love would that be?"

"The sort of love that is presumably foreign to you, monsieur—love for one's work."

"And for that he prostrates himself in the dirt? That seems less than convincing. How can he love his work, if he displays so little self-respect?"

"I have spoken with this man; I know him," Radominsky insisted.

"The letter is a white dove, a peace offering, in order to lull us into a false sense of security." His tone was hard, almost embittered. "Diderot wrote this letter to save his encyclopedia. He would rather betray himself than his work."

The Marquise de Pompadour recognized this tone: Disappointed lovers spoke this way of women who had spurned their love.

"What is your decision?" asked Malesherbes. "What should be done with Diderot?"

"What choices do I have?"

"Anything you desire, madame."

"Correct," Radominsky concurred. "The decision is utterly at your discretion."

"Whether to grant Diderot his freedom . . ."

". . . or have him executed."

The marquise frowned. "Is that the alternative?"

Both men nodded, one with the hint of a bow, the other with no expression on his face. The two very different men eyed each other tentatively. Radominsky was the only abbé at court who wore no wig; instead he dressed as an ordinary country priest in a silk cassock, although he was the father confessor to the queen. The complete opposite was Malesherbes, who, with a refined smile behind which he concealed his emotions as always, was just taking a pinch from his mother-of-pearl snuffbox.

"You mean Diderot loves his work more than himself?" La Pompadour asked at last. "So, it would be wiser to punish the work instead of the man. Perhaps that would be a lesson to him."

42

Sophie dipped the wooden spoon into the sauce to taste it one more time. Perhaps a bit more port wine? It also needed rosemary, and another spoonful of honey and quince marmalade wouldn't hurt.

For two hours she had been basting the duck on the stove. It was sizzling golden brown in the casserole, and the sweet, heavy aroma filled the whole apartment. Sophie had bought the roast with money from her nest egg, the secret savings she kept in her pouch under the mattress; even her husband didn't know about it. She wanted to surprise Sartine on his return from the journey with the most sumptuous feast he had ever eaten, prepared with sinfully expensive ingredients.

Sartine had truly earned such a reception. What other man would have sacrificed for his wife the first leave of absence he had ever received in his life? For so many years Sophie had tried to forget the past as if it were a bad dream she could dismiss as soon as she woke up. Only now, when the solution of the riddle was near, did she feel that she had been deluding herself the whole time. How could she be happy when the man who had Madeleine on his conscience was free? If Sartine had discovered his name, she would seek the man out, and who knows, perhaps she might even manage to see justice done on her mother's behalf, posthumously at least. Privately, Sophie begged forgiveness from her husband for the dark longings that sometimes came over her as she lay sleepless at night by his side. According to the timetable, his post coach should arrive in Paris before evening. She hoped that the fog, which had been rising in ever thicker clouds off the river for the past few days, had not delayed his journey.

She heard footsteps in the stairwell. Could he be arriving already? Hurriedly, she untied her apron to go and look. As she opened the door, her heart leaped with joy: before her stood Sartine. With a smile he handed her a box made of red cardboard.

"This is for you. A present from your home village."

"From Beaulieu? For me?" She gave him a kiss on the cheek. "But come, you must be exhausted from your journey."

She took his hand and led him to his favorite place, the easy chair.

"How lovely it smells," he said, sniffing the air. "And the table! You've set it like it's a holiday. No, let me," he said as she knelt down to pull off his boots. "Wouldn't you rather open your present?"

She took the package and undid the ribbon. When she saw what was inside she stopped short: a slender silver chain with a tiny angel carved from some sort of bright, polished material that reminded her of a skull.

"What . . . what is this?" she asked, annoyed. "Ivory?"

"I thought you'd know. It's a lucky charm, they told me in Beaulieu. There are many types of them. Don't you like it?"

"Of course I do, it's very . . . pretty," she said, trying to hide her irritation. "How sweet of you." She opened the clasp and put the chain around her neck. "Did you find it with the things belonging to my mother?"

Sartine shook his head. He took her hands and looked at her. His face, normally so carefully shaven, was covered with stubble.

"No, Sophie, I'm sorry. To tell you the truth, I found nothing at all. There is nothing left from your mother. The whole trip was—a failure."

"A failure? But why? Didn't you talk to anyone? Abbé Morel, Baron de Laterre—are they both dead by now?"

Sartine nodded. "And what's even worse—the church archive burned down, with all the books, deeds, and documents. That was two years ago."

"So that means . . ." said Sophie, incapable of finishing her sentence.

"Yes," he replied, squeezing her hand. "Everything was destroyed. We'll probably never know the truth about your mother—I mean, about the trial."

Sophie pulled her hand away. She had to sit down.

"And what would be the point, anyway?" said Sartine as she sank onto a chair. "Maybe it's better this way. It was all so long ago, and besides . . ."

"Besides what?"

"I mean, what good would it do to stir up all those past events?"

Sophie looked at him with incomprehension. "But I have to find out what happened back then. I can't just keep quiet because everything burned up."

"Why not?" he shouted, throwing his boots into a corner. "Sometimes it's better to keep quiet—and forget."

"That's your advice to me? I can't believe it!"

"Please, Sophie, be sensible," he said with noticeable impatience. "What's past is past! We can't undo what was done. Damn it, where are my slippers?"

As if there were nothing more important, he bent down to look for them, peering under the table, the chair, the stove.

"Here they are," said Sophie, handing him his slippers.

Instead of taking them, he looked at her, his expression uncertain, almost anxious; at the same time a peculiar fury was lurking in his eyes, like a warning. Sophie shuddered. She knew that look; she had seen it once before, on the night before he left, when he'd discovered her reading. And without knowing why, a question popped into her mind, an utterly nonsensical question that was no longer of any importance, though it had plagued her the whole time he was away. Suddenly she felt that she had to ask her husband, here and now, at this very instant.

"Why did you get a leave of absence?"

"Why do you want to know?" he said, both bewildered and agitated. "I told you it was a reward that had been promised to me long ago."

"Yes, but you didn't say what it was for."

"For my work, what else? The important thing is I was granted a leave of absence."

"But I'd like to know why."

"Why, why! Damn it all, I travel across half of France for your sake and spend a fortune, yet you ask me such foolish questions."

"Please tell me the truth."

"The truth, the truth! Why do you need to know? Is this an interrogation? Why does the truth concern you? It's a professional secret!"

"Please, Antoine."

"No!" he exclaimed. "Not a chance! Not in your dreams! Is that the thanks I get? After everything I've done for you?"

"I'm really very grateful, but—"

"But, but, but! You always say 'but'! Have you forgotten that you're a woman? Do your work and keep your mouth shut! Can I help it that everything burned up? Never mind, just give me my slippers."

In a rage he tore the slippers from her hand. Sophie bit her lip. He'd never behaved like this before. She no longer had any doubt why he was so worked up.

"The truth," she repeated firmly. "Was it you who saw to it that Diderot was arrested?"

"How do you know about the arrest?"

"From the Procope. That's all anyone is talking about."

"Indeed? Is that so? Really?" Dumbfounded, he looked at her. His lips moved but he couldn't make another sound. The next moment all his rage exploded. "Yes, by the Devil, yes," he yelled. "Yes! Yes! Yes! In the name of the Holy Trinity! I reported Diderot, and why not? He deserved nothing less. Or why do you think they pay me? So that criminals like that end up where they belong: behind lock and key."

"Then it's true," Sophie whispered, horrified. "And I told you his name. . . ."

"Yes, and so what? What's so bad about that? You should be glad. You can be proud of it. You have finally done something for me, at least this one damned time. Anyway, who are you, of all people, to reproach me? The whole time you were going behind my back and acting like you couldn't read when you—" He broke off in the middle of his sentence. His eyes were open wide, his nostrils flaring—like a beast that scents danger. The next moment he dashed to the stove and lifted the lid of the casserole.

"A duck? For us?" he asked, his fury suddenly under control but his voice cold and sharp. He picked up the bottle that stood next to the stove. "And port wine? Look at this! Where did you get so much money?"

"I saved it," said Sophie. "My nest egg. I wanted to surprise you."

"Saved it? You? From what?" He laughed out loud. "Don't try to fool me, I know where the money came from. It's also the reason for your sadness and your sympathy."

"I don't know what you're talking about."

"As if you didn't know. This Diderot gave you the money! He paid you!"

"Diderot?" said Sophie, completely baffled. "Paid me? Why?"

"Because you were under the covers with him. Because you . . ." He paused. "Because you're his whore!"

Sophie wanted to protest, but this unbelievable, astonishing accusation came so unexpectedly that the words stuck in her throat.

"If you could only see yourself," he said, speaking with the utmost contempt. "Shut your mouth. You can save yourself the trouble of answering, because it's written all over your face. Yes, you are his whore."

43

The fog was so thick that Sophie could see no more than twenty paces ahead of her. With no direction or goal she ran through the alleys dripping with milky patches of fog, as helplessly lost as she once had been in the labyrinth of Baron de Laterre. She had only one wish: She wanted to get away as rapidly as possible, away from the home that was no longer hers, away from her husband.

The buildings loomed around her as pale silhouettes, unreal as a dream, while the fog muffled the sound of footsteps and the calls of the fishwives and peddlers, the water carriers and shoeshine boys. Vehicles, coaches, and sedan chairs appeared before her out of nowhere, and she kept bumping into strangers who were also wandering aimlessly about; the burning torches fastened to the corners of buildings seemed only to accentuate the whiteout. Soon people would go to fetch the blind from the Hospice des Quinze-Vingts to lead the sighted through the city.

At the Pont Neuf Sophie crossed the Seine. A little later she heard a stifled howling and shouting that was obviously quite nearby but sounded muffled, as if coming through a wall of invisible rags. The acrid smell of a fire hung in the air and filled her nose. Where was she? The Châtelet must be only a stone's throw away; it was the seat of the law courts, and before its façade dancing shadows rose out of the fog. She hurried on. Suddenly, as if someone had pulled aside a veil, she caught sight of a fire sending flames high into the air, surrounded by a crowd of hundreds of people.

Sophie quickened her pace. No, she didn't want to see this! Whenever she could she avoided the square where the criminals of the city were executed: thieves and poisoners, church desecrators and murderers. But as much as she hurried to immerse herself in the all-concealing fog, she still couldn't tear her eyes away from the fire.

What sort of strange things were happening over there?

A procession of black-robed judges came filing out of the fog, followed by a tumbrel. But there were no chained prisoners behind the bars of the cart, pleading for mercy; instead there were books piled up in great heaps; Sophie had never seen so many books before. One of the judges reached into the mountain of books and took out a volume, then he mounted the steps to the Palais de Justice and handed the book to an executioner waiting at the top of the stairs, garbed in his hooded cloak. A servant proclaimed in a loud voice: "Denis Diderot!"

Sophie gave a start when she heard that name, as if it were directed at her. What did that mean? For a moment she thought she saw her mother through the wisps of fog and smoke, standing high up on the scaffold, her head shaved bald, wearing her shift of shame, chained hand and foot—exactly as she had seen her the last time. Horror clutched at her throat.

A deathly silence settled over the square. The executioner held the book in the air to show it to the waiting crowd, who watched him with greedy eyes.

"In the name of His Majesty the king, I hereby consign the writings of Denis Diderot to the fire! *The Indiscreet Jewels, Philosophical Thoughts,* and 'A Letter Concerning the Blind.'" With a single motion of his mighty arms he tore in two the book that the judge had handed him, stepped over to the burning bonfire, and tossed the pages into the blazing flames. Again Sophie saw her mother, as their eyes met; it was as though Madeleine's lips were moving once more, trying to form a word, a last message, that she wanted to call out to Sophie."

"Aaaaahhhhh . . ."

Like a sigh of deliverance a whisper rose from hundreds of throats. Sophie wanted to flee, leave this gruesome place, but she was unable to budge from the spot; she could not comprehend what was taking place before her eyes. The judges brought more books to the executioner, again and again, more and more. Every author, every title was announced to the people, who applauded and howled as the bonfire greedily devoured book after book, the flames dancing as if they wanted to obliterate all the life written in those books. Sophie stood there paralyzed and watched the execution. She didn't smell the stench of the fire, didn't notice that her face was wet; she saw only things that transcended her comprehension. She had to stay until the very end, to see with her own eyes how all the ideas, all the stories, all the questions and answers of the human beings who had thought up these books and written them down perished in the flames, lost for all time. A cat fled in long leaps from the steps of the Palais de Justice, as if chased by invisible demons. Sophie reached out, seeking something to hold on to, an arm, a hand.

"Why are you crying?"

When she heard those words she awoke from her paralysis. Through the veil of her tears she saw the face of a man. It was as foreign and familiar to her as her own life.

44

The fog enveloped both of them like a white, flowing tent, woven from myriad glittering spiderwebs, with no beginning and no end, as they immersed themselves ever deeper in the whiteout that protected and hid them like eternity.

They were the only people in the world.

"I betrayed you," said Sophie after a few moments, her face still wet with tears. "I don't know how it happened. All of a sudden I said your name."

"It was my fault," said Diderot, taking her hand, which she let him do without thinking. "I am the betrayer; I betrayed our story."

"I was so confused when I read what had happened to Mirzoza. She was so cold, so calculating. There was no love left between her and the sultan."

He stopped and looked at her.

"Did you read the story all the way to the end?"

She shook her head.

"So then you don't know how things turn out! Mirzoza passes the test; she is the only woman at court who truly loves her man. Mongagul doesn't learn this until the very end."

"That's what you wrote?" she whispered, gazing into his bright blue eyes.

"Yes, Sophie, I couldn't have done otherwise." He pulled her to him, very close. "It happened all by itself, almost against my will. In the beginning, I admit, I wanted the magic ring to betray Mirzoza too. But I couldn't make that happen; my arm and my pen refused to write down such an ending."

"Oh, if only I had known that! Can you ever forgive me?"

"There's nothing to forgive, Sophie. I deserved my punishment a thousand times over!" He took her face in his hands, without hesitation, as simply and matter-of-factly as if he could do nothing else. "There's only one thing you must tell me. Why did you marry? I felt like someone had stuck a knife in my heart."

"Don't you know?" Sophie asked.

"No. I thought about it over and over, but could find no answer. Please tell me, I have to know."

Sophie hesitated. Quite softly, as if from far away, she heard the waves of the Seine lapping against the riverbank. Then she said, "Because I was afraid of you, Denis."

"Afraid? Of me?"

Sophie nodded.

"But why?"

"Because . . . because I love you."

He looked at her without saying a word, but his eyes gave their answer to all the questions she still had inside her. Without shifting his gaze, he bent down to kiss her.

"How can anyone be afraid of love?" he whispered before his lips touched hers.

He wrapped his arms around her and then picked her up as she felt herself falling deeper and deeper and at the same time floating up toward the sky. He covered her face with kisses, stammering words of love and madness, stroking her arms, her shoulders, her neck. Yes, yes, yes! His hands slid down her back to her waist, her hips, as lightly and softly as a promise and yet so sure and powerful, as if she no longer wanted any other hands on her but his. At each caress she gave a start, with each caress she opened up. With a sigh she closed her eyes. All the longing that had burned inside her day after day, month after month, year after year, seemed finally to come to an end and yet at the same time begin in earnest; she was overwhelmed with longing, more strongly than ever before. Now she was all skin, feeling, and sensation; she was all flesh, need, and desire. Her breasts, her thighs—her whole body had thirsted for this pleasure, and now it was ready for him, ready with every pore, to take him in, to merge with him, become one with him, now and for all time.

45

Not ten paces away from them, hidden in the patchy fog that continued to rise up from the Seine, as if the river water were merging with the sky, Antoine Sartine stood staring into the impenetrable mist. Just as a sighted person follows the blind when all sight is impossible, he had followed the lovers from Châtelet to this place near the river.

He could neither see nor hear them; only now and then, when the haze seemed to clear for a split second, did he catch a glimpse of the couple, and then the sound of the words they exchanged reached his ear. And yet he saw everything, heard everything, felt everything—much more clearly and distinctly than was possible using normal sensory perception. For every image, every sound was paired with the forebodings that were gushing out of the gaping wound in his heart. His soul was afire as he lived through, suffered through the reunion taking place before him, only a shout away, and which he could not prevent. He knew the face of this woman, every blemish, every freckle on her skin, and knew the voice of the man who preached revolt in the coffeehouses of Paris. Tormented by unspeakable pain, Antoine Sartine sensed how the two embraced, how they caressed and kissed and began to undress under cover of the fog. Filled with a terrible sense of impotence and horror, he imagined the scene with ever greater certainty that his marriage was an utter failure. He should have known that a good end was simply impossible; never, at any time, could it succeed. Rather, everything would have to turn out the way it had in this moment. A sigh, then a cry in which all desire was released and tore through the fog. That was the woman to whom he had offered a home, in selfless love, without demanding anything in return, the woman who had vowed never to do him harm and who was now betraying him so shamelessly in the arms of his foe. He saw her red hair like flames in the white haze, saw the beauty of her body, which he had never enjoyed, felt her need, her desire, the boundless sensuality of her flesh, which he had never been privileged to arouse and which now ebbed away in a last sigh, robbing him forever of all joy in life.

Unspeakable was the rage that seized Antoine Sartine: rage at his miserable, useless body, rage at the women of this world.

Above all, rage at Sophie.

BOOK III

Forbidden Fruit

1751–1752

46

It was the dawn of a glorious June day, as radiantly beautiful as if the world had only just been created on this day. From a bright blue sky, in which not a single cloud obstructed the view of infinity, the sun was shining down on Paris in such extravagant measure, as if wanting to drown the city in its splendor. Armies of sparrows sang joyfully from the gables of churches and houses, praising the young day, while the rippling water of the Seine reflected the bright rays of the sun in millions upon millions of glints and flashes.

Blissfully the kraken of Paris stretched out its arms in the warming, life-giving rays, bursting with energy and the will to get moving. By nine in the morning everyone in the whole city seemed to be on their feet. On the street corners women poured sweet café au lait from big white tin pots for the crowds of workers and shopgirls who paused to pay two *sous* and drink the coffee from stoneware mugs on the spot. Also teeming with people were the alleys of the Latin Quarter, which took its name from the fact that here in the shadow of the venerable old Sorbonne university, the students and professors used the Latin language to preserve and add to human knowledge. Even at this early hour the area was full of restless activity, as if it were a matter of writing a new book of life.

"Watch out! Make way!"

Only by making a brave leap did a man manage to reach safety on Place Michel; he was almost struck by a cabriolet racing across the square, heedless of the other traffic. In fury the man shook his fist at the one-horse carriage as it dashed off. The passersby turned in astonishment to stare at him, because his appearance attracted even greater attention than his threatening behavior. Dressed in Armenian attire, he wore a bear-pelt cap despite the summery weather, and his angry eyes flashed from the matted tangle of his full beard, which covered most of his face.

Since early morning, even before the first shopkeepers had opened for
business, he had been roaming through the quarter where the libraries
and book lenders, the publishers and printers were indigenous. Himself
a *litteratus* of singular reputation, he eyed with suspicion the crowds
clogging the Rue de la Harpe; the queue stretched all the way from the
workshop of the publisher Le Bréton out to the alleyway. All the professors and students, the writers and abbés, the lawyers and philosophers
who usually argued so heatedly with one another as if they were on the
brink of a new era had only one topic on their minds: the first volume of
the *Encyclopedia*. It had been announced more than a year earlier and was
feared by some to be a missive from the Antichrist, while others longed
for it like a second Revelation. This morning it was being handed out to
subscribers.

As a dozen apprentices hurried through the throng with freshly
printed proofs, the Armenian tapped a student on the shoulder.

"I've heard that the book contains revolutionary articles on the topic
of music. People are even talking about a new system of musical notation."

The student turned around and looked at the man as if he'd come
straight from the Orient.

"Who cares about music?" he said. "The preface is the important
thing! Chains are being shattered! Curtains rent asunder! Doctrines
smashed to bits! Citadels razed to the ground!"

"How would you know that? The pages have just been printed."

"Everybody knows about it," replied the student, giving him a look of
pity. "But I want to read it for myself. With my own eyes."

The Armenian himself had known the preface by heart for a long
time—a text like a call to battle. Envy was eating away at him like acid
in his entrails. Why hadn't they let him write the preface, as they had
promised long ago? Instead of extolling this ludicrous mania for progress,
humanity could have proclaimed the truth: that everything society had
ever produced was now being used against nature; that the achievements
of the sciences and arts had been transformed over and over, becoming
sources of misery and destruction; that the compass, mining, and gunpowder had all increased the wretchedness of human beings as well as
adding to their happiness. But they hadn't trusted him. . . . He could not
forgive Denis Diderot this betrayal, even if the editor of the *Encyclopedia*
called him friend ten times over.

"Look out! Make way!"

This time the warning came too late. A huge mastiff running in front of his master's equipage knocked the Armenian down. The owner of the carriage barely even glanced at him. The fallen man lay on the ground, helpless as a beetle on his back. The student reached out a hand to help him up.

"You could at least say thank you," said the young student when the older man was back on his feet.

"I didn't ask you for help!" retorted the Armenian irritably, brushing the dust from his clothes. "Jean-Jacques Rousseau has never needed anyone else!"

47

"She really did it!" gasped the queen, looking up with anxious eyes from the book that lay open on her lap. "Even though her father probably had to flee abroad to escape the gallows!"

"Pardon me, Your Majesty?" asked her friend, the ancient Duchess de Luynes, holding her ear trumpet to her ear. Her brother, no less than Cardinal de Luynes, was snoring softly as he slept in an easy chair at her side; with his pointed nose and white, furrowed face with pink-powdered cheeks, he was the spitting image of his sister.

"La Pompadour!" shouted the queen, ignoring her slumbering guest. "The new court almanac lists her daughter, Alexandrine, for the first time. Like a real princess. Now there's nothing standing in the way of her marriage to the Duc de Picquigny."

"God preserve us!"

As the queen and her friend simultaneously made the sign of the cross, Father Radominsky, who was sitting over by the fireplace, went back to his own reading. The court almanac, a new edition of which came out annually, listed the entire nobility of the land, the gods on this earth, the ministers and marshals, the princesses and duchesses, all those favored by fortune. But the priest knew that the volume he was holding in his hands, a freshly printed copy of the *Encyclopedia* that his bookbinder had brought him that morning, was of much greater importance for the future of the monarchy than the compendium of vanities that determined the welfare and travails of court society.

"The philosophers have dared," he read in the preface, "to shake off the yoke of Scholasticism and with it all authority, prejudice, and barbarism. They are the first to summon the courage to revolt against a despotic and autocratic power, in preparation for a revolution that will lay the groundwork for a happier and more just system of government. . . ."

Every word was a call to storm the bastions of church and state. Radominsky vacillated between admiration and horror. The new tree of knowledge that adorned the frontispiece was a brilliant design—and at the same time it confirmed how dangerous the whole enterprise was. In the system of the Encyclopedists, reason and experience had taken the place of divine revelation as the source of all knowledge. Theology, which for centuries had been the highest of all disciplines, had withered to a tiny, inconspicuous twig on the tree of knowledge. Beyond the branches of this tree, as the unvarnished message stated, there was no longer any sure knowledge. With that the teachings of the church had been pushed beyond the boundaries of verifiable science, and the new border guards, who sought to supplant the theologians as guardians of the truth, were none other than these philosophers. Radominsky rubbed his temples with his fingertips. What a gigantic, misguided mind! What he and Diderot together could have accomplished! Instead he now had to join forces with the hated Jansenists, the old antagonists of the Jesuits in the church, at court, and in parliament, in order to deflect the menace of the philosophers. He cast a skeptical glance at the queen and her eldest son, Louis-Stanislas, the dauphin, whose pious horse-face was bent over his prayer book. The two were his most important allies. Would it be possible with their help to erect the necessary stronghold?

Radominsky heaved a deep sigh. How could he even hope for such a thing? The king was a spineless creature in the hands of a whore who flirted with the ideas of the rabble-rousers and shamelessly associated the liberation of the spirit with that of the flesh. In order to avoid the fate of her predecessors, who had each enjoyed the favor of the monarch for only a few months, La Pompadour had subverted all her own needs to the amorous services she sought to offer Louis. To enhance her lack of natural fire she took a strictly scientific approach. Everyone at court knew that her personal physician, Dr. Quesnay, prescribed all sorts of medicaments to kindle her passion, and together with her royal paramour she read the most obscene works printed in all of Paris. Every Wednesday Malesherbes, in his capacity as chief censor of the realm, supplied her with these texts. Yes, she had set up a regular seraglio for Louis, or as she called it herself, a laboratory experimenting in the arts of love.

No other mistress of the king had ever stooped to compensating for the inadequacies of her own body with the help of foreign love servants. In the Parc-aux-cerfs, a small pavilion at Versailles, La Pompadour gathered around her the lascivious creatures, which her personal valet procured from Paris just as the chef gathered game from the local forests for the dining room of the court. Petite and large, decked out and modest, submissive and willful, coquettish and proud, hotheaded and languid—all metamorphoses of Eve were gathered in the new pleasure palace, which was more deserving of this shameful name than any other place. With the help of this harem La Pompadour held in her slender hands control over the king and over France; the inclusion of her daughter in the court almanac was only one way of confirming the situation.

The queen stood utterly helpless in the face of this power wielded by the king's favorite mistress. Seven years older than her husband, Maria Leszczynska had given France ten children, but now her beauty had completely faded. Almost fifty years old, she showed no vestige of the scant charm with which God had once endowed her. At first she had worried about the love affairs of her husband, but later she had reconciled herself to not being the only woman in Louis's life and withdrew completely from the noise of the court—worldly amusements, she had confessed to Radominsky, were not created for her. Shut in her chambers in the midst of the feverish frivolities of a palace full of people, her existence followed the steady passage of time as if dictated by a cloister clock. She spent her mornings in prayer and edifying reading, then she painted a bit, went to mass, and visited her husband. In the afternoon she worked on handicrafts for the needy, while anticipating the high point of the evening. Abandoned by all the young people in her entourage, who fled to the apartments of her rival, the queen gathered her small group of courtiers around her: aged cardinals, wilted spinsters, and her pious son. How could this queen ever succeed in freeing her husband from the clutches of La Pompadour?

Cardinal de Luynes woke up with a loud snort that shocked Radominsky out of his reverie. The cause of this disturbance was Monsieur de Malesherbes, who was escorted into the room by a lackey. He presented his references to the queen with a bow.

"Your most humble servant, Your Majesty."

He was bowing over Maria's hand when his eyes fell on Radominsky.

"What are you reading there, *mon père*? The *Encyclopedia*? Well done! I haven't yet cut open my copy."

"Then it's high time you did," replied the priest. "Instead of sternly condemning the request to annihilate itself, the state has honored the work by granting the publisher a royal printing privilege. If every muddlehead gets hold of this inflammatory text and reads it—the consequences could be unimaginable!"

"Forgive me," said Malesherbes, "but my hands were tied. The editors dedicated the *Encyclopedia* to Count d'Argenson, the vice chancellor and keeper of the royal seals."

"But did he not refuse to take such a blasphemous work under his protection?" asked the queen. Turning to her father confessor, she said, "You told me that the book is teeming with attacks on our holy church."

Was this his chance? Radominsky fixed his gaze firmly on the sagging face of his queen and said, "As far as I know, Count d'Argenson had already refused the dedication, but after a discussion with your friend the Marquise de Pompadour, he developed second thoughts."

"Indeed?" said Malesherbes in astonishment. "That's the first I've heard of it."

"I myself was present at this conversation," Radominsky declared, firmly trusting that God would forgive him this alteration of the truth in the service of a good cause. "Only at the instigation of the marquise did the vice chancellor grant the Encyclopedists his permission."

"That is truly outrageous!" In her agitation the queen sprang up from her chair, knocking the court almanac to the floor and almost striking her lapdog, Mops, who had gone to sleep at her feet and now fled yapping to the other end of the room. "Monsieur de Malesherbes, what do you intend to do?"

"As I said, my hands are tied, Your Majesty." The smile on the censor's lips contorted to an embarrassed grimace, but when the queen did not release him from her gaze, he added, "Unless, of course, I should receive evidence that would make a ban on the work in question absolutely essential to protect the interests of the state."

The very next day Father Radominsky had already assembled his troops around him at the Jesuit church of Saint-Paul-Saint-Louis. They were superintendents and night brigadiers, inspectors, sergeants, and regular police informants.

"Bring to me everything you hear or read about the philosophers," he cried from the pulpit. "I want to see every article, whether handwritten or printed, and hear every idea that the rebels are circulating. No book, no sentence, no word—not even a semicolon can be allowed to elude us!"

48

And Sophie? Happy Sophie!

She was now twenty-two years old, and for the first time in her life she had the feeling of finally escaping from the labyrinth in which she had so often lost her way. Together with Diderot she experienced a time that seemed to her like a fairy tale, as if her father, Dorval, had made up a story, and she was the Cinderella whose life a good fairy had transformed with a magic wand. She still had to keep working for every piece of bread she ate and every sip of water she drank, like most of the other people on this earth, but she awoke each day as if to a wonderful promise, no matter whether it was raining or snowing or the sun was shining down from the heavens. People on the street smiled at her, even if she had never seen them before.

Was this happiness? Had she really reached the clearing in the labyrinth? Sophie didn't know. She felt only that it was the beginning of a new and different life, a life she could not even imagine. She felt she was at the start of a great journey, filled with boundless yearnings that strangely enough grew stronger the farther she moved away from the old shoreline and ventured out onto the open sea of the unknown.

Hardly a day passed that she did not see Diderot and hold him in her arms. They met mostly at Le Bréton's publishing house, where Diderot had a workroom, with his own place to sleep, divided off from the rest of the room by a curtain. But whenever she could, they left the building to make love under the open sky. They made love on the banks of the Seine, in the Tuileries gardens, in the Bois de Boulogne, and on Sundays they went out to the *faubourgs* outside the gates of the big city, to Montmartre or Vaugirard, where they would drink wine and dance barefoot in a circle until they were dizzy. As soon as Sophie saw her lover, or even thought of him, her jewel would call to him, and when he left her it never stopped dreaming tenderly of him. This magnificent sense of belonging, which persisted even during the hours when they were separated, filled her with a sort of inner music: Wherever she went, whatever she was doing—it was as if she were listening to a jubilant choir that no one else could hear.

How had she been able to live any other way for so many years?

After Sophie ran away from her husband, she never returned to his apartment. She had sent back in the mail the silver ring that he had given her on their wedding night, along with other valuables she had acquired during their marriage. She kept only the lucky charm from Beaulieu, the carved angel pendant that looked a bit like a skull—it was the only object connecting her with her home village. She kept the pendant among her underthings.

She had quit her job at Café Procope. She now worked in the house of a Monsieur Poisson, who was general director of the arts and construction commission in Paris; her former boss had recommended her, since Sophie knew Monsieur Poisson from the coffeehouse. Although he was not yet thirty years old, his portly yet elegant figure gave the impression of a man whose ambition allowed him to dine well three times a day. Sophie couldn't have been more fortunate. Her new boss treated her with a kindness that sometimes seemed like shyness. He appreciated her skill in the household and the kitchen, but even more he valued her talent for reading aloud from novels and dramas. With an obvious feeling of well-being he would listen to her read, sometimes for an entire evening, forgetting even to eat dinner. As a reward he largely released Sophie from the usual duties in the house, so that almost daily she could spend several hours with her lover.

After his release from prison Diderot had broken off his affair with Madame de Puisieux, but he was still living with his family on Rue de l'Estrapade. Little Didier had died in the winter from a feverish cold. Diderot's old father had come from Langres to the funeral, the first time since his son had left his hometown, and at Didier's grave he had made Diderot promise always to take care of his family. Even though the sanctity of the marriage was over, a sense of decency still had to be maintained—that was how the old man had expressed his demand. But Diderot's greatest wish, which he had confided to Sophie in a tender moment, was for her to give him another son.

"For a son from you," he said, "I would give up everything, even my work, even the *Encyclopedia*."

Sophie threw her arms around him, deeply moved by his words. Could there be a greater proof of his love?

"Yes, my beloved," she whispered. "You shall have a son from me. I promise."

One day Diderot asked her whether she would write out a clean copy of a manuscript for him—a text about the preparation of chocolate. Happy that he trusted her, she took the pages from him. In Monsieur Poisson's house she had her own garret where she could work undisturbed. The next day she presented Diderot with the finished copy.

"Were you able to read all of it?" he asked.

"Even the mistakes," she replied with a smile.

"Mistakes?" he asked, taken aback.

"You switched around the amounts of vanilla and cinnamon. You're not upset that I corrected it, are you?"

It wasn't long before Sophie became a regular collaborator on the *Encyclopedia*. She copied manuscripts for typesetting, made excerpts from scientific works, corrected galleys and proofread them against the drafts. What wonderful worlds opened up to her! There were animals and plants whose names she had never heard before, mountains that lay buried under eternal snow and ice, rivers that were wider than inlets of the sea. At the same time she came to know the ideas of the philosophers sooner than any subscriber. Eager to learn, she soaked up the new teachings: about the rights and duties of all human beings, about the various forms of their coexistence, but above all about their right to happiness. In this wonderful way Sophie began to create order from the chaos of the diverse fields of knowledge that she had assimilated over years of haphazard reading. As if the countless notes and pages, the snatches and fragments of poems and treatises, of dramas and leaflets that she had found at the Procope and saved in her little treasure chest, now began to take shape in new patterns—patterns with clear, recognizable contours, like iron filings on a piece of paper when a magnet suddenly pulled them into a pattern.

"Faith," she read in the draft of an article, "is being convinced of the truth of a fact without having examined it. But no one is ever content with himself if he makes no use of his reason. Whoever believes without having a reason to believe will always feel guilty, simply because he has neglected the most important prerogative of his nature."

The words struck Sophie like a personal accusation. Was this the reason for her discomfort whenever she thought about her past? Hadn't she too believed someone else's assertions without testing them in the light of her own reason? The suspicion that this might be true distressed her so much that she couldn't sleep all night.

When she met Diderot the next day, she decided to muster her courage. She had to talk about her earlier life, find answers to the big question from her childhood that still tormented her.

"Why did my mother have to die?"

Diderot lifted her chin and looked at her. "Don't you know?"

"The priest in my village said that she was destroyed by her own sins. Because she challenged God and sought to use the powers of evil."

"Superstition is the most terrible plague of humanity," said Diderot. "It works like a spell cast by fear on the soul. It is a tyrant that keeps people in a state of dread and terror in order to oppress them."

"You mean, it wasn't a damnation from Heaven?"

"God is not the clerics' executioner. It's a crime when people kill other people in His name."

"But what about the Host that I vomited up at my first communion? Wasn't that a sign?"

"The herbal drink that your mother gave you must have worked on your empty stomach like an emetic. What sort of sign is that? At most it showed that your organs reacted in a natural way."

Sophie listened to his words attentively. When he was finished speaking, she was silent for a while. Then she said, "Do you know how I feel? As if I had been locked in a narrow, dark room for years, and suddenly a door has been kicked open and I've entered a bright room flooded with light." She took his face in her hands and kissed him. "Thank you."

That's how Sophie conquered the superstition of her childhood, the prejudices and teachings of fear with which she had grown up and which had defined her world. She now ate from the tree of knowledge, but without fearing love or books, or life itself. What had frightened her for so many years had long since become reality: She was living the life of her mother, loving and reading and thinking, following her own heart and her own reason. But no bolt of lightning struck her down to punish her—on the contrary. The human happiness that Diderot and the philosophers proclaimed in the *Encyclopedia* was no fairy tale; it could be touched with one's own hands. Here on earth, right now!

But occasionally, following one of these encounters when Sophie had returned to her room at Monsieur Poisson's, she would think about Diderot's wife, and a scrap of terrible doubt would gnaw at her.

Hadn't Diderot once loved this woman as much as he now loved her?

49

The publishing house on Rue de la Harpe was buzzing like a beehive. Work on the next volume of the *Encyclopedia* was in full swing. Despite his enormous size, which seemed to keep increasing at the same pace as the work itself, Le Bréton was everywhere at the same time. With sharp eyes he checked the operations—the presses, the type, the printing ink, leather for the inking dabbers, candles, quills, spacers, galleys, forms, and a hundred other things—as he constantly barked instructions and orders over his shoulder to his employees. The work was dirty and loud. The presses screeched and groaned, the masters yelled at the journeymen and the journeymen at the apprentices, while the printing balls, filled with urine-soaked wool, spread the stench of a gigantic *pissoir*. To numb their senses, the men constantly took big swigs of wine from their bottles; now and then they also took swipes with their composing sticks at the cats who swarmed in the felted heaps of wastepaper.

Le Bréton was pursuing an ambitious goal. With the *Encyclopedia* he wanted to do even more lucrative business than he did with the court almanac, for which the king had granted him the commission as the first proper book printer. This lexicon of the nobility earned him thirty thousand *livres* annually—more than *The Odyssey* and the Bible put together. In order to reach his goal for both the *Encyclopedia* and the almanac, Le Bréton was aiming for the best-quality typography and printing. Pages that were overinked or soiled were plucked out along with those that came out too pale and hardly legible. He had also worked out a system that enabled him to offer the *Encyclopedia* for sale all over France. He sold subscriptions to the book dealers, and the book dealers in turn sold them to individual customers. In this way he granted the book dealers a considerable share of the proceeds, on a graduated scale according to the amount of their turnover, which gave them an incentive to make special efforts. But Le Bréton was placing his greatest hope on the publicity that the Jesuits would provide for the work through their attacks on the *Encyclopedia*. These attacks would come after the publication of the first volume as surely as the Amen followed a prayer in church.

The publisher's only worry was finding enough manpower. There were plenty of workers who could draw water from the well, but not many who were capable of operating the presses. Printing was an itinerant trade—the men went wherever they could find work, so they spent most of their lives on the road. In order to attract workers in sufficient numbers, Le Bréton had contracted an army of recruiters spread over the whole country: a bookseller in Marseille who canvassed the taverns of the port city, a civil servant in Strasbourg, a former smuggler in Dijon, a drayage agent and type founder in Lyon . . . They all enticed printers who made a decent impression on them with the promise of a generous travel allowance to go to Paris.

While on the ground floor the dabbers were being inked under Le Bréton's supervision to prepare the press for a new sheet of paper, Diderot received an important visitor from Germany in his editorial office. Melchior Grimm was his name, a journalist who made his living by dispensing information to the royal and princely courts of Europe about intellectual life in the French capital. He wanted to dedicate the new issue of his already famous *Literary Correspondence* exclusively to the publication of the *Encyclopedia*.

"How do you intend, Monsieur Diderot," he asked before even doffing his tricorn, "to publish such an enlightened work in a country as backward as France? Censorship has no greater power in any other land than here."

Abbé de Prades, a young doctor of theology with a thin, pockmarked face who had been working on the *Encyclopedia* for a few months, looked up from his desk, where he was busy editing a text.

Diderot poured his guest a glass of wine, saying with a smile, "Sometimes one must mislead people in order to disseminate the truth."

"I flatter myself that I speak your language fairly well, but I don't understand what you mean."

"If you did, then I would have done something wrong." Diderot set down the bottle, grabbed a copy of the *Encyclopedia*, and opened the book. "For example, take this article here: 'Anthropophagy.'"

"About cannibalism?" asked his guest in astonishment.

Diderot savored for a moment the bewilderment visible on Grimm's face before he ventured to explain.

"Do you see this little arrow here? It leads to the actual statements and theories with which we are concerned."

"See 'Eucharist,' 'Communion,' 'Altar,'" Grimm murmured as he read. Suddenly he seemed to understand. "My God, have you taken leave of your senses? What if the censors discover this?"

"The danger is not very great," de Prades put in. "At the oral exams for my doctorate, the professors were so deeply asleep that they didn't even wake up when the bell at the Sorbonne rang for the Angelus. And my dissertation contained more explosive material than the Paris arsenal. They put the doctoral cap on my head without reading a single line. *Jerusalem coelesti*—the 'heavenly Jerusalem' in the title—was enough to allow the gentlemen to sleep easily. They even congratulated me on my excellent Latin. The thesis was full of poetic images and metaphors."

"Yes," Diderot confirmed, "the arrogance of power is exceeded only by its ignorance."

Melchior Grimm regarded the two in disbelief.

"Nevertheless," he said at last, "aren't you worried that the matter might be discovered someday?"

50

Sophie devoted every spare minute to the *Encyclopedia*. Whenever Monsieur Poisson dismissed her for a couple of hours, she would make her way to Rue de la Harpe to meet with Diderot, or she would go upstairs to her room if she couldn't see her lover. How fortunate that she had her own room! Rented rooms were dirty, with peeling wallpaper and the wind whistling through the windows. But in her mansard room she could work in peace, undisturbed. Here she had set up a regular office, with a big plank for a desk and several smaller boards for shelving. There she piled dozens of manuscripts, sorted into neat alphabetical stacks, together with the first volume of the *Encyclopedia*. When she looked at these shelves she was always amazed. Wasn't this a wonder? The knowledge of the world here in her little room! Only occasionally, when she suddenly heard footsteps in the stairwell, would she wonder: What would her employer say if he ever read what she was storing under his roof?

She was busy working on copying an article when the door opened. Robert, Monsieur Poisson's valet, a man of almost forty with dark hair and an even darker expression, stuck his head in. Sophie didn't particularly like him; in the morning Robert went to mass, and in the evenings he got drunk. He also bowed his head deeper than necessary for the nobles—he was a lackey through and through. Instinctively she covered the manuscript with her hands, but as she tried to conceal the pages from his gaze, he simply reached toward the shelves, picked up the *Encyclopedia*, and began reading from it.

"'If Nature has created any kind of authority, then it is paternal power; but paternal power has its limits, and in the state of Nature it would stop as soon as the children were able to follow their own judgment.'"

"Put that back immediately!" Sophie shouted, jumping up.

Robert merely took a step back and kept reading: "'Is there then no unjust power? Are there no authorities which do not come from God, but are created contrary to His commandments and His will? Do the usurpers perhaps have a monopoly on God?'" Only then did he lower the book and gaze at Sophie, "What kind of book is this?"

"Why do you want to know?"

"Because it interests me. Have you ever read anything from it to Monsieur?"

"Do you wish to betray me?"

Sophie returned his stare. The other servants called him "Robert the Devil" because sometimes he had fearsome attacks of rage, especially when he was drunk. But right now he looked sad, as if Sophie's words had hurt him.

"I would just like to know what sort of book it is," he said again. "I . . . actually I like to read a good deal."

"A dictionary," said Sophie reluctantly. From his face she could see that her information didn't help him in the least. So she added, "It explains concepts, where they come from and what they mean. Things that people don't know but should."

Robert's dark eyes lit up. "I've always wanted a book like that." He paused for a moment, then he said, "Could you perhaps lend it to me?"

"I beg your pardon?" said Sophie, surprised.

"Not for very long . . . I mean, only if you don't need it right away. Because I'd really like to read some more of it."

Sophie saw how difficult it was for him to utter his request. He gnawed on his lip as he nervously shifted his weight from one foot to the other. All of a sudden she felt ashamed. Had she been wrong about Robert? Done him an injustice? Because she had blindly trusted the gossip in the house instead of forming her own judgment?

"Please," he said softly. "It was always my greatest wish to be able to learn and study. But I never got a chance to do so."

"Well, all right," Sophie said. "But you have to promise me that you won't get any spots on it or fold down the corners of the pages."

"I promise!" he exclaimed, beaming.

As carefully as if it were a baby, he took the book and held it to his chest. Sophie had to smile. Had she gained a new friend? For herself and the *Encyclopedia*?

"Oh . . . yes," he said over his shoulder as he left her room. "Monsieur is calling for you. You must come to the salon. Right away!"

51

❦

Monsieur Poisson was waiting for Sophie in the company of a woman with whom he was conversing animatedly. Her complexion was a dazzling white and her lips shimmered a pale pink, but her eyes were of an indeterminate color, a mixture of blue and black. As Sophie entered the room, the woman interrupted her chat with Monsieur Poisson and turned to her.

"So, you must be Sophie."

With a smile that revealed flawless white teeth and as if by magic produced two little dimples on her cheeks, she took a step toward Sophie; the movements of her body seemed to express both liveliness and grace. She seemed like a vision: Never in her life had Sophie seen such a beautiful woman.

"This is my sister," said Monsieur Poisson, "Marquise de—"

"The name is not important," she interrupted him.

"I happened to mention you to Madame, I mean to my sister, and she has come here today specifically to take a look at you, or rather, to get to know you." Poisson paused, as if not sure what else he should say or do. His cheeks flushed pink. Sophie could see the similarity between the siblings. Before he put on weight, Monsieur must have been as striking a figure as his sister.

Poisson cleared his throat and seemed about to speak again, but he merely opened his mouth and shut it again like a fish. "I think I'd better leave you two alone," he then said unexpectedly, and without further ado he left the salon.

"I'm really very pleased to meet you," said the woman as the door closed. "My brother has praised you most highly. Now I have to admit he was not exaggerating."

"By your leave," Sophie replied, feeling annoyed as she curtsied the way she had been taught.

The woman scrutinized her attentively with her bluish black eyes, as she made a full circle around her. Under this unrelenting stare Sophie began feeling more and more uncomfortable. What did they want with her?

"A conventional beauty you are not," said the woman, more to herself than to Sophie. "But that's no failing, there are more than enough conventional beauties. You have that certain something. The red hair, the freckles . . . Very pretty, very charming—a real tigress."

"Would you tell me, please, how I can be of service?"

"Why not?" The woman laughed. "All right, then listen. I want to propose something to you. I would like you to work for me in the future. My brother has had you all to himself for long enough."

"Good Lord." Sophie gave a start. "Is Monsieur no longer pleased with me?"

"There is no question of that."

"Then why must I leave? I get along very well with Monsieur."

"I have no doubt about that. My brother is indeed a person who is easy to get along with—although I do wish he would sometimes behave a bit more energetically." Suddenly serious, she said, "I run a little pleasure palace near Versailles. Only pretty girls like you are allowed to live there. I would be very pleased if you would join them, my child."

"A pleasure palace?" Sophie asked uncertainly. "I am honored by your proposal, madame—but . . . but what will Monsieur say?"

"Don't you worry about that! I've already discussed it with my brother. He's reluctant to let you go, of course, but in the interest of a higher good he is in principle prepared . . ." She paused and took Sophie's hand. "Come with me; you'll enjoy living with us. The girls have no other duty than to pamper a high-born guest who visits us from time to time."

Sophie's confusion grew with each word the woman spoke. What sort of strange offer was this? She couldn't imagine what it could mean, so she didn't know how to reply. "And what exactly would I have to do?" she asked at last, just to say something.

"I just told you." The woman laughed again. "It's all about sweetening the sojourn of a noble gentleman during the time he spends with us—be nice to him, fulfill his wishes, entertain him, so that he can relax away from his business dealings. You do know how to make a man happy, don't you?" She winked at Sophie. "It won't do you any harm."

When Sophie saw this wink, the scales dropped from her eyes. Someone had winked at her that way once in Faubourg Saint-Marceau. A fat woman with garish makeup had spoken to her when she was working at the tobacco shop, a matron who ran a public house. She tried to persuade all the pretty girls who owned a pair of shoes and a white petticoat to work in her establishment. Sophie could hardly believe it: Was the sister of her master that sort of matron? Was her "pleasure palace" a house of ill repute?

Without thinking further about her answer, she shook her head. "No," she said, "I would rather remain in Monsieur's service."

She wanted to pull her hand out of the woman's grip, but she refused to let go.

"Don't be stupid! You'll be well taken care of. You'll be given jewelry and wonderful clothes, and you won't have to work anymore."

Sophie shook her head again, although she was feeling less and less sure of her decision.

"Stop acting coy," said the woman, and her tone had suddenly turned sharp. "Or are you yearning to go back to Faubourg Saint-Marceau? That's where you came from, isn't it?"

"You know about that?" asked Sophie, feeling tears come to her eyes from sheer uncertainty. She bit her lip, hoping the woman wouldn't notice, but that just made her ambivalence even worse.

"Of course I know about that. I also know that your last job was at Café Procope. Do you think I would ask someone to join the house without knowing with whom I'm dealing?"

Sophie swallowed hard as she fought back her tears.

"I'm warning you!" The bluish black eyes that before had seemed to smile so kindly now skewered her, hard and cold. Abruptly the woman let go of Sophie's hand. "One word from me, and my brother will toss you out in the street. So decide. Either you come with me, or you can see where you'll end up."

Sophie lowered her eyes. A thousand thoughts descended upon her. She again pictured a furnished room, filth and garbage piled up in the stairwell; she smelled the foul stench and felt the damp, drafty cold that even in summer clung to the walls. And she saw the customers in the tobacco shop, the tanners and coachmen and latrine cleaners grabbing for her with their filthy hands; she smelled their sweat and their breath, felt their bodies greedily pressing against hers.

As the tears flowed down her cheeks, Sophie shook her head a third time.

"Please forgive me, madame, but I cannot come with you."

"You certainly can—but you stubbornly refuse!"

"No, madame, I cannot." Sophie's voice quavered, but she stood by her decision. "My heart . . . my heart already belongs to another man."

As she raised her eyes she expected to see a furious face. But all the hardness, all the coldness had vanished from those dark eyes. Pensively, almost fondly, the woman looked at Sophie; then she nodded almost imperceptibly, and her gaze seemed veiled, her eyes shiny with tears.

"I think I know how you feel," she said at last in a voice that seemed to come from far away. "I also felt that way about a man once, many, many years ago, but I made a different decision."

She took Sophie's hand and squeezed it, her expression full of sympathy. "I wish you all the happiness in the world."

Then she turned to leave. In the doorway she turned around.

"What a wonderful love that must be, since you prefer it to the love of the king."

Sophie was left with a feeling of utter bewilderment mixed with fear.

The love of the king?

It wasn't until late in the evening that she got an answer to her question. She thought that Robert would be able to answer the riddle. She found him in the kitchen, reading by the light of a candle, as he rested his chin in both hands. He was totally engrossed in what he was reading. Lying open on the table before him was the *Encyclopedia*.

When Sophie spoke to him, he looked up, his cheeks flushing bright red.

"That was Madame de Pompadour, the mistress of the king!" he said, anger and revulsion apparent on his face. "Didn't you know that the whore is our master's sister?"

52

When Sophie was alone in her room she felt so agitated that she couldn't sleep. Everything inside her longed for her lover, but Diderot had gone to Fontainebleau to meet with an author he was trying to recruit for the *Encyclopedia*.

She opened the window and looked out into the night. The noise of the day had died away. In the distance she could see the broad, glittering ribbon of the Seine, which seemed to be sleeping in the moonlight. A gentle breeze caressed her cheeks as somewhere the rumbling of a coach faded into the silence.

The peace of the dreaming city calmed Sophie, and her heart seemed to open as she stood at the window, simply breathing. She closed her eyes and saw the face of her lover, the way he looked and smiled, as if he wanted to say hello to her and tell her that he was by her side, forever and eternally, even though so many miles separated them.

Sophie nodded. Yes, this heart of hers already belonged to a man. Suddenly she was filled with an overwhelming feeling of happiness. She felt his breath, the warmth of his skin, his lips on her mouth, a full, deep kiss that sank into her, delving into her veins and her marrow; such a secret shudder of passion seized her that her heart seemed to stop, flooded with feverish joy and infinite tenderness.

Without thinking about what she was doing, Sophie went to her writing table and picked up a quill pen. She wanted to hold on to this moment, to capture her feelings in words. It was the only way to give expression to her yearning and at the same time to quiet her emotions.

"Love, wherever it appears, is always the master. It shapes the soul, the heart, and the spirit, each according to its nature. The heart and the spirit that love fills do not make it large or small; rather, love is measured by its intrinsic merit; and for lovers, love is what the soul is for the body of the person whom it fills. . . ."

Many times Sophie had asked how a text happened to come into being. What needed to take place inside a person to make the words under his pen coalesce into meaningful sentences? The process had always seemed like a miracle to her. Yet now she felt that no miracle was involved; in reality it was quite simple. The words simply had to come from the heart.

"Whoever is capable of love is virtuous. I even dare to claim that anyone who is virtuous is also capable of love. Just as it is an indication of failure when the body is incapable of reproduction, so it is a failure when the soul is incapable of loving. . . ."

Sophie heard neither the solemn bell that tolled midnight in the distance nor the monotonous song of the night watchman passing beneath her window with his lantern. The words and sentences flowed as if automatically onto the paper, expressing the deep, hidden truth of her soul, which poured out in this unstoppable flood of symbols to become real.

Eventually she put down her pen and read through what she had written. Oh yes, it *was* a miracle! All her feelings and sensations, all her longing and urgency that drew her toward her beloved was now revealed, and anyone who had a soul and later read these words and sentences would have to sense that with these symbols she had written nothing but her love.

Only one thing was missing. She took the goose quill and added her final thoughts.

"Like fire, love cannot survive without constant motion, and it is extinguished as soon as it abandons hope or fear. Because I fear nothing from love in terms of good morals, love cannot help but fulfill them. For those who love have become accustomed to transforming their will to meet the wishes of their beloved. It follows from this that true love is extremely rare. It is the same with love as with a ghostly apparition: Everyone talks about it, but few have actually seen it."

After Sophie had written down the last word, she took a tin from the shelf and sprinkled sand over the page so that the ink would dry. Without reading the text again, she folded the sheet of paper.

As tired and content as a person can be only when she has finished something entirely genuine, she stood up and went over to the window. On the heavenly vault, which had brightened imperceptibly, the stars were already beginning to fade. Somewhere the faint cry of a bird on a rooftop sounded, a timid chirp replied, grew bolder, rang out loud and pure and echoed from roof to roof.

Sophie suddenly felt bathed in glorious light, and as she raised her head she had to shut her eyes, blinded by the light of the sunrise. A range of purple clouds cast its bloodred glow over the waking city. Slowly the gigantic, flaming ball rose, broke through the bursting wall of cloud, and showered the sea of houses from horizon to horizon with its radiance.

At this moment Sophie made a decision, with the same inner certainty that had guided her pen earlier. Even though she also knew that she might one day be destroyed by this decision, she was more convinced that she was right than ever before: Should either of them, Diderot or herself, ever stop loving the other the way she had experienced it that night, she would leave her beloved.

53
❦

The next day Sophie read aloud to Monsieur Poisson from Montes-quieu's *Persian Letters,* in which two Oriental princes exchange their impressions from a journey to France in the drollest manner. Although the novel was one of her favorite books, the reading session had never seemed to drag on for so long as on this afternoon. She could hardly wait to show Diderot what she had written.

By the time Poisson finally dismissed her, twilight had already fallen outside. Sophie hurried over to Rue de la Harpe. The editorial office was empty, but on the desk stood a cup of steaming hot chocolate. He couldn't be far off. Sophie hurried to place the folded page of her manuscript next to the cup, managing to do so before Diderot entered the room. She was so excited that her hand was trembling.

"What's this?" he asked after they had greeted each other, picking up the sheet of paper from the desk. "An article about love?"

"No idea," Sophie said with a shrug. "Maybe one of your authors brought it by when you were out."

As Diderot began to read, the blood pounded in Sophie's veins so loudly that she was sure it could be heard throughout the room. Diderot continued to read her manuscript, the first actual text she had ever written in her life! Calmly and with concentration his blue eyes scanned the lines, but his expression did not betray what he thought of the contents. Finally he put down the page.

"Excellent," he said, his voice full of admiration. "A masterpiece!"

Sophie felt like cheering, but with an effort she managed to control herself. As blandly as possible she asked, "Indeed, you think so?"

Diderot nodded. "Every word is deeply felt, and at the same time it is all clear and precise. How happy a person must be to experience such a love. But who the devil could have written it?"

"Didn't the author sign it?"

He looked at the page, turned it over, and shook his head. "No. No name, no monogram, nothing."

Sophie could no longer suppress a smile. "I think we have no choice but to find out, together. Perhaps you should recognize the handwriting." She flung her arms around his neck and kissed him, and as their mouths found each other, her lips told him, and her tongue repeated, what she had long ago said with such abandon and passion that there was no longer any doubt. "Now do you know," she whispered as their lips finally separated, "who wrote that article?"

Diderot looked at her in disbelief. "Do you mean to tell me—"

"Yes, dearest, last night. You were so far away, and I didn't know how I would stand another hour without you."

She wanted to kiss him again. But he fended off her embrace.

"What's the matter?" she asked with some annoyance.

Diderot was suddenly quite serious. "Your article is wonderful, one of the best that I've ever received. But . . ."

Instead of finishing his sentence, he gazed at her. All tenderness had vanished from his blue eyes.

"But *what*?" Sophie wanted to know. "Come on, tell me!"

Diderot hesitated. "I can't print the article."

"You can't be serious!" she cried, trying to laugh.

"Yes, I am," he replied. "The readers would never accept a woman as a writer."

Her laugh stuck in her throat. He meant what he said; she could see it in his face. Sophie swallowed hard. She had secretly hoped that Diderot would accept the evidence of her love for the *Encyclopedia*, but he had no intention of doing so. She had never been so disappointed by him.

"But a moment ago you were envying people who experience such love," she said softly.

He took her hand. "You have to understand," he said. "I've already almost ruined the *Encyclopedia* once before with my novel—we barely managed to avoid disaster. I can't afford to make another mistake like that. Not now that we're having such success."

"Is success the only thing that counts?"

"Good God, Sophie—don't talk like a child. I've sacrificed everything for the *Encyclopedia*, written almost nothing else since I started on it, put all my energy into this work. Don't you understand?" And when she said nothing, he added, "The *Encyclopedia* means everything to me, more than my own life."

"So my manuscript is worth nothing?" Sophie cried. "My manuscript—and my love?" Her disappointment was mixed with anger. The happiness that she had felt and wanted to share with him had been simply dismissed. He had dropped it the way a careless customer in the coffeehouse would drop a glass, and now it lay shattered on the floor. She wasn't prepared to accept that, or the risk that she might have to quarrel with him. But if he wanted strife, then he would certainly get it!

She tore herself away from him and took a step back.

"If that's true, then I'm sorry I ever showed you my text—"

"Shhhh," he said, placing a finger to her lips.

Instead of replying she bit it.

"Have you lost your wits?"

"Are you ordering me to shut up?"

"Now listen to me, damn it! I think I have an idea."

"Really? I can't wait."

"It's like this: A female author writing for the *Encyclopedia* is out of the question. That's the way it is; end of discussion. But," he went on, when he saw she wanted to protest, "why do we have to tell the readers that a woman wrote the article?"

"What are you suggesting? Am I supposed to be in disguise?"

"Not you, but how about your name?"

"I don't understand a word of this!"

Diderot examined his throbbing finger. "How would it be if your article appeared under a man's name, say, that of one of my colleagues? For example, how do you like the name Jaucourt?" He looked up from his finger and grinned. "What do you think, would that be a solution?"

54

From that day forward Sophie regularly wrote articles for the *Encyclopedia*.

Diderot gave her a free hand in selecting her themes. He believed that the best way to get someone involved in a topic was to encourage their own interests. So Sophie worked on subjects that she wanted to learn more about. She wrote about the work of midwives and about fashion, about jealousy and about snoring. She displayed such talent that Diderot gradually entrusted even more significant assignments to her, and since she showed in her contributions an extraordinary competence in terms of expression and style, he soon gave her jobs editing the work of outside contributors. She would go over articles about brotherly love, about beauty and ugliness—and finally even articles on questions of philosophy and theology.

One day, when she showed him an extensive treatise with the title "Certainty," which she had spent all night editing, at first he didn't say a word.

They were lying in bed, both naked and dripping with sweat from the passion they had just enjoyed. Nestling among the pillows on her stomach she could feel the waves ebbing away in her body, as he read the article spread out on her back, as he used it as his desk. When he turned a page, the paper tickled her skin like a lovely memory.

Tensely she awaited his judgment. She had made several of her own interpolations in the article and added them to the manuscript.

"Well, what do you think?" she asked at last, when she could no longer stand it, turning her head to look at him.

"So you contend that there are no miracles on earth that we humans can interpret as signs of divine will?" He lowered the page and peered at her. "Are you quite aware of what this means? You're questioning something that's one of the fundamental tenets of religion. That could cost us both our heads."

"I merely deduced this conclusion from everything I have ever learned, from philosophy and from my own life, from reason and from experience, as mapped out on the tree of knowledge. And why are you giving me such a strange look?"

Instead of answering her, Diderot gave her the loveliest compliment that she could imagine. He bent over her, gave her a wonderfully tender kiss, and said, "You really *are* a philosopher."

Sophie turned over and threw her arms around his neck. "So you're going to print the article?"

"Do I have any choice?" he asked with a gentle smile.

She gave a loud shout of joy and pulled him to her, ready with every pore of her body to take him inside her again.

"Are you happy?" he asked.

"Yes," she said, clenching him inside her as hard as she could. "Yes, Denis, beloved—I am."

Then she closed her eyes so she would feel nothing but love.

The man with the plumed hat was now relegated to her past forever.

55

As he did every morning, Antoine Sartine started work at the main commissariat of the Paris police at precisely nine o'clock. Since his promotion to the position of secretary to the lieutenant general a few months before, he now had quite a grand office. If the performance of his duties had not required him to go out and investigate in the field, he would have spent almost all the hours of the day in this room, which the other civil servants respected as his private sphere and never entered without first knocking. Yes, anyone who served the state with the proper zeal could advance very far—Sartine had always known that. His residence, on the other hand, he used only for sleeping. The loneliness there was suffocating.

Luckily his work left him no time to worry about his feelings. He was responsible for monitoring all the bookshops in Paris—an assignment that required as much bureaucratic thoroughness as it did literary sensitivity. The whole country was seething with ferment. The populace was grumbling about the tax reform, and in the church the Jesuits were fighting with the Jansenists about which path led to the true salvation of the soul in Heaven and to the fattest *praebendi* here on earth. The arguments between the crown and the parliament over the powers of the state also seemed never-ending. In this heated atmosphere one spark would be enough to blow the entire powder keg sky-high.

Antoine Sartine was doing everything he possibly could to prevent such an event. On the shelves in his office were stored almost five hundred dossiers that he had written himself. They contained his judgment of Montesquieu's *On the Spirit of Laws* as well as Rousseau's *Treatise on the Sciences and the Arts* and Buffon's *Natural History,* but above all his views on countless major and minor scandalous writings from the fields of theology, philosophy, and jurisprudence. The authors were as different as their effusive texts. Most of them were merely striving to win a review in the *Mercure,* the most important newspaper in the city, while a few were seeking entry to the Comédie Française or a seat in the Académie. How they made their living was mysterious; some had a small pension or sinecure, while the rest seemed to live from hand to mouth. They came from all social strata of the populace and all corners of the kingdom; they published poems and won stipends, and they usually ended up as lawyers or civil servants. Unless, that is, they could keep their heads above water in the employ of a book dealer as a professional writer—such as Diderot.

The thought of this man wrested a sigh from Sartine's breast. He took the appearance of the *Encyclopedia* as a personal defeat—one that could have been avoided. In Sartine's opinion censorship was not being applied with enough firmness. Even worse than the general laxity, however, was an essential flaw in the procedure itself: it was that the manuscripts, not the printed texts, were the object of scrutiny. If there was anything in them to complain about, the censor could demand that changes be made, but what was actually done with the texts was another matter entirely— the censor never got to see the typeset galleys. To circumvent the censorship, all the author or the publisher had to do was promise to make the required changes. In the first volume of the *Encyclopedia* Diderot had shamelessly exploited this weakness in the system. Now the *Encyclopedia* was on the market, containing thousands and thousands of violations and heresies, but because the work was provided with a dedication written by the vice-chancellor and keeper of the seals, it was immune from any attack.

There was a knock at the door.

"Come in."

A workman entered the room, cap in hand.

"I believe I have something else for you," he said, pointing to his bag with a grin.

Sartine knew the man; he was on the list of those who regularly received payment from him, though he did not like him—he was a disgusting informer.

"Put the items on the table over there."

As the worker opened his bag and took out several galley proofs, Sartine pulled out his purse.

"Here," he said, tossing the man a coin. "And close the door behind you!"

As soon as the workman had left, Sartine hurried to the table to inspect the booty: a dozen new articles for the *Encyclopedia*. The galleys still smelled of printer's ink, fresh from the press. He took a paper knife and sliced them open, wondering if they would contain anything useful. Father Radominsky had demanded information about everything that the philosophers circulated: every book, every sentence, every word— even every semicolon. Sartine was determined to supply him with the necessary evidence. Even though his private life had nothing to do with his professional zeal, and his judgment as an officer of the police ought never to be influenced by personal feelings, it would be a pleasure for him to deliver up Diderot, the man who had robbed him of his wife and all happiness in life.

Sartine took the cut-open pages to his desk and began to read. Against his will the text won his admiration. What a cunning system the Encyclopedists had devised to deceive the authorities! All articles with suspicious titles, whether the content was religious or political, presented unassailable opinions. On the other hand, apparently harmless contributions such as "Deer" or "Eagle," which no normal censor would ever bother to read, were teeming with theories dangerous to the public, which a reader could discover by means of a devious system of cross-references. But Sartine had not been a police inspector his whole life for nothing—he refused to be led around by the nose! He almost enjoyed following the clues back and forth through the work. "Anthropophagy" was the name of one article; it said, "Feeding on human flesh. See 'Eucharist,' 'Communion,' 'Altar.'" The very listing of these concepts next to each other was blasphemy! As if the receipt of the Host were some sort of cannibalism. Unfortunately, a cross-reference was not a punishable offense.

Suddenly Sartine gave a start. What had he just read? "The miracles of the Bible can lay claim only to historical truth; even the miraculous healings of Jesus Christ have no real miraculous power, but they do share many characteristics with the normal healings of an Aesculapius . . ." Although Sartine was no theologian, he realized at once that this sentence was the most dangerous of explosives: Here the Holy Scriptures were denied as God's revelation. He moved his index finger back to the start of the line to check the source. The sentence in question was in an article entitled "Certainty," written by an author named de Prades.

Sartine raised his eyebrows. De Prades? He knew that name.

He got up from the desk and went over to his shelves. As expected, the dossier was filed under the letter *P.* Sartine pulled out the file and opened it. No, his memory had not deceived him. This de Prades had written quite a wicked treatise, a scandalous piece that was larded with the most terrible disparagements of the Christian faith, and he then had the effrontery to submit the work as a dissertation to the theological faculty of the Sorbonne. Stupid and lazy as the professors were, they found absolutely no reason for complaint and had conferred a doctorate of theology on de Prades. Sartine had reported this case at the time.

That very same day he set off to Place Royale. Before the portal of Saint-Paul-Saint-Louis he emerged from the coach and knocked at the door of an unprepossessing building in the shadow of the magnificent Jesuit church.

"Do you recall a writer named de Prades?" he asked Radominsky after the priest had asked him to take a seat in his office.

"Of course I do—*Jerusalem coelesti*. In his dissertation he violated a host of dogmas. I have already initiated proceedings against him, so that the philosophical degeneracy does not spread further in the temple of orthodox teachings. But why do you ask? Has the man attracted notice once again?"

"Indeed he has," Sartine replied. "Apparently he is working for the *Encyclopedia*. I have just read a galley proof that—"

"By de Prades?" Radominsky asked, leaning forward and clutching the armrests of his chair with both hands, as if he had to hold on to keep from jumping up. "The fellow is working on the *Encyclopedia?*"

"Yes, Reverend Father, it's an outrageous scandal."

"It most certainly is a scandal! And that's why it's an incredible stroke of luck."

"Pardon me? I'm afraid I don't quite understand."

Radominsky leaned back in his chair. "This is the best thing that could have happened," he said softly, almost to himself. A fine, almost imperceptible smile played over his lips as he steepled his fingertips before his face. "I believe we have them now. This will break the necks of the gentlemen philosophers." He closed his eyes and took a deep breath, as if to savor his words. Then he opened his eyes and said, "Well done, Sartine—very good indeed. Do you happen to have the documents with you?"

56

It was already growing dark on the last day of the year 1751, but the publishing house on Rue de la Harpe was still brightly lit. Even on this evening the printing presses on the ground floor were screeching and groaning as if trying to drown out the noise of fireworks and guns being fired; cloaked figures outside on the snowy streets were driving off the demons of the old year. In the meantime, in the editorial office on the top floor, they were celebrating a success that seemed to make superfluous every exorcism and prediction of the future, which was the custom on this day.

"Messieurs, to the *Encyclopedia!*"

"*À votre santé!*" replied d'Alembert to the toast from the publisher. "To bringing the work to a good conclusion."

"We can't complain about the past year," said Diderot.

"Certainly not," agreed Le Bréton, and a radiance transfigured his walrus face. "Today alone we received another thirteen subscriptions. And tomorrow the second volume will be released. I have word from a reliable source that Malesherbes has already signed—"

He broke off his speech, hearing loud footsteps in the stairwell. The next moment the door flew open, and in rushed Grimm, the German journalist, beet-red in the face and completely out of breath.

"Jerusalem has fallen!" he gasped, throwing himself onto a chair.

"Have you lost your mind?" Le Bréton asked. "We're in Paris, not in the Levant."

"The Sorbonne has stripped de Prades of his doctorate and thrown him out of the theological faculty. *Horruit sacra facultas.*"

"What?" cried d'Alembert. "That's impossible! His degree was conferred *summa cum laude.*"

"It's possible, all right. They've caught on to him. They accused him of defending natural religion and sensualistic heresies."

"Is that all?" Le Bréton heaved a sigh of relief.

"That's a serious charge," said Grimm. "They're claiming that de Prades has denied the miracles of Jesus."

Diderot gave a start. "Who says this?"

"The dean of the faculty. The professors are beside themselves; they feel disgraced to the bone. The reputation of the Sorbonne is at stake."

"Where's de Prades now?" d'Alembert asked, visibly nervous.

"He's in hiding somewhere outside Paris."

"For God's sake! Are things so bad that they're looking for him?"

"Much worse. The Jesuits are spreading the rumor that de Prades is part of a plot."

"A plot?" Le Bréton set down his glass, his face suddenly grave.

"Yes, they're talking about a conspiracy."

"And who else is supposed to be part of it?"

"The editors and authors of the *Encyclopedia*. As evidence they're drawing parallels between the dissertation and an article in the next volume of the lexicon."

"How the devil would they know what's in it? The second volume hasn't even come out yet!"

"How do I know? In any case it gave them the idea to take a closer look at 'Heavenly Jerusalem.' And when they did, apparently their expressions froze in astonishment."

"They're shooting at de Prades in an attempt to hit us." D'Alembert turned pale and his brown eyes grew wide as he gave Diderot a reproachful look. "I knew right away it was irresponsible to entrust such an important article to a man as inexperienced as de Prades."

Le Bréton turned to Diderot, who wasn't saying a word. In guilty silence he was already cursing his foolhardiness in deciding to send the text with Sophie's supplementary remarks to be printed instead of toning down what she'd written.

"Which article have we been talking about this whole time?" asked the publisher. "I'm probably the only one who doesn't know. So why are you all standing around? Do something, damn it! Something has to be done!"

57

❧ ☙

That same night Diderot wrote a letter to Madame de Pompadour.

> *A society of hardworking men, who make no other claim than to be use-
> ful to others, has devoted itself for several years to the editing of a lexicon
> that shall be a repository of human knowledge. The edifice is emerging, to
> the admiration of all of Europe. However, it is being attacked by obscure
> forces who are delivering blows all the more dangerous because the col-
> laborators of this lexicon spurn the very idea of refuting such suspicions.
> Meanwhile our restraint is starting to be viewed as weakness. . . . We
> seek no defender, we seek only a judge. Please be ours, Madame. . . .*

While Diderot waited for a reply from the marquise, his adversary was
preparing for a major counterattack. Scarcely had the second volume of
the *Encyclopedia* been published on New Year's Day when the *Journal de
Trévoux*, the Jesuit newspaper—which had no other task than to stir up
hatred against the philosophers—used the article titled "Certainty" as
an opportunity to ask whether the censorship office was even checking
the lexicon before granting its imprimatur to publish. With inquisitorial
severity the journal established proof of all the heresies perpetrated by
the editors and authors of the *Encyclopedia* and disseminated to date: the
preface criticized the principles of the church fathers; both the kings and
the saints were denied the space they were due in the work; the article
"Aius Locutius" called for freedom of speech and the article "Authority"
undermined the very foundations of the state.

"Hell has spewed forth its venom," intoned the archbishop of Paris
from the pulpit of Notre-Dame, "drop by drop."

Like the wrath of God the attacks descended upon the philosophers.
On January 29 the general assembly of bishops condemned the lexicon.

All over Paris placards were posted attesting to the holiness of Jesus' miracles and condemning the heresy of the Encyclopedists—they were charged with blasphemy, rebellion, and sheer audacity. Now the parliament of Paris, the supreme court of the land, also joined in. Forgotten was the strife that had been going on for decades between the Jansenists, who offered opposition to the king on the side of the parliament, and the Jesuits, who stood on the side of the crown—the adversaries united against a common enemy, as if hearing a battle cry from Heaven. After the order was issued to take de Prades into custody, the abbé protested, but in vain. In order to save his skin, he finally fled the country, first to Holland, then to Berlin, where with Voltaire's help he found refuge at Sanssouci, at the court of King Friedrich II of Prussia.

"Has La Pompadour finally responded?" Le Bréton wanted to know a week later.

Diderot shook his head.

"Then I'll probably have to go to Canossa," sighed the publisher. "Only Malesherbes can help us now."

"Should I come with you?"

"For Heaven's sake, stay where you are! You've already caused enough trouble."

As a sign of his contrition Le Bréton did not even take his sedan chair when he set off. There was only one argument that would put Malesherbes in a lenient mood: money. If the *Encyclopedia* were banned, all of Paris would feel the results—hundreds of people would lose their jobs.

But the director of the Royal Library and supreme overseer of the book trade would not even deign to see the publisher. Instead he issued a council decree on February 7 in which he officially condemned the volumes of the lexicon already published and prohibited the publication of the remainder, effective immediately:

"His Majesty has determined that the *Encyclopedia* contains maxims that aim to destroy the authority of the king, to promote the spirit of independence and revolt, and to incite misbehavior, the collapse of moral standards, irreligion, and lack of faith."

A deathly silence now settled over Rue de la Harpe. The printing presses stood idle and the typecases were abandoned; in the water basins floated remnants of putrid cellulose, while the paper rolls in the storerooms remained stacked uselessly to the ceiling. The groaning and screeching of the machines seemed to have been silenced forever, along with the cursing of the workers. The whole publishing building seemed like a haunted house, through which only a cat would wander now and then.

"Rousseau is behind all this," declared Le Bréton, who inspected the remnants of his troops like a defeated general after the battle. "They say that Malesherbes dotes on that jealous man."

"Impossible!" Diderot contradicted him. "Rousseau is my friend; he loves me like a brother."

"What's that supposed to mean?" Le Bréton asked. "Weren't Cain and Abel brothers?"

A messenger boy came stumbling into the print shop with a letter in his hand.

"For Monsieur Diderot! Your wife sent me. She says—"

"Hand it over!" When the messenger went on his way, Diderot looked at the envelope, which had a red seal affixed to it. "From Madame de Pompadour!"

"Thank God!" cried Le Bréton. "Finally, some good news."

58

"Watch out! Get out of the way!"

Along with a dozen cursing passersby Sophie sought shelter in a doorway as the water sprayed up from beneath the wheels of a coach rattling past. The crusty snow that had covered Paris all week long like a layer of gray frosting had now melted in a big rainstorm. A stream divided the street in two, so that it was possible to cross to the other side only by jumping over it.

Without regard for her shoes and stockings, Sophie hurried through the throng. She was furious—and disappointed. Madame Diderot had been in Langres visiting her father-in-law for the past week, and yet her lover hadn't had time for her. Day after day Sophie had restrained herself, but now her patience was at an end. Even if he was experiencing a hundred times more trouble than before—was that any reason to act as if she no longer existed? Sophie hadn't felt her lover inside her for five weeks, three days, and seventeen hours, and every minute of that time she felt was a minute too long. Her jewel was yearning for him as much as her heart.

She spent most of her free time with Robert, her employer's valet. He had read the *Encyclopedia* so thoroughly in the meantime that he knew many of the articles by heart. He was born into a farming family, but his father fell into poverty soon after his son was born, so Robert grew up with his uncle. He had hoped to learn a trade, but to survive he had to work, first as an orderly for an officer, then in a Jesuit college as a gardener and porter. The monks had separated him from his wife, whom he'd married shortly before, and sent her off to the provinces as a serving maid. He had hated the Jesuits ever after, and had become a fanatical Jansenist who went to mass each morning, even if he had drunk himself senseless the night before. When he whispered with tears in his dark eyes that his greatest wish was someday to meet the king and tell him how much injustice existed in his land, Sophie was overcome by such sympathy that she felt an urge to take him in her arms.

But what could she do with Robert? She wanted Diderot!

When she reached the hill of Sainte-Geneviève it suddenly stopped raining. She crossed the forecourt of the church and turned down Rue de l'Estrapade. On the ground floor of the tall building was a haberdashery shop. Sophie had visited Diderot here only once, when his wife was in the countryside. She wanted to see the room where he worked, but her presence made him so nervous that she had never gone back.

She entered through the back door and hurried up the stairs. She stopped in front of his door to catch her breath, so he wouldn't see what a state she was in. Then she opened it.

"What are you doing here?" He was bending over an open carton, a package of books in his hand. He looked at her as if she were a ghost. "For Heaven's sake, why have you come here? What if somebody saw you?"

She ignored his remark. "Is this where the great sultan Mongagul lives?" she asked, trying to sound as unconcerned as she could.

"Oh, Sophie, what's this all about?"

"I just wanted to find out whether he's forgotten all about Mirzoza. She hasn't seen him in weeks, and can't even remember what a kiss from him tastes like."

She went over to embrace him, but he didn't move.

"You know very well what's going on," he said, resuming his packing.

"Come on, put down your books, just for a moment. I won't stay long."

"I don't have time, I really don't."

"Not even for a kiss? Don't you always have time for that?"

He dropped the books into the carton and handed her a letter.

"Here, read it yourself. La Pompadour's answer."

Sophie took the letter and scanned the few lines. When she reached the end, she returned to the decisive statement:

I am unable to do anything in the matter of the encyclopedic lexicon. It has been claimed that the work contains principles that contradict religion and the authority of the king. If this is true, then it must be burned.

"But that's terrible . . ."

"Do you understand me now?"

Dumbfounded, Sophie put down the letter. Her anger was extinguished. She felt only shame.

"I feel horrible," she said. "It's all my fault. If I hadn't—"

"No," he countered, "I'm the editor. It's my responsibility to choose who writes each article—and who edits them."

"Nevertheless, I was the one who first set them on the scent. Without my additions nobody would have taken offense at that article."

"It makes no difference. What's done is done." He stroked her cheek, and at last his voice was again filled with tenderness. "I'm sorry if I've been—"

"Hush," she said, "I know what's been happening."

"Still, I shouldn't have allowed my fury to come between us," he said, bending toward her. "It was mean and contemptible and spiteful and—"

Sophie closed her eyes. She felt his lips on her face. Whispering tender apologies, he kissed the raindrops from her skin and her hair.

"Does Mirzoza still feel affection for the sultan?"

"What sort of stupid question is that? But he should watch out that he doesn't get soaking wet."

She threw her arms around his neck, and full of passion they shared a long kiss. For the first time in ages the midges at the back of her neck began to buzz.

"But tell me, why are you packing your books?" she asked as their lips parted. "Are you going to flee?"

"Voltaire has invited me to Prussia." He took her face in his hands and gazed at her. "Would you come with me if I asked you?"

"Is that what you want? Are you sure?"

Her heart was pounding with such surprise and joy. Traveling with Diderot! To a foreign country! The prospect was more lovely than any fairy tale. But before she could answer, a strange feeling suddenly crept over her. It was almost the same as when she had to use a pseudonym on an article that she'd written.

"And then?" she asked. "What will happen then?"

"No idea. I know only that I can't stay here. The priest of Notre-Dame announced from the pulpit last Sunday that de Prades doesn't even exist, and that *I* had written his damned dissertation. The Jesuits are trying to get their clutches on the *Encyclopedia* so that they can publish it themselves. Just imagine! D'Alembert is already thinking out loud of terminating my co-editorship. Good Lord, I had hoped so much that La Pompadour . . ."

He didn't finish the sentence as he looked at Sophie. All hope had vanished from his face. He shook his head in resignation.

"How am I going to find authors in another country? Who will print the texts? How are we going to get the books back into France?"

"I don't know," Sophie said, taking his hand. "All I know is—you can't give up now! Mongagul certainly wouldn't do that, and Princess Mirzoza would never allow it."

"Then what should I do? I've tried everything." He shook his head again. "I think this is the end."

"No, Denis! Don't talk like that!"

"Let's not fool ourselves, Sophie. This is reality, not a fairy tale from the Orient. If even Voltaire advises me to flee, then that means—"

"Don't listen to Voltaire! This is about *your* life, Denis. Ever since I've known you, you've been living for this book. You can't run away! You have to see it through to the end, and you can only do that here. You told me that yourself."

"But if I stay in Paris they'll arrest me. And I don't know whether I could stand being imprisoned again." His voice was now only a faint whisper. "Last night I couldn't sleep, and then they came back, creeping out of all the holes in the wall, the cockroaches, gigantic and black . . ."

Sophie looked into his eyes—those wonderful, incredibly blue eyes that usually shone as brightly as the sky on a spring day. Now they seemed as dark as a night full of fear.

All at once Sophie had an idea.

"Promise me that you'll wait a little while," she said. "Just a couple of days."

"Wait? For what?"

"Don't ask now, my love, just trust me!"

59

An outcry rose up through all of Europe, across every border. The *Encyclopedia* had been banned! In Holland, in Geneva, in Britain—in every country where freedom reigned, loud protests were raised. And in Russia and Prussia, where there was no freedom at all, even there the rulers protested against the verdict from Paris.

As Europe expressed its outrage, Sophie stood undecided in the house of her master before the door of the salon, ready to knock. But the longer she hesitated, the more her courage sank. On the other side of the door she could hear the voice of her master—and the voice of his sister, the Marquise de Pompadour.

"If you had only a spark of ambition, monsieur! You could be state councillor, maybe even a cabinet minister."

"I'm content with my life, dear sister, perfectly content, I might say."

"Your modesty is scandalous! As if eating and drinking were a profession. It's not a matter of your own welfare, but of the future of your niece."

Sophie was so agitated that she felt sick. She had told Diderot to trust her. But now, when the opportunity she'd been hoping for finally presented itself, she felt weak in the knees and her stomach was turning over. What had gotten into her to make such a promise to her lover? The hall where she stood suddenly seemed bigger than the cathedral of Notre-Dame, and she felt as tiny and lost as an insect.

Once more voices were raised in the salon.

"You have to establish yourself in a manner befitting your social standing. If you don't want to work, then you should at least marry!"

"Marriage is a dreadfully arduous undertaking. First the couple must feign two weeks of passion, and then spend years boring each other."

"I'm not making this demand for myself, monsieur, but for

Alexandrine. As the future Duchesse de Picquigny she needs a family. I'll give you a week."

At the same moment the door opened. Sophie hurried to take a step back. Before her stood Madame de Pompadour, as beautiful as the bright day. But her expression was clouded over.

"Were you listening at the door?"

"Please forgive me, madame," Sophie stammered. "I . . . I was waiting for you."

"Oh, have you changed your mind then? That would be gratifying, at least."

"No, no," replied Sophie in fright. "I would like to remain in service to Monsieur."

"Indeed? Then what do you want? Speak up! I don't have all day!"

Under the impatient scrutiny of those blue-black eyes Sophie grew even more nervous.

"I'd like to ask for your help," she managed to say with some effort. "Because I've read your letter."

"I write several dozen letters daily, but I can't imagine that any of them had anything to do with you."

"I mean your letter to Monsieur Diderot."

"I beg your pardon?"

"It's . . . It's about the *Encyclopedia,* the encyclopedic lexicon."

Finally she'd said the words. Cautiously, Sophie raised her eyes. La Pompadour seemed to be waiting for her to go on. So she plucked up her courage.

"I wanted to ask whether you . . . whether you might possibly reconsider your decision. You simply can't allow the lexicon to be burned!"

"And why not?" La Pompadour's face showed both amazement and amusement. "Can you tell me that?"

Sophie couldn't think of what to say. That the *Encyclopedia* was all about human happiness? About the future of France and the world?

Without thinking, she found herself saying, "Because I love Monsieur Diderot."

"Aha, so that's it," said La Pompadour as Sophie felt the blood rush to her face. "So is he the man to whom you've given your heart?"

Sophie nodded.

"And I was just asking myself why a maid would be concerned with philosophical problems." Then La Pompadour's expression turned serious again. "But it makes no difference—you know my decision. I have nothing more to add."

She turned to go.

"Is there no chance that you might change your mind?" asked Sophie in despair.

"And why should I?"

"Because . . . Monsieur Diderot has sacrificed everything for this lexicon, all his knowledge, all his energy." Sophie faltered, then added, "The *Encyclopedia* means more to him than his own life. If you ban the book, it would be like a death sentence for him."

La Pompadour shrugged her shoulders. "I'm sorry. The matter has been decided," she said and left Sophie standing there.

Robert, who had been waiting in silence at the front entrance, opened the double doors as a lackey hurried up to escort his mistress down the steps.

"I wonder . . ." La Pompadour had just reached the door when she turned around. "Perhaps there is a possibility, after all."

A faint spark of hope awoke in Sophie.

"Please tell me what I have to do. I'm ready to do anything. Whatever you require."

"Whatever I require? Is that right?"

"Yes, madame. If only you will revoke your decision."

"Very good. It's in your hands." La Pompadour took a step back into the hall. "If you accept my offer and come with me, I will reconsider the matter. And I promise that you will be pleased with the result."

Sophie did not comprehend at once. "Come with you? Where to?" Then she saw the twinkle in the other woman's eye. "You mean," she asked apprehensively, "to Versailles?"

"Correct, to my small pleasure palace."

Again that blue-black look. Suddenly Sophie felt like she had on the day of her First Communion: Everything again depended on her answer. But no matter what she decided—either way it would be the worst decision she could ever imagine.

She cast down her eyes.

"No," she whispered. "I can't."

"What? You know what you have to do to save Monsieur Diderot and his lexicon, and yet you refuse?"

Sophie couldn't say a word. Her knees buckled, and her stomach was churning. She felt so sick that she thought she was going to throw up.

"Didn't you just tell me that the *Encyclopedia* means more to Monsieur Diderot than his own life? Do *you* now want to pronounce his death sentence?"

"I . . . I cannot do as you wish," Sophie repeated softly as the tears flowed down her cheeks. "Even if I wanted to . . ."

"Is that your final word?" asked La Pompadour.

Sophie raised her eyes and nodded mutely. Her head felt as heavy as a millstone.

They both said nothing for a long moment, as the servants waited motionless by the open door.

Then La Pompadour said, "My God, I think you really do love him."

Through the veil of her tears Sophie saw a blurred image of the other woman's face.

It almost seemed that La Pompadour was about to smile.

60

It was one of those countless suppers at Versailles, the purpose of which was not so much the ingestion of nourishment as the dispelling of boredom experienced by the monarch. Father Radominsky, who sat at the royal table between Queen Maria Leszczynska and Madame de Pompadour, found the conversation as tough as the ragout that he was just cutting up on his plate. Once again the discussion revolved around the question of when the queen would finally name her husband's favorite to be her lady-in-waiting.

As La Pompadour dispensed her malicious remarks with a smile, which her friend the queen acknowledged with simple gratitude, Radominsky was thinking about what to do next. The fate of the *Encyclopedia* was sealed—the blow that he had dealt to the philosophers was not something from which they would quickly recover. But he wouldn't be satisfied with this triumph. It was his intention to take the entire enterprise in hand himself—*ad maioren Dei gloriam*, to the greater glory of God.

Such a takeover would solve two problems at once. First, it was a matter of finally chopping off the serpent's head before it could rise up again to spew its venom. But there was something even worse than the danger presented by the heretical articles on the questions of theology and philosophy. Radominsky feared most the scientific reputation that the Encyclopedists had acquired with their contributions to the explanation of natural phenomena. Blasphemy and lèse-majesté could be combated with the disciplinary measures of dialectics and justice; the simple laws of nature, however, eluded such subjugation. Particularly in their research, the philosophers were far superior to the Jesuits, as verified by the pathetic articles in the other lexicon that Radominsky's brothers in the faith had published in Trévoux. If they succeeded, however, in incorporating the *Encyclopedia* into their own lexicon, the radiance of scientific knowledge would shine down upon the Society of Jesus. The king had already sent word that he would be favorably disposed to such a takeover—as reward for the enthusiasm that the Jesuits had again exhibited in fighting the conspiracy against the church and the state.

"Who knows?" La Pompadour woke Radominsky out of his musings. "Perhaps all the recent arrests have been more harmful than useful. The country will be left bloodless if the best minds leave France."

"The best minds in France are sitting as always at this table," replied King Louis with a glance at Radominsky, who thanked him for the compliment with the hint of a bow. "If only I could say something equally praiseworthy about this ragout!" He dropped his silverware and clapped his hands. "Take it away! Let the pigs eat it—or no, better yet, give it to the cooks. That will teach them."

"What a wise solution," Radominsky agreed, glad that the conversation had returned to its usual banter.

The lackeys changed the plates, but La Pompadour refused to relinquish the topic that interested her most.

"Don't forget that as we sit here, Voltaire is already back at Sanssouci. The greatest philosopher in France is sitting at table with the king of Prussia instead of here with His Majesty."

"But you know how boring we find politics," said Louis with a pained expression. "We have entirely different concerns. We are exhausted from the hunt, exhausted and annoyed. My musket jammed. Just ask Du Bois." He pointed to his gamekeeper, sitting at the other end of the table. "He was there when it happened."

"His Majesty would have otherwise shot a capital twelve-point buck," said Du Bois. "What a terrible misfortune!"

Radominsky thought he noticed that the gamekeeper exchanged a brief glance with La Pompadour. Had he seen correctly or was he mistaken?

"Actually, it's quite inexplicable," said the king with a shake of his head. "I use a weapon every day without really knowing how it functions. Is there anyone at this table who can tell me why the shooting powder shoots?"

As the fawning courtiers gazed in embarrassed silence at their plates, La Pompadour again spoke.

"Why do you want to know, Sire? Is it any different with the powder that we ladies use daily? We too have no idea of what it is composed or how it works."

"Or does anyone know," put in the queen, obviously happy to be able to say something, "how those silk stockings are made that we women wear?"

Radominsky looked first to the left and then to the right.

La Pompadour was wearing an elegant *déshabillé* in which she generously displayed all the charms with which the Creator had endowed her; the toilette of the queen, however, was more reminiscent of the clothing of those impoverished souls for whom she did her needlework. No wonder she was parroting everything her rival said.

"But how useful it would be," said La Pompadour, "if one could look up such things in some book."

"Most certainly, indeed," the queen agreed with her. "That would be extremely useful."

Even the king nodded.

While Radominsky was asking himself what sort of odd comedy was being played out before his eyes, La Pompadour picked up a bell and rang it. The next moment the doors opened, and a servant brought in two elegantly bound volumes.

Radominsky gave a start. He had not the slightest doubt what books they were.

"Let us see," said Louis as the servant handed the volumes to him and his wife.

The royal couple turned the pages, read a few passages, and looked up in astonishment.

"That's simply incredible!" exclaimed His Majesty. "Everything is in this book: How a gun works, what powder is made from—"

"And how stockings are manufactured," his wife added with delight.

"May I point out that the dictionary of Trévoux also imparts similar information?" Radominsky put in.

But no one was listening to him. Completely immersed in his reading, Louis moistened his fingertip with his tongue and leafed through more pages. "Astounding, amazing . . ." Suddenly he laughed out loud.

"Would Your Majesty permit us to share in His amusement?" asked La Pompadour.

"With pleasure," he replied. "Listen to what it says here about marriage: 'One is bound to one's wife, but has a bond to one's mistress.'"

"How ingenious!" chortled Maria Leszczynska, but the giggle died in her throat when she saw the intimate look that her husband exchanged with La Pompadour. "Ingenious—isn't that what is said?" she said, turning to Radominsky for assurance.

But before the Jesuit could answer, the king said, "What a splendid work—a storehouse of the most excellent scholarship. And this is what we have banned?"

"Yes, so it seems," replied his favorite. "Although I might almost believe that Your Majesty had the book confiscated so as to be the only person in the kingdom who knows everything." The two most charming dimples appeared on her cheeks.

"That may well be true." Louis leaned over to kiss her hand. As he straightened up his glance fell on Radominsky. "Indeed, I don't know why people have been telling me such bad things about this book."

The priest refused to flinch under the king's gaze. "Because it contains bad things," he grumbled.

"That may be," replied Louis with a smile. "But should one mistake one small part for the whole? At supper today a ragout was served that was a total failure. Yet we dined well and did not instantly throw everything out the window. No differently do we wish to proceed with the *Encyclopedia*." He slammed shut the volume in front of him and clapped his hands. "Dessert! What are we waiting for?"

61

~☙ ❧~

"It is not the intention of His Majesty to withhold from the public a book that can be of great use to both the sciences and the arts; rather, their growth and progress are of the utmost interest to the Crown, and therefore His Majesty is pleased to announce that the printing of the subsequent volumes will be permitted to proceed."

The new edict, which immediately rescinded the council decree of February 7, had hardly reached the attention of the publisher and editors of the *Encyclopedia* when the old spirits returned to the haunted house on Rue de la Harpe. The printing presses began once more to groan and squeal, the masters and journeymen resumed their cursing, and Le Bréton had his hands full getting hold of enough paper. In order to meet his demands for quality, he processed only stock from mills in the Auvergne, which could not supply inventory fast enough to keep up with printing.

"However, it is the will of His Majesty that during the printing of said volumes a proof be pulled of each sheet and presented to one of the above-mentioned censors, in order to be further inspected and corrected, if necessary. The corresponding sheet is then to be signed and initialed by the censor who has examined it, and no copy of this sheet may be printed and disseminated unless it is so signed and initialed."

Although the decree placed the further dissemination of the *Encyclopedia* under the control of stricter censorship and in addition expressly confirmed the ban on the first two volumes, it was a terrible defeat for Father Radominsky. The Jesuit was appalled. What was King Louis thinking when he made such a decision? Was he not almost encouraging rebellion? Apparently the king of France had nothing other than roaring stags and lascivious women on his mind. Radominsky in any case had to set aside *ad acta* the dream of taking over the *Encyclopedia*. Alas, if only that damned supper at Versailles had never taken place!

The priest implored the queen to ask her husband to rescind the decree; he put pressure on the cardinal of Paris and the General Assembly of French bishops so that they would support him in his struggle; he intervened with Madame and with La Pompadour—but his efforts were all in vain. In order to complete his defeat, La Pompadour told him with her most captivating smile that the leader of the band of philosophers, Denis Diderot, would soon be presented as a candidate to the British Royal Society; the Académie Française was even considering admitting his accomplice d'Alembert into its honorable ranks—in recognition of services he had rendered to the *Encyclopedia*.

But Le Bréton was rubbing his hands with glee. Hadn't he known this would happen? Big business was made only with big ideas! The furious attacks of the Jesuits had ensured that the *Encyclopedia* would be as famous all over the country as the cathedral of Notre-Dame. The placards posted by the bishops still hung on the walls of buildings in Paris: "It pains us to observe, dear brothers in the faith, the disastrous progress that this so-called philosophy represents. These writers are no longer content to attack specific dogmas of the Christian church—no, they boast about a universal skepticism that respects nothing and questions everything, that endeavors to shake the very foundations of our holy faith. . . ."

Whenever Le Bréton spied a torn placard on a wall in the streets, he would haul his massive body from the sedan chair in order to reattach it with his own hands. The scandal had driven the number of orders to unimaginable heights—no advertising campaign could have produced a greater outcome! The third volume already had 3,100 subscribers, almost twice as many as at the beginning of the enterprise. And no one except the publisher knew that every single copy of the first two volumes had already been delivered to customers before the ban had gone into effect—they were all bought and paid for!

62

At the Palais Poisson sheer pandemonium reigned. Robert, the master's valet, had made off during the night with a box of valuable silverware—as well as the volume of the *Encyclopedia* he had borrowed.

But what did Sophie care? She was so happy that neither Robert nor his treachery could cloud her high spirits.

Monsieur Poisson had scarcely dismissed her before she left the house. It was such a marvelously lovely day, the kind that only the month of May could conjure forth. The mild morning air caressed her skin like silk. Not a cloud covered the sky, and as she crossed Place Michel a flock of pigeons fluttered up and accompanied her all the way across the square, as if the birds also wanted to celebrate the miracle that Sophie no longer doubted.

Ah, how wonderful life was! All of Paris seemed to be engaged in one big celebration. Street musicians played on every corner, the air was filled with a thousand sounds: from fiddles and flutes, oboes and drums. The shouts of the water carriers and the peddlers of rabbit pelts, of the fish-wives and junk dealers, that had once rung so frightfully in her ears that she could hardly stand it, today sounded like the most glorious music in the world.

The *Encyclopedia* would be published once again! Sophie could hardly wait to see Diderot. They had agreed to meet by the Seine, under the bridge where they had first made love. Sophie was full of plans and ideas—enough to fill a hundred volumes. But she had one more surprise for him, a gift that was more precious than all the books in the world, more precious than the *Encyclopedia* itself. This gift would bind them together as husband and wife forever, even if they could not be considered a married couple before God and the world.

All of a sudden the air smelled like a spring meadow. At the Pont

Saint-Michel the booths of the flower sellers lined the quay—blossoms in every color of the rainbow. Between pails full of lilies Sophie ran down the steps to the Seine, and she had scarcely reached the riverbank when she caught sight of him. Leaning against a buttress of the bridge, Diderot was waiting for her.

He caught sight of her at once and stepped out from under the bridge. She rushed to meet him, and then she gazed into his eyes, those incredibly bright blue eyes in which she felt as if she were drowning. She stood very close and could feel the warmth of his skin. The midges at the back of her neck were humming so loudly that they muffled the noise of the city. All at once everything seemed to stand still, and Sophie had only one more wish: to kiss this man. She closed her eyes, wanting to immerse herself in that paradise he had opened up for her with his first kiss. Then she heard his voice.

"I have to tell you something, Sophie."

"That you love me? But I already know that, my love!"

She looked at him tenderly. He shook his head.

"No? What then? That you desire me? That you want to have me? Right here and now?" She found the thought exciting, and her voice grew thick with emotion. "I must admit, I have nothing against such an idea."

She wanted to stroke his cheek, but he backed away from her touch.

"You're not going to like what I have to say to you, Sophie. But . . . but I have no choice." He swallowed before going on. "You can't work with us anymore."

"Can't work with you? What do you mean?"

"The *Encyclopedia*. It's impossible for you to continue working with us. I mean, you can't write or edit any more articles, or—ah, good God!" he exclaimed loudly. "You know exactly what I mean."

His silence was as sudden as his outburst. He lowered his eyes and his face turned red.

"You . . . you can't be serious," she stammered, grasping the meaning of his words only with great effort.

"But I am, Sophie. I've thought about it for a long time, and it's damned hard for me to say this, you must believe me—but it's the only option. It's simply not possible for a woman—"

"For a woman *what*?"

"For a woman to work on the *Encyclopedia*. Either under her own name or some other. We've tried it, and it just doesn't work. It's like a . . . like a natural law. And we have to abide by it."

Sophie felt like someone had dumped a bucket of water over her head.

"You dare say this to me? After all we've been through?"

"Yes. Forgive me, Sophie, but there's no other way out. Damn it all, why are you making this so hard for me?"

"What? I'm making it hard for *you*? Do you have any idea what you're saying?"

"Of course I do! You came close to ruining the *Encyclopedia*! You inserted the worst heresies into de Prades's article. Your comments brought the censor down upon us—as you yourself admitted. Or have you forgotten that?"

His expression was like that of a father trying to drum reason into an intractable child. Sophie was so distressed that she had to struggle for words as she gasped for air.

"Ruined? I did everything I could to save your work. Why do you think you suddenly got permission to keep going?"

"How do I know? Despots don't have to account for their decisions."

"Then I'll tell you: Madame de Pompadour put in a word for you with the king."

"La Pompadour? Don't be ridiculous! She wrote and told me herself that she could do nothing for me."

"She reconsidered." Sophie hesitated, then added, "Because I asked her to."

"You?" Diderot laughed. "You know how much I treasure you, but surely you don't believe your own words. Why would the favorite of the king change her mind about such a serious matter because a mere maid asked her to do so? That's ludicrous."

"You have no idea what happened!"

"Then please explain it to me. How did you convince her?"

The answer was on the tip of Sophie's tongue. *With my love for you!* But at this moment, when he was expressing such disdain, she would sooner bite off her tongue than confess her love for him. So she said nothing.

"Out with it!" he insisted. "Tell me, don't break me on the rack!"

Her heart, her jewel, everything in her was longing to cry out the answer to him. But Sophie controlled herself and kept silent.

"You see?" he snorted at last. "You have nothing to say. How could you?"

He gave her such a disparaging look that Sophie felt cold all over. She suddenly recalled Diderot's wife, how in the middle of the night she had once appeared before her, carrying a babe in her arms. The memory opened her eyes, and the realization was as bitter as gall. What she had always feared the most, more than illness or death, was happening right now: He was treating her as unkindly as he always treated his wife.

"Come, calm yourself," he said, trying to smile. "I didn't mean it like that."

He stepped closer and reached out his hand, wanting to caress her, but she shook her head as vehemently as if he had tried to threaten her.

"Don't touch me! Not now!"

"But why not? Come, let's be friends."

He bent down as if to kiss her. She took a step back and gave him such a sharp look that he stopped short.

"Answer me one question," she said.

"Anything, as long as you stop being mad at me."

"What's more important to you: the *Encyclopedia* or our story?"

He bit his lip and looked at the ground.

"It's a simple question, Denis."

He said nothing and refused to look at her. From the quay a breeze carried the scent of flowers toward them. It almost made Sophie feel sick.

"There are only two possibilities. Decide!"

Finally he raised his eyes. They were as bright and pure as water. He cleared his throat and said, "The *Encyclopedia* is more important than us. More important than any single human being. More important than anything else in the world."

"More important than love?"

Diderot nodded. "Even than love."

Sophie closed her eyes. *Even than love.* Those three words clattered in her head like a handful of gravel in a tin can. Those words kept echoing as in a nightmare: *Even than love.*

Sophie took a deep breath. Those three words had decided everything. She opened her eyes and said, "Go straight to Hell!"

Without another word she left him standing there.

She hadn't told him that she was expecting his child.

BOOK IV

The Expulsion

1757–1759

63

There was a mighty ferment in the belly of the great kraken. While in the churches of Paris five thousand masses were conducted daily to accompany the dead souls on their way to Paradise, in the streets and alleys the stench of sulfur was spreading. Rebellion and strife everywhere! As the priests intoned pastorals from their pulpits, forbidding the consumption of eggs during the Lenten fast, freethinkers in the salons denied the existence of Almighty God. As the rich rode through the Bois de Boulogne by day, flaunting their resplendent carriages, by night they were afraid for their lives, as marauding bands went on raids under cover of darkness. In the same building one resident might be contemplating where to invest his millions, while his neighbor didn't know where he could borrow a few *sous* to feed his children for another day.

Had these outrageous differences been decreed by God? Or did they arise from the hierarchies that humanity had established over the course of centuries? As if separated by invisible barriers, the inhabitants of Paris were divided into sharply distinct classes: the fewest but in no way least important were the princes and great noblemen; then followed those who wore cassocks, the financiers, the shopkeepers and peddlers, the artists, the craftsmen, the salaried workers, and the lackeys, with the lowest class consisting of the indigent. But how were the indigent actually identified? There were good-for-nothings and idlers in every class. Like many of the noblemen who could trace their lineage back to Adam and Eve, such people avoided work like moles avoided the light. Then the nobles of the second rank, who had inherited their titles from the heroic deeds of a long-expired forefather, allowing them to rest on their laurels for all time; in addition, the cohorts of clerks, court bailiffs and scribes, the many thousand pompous subordinates, who as servants of the state did nothing but increase the tax burden. The church indulged countless seminarians, who poured forth from the colleges like black clouds without ever serving a single human soul. The physicians went from door to door with their cupping glasses to bleed everyone, sick or healthy, for good money; while the financiers, from the wealthiest landlord to the small corner pawnbroker, fell upon their prey like a brood of vipers to suck their blood. Added to these groups were all the people whose daily efforts brought nothing but misery: all the landlords and rent collectors whose occupation allowed them to doze the day away; the corrupt judges and lawyers; as well as the coachmen, postilions, and stableboys. To this army of do-nothings could also be counted the endless hordes of monks, canons, and curates. Contemplating the activities of all these people was enough to make one realize with horror the true state of the kingdom's capital!

The authorities had their hands full keeping this churning vat under control. If the people of Paris were given free rein, if they didn't constantly feel behind their backs the mounted guards and patrols, the gendarmes and inspectors, then soon they would lose all sense of restraint and there would be no stopping them. For this reason, vigilance was crucial. The police regiments, the troops of guardsmen, the royal life guard—they were all stationed in their barracks, ready to be called out to nip any insurrection in the bud. Thank God their mere presence in the city obviated any riotous assembly almost entirely. Usually only one squadron was enough to disperse a crowd of five hundred men, and all would be peaceful again once the soldiers had put two or three hotheads in chains. In this way the authorities kept the peace in Paris, and the longer the calm lasted, the less likely it seemed that it would be disrupted.

But somewhere the accumulated gases and vapors of this ferment had to find an outlet from the bowels of the great kraken. So the smoldering unrest was no longer restricted to Paris alone. And gradually, almost unnoticeably, the kraken stretched its arms toward Versailles.

64

Dominos and shepherdesses, Chinese mandarins and Greek goddesses, pharaohs and South Sea islanders filled by the hundreds the Hall of Mirrors, resplendent in the glitter of the chandeliers. Madame de Pompadour had issued invitations to a masked ball, and for hours the court of Versailles was preoccupied with amusing itself. The ceilings, adorned with gilt and plaster ornamentation, resounded with intoxicated glee and laughter, while seductive glances flashed from behind handheld masks. Even the monarch—dressed as Mars, the god of war, as a sign of ultimate solidarity with the kingdom's soldiers, who were currently taking the field against Britain and Prussia—seemed to be amusing himself. Constantly surrounded by a dozen harem ladies, Louis had yawned only three times during the evening.

Sophie was the only woman among the guests wearing neither a costume nor a mask. For her the towering wig that she balanced on her head was disguise enough. Although by now she had been at court for three years, she had still not gotten used to the artificial hairpiece; nor was she used to the thick layer of powder on her cheeks that covered her freckles.

Madame de Pompadour had hired Sophie to read aloud, immediately after her only daughter, Alexandrine, had died of tuberculosis at the age of ten. Taking leave of Monsieur Poisson had not been easy for Sophie, but the mistress of the king treated her with even greater kindness than her former employer—almost like a younger sister, in fact. Sophie sometimes felt that the marquise wanted to make up to her what fate had withheld. As for the original proposal that Sophie should move to the pleasure palace at the Parc-aux-cerfs, the king's favorite had never mentioned it again.

"I'd like to introduce you to someone."

Sophie turned around. Before her stood La Pompadour in the

costume of a female gardener. On her head she wore a straw hat, and in her hand was a bouquet of hyacinths.

"Please don't," said Sophie. "You know I'm not interested."

"Fiddle-faddle! A woman needs a patron at court. If not for your pleasure, then at least to offer you protection."

La Pompadour stopped a monk who happened to be passing by. His head was covered by a cowl, his arms hidden inside the wide sleeves of his cassock.

"Ah, monsieur, do you know my friend Sophie?"

"I have heard a great deal about her," said the monk, bending over Sophie's hand. "Her skill at reading aloud is known throughout the court."

As he straightened up, Sophie recognized the man: The cowl concealed Monsieur de Malesherbes, the director of the Royal Library. She wanted to return his compliment at once, but the music started up.

"May I?" he asked, offering her his arm.

"Do you really dare?" La Pompadour was amazed. "Don't forget, monsieur, when dancing the feet take over from the brain!"

"I shall forbid them to do so by council decree."

Malesherbes led Sophie to the dance floor past an artificial pond in the center of the ballroom, where two lonely swans were swimming in circles. There beneath garlands of hyacinth blue a few couples were taking up position for a minuet. As she took his hand, Sophie recalled for a moment those distant Sunday afternoons in Vaugirard, where she had danced in a circle barefoot until she was completely dizzy. But that was only a memory. Her jewel was as mute as if it had never spoken to her.

The dance master raised his staff, and the first reprise of the minuet began.

"I only hope," Malesherbes said with a sigh, "that the king doesn't see me. I feel as lost on the parquet as in the land of the Cacouacs."

"I would gladly offer you my sympathy, monsieur. But in what land do these people reside?"

"You don't know of the Cacouacs?" He gave her a searching look. "In Paris people are talking of nothing else."

"I haven't been to the city in months."

"Well, then it's no wonder that you haven't yet encountered them. Unless some have strayed into the court."

"You mean, the Cacouacs live in Paris?"

"Precisely. And yet no one understands their quacking." When he saw her quizzical look, he added with a wink, "Only a parody, madame. It recently appeared in the *Mercure,* and of course it was the philosophers who were meant."

For a second Sophie lost track of the rhythm.

"Whoops! Have you perhaps already been thinking with your head instead of with your feet?"

"You mentioned the philosophers?" she replied. "What . . . what do they have to do with the Cacouacs?"

"Quite simply, they behave like the friendliest creations of God, at least at first glance. But as soon as they start to quack, their tongues spray deadly venom."

"What an astute comparison," said Sophie with a hint of bitterness. "I assume that His Majesty's censor is speaking here?"

With pressure from his hand he bade her do a turn. She had to duck her head a bit to step through under the wide sleeve of his cassock.

"Even though I am flattered," he said when she was once more at his side, "my opinion really does not matter. The time when the royal court determined public opinion is gone. In the past, all of Paris trembled at every word that our sort happened to utter about a book, a play, or a painting. Today the opposite is true. The court waits to hear what the capital is saying, and that's a good thing. True censorship is being practiced by the public. In matters of art and literature it is the only judge that really counts."

"And . . . how does the public judge the Cacouacs?"

"With laughter. And believe me, that's a very serious matter. This little parody could have much greater consequences for the Encyclopedists than any council decree. At any rate, I wouldn't want to be in Monsieur Diderot's shoes. Oh, *pardon!*" he said as Sophie stumbled. "Did I step on your hem?"

"No, no. I'm afraid it was just my own clumsiness."

He gave her a sympathetic smile. "They say that dancing is the poetry of the feet. But I have the impression that we two aren't much good at versifying." He nodded to her. "Shall we make do with one stanza?"

"To tell the truth, you would be doing me a favor."

He led her to the far end of the ballroom. Behind a grotto constructed of papier-mâché, out of which a waterfall tumbled gracefully, they found themselves a bench tucked away in an arbor.

"I think we'll be safe here," said Malesherbes, taking two glasses of wine from a tray standing ready in the arbor before a mirror. "To the health of the favorite, who introduced us to each other!"

They began to chat. Although the minuet had been a catastrophe, Sophie no longer regretted that Malesherbes had asked her to dance. She liked the director of the Royal Library; he was charming, and his jokes sparkled with wit, even when he was speaking of the most mundane things. Above all he knew how to keep his distance. He neither pestered her with suggestive remarks nor attempted to whisper words in her ear, as was the normal practice at court as soon as the first five minutes of a conversation had passed. Only occasionally did he stare at her in an odd fashion, as if he were searching her face for something, though it was not apparent what that might be. Sophie wondered whether her wig was crooked, but a glance in the mirror told her that this was not the reason for his scrutiny.

Had he perhaps noticed her irritation when he spoke of Diderot?

"To be frank," he said, as if reading her thoughts, "you are a great riddle to me."

"That doesn't surprise me," replied Sophie with a smile. "Men find every woman to be a riddle, and they are constantly seeking the answer, from one woman to the next."

"In my case, you don't have to worry. A long time ago I promised myself the privilege of being my own greatest riddle." All at once his expression turned serious. "You are the only woman at court who has no lover. Why? You are surely the only one who is capable of real love."

"How would you know that?" she asked, astonished by his sudden openness.

"If I am correctly informed, there is natural proof of what I said."

Sophie knew what he was referring to and kept silent.

"Might I pay you a visit," he asked, "if I happen to be at Versailles?"

As Sophie reached out her hand in parting to Malesherbes, outside a bird was already chirping to greet the new day.

65

A furniture wagon with two mighty Belgian draft horses harnessed to it waited outside the house on Rue Taranne. Half a dozen men were running up and down the stairs, unloading furniture.

"That goes in the bedroom!" called Nanette to two movers who were just hauling a chest of drawers through the front door.

"Watch out, man! It's all brand-new!"

With her hands on her hips, she stood on the landing and craned her neck so she could keep an eye on everything at once. While in the Latin Quarter the laughter was still raining down over the Cacouacs and her husband, Nanette Diderot was setting up their new residence. Finally they had escaped the cramped confines of Rue de l'Estrapade! The house into which they were now moving in the neighborhood of Saint-Germain-des-Prés was big and beautiful and almost grand. For Nanette a dream had at last come true. She was as happy as on the day her husband had finally married her.

"The chairs go in the salon—not in the kitchen! How many times do I have to tell you?"

As she directed the work with glowing cheeks, Diderot furtively climbed up the stairs like a thief in the night. High up under the roof, in the mansard, he had a garret room all to himself. When he closed the door behind him, all worry fell away. Content, he surveyed his new kingdom: a chair with a woven straw seat, a simple table, bookshelves made of fir. That was all he needed. The framed copperplate engravings that he would later hang up were still leaning against the wall among plaster busts of Horace, Homer, and Virgil. Although they had been in the new house for less than a week, up here he already felt at home. No cockroach in the world would be able to follow him up to the sixth floor.

The new contract with Le Bréton had made the move possible. Diderot was now earning almost twice what he made before. The publisher could afford it—business was booming, not least thanks to the Jesuits, who never tired of launching highly vocal attacks against the *Encyclopedia*. In the meantime the lexicon had more than four thousand subscribers, and each year a new volume appeared containing articles beginning with the next letter of the alphabet. Only with the letter C had there been difficulties, stemming from the article "Constitution," which dealt with the question of which higher authority should decide in doubtful cases: the king or the church? The head censor of the book trade, Chrétien de Malesherbes, had requested that the article be corrected but then had apparently left it forgotten in his drawer. A few weeks later d'Alembert had been admitted into the Académie Française. Diderot was sure about one thing: The outcry over the Cacouacs would most likely die down once he had settled into his new accommodations. He slipped on the old scarlet-colored robe that he had rescued from his former lodgings and sat down at his writing table. Documents were stacked all around him. The original twenty cartons of notes and manuscripts that were half finished or completed had in the meantime metamorphosed into more than a hundred. The *Encyclopedia* had assumed such proportions that Diderot increasingly had to take on the tasks of both editor and organizer—he hardly had time to write his own articles. Thank God the Chevalier Jaucourt, a philosopher from a noble family, was able to assist him. He had studied theology and physiology in Geneva as well as mathematics and philology at Cambridge; as a student of the famous Boerhaave in Leyden he was awarded an M.D. Now his life belonged to the *Encyclopedia*. He compiled, excerpted, and wrote— modestly, industriously, unobtrusively. His participation was a stroke of luck for the enterprise.

Diderot reached for a quill and wiped it on his robe. Then he took a sheet of paper and dipped the quill in his inkwell.

Dear Sophie. I am writing blindly. I have arrived; I wanted to kiss your hand and then go. I will have to leave without this reward. But is it not enough reward for me that I have shown you how much I love you? I am writing to tell you that I love you, or at least I want to write it to you, but I know not whether my pen will bend to my will. Why do you not come, so that I can say these words to you?

It had been almost seven years since he had last seen Sophie, yet not a day passed without him writing to her. He told her about his hopes and sorrows, about the progress of the work, about the *Encyclopedia*; he asked after her health and her life at court, asked her whether she now had to wear spectacles as he did, and begged her, no, beseeched her to meet with him on the bank of the Seine where they had first kissed. But he never sent any of these letters.

Then why did he write to her?

Diderot knew that what he was doing was absurd. But he could do nothing else. She had sent back his first letters unopened. He understood the gesture and had not sent her any more. And yet he did not stop writing to her; it was the only way he could be close to her and feel her presence, after she had disappeared from his life almost without a trace—the only way he could make sure that she still existed. Sometimes he asked himself whether she did indeed exist or was merely a figment of his imagination.

Does your heart not tell you that I am here? I feel only one thing: that I am incapable of leaving here. The hope that I might see you for a moment holds me back, and so I converse with you and do not know whether these are real words that I am writing. Where nothing is written, read that I love you. . . .

Under the table something moved. Diderot put down his pen and looked down. The brown eyes of a child were looking up at him.

"Angélique! What are you doing there?"

His daughter's four-year-old face was beaming.

"I was hiding underneath you."

"Well, come up onto my lap."

"No," she said, shaking her brown locks. "I can't."

"Why not?"

"Because I have to finish writing my book."

She made a very serious face. Only now did Diderot see that she was holding a sheet of paper and a pen in her little hands.

"But you can give me a kiss first, can't you?"

"Only if you promise that I'll get a little brother to play with."

Her request pierced his heart. Sophie had told him in two lines that she had given birth to a son by him, that the boy's name was Dorval and that he lived with her at court. Only those two lines—no more.

Angélique pinched him on the calf.

"Do you promise?" she repeated.

"Nobody can promise something like that, my little angel."

"Then you won't get a kiss either."

She looked at him, her tiny brow knitted in angry furrows, but when she saw that he was no longer trying to win her over, she crawled back under the table.

Diderot sighed. Would she ever get to know Dorval? He tried to imagine how Angélique and his son might one day meet. . . . Where would that happen? Under what circumstances? An idea came to him: Could that be a story? Or a play?

"Well, then see about finishing your book," he said as he jotted down his idea on a piece of paper. Then he grabbed one of the cardboard cartons to get started with his work at last. At that moment there was a knock at the door.

"Come in!"

Jaucourt stood on the threshold with his tricorn in hand. He was so out of breath that he couldn't utter a word as he waved his arms about in excitement.

"What is it?"

"Have you heard?" he finally gasped, his voice breaking. "Somebody has killed the king!"

"Whaaat?" shouted Diderot, jumping up from his chair.

"I just came from the Procope. A customer there saw the whole thing with his own eyes. An attack. They have murdered Louis."

They stared at each other, both of them stunned and mute.

Although he was innocent, Diderot suddenly felt afraid.

66

Three days later, Antoine Sartine appeared to give his report to Father Radominsky. In the ensuing years Sartine had become a well-established police superintendent in command of a whole army of inspectors and sergeants.

"How could this happen?"

"It happened at exactly a quarter to six in the evening. The king was returning from a visit to Madame. The perpetrator fell upon him with a knife just as His Majesty was climbing into his coach to go celebrate the Feast of the Three Holy Kings at the Trianon."

"At the pleasure palace of his mistress?" asked Radominsky in disgust.

"Precisely. The man had been lurking beneath the vault of the church and then slipped into the compound unnoticed with His Majesty's guard. The knife blade was about five inches long and penetrated the king's body in the side between the fourth and fifth ribs. The thrust was made in an upward direction. At first the king thought he'd been hit with someone's fist. Not until the blood began to flow did he realize that he'd been wounded. His Majesty was taken at once for bloodletting, exactly at a quarter past six."

As Sartine went on with his report, Radominsky attempted to imagine the consequences of this disaster. Was the attack a sign from Heaven? A reason finally to intervene with all severity against the rabble-rousers and sinners in the country? Ah, if only it were so! But the attack on Louis was committed not only to send France into a deep crisis but above all to deliver a blow to the defenders of the true monarchy in France; they, by the grace of God, were the sole guardians of royal power—the Order of the Society of Jesus.

Radominsky's fear was more than justified. France had already been weakened to the core by the armed conflict with Britain and Prussia;

now a war of faith had been incited such as the country had not experienced since the expulsion of the Huguenots. The damned Jansenists were to blame. They followed only the crowing of the Gallic cock instead of listening to the voice of Rome, declaring the claims of the crown with regard to the church as inviolable—an affront to the Pope, who with his *Unigenitus* bull had branded Jansenism as heresy. But was this display of impudence any wonder when the parliament, the foremost jurisdiction in the land, took the side of the rebellion? Although the archbishop of Paris had ordered that no disciple of Jansenius should be allowed to have the last rites administered unless he first renounced the heresy, the parliament had countermanded his order. Parish priests were to administer the proper sacraments to all the dying who professed the Catholic faith; otherwise an arrest warrant would be issued for them. Yes, the parliament even had the effrontery to condemn God's representative on earth, Pope Benedict XIV, because Rome had promised the king the support of the church in this conflict with its adversaries. Louis, to finance the war, decided to raise by two *sous* the tithe on every *livre*.

And now, amid all this turmoil, came the attack! His Majesty's blood had not yet dried when the land was already reverberating with the most lunatic rumors about the perpetrator and the men who might be behind him. Conspiracies were suspected both in France and abroad, and no faction trusted any other; the parliament suspected the court, the court the people, the people the warring parties—nor was a secret plot by the Russian tsar ruled out. But the Jansenists spread the most evil, vulgar, and offensive rumor. It was making the rounds everywhere, in the city as well as at Versailles: The attack on King Louis, called "the Much Beloved" by the people, concealed in reality a plot devised by the Jesuits . . . What shameless infamy! No atheist could have dreamed up a more insidious idea—the mere suspicion threatened the existence of the order. As explanation for the appalling insinuation, the Jansenists referred to the old precept of the Society of Jesus, which stated that the murder of a tyrant was justified before God. Radominsky groaned. If only the perpetrator had achieved his goal! The rumors of the death of the king, which had been coursing throughout Paris all day long, had proven false. Despite the blood that had gushed out of the wound, no vital artery had been hit—two thick coats and the fur that the king was wearing had dulled the force of the stabbing. But no matter whether Louis was now dead or merely wounded—the slanderers had the presumption to claim that the king's life was no longer safe as long as there was a single Jesuit at Versailles. The Society of Jesus was supposedly doing everything it could to install on the throne the sanctimonious dauphin, the favorite son of the queen, in order to ensure the hegemony of the church over the crown. No doubt the Jansenists no longer wanted to be content with their supremacy in parliament; they sought to exploit this calamity in order to seize power at Versailles as well.

No, Radominsky had no illusions. The attack could mean that the Society of Jesus would be banned forever in the kingdom of France. Unless, that is, irrefutable evidence was found that the endangerment of the state came from a completely different source.

"The man wore a green velvet waistcoat and red plush hose," Sartine reported. "The weapon was found in his pocket, a folding knife with two blades, one quite ordinary and rather sharp, the other like a penknife. In his hand he carried a prayer book. He explained that he'd been given it by a monk."

"Good Lord!" Radominsky whispered in horror.

"In his pockets was also found a considerable sum of money, thirty-seven *louis d'or*, as well as some silver coins."

"The details do not interest me," Radominsky interrupted him, drumming his fingers impatiently. "It's all in the newspaper. I must penetrate to the heart of the deed. What sort of man is the attacker? What do you know about him? Where does he come from? What are his motives?"

"The man's name is Damiens," replied Sartine, "a former lackey."

"Who are his accomplices?"

"He claims to have none. Even under torture he stuck to this story. They tried to burn the names out of him with red-hot pincers, but in vain."

"In the *Mercure* it was claimed that he is feebleminded. Do you share this opinion?"

Sartine shook his head. "No, I don't believe that. I interrogated him several times in private. It's true that sometimes his speech was rather confused, and he stammered incoherent babble, saying he had to *hit* the king, *touch* the king, and that sort of thing. But he could also speak remarkably clearly, in complete sentences, as if ready to be printed."

"Printed? From an uneducated lackey?"

"Pardon me for contradicting you, but I consider this man in no way uneducated. Rather, I have the impression that he has enjoyed *too much* education, probably more than is good for him. His manner of speaking reminds me of some devout women—I don't know whether the comparison is apt, but . . ."

Sartine hesitated and gave Radominsky a questioning look, who gestured for him to go on.

"How should I put this? When he says certain sentences, and he keeps repeating them, it sounds like an old lady in church rattling off the Lord's Prayer. Each word is spoken in the proper order, but they all come out with no underlying sense, as if he had memorized a text that he doesn't fully understand."

"What sort of sentences are they?"

"Just a moment, please, I wrote down a couple of them." Sartine pulled out his notebook and opened it. "For example, this one. He says this over and over: 'Power that is attained through force is usurpation and lasts only as long as the strength of the one in command exceeds that of the one who obeys.'"

Radominsky grabbed the armrests of his chair so as not to jump up. He recognized this sentence! He could positively hear the voice of the man who had written those words, could see his face, his eyes, his mouth—as clearly and distinctly as if he were sitting here in this room.

"And he asked questions," Sartine went on, "always the same ones. 'Is there then no unjust power? Are there not authorities that do not originate from God, but are created contrary to His commandments and His will? Do the usurpers alone have God on their side?'" The superintendent closed his notebook and looked at Radominsky. "I think I know where these sentences came from."

"So do I," said Radominsky, getting up from his chair. "Search the dwelling of this man at once! Confiscate all books and brochures that you find there. Turn the whole place upside down. I want every damned printed word you find in that fellow's possession!"

67

Dark clouds hung over Versailles, and in the most magnificent palace in all of Europe—usually filled twenty-four hours a day with noise, music, and laughter in order to drive off the fog of boredom—the courtiers and lackeys now dared only walk on tiptoe.

The normal routines had been abolished. Although the king's skin had only been scratched, Louis imagined he was at death's door. The horse-faced dauphin, Louis-Stanislas, thoroughly unfamiliar with the business of ruling a country, was forced to lead the meetings of the royal council instead of going to the fair with his mother. In the meantime the monarch summoned his father confessor, Desmarets, and had the last rites administered on a daily basis. Between absolution and extreme unction he sent off remorseful letters to his wife, Maria Leszczynska. His mistress, on the other hand, got nothing of the sort, not a single note. La Pompadour remained in her quarters, receiving no news at all. As if that weren't humiliation enough, enraged threats were shouted at her from outside; beneath her window the people had formed a mob. It was commonly thought that she bore the blame for the entire unfortunate affair. Allegedly, it was the wish of the king that she leave Versailles forever.

The favorite wept, fell into a swoon, began crying again, and swooned once more. Too distraught to hold a glass, she lay on her ottoman and sipped orange blossom water that Sophie cautiously poured into a silver goblet. In her agitation and her pain La Pompadour thought seriously of packing her bags. But before taking such drastic measures, and whenever she had regained her strength for a few hours, she consulted with the few friends she had left at court. She sought the advice above all of her confidant of many years, Bernis, who was both a free spirit and a cardinal, and could be counted among the clergy of the Jansenist party. He consoled and calmed her, assuring her that a man in the king's condition who felt less sorry for himself would certainly be fully capable of going to the ball that evening.

"Rest assured, madame," he added, "that as soon as the delusion of death leaves him, His Majesty will once more be as wild as the Devil."

Sophie spent the little time she had, when her mistress did not need her, worrying about her son. Although he had only just turned five years old, Dorval was already finding his way around the vast labyrinth of Versailles better than Sophie did. All by himself he would run from the Salon of Diana to the Salon of Plenty, from the Salon of Mercury to the Salon of Venus, and from there to the *oeil-de-boeuf*, where a gigantic nurse who fended off anything that might disturb the king grabbed the boy by the collar and sent him back to his mother. Dorval was the terror of the lackeys and table servants, whose low bows he imitated in the drollest fashion. All the grand splendor at court still seemed foreign and overwhelming to Sophie. But her son had never seen the poverty and misery in the alleys of Paris, or the damp tenements, the stinking sewers, and filthy tobacco taverns; he knew no other world. The suites of rooms and the magnificent halls impressed him as little as all the paintings, statues, and antiquities. He wasted no time admiring the many gilded mirrors or the expensive baldachins or the countless courses that were served at table; and he paid no mind to the coaches adorned with coats of arms that passed as he played outside in the gardens. The boy noticed only the captain of the Swiss Guard, a small, pale-faced little man with spindly legs, whose soldiers, all six feet tall with mustaches and armed with halberds, obeyed his slightest command despite their physical superiority.

From morning till night Dorval ran around in the palace and in the park. Even greater than his lack of respect was his thirst for knowledge. Everything he saw or smelled or touched aroused his curiosity. The cooks in the kitchens had to explain to him how they prepared the different dishes; the cartwrights in the outbuildings recounted how they mounted the wagon wheels on the axles of the coaches; the smiths in the stables demonstrated how they shoed the horses. The fairy tales of Perrault that Sophie used to read to him at night had long become inadequate; even the fables of La Fontaine couldn't hold his interest. He was not satisfied merely to listen to his mother read; he wanted to read the books himself. He was firmly convinced that behind the printed letters and words were concealed much more exciting things than Sophie revealed when she read aloud.

So she had decided to teach him to read—as her own mother had done many years before. As a textbook she chose a multivolume work that contained answers to many more questions than even Dorval thought to ask. One article had made a particular impression on him.

"The Indians, who had known of this drink since primeval times, prepared it in a very simple manner. They roasted their cacao beans in earthenware pots and, after shelling them, ground them up between two stones, then dissolved the pulp in hot water, and spiced it with allspice. . . ."

Without faltering, Dorval summarized the whole article, explaining where chocolate came from and how it was prepared. When he finished, he asked, "Where do the Indians actually live, Mama?"

"Why ask me? You can read it for yourself."

Under the letter *I* she looked up the headword for him. With glowing cheeks Dorval immersed himself in the new article, and he had scarcely finished before he paged onward, following the cross-references in the text. Each answer awakened new questions in him, and like a tracker he followed the trail through the thicket of knowledge, searching on and on from one article to the next.

"The man who wrote this book must be the smartest man in the whole world," Dorval said reverently.

"I think you might be right," replied Sophie with a certain wistfulness.

Dorval looked up in surprise from the *Encyclopedia*.

"Why would you say that? You don't know him." And when she didn't answer, he added, suddenly very excited, "Or do you? Maybe you do know him."

With a smile she stroked his reddish blond hair.

"Ah, Dorval, what does 'know' mean?"

Now he could no longer sit still. He jumped up, hopping around her like an Indian, and cried out, "Come on, Mama, tell me! Do you know the man who wrote this book? If you do, you have to tell me."

"You need to calm down," said Sophie.

"But you have to tell me, you have to!"

He was literally incapable of standing still. Although she was holding him by both arms, his whole body was wriggling with curiosity and excitement. His cheeks were flushed red, and with his incredibly bright blue eyes he gave her a look so pleading that she could hardly stand the sight. He had asked her so often about his father, but she had always managed to evade the issue. Did she have a right to do that? Without pondering it any further, she decided to tell him the truth.

"Yes, Dorval, I do know the man who wrote the book."

"Really, Mama? Who is it? What's his name?"

"The man's name is Denis Diderot, and he is . . . your father."

"My father? But I thought . . . You always told me that . . ." He was so confused that he was speechless.

"Yes, I always said that he lived far away—and he does. He lives in Paris. It's four leagues from here, and on foot it would take half a day to walk there."

"But why does he live in Paris? Why isn't he here with us? Doesn't the king like him?"

Before Sophie could answer, the door opened and in came a servant, followed by Monsieur de Malesherbes.

"Do you know who wrote this book?" shouted Dorval, running up to him.

Malesherbes cast a glance at the volume, which still lay open.

"The *Encyclopedia*? But of course. It's by Diderot." He frowned with concern. "Tell me, young man, do you mean to say that you're reading this book?"

"Did you hear that, Mama?" Dorval yelled, beside himself, as Malesherbes greeted Sophie. "He knows too! He knows who wrote the book!"

He was bouncing as high as a rubber ball, pulling and tugging at her clothes and her hair.

"Dorval! Have you lost your wits?"

Too late. He had gotten hold of one end of her wig, and before she could stop him, the hairpiece lay on the floor. As she was bending over to pick it up, Dorval grabbed the *Encyclopedia*, and although the volume was almost as big as he was, he started lugging it away.

"Where are you going?"

"To the smithy. And to the kitchens. And to the Swiss Guard!" he called, already at the door. "I have to tell them who wrote this book!"

As Sophie turned back to Malesherbes, she caught sight of his expression. He seemed terribly annoyed. He looked at her as if seeing her at this moment for the first time. Involuntarily, Sophie grabbed her hair.

"What wonderful red tresses," he said. "How strange. It feels as though I've seen you somewhere before."

"I should hardly think so." Sophie laughed, half bewildered, half amused, and put her wig back on. "Unless you were in Café Procope, watching the waitresses. But tell me, monsieur, to what do I owe the honor of your visit?"

"Ah yes, I'd almost forgotten." As she secured the wig with a hairpin, Malesherbes took a letter from his pocket. "An invitation to dinner at Baron d'Holbach's. Would you do me the honor of accompanying me? I promise you most sincerely that no one will ask you to dance."

68

The Palais d'Holbach was located in the most elegant quarter of Paris, on Rue Royale, where entrenched wealth was manifested in buildings that were equally solid.

The baron, born in the Rhineland Palatinate, was a grumpy-looking man who was married to a charming, friendly woman of even disposition. Although he was known to be a bad loser at the dice game of *trictrac,* he had an even bigger reputation as a magnificent host. The dinner parties that he held every Sunday and Thursday in his five-story house were renowned at court as well as in the city. Because of these regular get-togethers the palais was also known as "the synagogue."

On the Sunday when Sophie was a guest the menu consisted of lobster, veal, and pheasants, garnished with fruit and vegetables, and a dessert of almond-and-raisin pudding, served with wine from the Palatinate. At the table were gathered two dozen ladies and gentlemen, who vied with one another to display their wit with their bons mots. Only the sisters of the baron, two aging spinsters who kept jabbing each other in the ribs as they blushed, did not participate in the conversation. But they did listen attentively to every word that Malesherbes, seated next to Sophie, exchanged with the host's mother-in-law. Madame d'Aine was a peevish elderly woman who with her remarks brought the whole company almost to tears from laughter, as she attacked the meat on her plate with her silverware as if she were vanquishing her most evil foe.

"Why do you pray to God?" Malesherbes asked her.

"My goodness," replied Madame d'Aine with a shrug, "how do I know?"

"But you attend mass. For what purpose?"

"One day I believe, the next I don't."

"And on the day that you do believe?"

"Then I'm in a foul mood."

"Do you go to confession?"

"Only out of habit—what else can one do?"

"Everyone should confess his sins, of course," said Malesherbes reproachfully.

"I commit no sins. But if I did and confessed them to the priest—would that undo them?"

"So you aren't afraid of Hell?"

"As little as I hope for Paradise. I know only this: If I am to be damned, I won't be alone—down there nothing but good old friends are waiting for me. Ah, if I had only known that when I was still young! I would have done many things that I unfortunately refrained from doing."

Sophie gradually began to comprehend why the Palais d'Holbach was known in Versailles as the citadel of the atheists. As the dinner progressed from one course to another, she listened to the freest conversation she had ever heard—there was no question too delicate to pose, no answer so confusing that it was not voiced. But to finish the meal the baron had thought up something quite special: the premiere of a new play. Malesherbes had already mentioned it on the way over. The drama to be staged was called *The Natural Son, or the Tests of Virtue.*

"May I?"

Malesherbes escorted Sophie through a richly stocked library, where wonderful Flemish oil paintings hung between the shelves, into a large hall that was arranged as a regular theater. She hoped that the presentation would not last too long—she wasn't fond of the theater. On stage the actors always moved like puppets; it was forbidden to raise the hands above a certain height, and the distance they could move their arms away from their bodies was strictly prescribed, as well as how deep they could bow, which was measured as if by a circle. What normal human being behaved like that?

"Aaahhh," the audience exclaimed.

As the curtain went up Sophie couldn't believe her eyes. What she saw was no artificial puppet stage—it was real life! No noble salon, but the home of regular citizens. No actors who stood stiffly and symmetrically in a circle, but women who had put aside their hoop skirts and men who had removed their wigs. They appeared in the whole disarray of their emotions, like people of real flesh and blood, with tousled hair and gestures that seemed to come straight from the heart.

As if bewitched, Sophie followed the drama, which seemed to originate from her own experiences: she witnessed the fate of a young man who fell deeply in love with a maiden—only to realize in the end that she was his own sister.

When she heard the name of the young man, she closed her eyes.

His name was Dorval.

"May I introduce you to the author?" Malesherbes asked.

Sophie hadn't noticed that the curtain had fallen—the piece had affected her so strongly. She looked up, but when she saw the countenance of the man to whom Malesherbes was introducing her, the blood drained from her face.

69

"How are you?" Sophie asked when they were alone.

"Are you asking *me*, madame, or Sultan Mongagul? By the way, my compliments—the wig suits you admirably."

"Please, forget the wig," she replied. "I'm asking *you*, Denis."

The grin on Diderot's face vanished.

"What can I say? The *Encyclopedia* is making good progress, although our enemies are doing their best to make life difficult for us. I hear that the laws will soon be tightened drastically."

The two had waited until the other guests had withdrawn to the salon. Then they had retreated to the empty stage behind the curtain, so that they could speak to each other in private. The candles were almost burned down, and the set seemed like unreal shapes in the flickering light: a piano, a couple of chairs, a *trictrac* game on a table, an embroidery frame, and a settee.

"And . . . how is the sultan?" Sophie asked after a while.

Diderot's shoulders sagged. He seemed so helpless that she had to swallow.

"Did you write this play about that?"

"Yes, Sophie," he said with a nod. "I wanted to see you again. Baron d'Holbach is a friend of mine. He arranged everything."

"Life is not a stage play, Denis."

"I can't imagine it any other way."

He tried to smile but failed. He had grown older, just as she had. His hair had lightened, and the creases around his nose and mouth were sharper than she remembered—they were no longer only the result of laughter. But as always, his small head on those broad shoulders moved like a weathercock on a church steeple, and his blue eyes were still so bright and clear that she thought she might drown in them.

Sophie could feel the midges begin to dance.

"Please don't look at me like that," she said, at the same time hoping he wouldn't stop looking at her that way.

He reached for her hand and held it.

"Come back to me, Mirzoza. We belong together."

She pulled her hand away.

"No, Denis. There . . . there isn't any Mirzoza anymore."

"But why not? I love you, and you love me. I can see it in your eyes."

Sophie shook her head.

"Anyone who has been in paradise can no longer return to the earth. We would only destroy what we had."

"Sometimes you have to destroy one thing to create something new."

"Even in love? Do you really believe that?"

Again he took her hand and dropped to his knee before her.

"*Love, wherever it appears, is always the master,*" he said fervently, like a prayer. "Those are your own words. Have you forgotten them?"

"How could I?"

"*For lovers, love is what the soul is for the body . . .*"

"Stop torturing me!"

"*Whoever is capable of love is virtuous . . .*"

Sophie said nothing. She knew that she shouldn't allow him to hold her hand, but she didn't have the strength to pull it away a second time. Everything in her was yearning to kiss him. He raised her hand to his lips.

"Mirzoza, Sophie." His voice caught as he covered her fingers with his kisses. "Please, I beseech you! You mean everything to me, my entire happiness, more than my own life."

"You said that once before."

"Yes, I know, and I also know how deeply I hurt you. I broke my promise—it was the worst mistake of my life. But believe me, I regret it with every breath I take."

"You made your decision, Denis. We can't go back."

"I'm no longer the same man; I've changed. I'll agree to everything you demand. If you want to punish me—hit me, I deserve it. There's only one thing you must not do."

"What?"

"Betray our love."

His expression was full of despair, his eyes shimmering with tears.

Sophie looked away. She saw the unfamiliar room they were standing in: the sheets of music on the piano, the cards on the playing table as if the game had merely been interrupted, the embroidery begun on the settee. How often had she dreamed of living in such a home with Diderot?

"Please, get up," she whispered.

"First you must give me an answer."

She shook her head. "It was you who gave the answer long ago."

"But I told you that I'm not the same!"

"You have a daughter, don't you?"

"How do you know that?"

"Is it so hard to guess? I saw your play."

"Yes, you're right. I have a daughter."

"What's her name?"

"Angélique. She's four years old. She . . . she means everything to me."

Sophie took a deep breath. "You see?" She nodded. "Be reasonable, Denis. Things are good the way they are."

"No, Sophie, they are not!" He jumped up and grabbed her by the shoulders so hard that it hurt. "What can I do to convince you? Tell me, and I'll obey. I'm ready to do anything."

He hesitated a moment, then added, suddenly quite calm, "If you want me to, I'll leave my family—at once. My only wish is to be with you."

"Stop it, Denis! Please. You're frightening me."

She could hardly hold back her tears.

"Then tell me that you forbid me to leave them."

"I . . . I forbid you to do it," she whispered, barely able to speak.

"You're lying! I don't believe a word of it."

"No," she said, "I forbid you. You must not leave your family. Think of your father. You . . . you always wanted to . . ."

Her voice failed her. She was trembling all over. Diderot was silent as well. The tears were running down his cheeks.

"At least may I see you again?" he asked finally, his voice gentle.

Sophie shook her head one last time.

"No, Denis. It would only hurt—both of us."

She tore herself away from him and stumbled from the stage. She had to get away as quickly as possible, before she did or said something foolish.

Without knowing how she found her way through all those rooms, she suddenly stood in the library. The host's mother-in-law, Madame d'Aine, was just saying good night to Malesherbes. As if in a dream Sophie heard their voices.

"Please excuse me, monsieur. But I must leave now to say my evening prayers."

"I thought you said that you didn't pray to God."

"Well, it's customary to kneel down before going to bed."

"So you also have moments when you believe?"

"Of course I do. I think that we women continue to have such moments of belief until the grave. It's the last sign of life in us."

70

A rumor was making the rounds of the court at Versailles, such an outrageous piece of news that even the attack on the king was pushed into the background. Hands were discreetly held up to pass along the news in a whisper, with either dismay or relief according to the society in which one found oneself: The Marquise de Pompadour, it was said, had suddenly turned pious.

Was it remorse? Was it calculation? Was it her advancing age? No one could say with certainty. Regardless: All at once they heard the marquise speaking of the Catholic religion. Quite seriously she explained that she was attending to her salvation and wanted to live according to the prescriptions of the Christian faith—the death of her daughter, Alexandrine, had caused her to stop and look into her heart. And in a sorrowful tone she added that even if she might not yet have found the path to true devotion, she was full of confidence that she would do so through prayer.

She was now actually seen at mass every day—not on the balcony that had been built especially for her use above the sacristy, but down in the nave among her people; after the rest of the congregation left she would stay behind alone, kneeling before the altar, immersed in endless worship. Many people talked of the divine grace that had come over her—and as proof of this they referred to the fact that the connecting door between the apartments of the king and that of his favorite had supposedly been walled up on their instructions. But others said instead that they believed it was a physical malaise that was the cause of this astounding transformation. They cited the anemia of the marquise and maintained that her personal physician, Dr. Quesnay, had prescribed donkey's milk, a glass every hour, to cure her of the consequences of dissipation.

La Pompadour ignored all these rumors. No matter what was said about her, she knew what she was doing. She was determined to end the scandal surrounding her person once and for all, and she was already thinking about a suitable public ceremony to demonstrate her conversion.

One day, as she returned from her devotions, she found an unexpected visitor in her boudoir: Father Radominsky. The priest was engrossed in looking at a picture that stood on an easel by the window. La Pompadour stopped short. The father confessor of the queen? What did he want with her? When she cleared her throat he turned around.

"I hear that it's your intention to be allowed to take communion once again—am I correctly informed?" he asked without further preamble as soon as they had greeted each other.

"Yes, *mon père*. It is my ardent wish to return to the bosom of the church. The misfortunes that have followed me even in my greatest happiness have shown me that I can never achieve true joy through the acquisition of the goods of this world, no matter how abundant my possessions."

"Your insight is as gratifying as it is laudable, madame. It is also being said that you intend to renew your marriage vows to your husband."

"That too is correct. Though Monsieur d'Etiolles is still hesitant about giving his consent. He seems to have become quite used to his bachelor life and shows no inclination to replace all the pretty young dancers and *grisettes,* whom he has been receiving in his house for years, with an old wife who has grown ugly and, garbed as a penitent, begs to be admitted."

At this point the rules of etiquette demanded a compliment. But Radominsky was unmoved and replied, "There are always ways and means. As long as your marital situation remains unresolved, you are barred from the sacraments. Do not deceive yourself that you can reconcile with the church and at the same time maintain your relationship with the king."

"I have taken measures that are eminently clear. My apartment is an absolute construction site. Stairways have been moved, entrances walled up. Now the king can reach me only through the reception room."

"I admit, that is more than a beginning."

"My only desire is to be close to His Majesty in pure, chaste affection, without being subjected to the suspicion of a weakness that I have long since renounced. In this spirit I have already written to the Holy Father in Rome, in order to ask for his blessing."

"It is precisely because of that letter that I have come. I wish to offer you my assistance. It is my duty to encourage true repentance wherever I encounter it and to offer penitent sinners my hand. Who knows, perhaps there is a resolution that would serve your interests as well as those of the church."

La Pompadour pricked up her ears. But instead of explaining what such a resolution might be, Radominsky paused and returned to the easel to look at the picture there. It was a portrait of La Pompadour as she looked up from reading a book. The painting showed off her beauty to such advantage that she herself was almost envious of it. One could not imagine that this beauty would ever fade.

"It's a shame," said Radominsky, "that your artistic sense has not developed in the same manner as your moral powers of judgment."

La Pompadour had an inkling of what the Jesuit might be getting at, but she wasn't sure.

"The portrait is by La Tour," she replied. "He is considered the most important painter in France."

"I'm not speaking of the brushwork skills, madame, but of the decorative content. You allow yourself to be portrayed holding a volume of the *Encyclopedia*?" He turned and shook his head. "The Bible would have been more becoming to you."

She regretted her carelessness at leaving the half-finished work uncovered in her boudoir. But there was nothing to be done about it now.

Aloud she said, "I have also had reservations and wonder whether to have the work finished at all."

"If you'd like my advice—you would do better not to show yourself in such company. General public opinion is against you, and now the investigations by the police have determined that the man behind the attack on the king is a former servant in your brother's employ."

"My brother?" she repeated in horror. "Monsieur de Poisson?"

"Quite right, and that's not all," Radominsky went on. "They found a copy of the *Encyclopedia* in his room. When questioned he quoted freely from it to justify his hideous deed. Is any other proof needed of how dangerous this book can be?"

La Pompadour reached for the arm of a chair to support herself.

"Is that why you came to me, Reverend Father?"

Radominsky nodded.

"What would you have me do?"

"It is time for the government to step in and take stern measures

against the Encyclopedists. I have already spoken with Monsieur Maupeou, one of the few reasonable men in parliament. He recognized the
seriousness of the matter and introduced a draft bill. All writings that
incite revolt against the church or the state shall henceforth be punishable by death. I need your help in persuading the king to support this
bill."

"I'm afraid you overestimate my powers," she said uncertainly. "I no
longer have access to His Majesty."

"You mean the walls, the staircases? I already said that there are always
ways and means. So do not disappoint me!" He gave her such a harsh
look that she thought she could feel his gaze burning her skin. "You must
decide, madame, on which side you stand: on the side of faith or on the
side of revolt."

71

Sophie stood at the window of her small apartment, looking at the garden. Outside everything was cold and gray, as if winter would never end. In a corner of the boxwood hedge that divided the garden in front of the window, Dorval was at that moment busy setting up a birdhouse. For this he had mobilized a whole troop of craftsmen from the royal workshops, his two best friends, the smith and the cartwright, and also two journeyman carpenters, all of whom he was now directing with loud yells and vigorous gestures. His little face was red from the cold and excitement. A couple of days earlier he had been shocked to see a stray cat catch a bird in a tree and kill it. Since then he had decided to protect all the birds of Versailles from the poaching cats, which prowled through the gardens and parks by the hundreds.

Seeing Diderot again had affected Sophie deeply. As she watched her son outside, her thoughts kept going back to their meeting at the Palais d'Holbach. Had it been a mistake to turn him away? Although the longing still burned inside her like an open wound, she believed she had made the right decision. He had betrayed her love, and now every attempt to revive it must end in disappointment. True love, as she herself had written, was rare. It was the same as with visions of ghosts: Everyone talked about them, but very few people had ever seen a ghost. . . . Sophie tried not to feel the pain. No, love was not the only thing. She had a son, and it was her duty to care for him so that he might receive from her everything he would need later in life. Her own feelings had to take second place; emotions were not important. She needed rest, not a man. She wanted to follow the example of her patroness.

Sophie was waving to Dorval just as La Pompadour came in. Her face seemed pale even beneath the thick layer of powder, and her bluish black eyes looked both tired and nervous. With a guilty conscience it occurred to Sophie that she had completely forgotten to bring her mistress the hourly glass of donkey's milk.

"Don't worry about it," La Pompadour said dismissively. "I only drink the milk so that the court will have something to talk about."

"Please excuse me, madame, but you look as though you might need to see the doctor. If you'll permit, I'll fetch Dr. Quesnay."

"Do you think he could help me? No, it would take a miracle to do that. My enemies have joined forces to press me from all sides. They're demanding a sign from me."

"Isn't the wall in your apartment sign enough?" Sophie asked.

"Ah," sighed La Pompadour, "that's the most superfluous wall in all of Versailles. The king hasn't used the connecting door in months." Her eyes filled with tears, and her gaze seemed to be lost in boundless emptiness, as she said wistfully, "Whether the door is open or not makes no difference. The king ceased his visits to me long ago."

Sophie touched her hand softly. "Tell me how I can help you."

La Pompadour briefly closed her eyes. Then she looked at Sophie. "If you want to do something for me, then accompany me tomorrow to the Châtelet."

"To the seat of the law courts?"

La Pompadour nodded.

"Yes, Sophie. Tomorrow they will execute the man who tried to kill the king. They expect me to attend, as a sign of my devotion. With my entire court household."

"Please, madame, spare me this . . ." Sophie stammered. "I am prepared to do anything you ask of me. But an execution, please . . ."

"I know what you're trying to say," replied La Pompadour. "It's because of your mother. Nevertheless, I cannot show any weakness—they're watching me, hoping for some pretext to chase me out of Versailles. No, I can tolerate no disobedience," she declared, as Sophie sought to object. La Pompadour's expression had conveyed the misery of a betrayed and humiliated woman, but now her face seemed to freeze with harsh resolve. "You shall accompany me tomorrow!"

72

Thousands of people were crowded before the Châtelet; the babble of voices rose over the throng like the rumble in the sky before a thunderstorm. From the neighboring streets and alleys more hordes of people pushed their way forward; the whole square seemed to surge back and forth as a massive entity. The windows of the buildings were black with clusters of people, and as far as the eye could see, the rooftops and trees were full of gawkers; they had climbed up to the chimneys, squatted on dormer windows and roof ridges, risking their lives. Everyone craned to catch a glimpse of the scaffold that had been erected three feet above the ground in the middle of the square. But there was still nothing to see except for the mounted guards and the ranks of soldiers, who despite fixed bayonets and shiny drawn sabers were having great difficulty keeping the impatient crowd in check. The lieutenants bawled orders at the sergeants, the soldiers braced themselves against the people. Whether men or women, old folks or children, all were eager to see the blood, the death struggle, and the bursting eyes.

And Sophie? She sat at a window directly across from the scaffold and had a clear view of it, as from a platform. Her palms were damp with nervousness. She had tried vigorously to escape this obligation, but her mistress would not hear of it. Especially for this occasion the Marquise de Pompadour had rented a floor in a merchant's house on the Place de Grève, in order to view the execution with her entire household and a few guests. She had paid quite a few *louis d'or* to secure these box seats; with the receipt the landlord had committed himself to refund six hundred pieces of silver in the event of noncompliance with the contract. As everyone looked for a good seat, Sophie fidgeted nervously with the tiny carved angel hanging on a slender silver chain around her neck. It was the first time she had worn the chain. Dorval had found it the night before among her undergarments—now she was happy to have it as a diversion.

"*À votre santé!*"

"*Je vous en prie!*"

Outside, raucous laughter was heard. What a revolting spectacle! Sophie could hardly watch. A torturer staggered over to the scaffold, a bottle in his hand and drunk as a sailor; the shouts of the public goaded him on, while the executioner and his assistants were busy lighting brushwood to start the bonfire made from logs piled up to the height of a man. The executioner drove his men hard, in such a loud voice that his curses carried all the way up to the window.

"What a pile of junk, you louts! Nothing but damned rotten wood! Maybe good enough to roast dogs or cats over! Nothing prepared! Nothing ready! No lead, no sulfur, no pitch, no wax! Run and fetch the stuff! Buy it or confiscate it—but be quick about it!"

Thick gray smoke rose over the square from the damp wood. Sophie shivered, but not from the cold weather, which still prevailed on this 28th day of March in the year 1757. She was picturing the village square of Beaulieu, many, many years ago, the way Abbé Morel had led her through the rows of villagers who had all come to see her mother executed; she heard the squeaking of their galoshes in the muck, smelled the smoky fire. The memory numbed her like a dull pain. The fire caught and then went out; the spectators mocked and ridiculed the executioner and then began pelting him and his men with rotten fruit. Sophie wished it were evening already.

"I'm afraid it will be a while yet," said La Pompadour. "But fortunately we have you, Signor Casanova. Help us pass the time and tell us of your journeys. We are eager to hear your adventures."

Grateful for the diversion, Sophie turned around. Behind La Pompadour's chair stood a man who drew the attention of everyone present: a thin Italian with a sharp nose, an olive complexion, and large, protruding eyes.

"What can I contribute to pass the time, Marquise? I fear I would only bore your guests."

"Set your mind at ease, Signor Casanova. Is it true that because of a love affair you were incarcerated in the leaden chambers of the Piombi? Is that why they banished you from Venice?"

"What an ugly word, madame. Let us say instead that for the sake of my physical welfare it is best for me to remain far from my home city for a while. Besides, I love Paris. This is the center of all life, civilization, and enlightenment. Here a new era is being proclaimed."

"In spite of the threat from our enemies?"

"You mean the English and the Prussians?" Casanova said with a sympathetic frown. "The former do not know how to cook, and the latter know nothing of love. How could such nations present a danger to France, which has cultivated both arts to perfection?" He paused and then said, "But I think our central figure is now approaching."

The remark brought Sophie back to the present. All of a sudden she felt ashamed. Down below, not a stone's throw from them, preparations were under way to kill a human being, while here the conversation was the sort that might be heard at a supper party at Versailles. And she had been listening with interest like all the others, merely to take her mind off the execution.

Loud howls and shouting rose up to them from the square. Sophie grabbed for her pendant. The gruesome drama began. Not far from the Châtelet, a gate guarded by several pairs of sentries was opened. A man chained hand and foot stumbled into the open air. With bayonets thrust out before them, the guardsmen cleared a path through the crowd as four soldiers dragged the offender toward the scaffold. La Pompadour's guests crowded at the window, bending so far over the balustrade that they almost fell out, shoving and squeezing forward just like the commoners below.

"There he is! The man who tried to murder the king!"

Sophie could no longer see; her view was suddenly blocked by heads and shoulders, wigs and hats. Without thinking, she jumped up from her chair and forced her way to the window. Between the backs of two people standing in front of her she caught sight of the convicted man. He sat motionless on the scaffold, waiting for his sentence to be carried out, as alone as the first man in creation despite all the milling people who had come to watch him die. Only his legs were twitching. At his feet peddlers were selling fruit and refreshments to the spectators from their sales trays, while the executioner stood behind the prisoner, preparing his instruments. Over the still smoking fire hung a gigantic cauldron in which a dark liquid was boiling.

"Nineteen torturers," someone said. "I counted them."

"A poor bargain for the executioner," replied another. "He won't earn much from such an execution."

Sophie wanted to turn away, go back to her seat, take refuge behind the heads and backs and shoulders, in order to shield herself from what was coming. Her hands were now wet with sweat and her whole body was trembling. But why? She tried to calm herself, convince herself that it was a perfectly ordinary execution that she had to watch, neither the first and probably not the last to be conducted in Paris. What did the stranger matter to her? Hadn't he deserved his punishment? Hadn't he committed the most heinous crime a person could commit? He had tried to kill the king, the monarch, whom God had appointed as ruler of all the French people.

She took a step back toward her chair—and then the condemned man raised his head. He looked straight in her direction.

When she saw his face, Sophie froze: a shock of dark hair and below it an even darker gaze. How many times had she looked into those eyes? And there she now saw the misery of all humanity.

It was Robert, the former valet of Monsieur Poisson.

"Now! It's starting!" came the whispers and hisses all around her. "Pay attention! They're going to begin!"

All at once it was so quiet on the square that they could hear the twittering of the birds. In Sophie's head only one thought kept churning: Robert . . . The condemned man was Robert . . . "Robert the Devil," the man who had stolen her book. . . . Like a poisonous potion the realization seeped into her soul, slowly, gradually, insidiously . . . Her hands clutched the windowsill; she was unable to take her eyes from the doomed man. Time stood still as she stared at the scaffold, and not another sound reached her ears. She was aware only of her own breathing and this man, who was now lifted up by two helpers and undressed.

Robert . . . Like a puppet he let events take their course, defenseless and delivered up to the brutal powers. His body was pale, with only a cloth covering his loins, as they laid him on the platform, gagged him, and fastened his arms and thighs with iron bands. As Sophie saw his naked body stretched out so shamelessly before her, she felt a brief, intense excitement as if in anticipation of an act of love. She swallowed hard to stifle the feeling.

A judge walked over to Robert.

Loud and clear he raised his voice over the crowd: "Tell us the names of your accomplices!"

Sophie gave a start when she heard Robert's answer.

"I am innocent!"

"Relieve your conscience so that you may find grace in Heaven."

"I will greet my family and pray for them!"

"Divulge what you know to us, for the sake of your soul's salvation."

"I am full of faith, and my only wish is to serve France."

Suddenly Sophie's heart began to pound wildly and the blood throbbed in her veins. How could Robert talk like this in the face of death? The judge consulted with the executioner, who made a sign to his men.

"Astounding," said Casanova. "Normally they try to postpone the end, if only for one more breath."

Her whole body in shock, Sophie looked down on the square. A cry rose from her breast into her throat, but there it stayed. Robert did not move. Only his dark eyes shifted restlessly. With attention, almost curiosity, he gazed at his torturers, following their every move. The seething sulfur in the cauldron filled the air with its sharp odor. This was what it must smell like in Hell, she thought. Robert coughed a few times as a helper tied a knife to his right hand.

"Is that the hand that attempted the murder?"

"I assume so," said La Pompadour. "The hand of the murderer."

Then a scream rang out across the square, a scream so loud that it must have been heard in the remotest alleys of the quarter. The executioner was holding a pan of hot coals under Robert's hand to burn it with sulfur fire, and he screamed and screamed and screamed. Sophie shut her eyes. She recognized this scream; she had once screamed that way herself. . . . Applause broke out; the tension that had been building to unbearable heights among the spectators seemed to be released.

Sophie opened her eyes again only when the applause ebbed away. Robert was silent. When she looked at him she gave a start. Only a charred black stump remained of his hand; he looked at it with a vacant stare, absently, almost indifferently, the way one looks at a foreign object, as if the stump didn't belong to him. He moved his lips without a sound, but Sophie thought she could hear the words: "What did I do? Tell me what I did."

The executioner rolled up his sleeves and then took a pair of red-hot pincers from the fire and went over to Robert. Sophie heard the hiss as the pincers touched his skin, and saw the smoke rising from Robert's body, a small, merrily curling tendril of smoke. What horrendous pain he must be suffering! The executioner proceeded with gruesome slowness, tormenting Robert's legs with his pincers, one after the other, first the calves, then the thighs. After that he started in on the man's torso, tearing at his arms, his shoulders, his nipples, turning and twisting the pincers in order to rip off the bits of flesh that refused to yield from the convulsing body, leaving wounds the size of a large coin. At each bite of the pincers Robert howled. But he would then gaze at the wounds as he had at the charred stump of his arm, and his screaming stopped as soon as the pincers stopped tearing at his flesh.

"Tell us the names of your accomplices!"

Sophie sent a quick prayer to Heaven that Robert would finally speak. But he just kept shaking his head at each question and each demand. He was as obstinate and unrepentant as a heathen who refused to denounce his false gods. No confession could be wrested from him, no plea for mercy, no lies to save his skin, not even a curse. Enraged, the executioner called over his assistants. They brought him their roiling medicaments: molten lead, boiling oil, burning pitch, wax, and sulfur, which they dribbled into Robert's open wounds.

"My God, give me strength! Give me strength!"

Sophie bit her lip so as not to cry out along with him. Why didn't God hear his pleas? Could the Lord close His ears to these cries that could melt even a heart of stone? When Robert screamed, his eyes nearly popped out of their sockets and his hair stood on end. But between the cries he always raised his head to look at his body as the executioner poured new liquid into his wounds with an iron spoon. Sophie moaned. Was it really God who was conferring on him such fortitude? It would have been more merciful to take away his strength so that he might come to a more rapid end. Or was it the intoxication of pain, experienced in moments of mute observation even more terrible than his screams, that made him numb to these torments?

"The Devil has spewed him out!"

"Only a monster could tolerate such pain!"

Sophie turned around. A dreadful admiration was evident on the faces of the courtiers looking down into the pit of Hell with raised eyebrows. Could it be that they were reveling in this inferno? Suddenly she saw something that exceeded all bounds of comprehension. Quite close to her, only a couple of arms' lengths away, Signor Casanova was fiddling with the skirts of a lady who was leaning out the window in front of him, apparently completely engrossed in the cruel drama that was taking place down in the square, but actually busy with something else entirely. Her slim hand grasped a swollen red member that for a second shot out of a golden fly before vanishing with a twitch beneath her skirts.

"Give me more! More, more, more!" It was Robert egging on his tormentors to increase the torments. With a voice that no longer sounded at all human, the cries burst out of him like pain made audible. Had he gone insane from the torture? Had his mind finally snapped? Sophie no longer wanted to watch him suffering, and yet she couldn't tear herself away; her muscles refused to obey her command, and she had to turn her eyes to Robert's misery again and again and again. Now they stretched his body out on a wooden cross. He was bleeding from a hundred wounds and yet in an eerie way his body still seemed intact. A priest stood at his side and spoke to him, holding a crucifix before Robert's face, which he kissed over and over again. Then the executioner's assistants tied the towrope of a horse to each of his arms and legs.

"Have mercy, Lord!" Robert roared as the horses began to pull. "Have mercy!"

The scream seemed to be coming from Sophie's own heart. She held her hands to her ears so as not to hear, but she couldn't help looking at him, as if she were damned to share in Robert's torments, to bear her cross with him as Simon of Cyrene bore the cross of the Savior. A helper had seized the reins of each horse while another stood behind and swung the whip. The four-horse team started to move. Sophie could hear the snorting from their nostrils and the thump of their hooves, beneath which the iron sprayed out sparks. Suddenly one of the horses fell to the cobblestones.

"Look at that—the poor horse! Look!"

Sophie let her hands drop, powerless and exhausted. The people howled with excitement. Robert's muscles and sinews had somehow withstood the dreadful strain. Instead of breaking his limbs, the beasts had stretched him grotesquely—his arms and legs seemed almost twice as long as they were before. Again the horses set to work with all their might, driven by the whips and shouts, and again they were pulled back. And still there was life in Robert's ravaged body. Sophie could hear his breathing like the bellows in a smithy.

At some point she lost all sense of time. Did it go on for minutes? Hours? Or was it only seconds in the hell of darkness. As if in a dream, unreal and surreal at the same time, things were taking place before her that she saw with her own eyes and yet could not comprehend, while tears of sorrow, rage, and helplessness ran down her cheeks. . . . Now they had the horses pull in the opposite direction: those at the arms toward the head, and those at the legs toward the arms. The priest slumped in a faint, the court clerk hid his face in his robe so as not to look any longer, as the crowd began to grumble. They could feel that twilight was about to fall. Two more horses were hitched up, and now four helpers whipped each of the six animals. Robert's bones creaked in his joints, but his body still held together, as if no power in the world could tear apart his limbs.

"Pray for me!"

Lonely as a shout in the desert, Robert's plea drifted over the thousands of heads in the crowd. Sophie grabbed for the angel hanging from the silver chain at her throat, as if it might still avert disaster. But through a veil of tears she now saw the executioner conferring with the judge, whereupon the judge called over a physician, the physician called a surgeon, until finally they put all their heads together, five of them, then six, then a dozen, without reaching a conclusion.

"What a farce!" whispered La Pompadour, her cheeks drained of blood beneath the rouge.

"Most certainly," Casanova agreed with her. "The execution is supposed to serve as a deterrent. How will that be possible after dark?"

Sophie clasped the angel in her hand. Finally, finally they would have mercy! With a long, shiny steel knife the executioner got to work cutting through Robert's shoulders and hips, slicing the tough tendons that had prolonged his agony. The angel felt cool in her hand, like the beads of a rosary. Sophie could not feel the points of the carving penetrating her skin; all her senses were with Robert, who raised his head one last time and stared with glassy eyes at the executioner, as if he could not get his fill of his tormentor's work. He watched every move, staring and staring until his thighs and shoulders were cut through. He had lost even the strength to scream.

"May God have mercy on your soul," Sophie whispered. She kissed the angel on her chain and made the sign of the cross. Once again the horses pulled mightily at the harnesses. There was a faint sound of cracking and breaking, and Robert's body finally gave up as the limbs tore loose from his torso; first an arm, then a leg, then another leg and the second arm. . . . Finally Robert Damiens had breathed out his life and was dead for now and all eternity. Only his jaw still moved, as if he wanted to shout something, while his eyes, two glassy, burst balls, seemed to gaze up at Sophie.

"Bravo! Bravissimo!"

As if waking from a nightmare, Sophie turned her head. With gloved hands Casanova was applauding, while the lady in front of him at the window calmly straightened her skirts as if she were only arranging the fall of the folds. Casanova gave her a friendly nod; he seemed cheerful, refreshed, and calm. All of a sudden Sophie thought she saw her mother's face: a grinning caricature bobbing up and down.

Her hand clasped around her pendant, Sophie sank onto her chair. And fainted.

When she awoke from her swoon, she was gazing into a deathly pale face: Malesherbes was bending over her with a sympathetic gaze.

"It is finished," he said and offered her his arm.

Only now did she notice that her hand was bleeding.

73

For the first time after weeks of tedium there was again life at Versailles. While at the execution site Robert Damiens's ashes were scattered to the four winds, all the rooms in the palace were illuminated. Everywhere people were standing together in groups until deep in the night, and wherever two courtiers were speaking to each other there was only one topic: the just end of the king killer.

When had they last conversed with such enthusiasm? As they enviously surrounded the few eyewitnesses who had enjoyed the privilege of attending the execution in person, Louis retired to his private chambers so that La Pompadour could relate to him in minute detail the events of the day. He wanted to know everything that had happened at Place de Grève, and she must not omit the slightest detail. When she demonstrated for him how the assailant had been torn asunder, the king uttered loud cries of pain, threw himself on his bed, and wept like a child.

"And when they picked up the torso," he asked with tear-filled eyes, "was the man really still alive?"

"The executioner said so, Sire. He seemed to have nine lives, like a cat. They tossed the torso and the limbs into the bonfire. It took four hours for the pieces of flesh to burn up."

"That is simply appalling, madame, utterly appalling!"

It took until the next day for Louis to recover from the shock. Not until noon did he consider himself capable of meeting the foreign envoys whom he received in the Hall of Mirrors as if he had been raised from the dead. But he knew his duty and was tireless in telling them in copious detail about the execution of "his murderer," all the while reproaching the indifference of his subordinates, who after the attack had shown him scant proof of their love.

The bishops and priests all over France took full advantage of the situation. Even as the dogs tried to warm their muzzles on the pavement where the bonfire had been, before being chased away from the execution site, masses of thanksgiving were held in the churches for Louis's miraculous deliverance. Countless parishes undertook celebrations to express their allegiance to the king.

The parliament was not to be outdone by the church. Already on the day after the execution the law court ruled that the father, wife, and daughter of the assailant must leave the kingdom without delay. If they failed to do so, they would be hanged and throttled. The judges also prohibited, under penalty of the same punishment, any other relatives from bearing the name Damiens in the future. Upon hearing of this ruling the city of Amiens humbly begged permission to change its name to Louisville in honor of His Majesty, so as not to remind anyone of the murderer. The house where he was born had already been burned to the ground by Louis's soldiers.

"When will it be enough?" asked Sophie. "Can a crime be so abominable as to deserve such extreme punishment? Where is the law?"

"The law is a chameleon," replied Malesherbes, "perhaps the most changeable of all. It can assume any imaginable color and will stop at nothing, no matter what its master may demand of it."

They were alone in Sophie's apartment. Dorval was already asleep; she had put him to bed before Malesherbes knocked on her door. Ever since he had escorted her home from Place de Grève, his visits had become almost a daily occurrence.

"I hope that your hand has stopped hurting by now."

"The wound has long since healed; it was only a scratch."

She turned to the window. Darkness had descended upon the garden, and everything seemed to be sleeping. Dorval's birdhouse was visible only as an indistinct shape against the black background of the hedge, a small, peaceful place of refuge in the dark night.

"Sometimes I almost think," she said softly, "that there's a curse on the book."

"May I inquire of which book you are speaking?"

"The *Encyclopedia*. It was supposed to enhance the happiness of humanity, and now it has hurled so many people into misfortune. Who knows, perhaps without that book things might not have reached such a calamitous end."

"You mean, because Damiens referred to a couple of sentences from the book?"

"I worked in the same house as he did, for Monsieur Poisson, the brother of Madame."

"I know that you knew him. It must have been horrible for you to witness the execution."

"You know nothing, Monsieur Malesherbes." She turned to him and looked him in the eye. "I gave Damiens the *Encyclopedia* to read."

"You did?" he asked in surprise. "But how did that come about?"

"It's not important; I happened to have a copy in my possession. I . . . I have to know something else, and I beg you to answer me honestly." She paused before asking the question. "Do I share in the blame for his demise?"

Malesherbes was quiet a long time before he said, "A book is a mirror, Sophie. If a thief looks into the mirror, no apostle will look back. Every reader derives a different conclusion from what he reads; I have learned that in my years as censor." He gently touched her shoulder. "No, believe me, you bear no guilt."

"But shouldn't I have been able to foresee the results? I knew Robert, after all, and I knew how fanatical he was."

"Would you make Jesus responsible when people are killed in the name of the Bible? No," he repeated, before Sophie could object, "books are like knives. You can use them to cut bread or to kill someone. But—there is something I have long wanted to ask you," he said, suddenly changing the subject. "What is that pendant you're wearing around your neck?"

"You mean the angel?"

"It goes wonderfully with your hair. May I?" Malesherbes reached for the ornament to examine it. "What sort of material is this? Ivory?"

"I don't know—it's merely a talisman. It's from my home village. The only keepsake I have from there."

"A talisman?" he asked, sounding annoyed.

"Yes, is there something special about that?"

"No, nothing. It's nothing," he stammered, confused. "It's only that in my hometown we have similar talismans."

He let go of the angel and looked at her, embarrassed and searching at the same time, scrutinizing her with his gray eyes just as he'd done when they first met. He seemed to be seeking something in her face, but he had only a vague inkling of what he was looking for.

"I have another question, Sophie," he said at last. "You've never told me where you come from."

"You wouldn't know the place, it's only a tiny village. Beaulieu is its name, on the Loire River."

"Beaulieu near Roanne? But of course I know it; that's only a day's ride from my family's castle. Strange that I didn't hear it in your speech, but you don't have a trace of an accent. One might almost think that you wished to expunge your origins."

Suddenly his expression turned serious. His lips moved a few times as if he were having a hard time deciding whether to speak, as if he had to overcome a certain reluctance. But then he said, "Sophie, why have you taken such an interest in Damiens's fate?" And when she hesitated, he said, "I'm right, aren't I? There is a reason, a special reason, isn't there?"

Sophie felt a flood of memories welling up inside her, all the images and feelings that she had been holding back for days, out of fear that they might overwhelm her.

"It wasn't the first execution I've seen," she replied haltingly. "I was forced to witness one before, in my childhood. . . . Then too a book was the reason that a human being had to die."

"Who was this person?" he asked softly. "Someone close to you?"

Sophie turned away. It was all there again inside her, more than she could stand, trying to burst out of her. And as she peered into the dark garden, the words came streaming from her lips, words that described her whole life, the happiness and despair, the love and the death, and the eternal longing to understand at last what was impossible to understand—her life. She told him about her mother, about her childhood, about their little house at the edge of town. How Madeleine had cared for her and protected her and taught her to read—until the day of her First Communion. She told him about Abbé Morel, about Baron de Laterre, about the man with the plumed hat. About the endless long days of waiting and uncertainty at the castle, while a distant court decided her mother's fate. And about the long way back to the village, holding the hand of the old priest. . . .

"My God," Malesherbes whispered when she had finished. "My God . . . My God . . ."

He put an arm around her shoulders. She looked at him. His eyes were bright with tears. He took her hand and, struggling for words, he said, "I promise you, Sophie, whenever you need a friend, you can count on me. I will do anything for you, anything. For you and for Dorval."

Gratefully she squeezed his hand in return. And as he held her hand, she had the feeling that all the grayness would disappear, forever banished, as long as they stood there together, with her hand clasped in his.

"There's just one thing I ask myself," she said after a long while, "if a book can do so much harm, wouldn't it be better to ban it?"

"Perhaps you're right," he said, without letting go of her hand, "and it should be banned. Then again, perhaps the very opposite should be done."

"The opposite?"

"Yes, Sophie, as cruel as it may sound. Perhaps there have to be books for which people lay down their lives, so that such crimes never happen again."

74

"Such an intensification of the laws is absurd! The death penalty for books would be a disaster for France."

"Attacks on the king are a disaster. As are the books that incite such actions. It amazes me that I have to remind you of this, since you are His Majesty's censor."

"Quite true, I am the censor, not a policeman! A country in which people read only books that are published with the approval of the government will remain a century behind the times."

Radominsky didn't recognize Malesherbes anymore. Just the day before he would have wagered the church of the Jesuit order that the director of the Royal Library would accept the new view of things— until now he had always flown his banner in the prevailing winds. But an hour ago Malesherbes had shown up at his door, unannounced, seeking to intervene against the legislative initiative. No doubt the career-minded man with no scruples had turned into a determined party supporter. And what was even worse, he seemed to believe his own words.

"It wasn't very long ago," said Radominsky, "that you forbade the *Encyclopedia* with a council decree. What causes you suddenly to take the side of the philosophers with such vehemence?"

"Monsieur d'Alembert, a man who is above all suspicion, has written to request my assistance. He views his work as endangered, yet it will contribute more to the glory of France than does the war against England and Prussia."

"I know that letter written by d'Alembert." Radominsky laughed. "He demands that the government safeguard the Encyclopedists from the yellow press, using the tools of censorship! He wants us to put a gag on his critics. What pitiful hypocrisy!"

"D'Alembert is a member of the Académie Française. He justifiably fears for his reputation as a mathematician."

"He still feels insulted by the Cacouacs affair. He and his band of philosophers were exposed to ridicule. That's all it is."

"He has rendered outstanding service to the Catholic faith. His article on Geneva in the *Encyclopedia* is the most astute condemnation of Calvin I have ever seen."

"His friend Voltaire, who has made himself at home in Geneva and now wants to set the tone there as he previously did in Paris, has guided his pen. In addition, surely you must have noticed that the article is not directed at Calvin alone, but against every form of Christian faith. But why are we wasting our time arguing about these pederasts?"

"I don't know who you're talking about."

"D'Alembert, of course! Don't you know about his unnatural tendencies?"

Malesherbes was so irritated that he took a pinch of snuff. But his agitation lasted only a few seconds. After he had blown his nose, he said, "Socrates loved boys, too. If you want to impose the death penalty for that, I fear for the sleep of many of your fellow brothers, *mon père*. You could end up in Paradise faster than you'd like."

"Stop digressing," replied Radominsky, unmoved. "If I demand the death penalty for certain books, it's only for the purpose of fending off disaster for a great number of people. On this topic, by the way, I know I'm of the same mind as your father, the chancellor."

"My father and I see each other occasionally, so you don't have to explain his views to me," said Malesherbes, taking another pinch. "But if you want to challenge me, I must ask you directly and without further ado: Is it really your wish to draw and quarter writers and burn them at the stake like the murderer Damiens, just because they've written books that you don't like?"

Radominsky didn't need even a second to consider his answer.

"If by doing so we protect the church and the monarchy from future Damiens—yes!" He got up from his desk and began to pace back and forth. "So what needs to happen, Monsieur de Malesherbes, to make you finally admit the correlation? The attack on the king is proof enough, after all: The *Encyclopedia* is nothing more than a conspiracy to destroy religion and undermine the state, as it has been bestowed on us by God. And the pernicious seed continues to germinate, it blooms and thrives.

Have you read *On the Spirit,* by the way, the latest defamatory writing of
the philosophers? The author, a certain Helvétius, states that the interest
an individual exhibits for himself is a main principle of human behavior.
Self-love as the source of morality!"

"I know that book. It's an attempt to bring into harmony the happiness of the individual with the general welfare of the community. A com-
mendable undertaking."

"The book is a summary of the *Encyclopedia*—an absolute call to
rebellion. This Helvétius, or whoever is hiding behind that name,
polemicizes against everything that is sacred: against the church, against
the law, against the cloister system, against the belief in miracles—even
against road building and the merchant trade. No load of sugar, so he
claims, arrives in Europe that is not tainted by blood." Radominsky
stopped in front of Malesherbes and stared at him. "Don't you realize
that we have to take action against such writings? If we don't, we'll be
committing a sin against the God-given order of things; the king is an
affirmation of God's will on earth, and we would be digging a grave for
the monarchy, which is graced by God."

Malesherbes returned his gaze without flinching. Then he shook his
head. "You will not succeed with your initiative. Even if you have Maupeou and the parliament behind you."

"You're forgetting your father, the chancellor."

"Even he can't help you. Because you're lacking *one* specific power in
the state."

"And which one would that be?"

"The crucial one." Malesherbes paused to savor the moment and took
a third pinch of snuff. "Madame de Pompadour, the favorite of the king."

Radominsky shrugged. "Madame de Pompadour has already promised
me her support."

"I find that hard to believe. Why would she do that? The marquise is
a friend of philosophy."

"That could be," responded Radominsky with a smile, "but above all
La Pompadour is a friend of La Pompadour. Fortunately I succeeded in
arranging for her a small favor. Yesterday the queen officially appointed
her to be her *femme d'honneur.* Did she not tell you about that?"

75
🙰 🙱

"What is man, that he must continually make plans?"

Diderot had accepted an invitation from Melchior Grimm to La Chevrette, an idyllic little village where Louise d'Épinay, the wealthy mistress of the journalist, had a comfortable estate with many guest rooms. There, in the peace and seclusion of the countryside, far from all the tumult of the capital, Diderot sought to work. But instead of reading and writing, or simply daydreaming without having a typesetter's apprentice waiting by his door for the manuscript, he found himself from morning till evening subjected to Rousseau's pestering. His old friend had moved into a cottage in the neighborhood with his wife and mother-in-law, and he had discovered a sentence in Diderot's novel *The Natural Son* that he took as a personal criticism: "Only a bad man lives alone."

Since this discovery La Chevrette had turned into a madhouse. Rousseau seemed out of his mind; whoever he managed to buttonhole—whether Diderot himself or Grimm or even Baron d'Holbach, who sometimes came to visit—he inflicted upon everyone his tirades and delusions in an attempt to convey the reprehensible state and depravity of a life gone astray. He extolled nature as the only possible seat of human happiness and condemned society, from which all evil proceeded; he pilloried the corruption of morals, the intrigues and dissembling that proliferated like weeds in the cities and defiled the original and sincere relations that human beings could have with one another. Rousseau regarded as his enemy anyone who refused a life in nature. Anyone who did not follow his teachings was a traitor and intent on destroying his innocent bliss. Even the fact that Voltaire had settled in Geneva was something he took as a personal attack: It meant that he was banned from his homeland forever. But Rousseau had developed a passionate love for Madame d'Houdetot, a relation of their hostess who had an incredibly ugly face but bosoms as big as udders, which had become the focus of the brilliant author's ardor. This was the only reason Diderot was able to find a few moments' respite when he could spill out his heart in a letter to Sophie. Even if he never sent the letters, they were his sole opportunity to forget the madhouse all around him.

He had just sat down to write a few lines when a servant brought him a dispatch.

"From Paris?"

Diderot furrowed his brow. The handwriting was that of his publisher. Impatiently he opened the envelope. The letter contained only a few lines, but they were enough to alarm him in the extreme:

> The parliament has forbidden the sale of the *Encyclopedia* and has set up a commission of inquiry. Come back at once! Come now! Drop everything!

With the next post coach Diderot set off. He arrived in Paris at the crack of dawn. Even before going home to change his clothes, he stopped off at Rue de la Harpe.

At the publishing house the mood of crisis was palpable. Usually when he entered the ground floor of the print shop, all the journeymen would doff their caps in greeting. Today they merely stared at him with crooked grins, and he had scarcely turned his back to them to ascend the stairs when he heard them whispering.

Le Bréton, who was waiting for him together with d'Alembert in the editorial office, greeted him with a book in his hand. The title resplendent on the binding was like a signal: *On the Spirit*.

"Did you concoct this shit?"

"What gives you that idea?"

"There's a rumor going around," said d'Alembert, "that no one but you could be hiding behind the pen name Helvétius."

"Who says that?"

"The Jesuits. In the *Journal de Trévoux*."

"Tell me the truth!" Le Bréton bellowed. "And woe to you if what those evil crows claim is true. I'll strike you dead!"

Diderot suddenly felt as if he were on trial.

"I don't know what you're talking about. I've spoken with Helvétius a couple of times, and I might have given him the occasional manuscript to read—I can't remember every encounter, for God's sake! What are you getting at?"

"What I'm getting at?" Le Bréton snorted. "I can tell you, Diderot: a rope, a beautiful rope. A perfect fit for your neck and mine." He grabbed his throat as if he could already feel the noose. "If the king agrees with the vote of parliament, we're finished."

"We could always go abroad," d'Alembert whispered, his face pale as the wall. "Voltaire has always said—"

As he was speaking the door opened, and in came Jaucourt.

"Rousseau has switched sides!" he shouted. "He's attacking us in public!"

"What are you babbling about?" said Le Bréton. "What do we care about Rousseau?"

"He's written a reply to the 'Geneva' article." Jaucourt pulled a pamphlet from his pocket and handed it to d'Alembert. "There—read for yourself!"

Before d'Alembert could react, Diderot snatched the pamphlet from his hand.

"What sodomite did you incite to libel the people of Geneva?" Le Bréton hissed at d'Alembert, who had written the article on the Swiss city for the *Encyclopedia*. "They were always good customers."

While the others argued about whether Rousseau was ill or insane, Diderot scanned the pamphlet, which he held with trembling hands. The text was an absolute declaration of war. To save the virtue of his hometown, Rousseau condemned everything that was sacred to the philosophers: reason, theater, and atheism. Instead he proffered a new piety, appealing to the heart and the starry firmament, and accused his former allies of treason. The view he voiced was so despicable that Diderot felt ill. Rousseau must have been setting this disgusting smear campaign to paper in La Chevrette at the same time that they were seeing each other on a daily basis.

"This is unbelievable," said Jaucourt. "The opera composer condemns the theater. He must be out of his mind!"

"He's ill," d'Alembert retorted. "A sick man with plenty of spirit, but he has spirit only when he's feverish."

"His urine has gone to his head because he can't piss!" Le Bréton said, rolling his eyes. "I've always hated that skunk. But forget about

Rousseau. What about the others? What are they saying at the Procope?"

"At the Procope hardly anybody dares say anything anymore," said
Jaucourt. "They're all afraid of each other. Afraid of the informers, of
their tablemates, of themselves. Duclos, Marmontel, and Turgot have
quit the *Encyclopedia*."

"Th—that can't be true!" stammered d'Alembert. "Three of our most
important authors . . ."

"The rats are fleeing the sinking ship." The news struck Le Bréton
with such force that he sank down onto a chair. "These damned traitors!
May plague and cholera take the whole bunch of them!"

Diderot put aside Rousseau's tract.

"They're no traitors, Le Bréton. They're just scared."

"Nonsense! If anyone has a reason to be afraid, it's me. The next
volume is being typeset, the whole storeroom up to the ceiling is full of
paper. If I can't print I'll be ruined."

"It's not about money."

"Not about money? What's it about then?"

"People are afraid for their lives. The scaffold threatens you—as it
does all of us."

Suddenly they all stopped talking. The echo of Diderot's words only
emphasized the uneasy silence in the room, as the groaning and screeching of the printing presses rose up to them from below as if from another
world.

D'Alembert cleared his throat. He looked at Diderot with his big
brown eyes, timid and frightened as a deer.

"I . . . I don't think the *Encyclopedia* will ever be completed." He faltered, then added, "At least, not with my help."

"What are you trying to say?" Diderot asked.

"I'm sick of it—sick, sick, sick! The ridicule in the newspapers, the
sermons from the pulpits, and every night the fear that the police will
come knocking on my door. I'm a scientist, not a soldier!" D'Alembert
took a deep breath. "Gentlemen, you are free to appoint my successor. I
resign my position as editor."

He nodded curtly to the others, then turned and left the room.

76

"You have to do something, madame! Diderot's life is at stake!"

"I'd love to help you, Sophie," replied La Pompadour, "but my hands are tied."

"Do you want to watch as they drag him to the scaffold?"

"What do you want from me? I'm under the harshest scrutiny. I've even asked Monsieur de la Tour to stop working on my portrait. Although I have no idea how long my looks will be worth committing to canvas."

Sophie had to accept that no help could be expected from the king's mistress. Madame de Pompadour was not ready to jeopardize her resurrection at court, which she had contrived with such difficulty. Not only had she walled up the connecting door to the king's chambers, but she had also cut off all access to her heart. Now there was only one person to whom Sophie could turn: Monsieur de Malesherbes, the director of the Royal Library and chief censor of the book trade. When he next called on her, she shared her worries with him.

Malesherbes took a pinch of snuff and slowly shook his head.

"Diderot should leave Paris; that's the only advice a reasonable man would give him. Unless he follows d'Alembert's example and distances himself from the *Encyclopedia*."

"Do you think a man would give up his life's work to save his life?"

"You seem to know human nature. I visited Diderot and advised him in person to flee. He reacted just as you suspected."

"You saw him?" said Sophie in surprise.

"By your leave, two days ago."

"What did he say?"

"He thinks that if he fled it would be perceived as an admission of guilt. So he has no intention of leaving Paris. He even refuses to visit his father, who is deathly ill in Langres; he doesn't want to give his opponents the slightest opening."

"But that's insane!"

"I would not venture to contradict you."

Sophie looked at Malesherbes. "If Diderot doesn't comprehend the danger he's in, others will have to act for him. We can't leave it to fate."

"What do you want me to do?"

"Lift the ban on the *Encyclopedia*, Monsieur de Malesherbes. No one can be persecuted because of a book that has been vouched for by the chief censor of France."

"I'm afraid you overestimate my powers. Forces are at work here against which I have no control. The very monarchy is at stake. There's no end in sight for the war with England and Prussia, and now it's raging in far-off America. The treasury is empty, the people are rebelling against the court—the whole country is in seething ferment. France is a powder keg."

"Is that the fault of the Encyclopedists? Or should we blame the ministers and their government?"

"This is not a question of placing blame, it's about power, Sophie, and the more the state sees its power threatened, the more vigorously it will defend itself. In that sense, it's like a wounded animal."

"Then we must find a way to appease it, soothe it, calm it."

"I'm afraid it's too late for that. The church and the parliament have formed an alliance against which no power on earth can fight—at least no power in France. Up until now Madame de Pompadour was still able to exert an ameliorating influence on the two parties, but now that she finds herself forced to fight for her own position. . . ."

"Won't you make an attempt, nevertheless?"

"I am a censor, hardly more than a police officer—"

"And if I beg you?" She pressed his arm. "For my sake . . ."

He returned her smile but then grew somber.

"Why do you take such a strong interest in the *Encyclopedia*?" he asked.

Sophie felt the blood rise to her cheeks. "You know that I knew Damiens."

Malesherbes shook his head. "You said that when you were in the employ of Monsieur Poisson, you possessed a copy of the lexicon. That is rather unusual for a maid." He gave her a searching look. "Where did you get the book, Sophie?"

Under his gray eyes it was no longer possible for her to lie. As hard as it was for her, she returned his gaze as she said in a hoarse voice, "Dorval is Diderot's son."

Malesherbes nodded. "I thought as much. You taught him to read using the *Encyclopedia*. Only love could inspire such an idea."

"Will you help me?" Sophie needed all her courage to ask this last question. "Will you help us anyway?"

77

※⟩ ⟨※

"What have I done to deserve this? This is a disgrace! Even the neighbors know that you're being forced to clear out!"

Diderot was hardly listening. Nanette stood behind him, lamenting over and over the fate that had chained her to him, while he packed his things. In feverish haste he looked through the papers scattered around the room—traces of his work and his life, all possible evidence for the prosecution. Wherever he looked he found incriminating material, in every box of notes, in every drawer, more than enough to put him away for the rest of his life in the fortress of Vincennes, if he were not led straight to the scaffold. What the alliance of church and state had not been able to accomplish in so many years had now been achieved with the cooperation of his old friend Rousseau: The *Encyclopedia*—the advance artillery of reason, the armada of philosophy, the siege engine of the enlightenment—was destroyed.

"Where's my dressing gown?"

"You want to take that old rag with you?"

"Without it I can't think."

He had resisted fleeing until the last moment. Le Bréton had actually done all he could to keep him in Paris; the old miser had even offered him a new contract—Diderot would earn 2,500 *livres* per volume in the future. But what had occurred in the past few weeks had exceeded the worst fears of the Encyclopedists. Defeat at every turn. An absolute triumph of reactionary thinking. The author of the essay "On the Spirit" had been the first to trigger the catastrophe, yet Helvétius, thanks to his protection by the court, had escaped virtually unscathed. In the meantime the *Encyclopedia* came under ever more intense fire. The director of the Royal Library was now the driving force behind the annihilation of the lexicon. Obviously the inconstant Malesherbes had finally cracked;

perhaps his father, the chancellor, Lamoignon, had had a powerful word to say. In any case, by council decree father and son had rescinded the printing permission and officially prohibited Le Bréton from continuing the project, stating that any benefits the arts and sciences might gain from the *Encyclopedia* were outweighed by the damages suffered by religion and morality. And the general advocate of parliament had asked the supreme court of the land to take action to the full extent of the law against those men who had misused the aims of philosophy to declare war on society, the state, and religious faith. The church had come down equally hard on the Encyclopedists. On March 5, 1759, Rome had put the *Encyclopedia* on the Index of forbidden books, and the pope had ordered all Catholics who owned copies of the banned volumes to have them burned by a priest—anyone who did not obey this order would be excommunicated. No book could be more unequivocally condemned.

"Damn it all! Who hid my dressing gown?"

"What do I care about your dressing gown? Tell me where you're going. What should I do if I need money? How can I reach you?"

At the Procope rumors had been circulating for days about an imminent wave of arrests. Superintendent Sartine, secretary to the lieutenant general of the Paris police, had been put in charge of the action, with a mandate to put an end to the conspiracy once and for all. But where could Diderot flee? To Geneva, to Voltaire? After the resignation of his friend d'Alembert, Voltaire had not only terminated his cooperation with the *Encyclopedia,* he had also demanded the return of all his manuscripts. To Berlin, to de Prades? The abbé had returned from exile and was already in prison, despite renouncing his earlier theses. Diderot had spent days and nights in dread and uncertainty before he finally decided to flee. When he awoke, a cockroach crawling across his blanket had triggered this decision.

"I want to try and reach the coast, and then take a boat to England," he told his wife as he leaned down and continued the search. "Thank God, here it is!"

He reached for the scarlet corner of the robe sticking out from under the table—and discovered his daughter, Angélique, who had been hiding at his feet under the dressing gown.

"England?" she asked with eyes wide with worry. "Where's that, Papa?"

"Across the sea," Nanette cried before Diderot could answer. "Far, far away—much farther than a person can swim."

Horrified, Angélique let go of the robe and flung her arms around Diderot's legs.

"You can't go to England, Papa!" she cried. "You mustn't, I won't let you!"

He almost had to use force to pry her off him, she was holding on so tight. His wife never stopped her grumbling and complaining.

"For a lifetime you've been ashamed of me, because you think I'm too stupid for your learned friends. All I was allowed to do was bear your children. But the whole time I always loved you and hoped that you would have some small affection for me. Now you finally have an excuse to leave me—"

All of a sudden Nanette stopped talking, and the next moment a calm, deep masculine voice was heard.

"Monsieur Diderot!"

He turned around. In the doorway stood Malesherbes, state councillor and chief censor of the king, flanked by two guardsmen.

78

Rumors of the raid had reached Sophie at Versailles, but they were so contradictory that each bit of news placed the previous claim in question. Could the truth be worse than this uncertainty? Upon leaving early mass the dauphin, Louis-Stanislas, had told his mother that the head of the serpent had been crushed underfoot and the danger forever averted. Sophie, walking behind the queen and her son as they exited the chapel, had been shocked almost to death. She knew that he could only mean Diderot.

Her hand was still trembling when a quarter of an hour later she handed her mistress a glass of donkey's milk. On orders from Dr. Quesnay, who was unable to diagnose the malady, some time ago a white mare donkey had been acquired, which Dorval looked after in a paddock behind the royal stables and milked twice a day. The night before, La Pompadour had suffered another severe attack of fever, the third in just a week. But the drink still showed no effect. While Sophie attended mass, La Pompadour had attempted to write a letter to the Duc Aiguillon to congratulate him on the victory over the British at Saint-Cast. But her strength had not been sufficient to guide the pen. Now, an hour later, she was resting on her ottoman, her eyes closed and her hand on her forehead.

"I feel unspeakably sorry for you," she said, taking the glass. "Ah, if only I could help you. But you can see what has become of me."

Sophie could see from her face that she was expressing genuine sympathy. As the marquise drank, Sophie said, "Monsieur de Malesherbes claimed to be my friend. So how could he do such a thing?"

La Pompadour put down the glass and looked at Sophie. "No one is more dangerous than a man who when courting a woman must take second place to another man. Jealousy is a far stronger motivation than greed or fear."

"I only hope that Sartine wasn't leading the search. He must hate Diderot. When I think what he might do in his rage . . ."

A servant cleared his throat at the doorway. Following him was a man in middle age who entered the room hastily, his tricorn under his arm. Sophie knew him slightly—it was the German journalist Melchior Grimm. As editor of the *Literary Correspondence,* a magazine with which he kept the courts of Europe informed about the intellectual life in the French capital, he was a frequent guest of La Pompadour. He seemed completely out of breath.

"They searched Diderot's house!" he blurted out, gasping for air while he was still bowing.

"You are speaking of the visit of Monsieur de Malesherbes to Rue Taranne?" asked La Pompadour. "We have already been informed of this."

"Malesherbes? No, a high-ranking police officer named Sartine, the secretary to the lieutenant general, led the action. He spent the entire day there, turning everything upside down, the study, the archives, the residence, the whole place!"

Sophie exchanged a horrified look with the marquise.

"Please, tell us exactly what happened," said La Pompadour, motioning her guest to a chair.

"Gladly, I wish nothing better."

But instead of telling them, Grimm had hardly taken a seat before he suddenly burst out laughing, giggling and chuckling foolishly like a child as he held his hand to his mouth; he even doubled over with merriment, as the tears ran down his cheeks.

Sophie no longer understood a thing. La Pompadour's expression darkened.

"If you would be so kind as to explain the reason for your boisterous joy?"

"They found nothing, madame!" Grimm finally burst out. "No manuscript, no notes, not a single word—it was all gone!"

"Pardon me?"

"Yes, madame. Just imagine. Diderot's workroom was as empty as the grave of Christ on Easter morning! Ah, how I wish I'd been there to see it. . . ."

79

❧ ❧

Diderot stood by his father's grave. He had folded his hands, but his lips remained silent. The grave was still fresh; it smelled of earth and withered flowers. A letter from his sister Denise, who lived with their parents in Langres—along with their younger brother Pierre-Didier, an intolerant, quarrelsome abbé—had called Diderot back to his birthplace, but by the time he arrived his father was dead. Now all he could do was attend to the inheritance matters.

With an air of gloom he looked at the simple gravestone. *Didier Diderot, cutler of Langres, 1695–1759.* The old man had died as he had lived: All his debts were paid, and a considerable fortune was left—real estate, pensions, inventories—which his heirs could now divide. Diderot knew that he would have no worries about money from now on.

He looked up from his father's grave and let his eyes wander. The cemetery was situated atop a hill overlooking the valley. It was the height of summer, and the whole countryside spread out before him in the shimmering sunlight was bursting with glorious bounty. As far as the eye could see stretched vineyards and undulating fields of grain, in which there was a humming of a million creatures—bees, other insects, birds—searching for mates and procreating. He hadn't been here in so many years. Should he ever have left?

The old town nestled gently at the foot of the hills. It seemed like a quiet corner of peace in the midst of the burgeoning landscape. Diderot saw the town hall, the cutlery, the Jesuit college that he had attended in his youth. With what pride his father had always received him when he came home with some new honor. . . . Didier Diderot had been a diligent craftsman who kept order in his house and at his workshop, a patriarch with a solid faith in the church. Denis would have become a priest or a craftsman if things had gone according to his father's wishes. The old man had admonished and exhorted his son; he had even had him locked up with the full power of fatherly authority, so that the Jesuits could cut his hair into a tonsure. And yet his father had always been an exemplar for him, despite all the tensions and conflicts between them—the best of all fathers. From him Denis had learned that agreements must be honored, and once taken on, jobs had to be properly carried out. Diderot thought he could still see his father sitting in his armchair, with his calm demeanor and his serene face, and he could still hear his voice.

"Denis Diderot?"

He turned around. An old, shriveled face was gazing at him. Diderot recognized the man at once in spite of all the wrinkles and creases.

"Père Lumière, the sexton, isn't it?"

The old man nodded. "Monsieur Diderot," he said, touching his arm, "you may be a good man, and in Paris you are perhaps even a famous man. But if you believe that you can ever measure up to the standard of your father, you are mistaken."

Without waiting for a reply he turned away and walked down the path toward the church, wagging his head. As Diderot watched him go, deep inside he had to admit that the man was right. His father had been an honest and upright man, always concerned with being of use to others. Yes, to be of use—that had been the main goal of his life. Diderot remembered a promise that he'd been forced to make to his father ten years earlier, as a condition for his father to support his family while he was imprisoned in the fortress of Vincennes: He had to promise to write with his pen a "decent work," using it to gain the blessing of Heaven and to win back the affection of his father.

Diderot ran his hand over his thinning hair. Had he created such a work with the *Encyclopedia*? Yes, he had done so, and this certainty filled him with pride. But he also knew that many times he himself was to blame for jeopardizing this work. Three times he had exposed the *Encyclopedia* to menacing attacks, each time caused by other books that were not worth the risk, and if the latest crisis did not mean the end of the lexicon, it would be a miracle—a miracle for which he could thank Malesherbes.

The panic that had shot through his limbs at the sight of the censor and the two guardsmen had lasted only a few seconds. Malesherbes had not come to Rue Taranne to seize him, but to warn him of his impending arrest. In a few hours, Malesherbes had told him, Superintendent

Sartine would appear with a dozen officers to search the house—he must get rid of all incriminating material immediately, on the spot!

"But where shall I put hundreds of manuscripts?" Diderot had asked. "Who could I find in such haste who would be willing to hide these papers? And with whom would they be safe?"

"Bring them all to me!" Malesherbes had replied. "No one will look for them in my house."

Then the censor had set off for Rue de la Harpe, to Le Bréton, and there he demanded that the publisher let him confiscate the texts, which were then transported off to his house as well. The last cartons were barely on their way before Sartine and his officers had knocked on Diderot's door. A few minutes sooner and the whole scheme would have been discovered.

Diderot turned back to his father's grave. As he directed his gaze at the fresh mound of earth with the wilted flowers, he raised his hand: Never again, so he swore to himself and to the old man, would he publish books that might endanger the *Encyclopedia*, not dramas or novels or pamphlets, even if he had to give up all hope of publishing his unwritten works!

The *Encyclopedia* was more important than any other book.

It was his life.

His world.

The new world.

80

❧ ❧

Seldom had Sophie been so happy to have been mistaken. Her despair over Malesherbes's supposed betrayal had given way, after learning of her error, to enormous relief. With a feeling of embarrassment she climbed into the coach and set off to thank the director of the Royal Library.

She entered the city through Porte de Saint-Cloud. It was the first time in months that she had been back to Paris. She hadn't realized how much she had missed the bustle of the capital. How wonderfully loud and colorful life was here compared to Versailles, where all events took place as if on a theater stage, at once artificial and contrived, stage-managed by the ailing and the ancient who feigned a lust for life, although beneath the garish makeup on their cheeks all the blood had long since drained from their veins. Sophie opened the window to hear the cries of the street merchants, who drowned out the noise and tumult of the intersections as they sang the praises of used hats, rusty pots, and torn rags. Water carriers, with a pail hanging on either side of them, hurried through the throng and vanished into the houses, where for two *sous* they lugged their load all the way up to the mansard. As the coaches drove along the quays, where rogues and pickpockets teemed among the shopkeepers' booths, Sophie breathed deeply of the street air. All the old familiar smells, the mist off the Seine, the stink of fish and rotten vegetables, of garbage heaps and cesspools—now they seemed to her the thousand lovely aromas of the Orient.

Suddenly a great bellowing commenced, giving Sophie a start. The next moment the coachman reined in the horses, and with a jolt the coach came to a halt. Sophie leaned out the window. In the middle of the street in front of a butcher shop an ox was writhing in the ropes tied to its horns and legs, with which two apprentices were trying to bring the animal under control. A gigantic butcher, his arms bare, his neck fat, stepped before the beast with his blood-smeared apron, swung back a heavy club, and smashed its skull. With a loud groan the ox sank to the ground, its mighty body twitching and thrashing. Even as the legs were still kicking, the butcher fell on the beast again and hewed his broad knife into its throat. Blood gushed out and covered the street in a torrent, steaming as it flowed into the gutter, where the cheap whores squatting on the curb watched the blood color the shoes of the passersby red.

Feeling sick, Sophie pulled the curtain closed. Why was there no law to forbid slaughtering on the open street? Fortunately the horses soon set off, and the journey continued. At the Pont Neuf they crossed the Seine. The closer they came to the Tuileries, the more the noise outside diminished. Soon Sophie could even hear the twittering of the birds.

"Whoa!"

The coach stopped on Rue Vivienne. Sophie looked up at the façades of tall, imposing buildings. All the banks of Paris were located on this street. Here there was more money to be found than in the entire rest of the city. The portal of the Palais Malesherbes, which loomed kitty-corner from the discount bank, was guarded by two doormen in livery. Sophie opened the door and descended from the coach. Madame de Pompadour had told her that Malesherbes's wife lived in the country with the children.

The director of the Royal Library received her with a kiss on the hand.

"What an undeserved honor."

"I came," Sophie replied, "to beg your pardon."

"I? Pardon you? But why?"

"I gave outward appearances greater credence than my inner conviction. I thought you wanted to destroy Monsieur Diderot."

"The father of your son?"

He was still holding her hand as he gazed at her with his gray eyes. She decided not to pull her hand away.

"You must have misunderstood my actions, Sophie. But how else could you have interpreted my ban on the *Encyclopedia*? I am the one who must beg your pardon," he insisted when she tried to argue. "But believe me, the only way I could save the lexicon was to prohibit its distribution. Public opinion needed a scapegoat, and I had to do something to pacify the populace. That's the only reason I rescinded the printing privilege."

"I still reproach myself," said Sophie. "Even if appearances spoke against you—I should have known that you were not capable of such a betrayal." She gratefully squeezed his hand. "You put your career at risk, Monsieur de Malesherbes. They could have denounced you for high treason; Sartine would not have wasted a second if he had arrived—"

"Shhhh . . ." he said, placing a finger to her lips.

Indignantly she shook her head—she hated this gesture. But then she saw his face.

A warm smile filled his gray eyes. His gaze embraced her like a gentle sunset after a long, stormy day. She saw only understanding, tenderness, love; a feeling of warm, sincere security flowed through her.

Sophie closed her eyes and waited for his kiss.

BOOK V

Thistles and Thorns

1760–1766

81

The sweet smell of decay hung over Paris, drifting through the streets and alleys, settling over the marketplace squares of the magnificent city, fermenting and coagulating into a stifling, viscous stillness. Since the attack on the king it seemed as though life itself had retreated from Paris. A leaden calm had overcome the great kraken, under which the inhabitants grew weary, as if anesthetized for all eternity.

Not a breeze stirred to freshen the air and fill it with new life. Where would a breeze come from? Narrow, winding streets made free circulation of the air impossible; it was contaminated by the ever-present stink from the slaughterhouses and fish halls, the cesspits and cemeteries. The bridge houses over the river blocked the wind from moving from one end of the city to the other and carrying away the bad air filling the streets. No one could take a step or a breath without being followed by the stench of extinguished life rising up from the mire and garbage, the excrement and spilled blood.

Most to blame for the infernal vapors were the open privies in all the buildings. Yet every family demanded use of its own latrine, as if it were a matter of class privilege. It wasn't enough that the most abominable stench came from the countless fecal pits; many sewers were so absurdly located that their contents seeped into the adjacent springs. The bakers were dependent on the springwater and could not do without it, so even the bread, the most common and everyday foodstuff of the people, was rife with the traces of death.

When the latrines were emptied the smell of manure spread through the city even at dawn. With ashen faces as pale as the grave, the sewer cleaners climbed down into the interior of the pits. Ravaged by the poisonous gases, they fortified themselves with liquor so as not to succumb to the pestilential miasmas of the underworld; incapable of ever escaping their fate, they damned their return into this hell day after day. In order to save themselves the trouble of transporting the sewage outside the gates of the city, they poured the brown effluvia that they brought up to the light from the stinking darkness into the drainage ditches and gutters. In this way they emptied it out in the direction of the Seine and contaminated the banks of the river. That was where the water carriers dipped their pails into the water, which they then brought back to the houses for the Parisians to use for washing and drinking.

But most disgusting was the stink exuded by the churches. Many houses of God were so polluted by the odors coming from the corpses laid out on biers that the faithful refused to set foot inside. So as not to lose their loyal following, the priests claimed that what they thought was the smell of death was in reality only a harmless musty odor lodged in the old masonry. Every corpse, they assured the congregation, was taken on the night after the funeral to the cemeteries, and not a single one remained inside the church crypts. But who would give credence to such protestations? The stench of dead bodies poisoned every worship service and every mass, while outside the churches, fires were kept burning to drive off the evil Mephistophelian vapors. Those fires were like impotent flickering purgatories that offered not the slightest remedy for the intolerable social evils.

So the great kraken continued to vegetate, anesthetized by the corpse-like stench of its own body, which seemed already in a state of decay, even before the kraken had breathed its last. Would it ever again have the power to rise up from its muddy bed? To shed its putrifying odor and renew itself, sprouting a new head and limbs?

82

The tower bells of Saint-Germain-des-Prés were already summoning the faithful to the angelus when Diderot left his house on Rue Taranne. He had to hurry to make his appointment at seven with a watchmaker on the Quai de l'Horloge; he wanted to be there on time. If he arrived too late, the master might have begun the work, and his efforts would be in vain.

The first lemonade waiters were already carrying their trays, as in the wan light of the breaking day the nighttime carousers were returning home from their rendezvous with prostitutes. They looked pale and the worse for wear as they dragged themselves across Place Taranne. All day long they would rue the squandered night, just as the gamblers would; they were only now leaving their dim caves, although the bright hammering of the tinkers could already be heard. Diderot had nothing but contempt for idlers. If they were the ones who decided things, all the smiths who scraped their files in the morning, all the wheelwrights who riveted iron hoops onto wheels, and all the peddlers who wandered through the alleys hawking their wares would be banned from the city. The bells could no longer toll, the drums of the guard would fall silent, and the streets would have to be upholstered so that the coaches could roll along the pavement noiselessly, waiting for these layabouts to climb out of their old beds.

Diderot was an early riser, like the workmen and craftsmen streaming out of the buildings everywhere, keeping him company as they set off to work. What luck that he was able to continue his work on the *Encyclopedia*! He had Malesherbes to thank for this miracle. The censor had not only decided tacitly to tolerate the publication, but he had also made possible its continuation through arrangements and agreements that effectively canceled all official sanctions. To be sure, Malesherbes

had obliged the publisher to pay seventy-two *livres* to each subscriber as
compensation for the canceled volumes that now could not be printed,
but in order to circumvent his own ban, which would have unquestion-
ably ruined the entire enterprise, he had simultaneously given Le Bréton
permission to satisfy the claims of the customers by supplying graphic
works. In addition, he had granted permission to print *A Collection of a
Thousand Plates on the Sciences, the Free Arts, and Technology,* an apparently harmless title that happened to conceal the graphic volumes of
the *Encyclopedia*. Because the subscribers were also content with this
settlement—not one had demanded a refund from Le Bréton—the work
could therefore be carried on under the protection of the censor, as if
there had never been any prohibition of the *Encyclopedia*.

Diderot had worked out the following plan with his publisher: As
they delivered the officially approved graphic volumes year after year so
as to keep the subscribers happy, they would at the same time finish work
on the remaining but prohibited ten volumes of text. These they would
produce at a fictitious printing location "abroad," such as on the island of
"Cythera" as had been done years before with *The Indiscreet Jewels,* and
then offer them all at once to the public as "imported" works—in the
hope that by then the fury on the part of the government and the church
would have subsided.

In order to reach this goal, Diderot worked like a man possessed.
From morning till night he was occupied with his work. His primary
ambition, of course, was the production of the graphic volumes. These
were supposed to be put into the hands of experts in the various fields,
such as his father; into the hands of craftsmen and engineers who were
familiar with every little line and would want to work from the draw-
ings to improve their products. The illustrations would depict the status
of technology more exactly and vividly than any work ever before, as
well as uniting the beauty of the rendering and the scientific precision
in new ways. Every day Diderot sought out craftsmen for this purpose,
visiting the workshops of hosiers, tapestry workers, and cabinetmakers,
asking them about their tools and methods, delving into the secrets of
looms and the mechanics of block and tackle; he listened to lectures on
chemistry and physics, made his own sketches and models, instructed
the draftsmen and graphic artists, so that everything would be depicted
as precisely as possible. In the meantime, Jaucourt, busy as a bee, would
deal with editing the text volumes. He excerpted, compiled, and wrote.

One entry after another, reviewing contributions, working indefatigably day after day, without ever tiring of the onslaught of articles, as if God had created him specifically for this activity—yes, the *chevalier* even sold one of his own houses in order to hire half a dozen scribes at his expense, thus ensuring the survival of the *Encyclopedia*.

At the Hôpital Bicêtre, Diderot had to hold his sleeve over his mouth, the stench was so revolting. Workers wearing masks had recently tossed out the pieces of dismembered corpses on which young students of anatomy had practiced their essential art. The loaded cart now stood before the entrance of the hospital, bound for the cesspit. Diderot was indignant: When would the city finally begin to combat the devilish air and its deadly effects with the modern methods of chemistry?

Each month dozens of people died from the poisonous vapors and emanations of the city. New experiments had been promised to study the subversion of the air and gain the upper hand over the stinking scourge. What a dereliction of duty on the part of the magistrate to close his eyes to the miracles of chemistry! Could there be anything more important for a government than promoting the health of its citizens? Didn't the strength of future generations depend on such municipal services? Far better now, using the methods of science, to reduce the number of accidents and diseases caused by the emptying of latrines and cesspits, than to support the victims of the polluted air with alms and hospital beds later on. Diderot decided to write an article on the topic.

When he reached the quay a fresh morning breeze was rising off the Seine, which for an instant seemed to drive off all the stink of filth and decay. Diderot remained standing next to the riverbank wall. He inhaled the clean air as deeply as he could, feeling it stream into his lungs and give him new vitality. Would the *Encyclopedia* someday, like this breeze, chase away the degeneracy and decay from the minds of men and the chancellery chambers of the government?

Only a stone's throw away were the steps leading down to the Seine. The sight of the place pierced his very soul. That was where he always used to meet Sophie. Since their last encounter at the Salon d'Holbach after the performance of *The Natural Son,* Diderot knew that she would refuse any further contact with him. Did he want to see her again? It was said that in the meantime she had become the mistress of Malesherbes. That made the answer to his question superfluous.

The bells of Notre-Dame struck seven times. Diderot turned to continue on his way. No, he had decided to pin all his hopes and efforts on the success of the lexicon. His dream was that the *Encyclopedia* would someday be among the most requested works from the booklenders, copies that would be dirty and torn, dog-eared and covered with grease spots, well worn from the eager hands of the masses: a repository of all knowledge that enlightened people would use daily just as the women at church used their prayer books. No power in the world would prevent him from realizing this dream.

But above all he dreamed of one day handing over the completed work to his children, Dorval and Angélique: all the knowledge of humanity, the pure, complete truth, the map to paradise on earth—as his legacy to his descendants.

83

❧ ❧

Escorted by Malesherbes, Sophie entered the Comédie Française, where her companion retained a box in his position as the director of the Royal Library. But why did the theater seem to be occupied like an army field camp? At the entrance a whole company of sentries with shouldered muskets received the theatergoers as if expecting an enemy, although the performance was only a comedy by Voltaire. The grim expression of the guard major as he loaded the barrel of his musket in full view of the audience gave no doubt of his determination to defend the theater like a fortress against any attack.

Today was the anniversary of the day that Sophie had entered into a liaison with Malesherbes at the court. The fact that the state councillor had been married for more than ten years did not stand in the way of such an arrangement. A marriage, as Madame de Pompadour had explained to Sophie, was not witnessed in Heaven but before the notary; the deciding factor was not love, but reason. Every man had a mistress, every woman a male "friend of the family"; that was the custom to which no one with a little *savoir-vivre* could object. Sophie had gradually gotten used to these arrangements between the sexes just as she had the wigs on her head and the thick layer of powder that now covered the freckles on her cheeks.

No, she had not regretted for a moment that she had followed the advice of her patroness and yielded to the director of the Royal Library. Malesherbes was a man as intelligent as he was loving, and not only did he take care of her in a charming manner, but he also showed the most touching concern for her son, Dorval, almost as if the boy were his own flesh and blood. Besides, Sophie and Malesherbes felt bound to each other by their common interest in the *Encyclopedia*. The fact that she had once been Diderot's lover did not prevent the censor from supporting the other man's lifework to the best of his ability. La Pompadour claimed that Malesherbes was even going to back Diderot's candidacy for the Académie, which Voltaire had recently proposed. Such public acknowledgment would put an end to the constant attacks on both the *Encyclopedia* and the character of its editor.

In the theater parterre an awful shoving and jostling was going on as Sophie and Malesherbes took their seats in the box. The crush was so great that people were fighting with loud curses over the seats in the parquet, threatening to crack one another's ribs. A fusilier with a big mustache began herding the spectators in rows like chickens on the roost and using the power of his position to decide how many backsides could fit onto each bench. In the meantime, in the box a lackey served ginger confections and champagne. Malesherbes declined both, taking out instead his tin of snuff.

"Now tell me what's on your mind," Sophie demanded with a laugh after she had taken a nip from her glass. "If you need to take a pinch, it must be something serious. Is it perhaps that you are considering using the informal *tu* with me at last?"

"How well you know me," he replied. "Yes, Sophie, the intimacy of addressing each other as *tu* is my most ardent wish, but I do not yet dare ask this of you. I would rather propose something else, a suggestion that concerns our life together."

"So solemn, Monsieur de Malesherbes? Does your proposal perhaps have something to do with our first anniversary together?"

"Not directly, but today seems to me a suitable time to voice my suggestion—"

He was interrupted by loud applause and howling coming from back in the parterre section. Sophie gazed over the railing at the stage below. She was no less curious about the announced comedy than she was about the audience, which the guardsmen managed to control only by using their fists.

Finally the curtain went up. The name of the play was *Les Écossaises*, and in the program it was noted that the title was a translation from the English phrase "The Scottish Ladies." But actually the play was Voltaire's answer to the libeling of the philosophers by the self-appointed savers of souls in the churches, the hussars of the pulpit and cannons of God, who never tired of taking the field against the *Encyclopedia*. This time the Jesuits were again on stage, to be presented as toads, serpents, and spiders—a zoological garden of malice populated by all the creatures that God had excluded from His love.

"So that must be why there's such a contingent of soldiers here!"

As Sophie again regretted that Madame de Pompadour had not been able to come along because of a feverish indisposition, the audience in the parterre was raising a ruckus. The spectators were yelling and whistling so loudly that the actors could hardly be heard; they threw fruit and vegetables and kept interrupting the performance with frantic applause, so that the guardsmen had to intervene every couple of minutes to quell their enthusiasm.

"Do you remember, Monsieur de Malesherbes, what you told me about the audience at our first encounter?"

"That it's the only authority that is always right?"

Sophie nodded. "I think that today I understand the reason: Each individual in the audience may be an idiot, but taken as a whole they represent genius."

"Indeed," Malesherbes agreed with her. "The spectators in the parterre should be allowed to clap and whistle as they please. That won't make us attack the enemies of the state any less decisively when we catch sight of them. But what are you looking at?"

It had not escaped his notice that Sophie was barely listening. She was distracted by the gaze of a man who was also watching the events, from a neighboring box: Father Radominsky, the father confessor of the queen. With a stony face he witnessed the performance, alone in the lion's den, while the actors on stage mocked him and his kind.

"To think he has the courage to show himself here," said Malesherbes. "I must respect the man!"

"Indeed," replied Sophie. "But if I'm not mistaken, you wanted to make me a proposal regarding our life together?"

Instead of answering at once, Malesherbes awkwardly took another pinch of snuff. Annoyed by this unusual show of solemnity, Sophie put her hand to her throat as she returned his glance. But her fingers found nothing to grasp. He had asked her to leave the talisman at home this evening. He did not care for the little carved angel.

Finally he blew his nose. Then he gazed at her and said, "Have you ever considered, Sophie, getting a divorce from Monsieur Sartine?"

84

Father Radominsky stood at the front of his theater box and stared at the stage; his hands gripped the railing as if wanting to crush it. His face betrayed no hint of the turmoil going on inside him. He had to force himself not to vomit, so violent was the revulsion engendered by the vulgarity displayed below him on the stage. The play being performed by a horde of garishly made-up actors signified a repudiation of all the values he had fought for his whole life. The Word of God, the revealed truth, was being sacrificed on the altar of human reason, with unforeseeable consequences for the faith and the kingdom.

Radominsky's gloomy thoughts were no figment of his imagination, no narrow-minded reaction to the personal affront he was witnessing here. The play, which delighted the audience members like swine at a trough of stinking offal, was more than mere theater. The godless subversion that was being perpetrated in public had already had an effect that reached beyond the stage—it had penetrated deep into the heart of the Catholic Church, spreading like a cancer. Even the pope and his cardinals had been affected by it, not to mention the king of France and his ministers, incapable of distinguishing between friend and foe.

As Radominsky watched how he and his brothers of the faith were ridiculed, he asked himself a bitter question: Had the alliance with his enemies, the Jansenist heretics, been the biggest mistake of his life?

After the assassination attempt on the king and the execution of the assailant, the Society of Jesus was no longer given any peace. Previously the group had been regarded as an unshakable power in the state and the rest of the world, with great influence in the royal courts, endless reserves of funds, with the Holy Spirit on its side. But now the order was fighting for its very survival. This time it was not only the familiar antagonists of the faith threatening disaster; the decisive blow had been delivered by forces that had been reliable supporters of the order for more than two centuries.

Everything was connected to everything else—it was as though some- one had spit in the ocean on the other side of the world, and now the waves propagated by this inconspicuous event threatened to inundate all of France. The storm had started in the Jesuit colonies of the New World, on the Lesser Antilles in far-off America, where a few hun- dred thousand *Indios* had led an almost vegetative existence under the leadership of industrious priests, ruled by the clock from morning till night. But a curse had hovered over this quiet corner of the globe; the enterprises of the pious community had been haunted by misfortune. A scourge had raged among the *Indios*; there had been uprisings and bloody campaigns to remind the natives of their destiny to serve their white masters as slaves—though without success. A bank that had financed the Jesuit mission had collapsed; the order, previously so wealthy, was sud- denly oppressed by huge debts, which now had to be paid back by all the provinces of the Society of Jesus, even if they had nothing to do with the colonies. The consular court in Paris had ruled that the mission admin- istrator must make a payment of 30,000 *louis d'or* because the Jesuits all over the world were led by *one* general, and therefore each province must assume responsibility for all the others—otherwise the creditor could appropriate all assets of the Society in France. The Paris Provinciale had immediately lodged an objection to this judgment, but the supreme court of the land, the parliament, which was infiltrated by Jansenist lickspittles and traitors, had decided in favor of the shared liability of all sectors of the order.

What a devilish plan! In order to distract the populace from the unfortunate war that France had been waging for years against Prussia and Britain with no end in sight, the government had decided to perse- cute the Jesuits in the dubious hope of alleviating the financial straits of the state by seizing the assets of the order. As it focused on the annihila- tion of the Society of Jesus, the parliament heaped the most offensive calumny and accusations on the priests, ranging from blasphemy and lies regarding magic and murder to accusations of whoring and pederasty. Twenty-four Jesuit works were condemned because they allegedly justi- fied regicide and denied the Gallican freedoms of the Catholic Church in France. At the same time the court forbade the order to take in novi- tiates and offer public or private lessons. This led to the unfortunate consequence that even the Holy Father in Rome voiced accusations against the Society of Jesus.

"There! Look at the black crow!"

An object came flying toward Radominsky, barely missing his head. Suddenly he was looking down at hundreds of faces staring up at him with lascivious and greedy expressions, as if at an execution. Men and women shook their fists at him, whistled and jeered. Would the curse of Francesco di Borgia, the third general of the order, be fulfilled? "There will come a time," the holy man had prophesied to his brothers in the faith, "when your pride and ambition will know no limits, and you will think only of heaping up riches and gaining influence, but you will neglect to practice the virtues. Then there will be no power on earth that can lead you back to your original perfection, and if it is possible to annihilate you, it will be done."

The soldiers drew their swords to keep the rabble under control, but the shouts in the parquet only grew louder.

"Down with the priests! Hang the vultures in cassocks from the lampposts!"

An egg smashed against Radominsky's cassock. But the man of God did not shrink back—he had never before retreated from his enemies. With head held high he endured all that was hurled and shouted at him, defiling his priest's vestments and his honor with rotten fruit and disgraceful epithets. The order of Creation was at stake, but as long as the Lord God gave him strength, he would defend His works in the certainty that in the end Providence would triumph over the Antichrist.

No, Father Radominsky did not falter. As he endured the attacks without complaint, he prayed to the Lord God for a sign that the time of trials would soon come to an end.

Not until the curtain finally fell did he turn away and leave his box. He did not acknowledge the Judas kiss of Chrétien de Malesherbes, the chief censor of the land, who nodded to him from the box nearby.

85

"What do you mean—adopt?"

"To take you as his son, like a father."

"But I already have a father; he wrote the great book, the *Encyclopedia*! Why should I have a new father?"

The incomprehension of his youth spoke from Dorval's bright blue eyes; he was only eight, after all. For the past half hour he'd been pelting Sophie with questions because he couldn't grasp what she was trying to explain to him. And was that any wonder? She herself had recoiled in shock from the proposal that Malesherbes had made last evening at the theater: The director of the Royal Library wanted to adopt her son, as a sign of his devotion to her. So he had asked her to consider getting a divorce from Sartine, since Dorval was still legally considered his son.

"I don't want a new father," Dorval repeated. "Why can't I be with my real father?"

"You know that he lives in Paris. He has to stay there to finish writing the great book."

"Then we should move to Paris. Maybe I could help him."

"That's impossible. Madame de Pompadour is ill, and she needs my help to get well."

"Then my father should come here. We have plenty of room."

"How can you say such a thing? There's no work for him to do here. How would he earn a living?"

"He can help me milk the donkeys. Then Madame would certainly have nothing against him coming here. And don't worry about food. The cook is a friend of mine." Dorval was so excited that he was gasping as he talked. "You still love him, don't you?" he asked suddenly.

Sophie had to swallow hard, the question came so unexpectedly.

"Love," she said, "is the most beautiful thing in the world, but it seldom lasts for a whole lifetime."

"I don't believe it!" he exclaimed. "I'll always love you, for as long as I live. Even if the king forbids it!"

"That makes me very happy, my dear, but it's not the same. Parents and their children always love each other for their whole lives. But it's different between men and women."

"What's different about it? If you love somebody, then you love him."

"Ah, how can I explain it to you?" She took him by the shoulders and looked him in the eye. "So you don't like Monsieur de Malesherbes at all?"

"I do. He's always very nice to me. But—I don't want to have two fathers."

Sophie couldn't meet his gaze any longer. She had an uneasy feeling. Everything spoke in favor of accepting Malesherbes's proposal, above all in view of Dorval's future—such an adoption would elevate him to the nobility. Nevertheless the idea still seemed wrong to her. Malesherbes had recognized her ambivalence and suggested that she allow Dorval to decide for himself; she simply had to give him the opportunity to understand the advantages of adoption. But how could she succeed in that if she wasn't sure of her own view on the matter?

"Now listen to me," she said at last, "I want to tell you a story."

"A story?" Dorval asked, surprised.

"Yes, listen to this." She sat down on a chair and took his hand. Reluctantly he allowed her to hold it as she began the story. "Once upon a time, many, many years ago in the Middle East, there lived a poor beggar boy. He lived all alone with his mother in a tiny hut on the edge of the village. The boy's name was Dorval and his mother was Sophie, and both of them loved each other more than any two people in the world. And yet they were missing something that would make them truly happy—a family."

"Why are you telling me this, Mama?" Dorval asked in annoyance, pulling away his hand. "We're not poor at all. And . . . and we don't live in the Middle East either."

When Sophie saw his reproachful expression, she felt ashamed. She had tried to explain everything to him the way her father would have done, or like Diderot—with a story.

"You're right," she said. "You're too big for fairy tales."

"Why do you want Monsieur de Malesherbes to be my father?" he asked solemnly.

She decided not to make any more excuses. "Because I think there would be no better father for you. As his son you would belong to one of the most powerful families in France. Then you would be a real prince."

"A real prince?" His eyes lit up for a moment. "With my own castle?"

"Not just one! As far as I know, Monsieur de Malesherbes has half a dozen castles. One of them is even in my hometown, on the Loire. Then I could show you where I used to live."

"He has a castle on the Loire?"

"Yes, with vineyards and meadows for the horses, and of course many, many craftsmen."

"Cooks and smiths too?"

"And cartwrights, and I even think he has his own Swiss guard."

"With a real captain?"

"A real captain of the guard!"

As she spoke she could see the idea gaining ground inside him. The growing light in his eyes almost broke her heart. Although it cost her a great effort of will, she said, "Do you believe me now, that there could be no better father for you?"

"Except my real father," he said softly.

"Naturally," she said, and had to hold back her tears. "So what do you say, shouldn't we at least give it a try?"

Timidly, almost imperceptibly, he nodded.

"But you must tell me one thing, Mama . . ."

"What is it, my darling?"

"Can I keep living with you even if Monsieur de Malesherbes adopts me?"

"But of course! Did you think I would let you go?"

"And can I keep on milking the donkey mare and feeding the birds?"

"Every day! Morning and evening."

"And we'll keep living here, and I can visit the cook in the kitchen and the smith in the stall and the cartwright and the captain?"

"As often as you like."

Dorval fell silent. He was thinking so hard that a frown settled over his little face. Finally he said, "Would you be very happy if I said yes?"

Although every fiber of her being resisted, Sophie nodded.

"All right then, Mama, I agree."

Without a word she took him in her arms and hugged him tight so that he wouldn't see the tears running down her cheeks.

86

Antoine Sartine was leafing through a file that he had just taken from the shelf after he made sure that the door to his office was locked. He had compiled this file expressly for his personal use, without the knowledge of his superior, and had made all the entries in his own hand. Since his promotion to magistrate, he was now the third-highest officer in the Paris police and had several secretaries under him to whom he normally dictated his reports. This dossier concerned none of the usual garret scribblers or coffeehouse philosophers, with whom his investigations usually dealt—this dossier was about a man who seemed above all suspicion and yet who for some time had been the cause of considerable irritation: Chrétien Lamoignon de Malesherbes, son of the chancellor and chief censor of His Majesty the king.

Could this man still be trusted? Sartine had begun keeping the dossier after his unsuccessful raid on Diderot's house. Rumors had been circulating in the police ranks, highly confusing rumors about the role that the director of the Royal Library was said to have played in this action. Since then Sartine had been writing down in this dossier everything that seemed noteworthy about the chief censor. In only a few months it had turned into one of the most problematic files that he had ever assembled, full of contradictions and inconsistencies. Malesherbes associated with the archbishop of Paris as well as with shadowy figures such as Rousseau and d'Alembert; in the morning he was always present during the king's *lever* audience in Versailles, and in the afternoon he attended lectures at the Académie des Sciences. He had once warned of the rebellious gazettes from Holland that were being disseminated in France and threatening to set the entire kingdom aflame; yet he held his protective hand over the *Encyclopedia*, which was causing greater damage than all the publications in the rest of Europe.

But most bewildering was the "Memorandum Concerning Freedom of the Press," which Malesherbes had personally drafted at the request of the dauphin. The pamphlet offered a few sentences on the defense of the state and church against the attacks of the philosophers; accordingly, all books were to be forbidden that "disparaged individual persons, endangered the government, or took positions against good morals or religion." This was followed by a whole flood of sentences that were nothing but blatant incitements to rebellion. "We live," it said, "in a century and in a country where it is concomitant to a crime to make efforts on behalf of the public welfare . . . It is political unrest that has led to a lack of restraint in what is published; the texts are not the cause of the unrest . . . If we prohibit the spread of erroneous thinking, we will obstruct the promulgation of truth, because new truths are always considered erroneous ideas for a certain period of time . . ."

Sartine read through the entire dossier carefully; he had compiled under six different headings all the information about his superior that he'd been able to gather in recent months. Even though he had no idea what awaited him this afternoon, it was always beneficial to study a person in detail before meeting him. Malesherbes had summoned him to his city residence on Rue Vivienne at five o'clock. An unusual place for an official discussion.

Two hours later the director of the Royal Library welcomed him to his elegant salon. "How nice to see you. I suggest we have a little glass first."

"Gladly," replied Sartine, although he otherwise never touched alcohol on duty.

A lackey offered him a glass of sherry from a tray, as if he were a good friend of the host—another reason to be irritated. As Malesherbes motioned him to take a seat, Sartine looked around. On principle he had vowed never to question the possessions of others, but rather to rejoice in what he himself had achieved. But here he was faced with luxurious mirrors and lamps, decorative gilt and plaster, paintings and tapestries, expensive furniture, and carpets into which his feet sank; for a moment his principle wavered. Would he ever possess such a house? Certainly not, no matter how many sacrifices he made in the discharge of his duty. In order to maintain such a house as a police officer, he would have to become the lieutenant general himself. But such a position required a noble title as well as a personal fortune, and was beyond his reach.

"It is a great honor for me to be received here by you," Sartine said, without taking the proffered chair. "May I ask the reason you have summoned me?"

"But of course, naturally, why not, I was just about to get to that," replied Malesherbes more verbosely than was his custom. He got up from his chair when he saw that his guest made no move to sit down. "You have done me some important services in the past, Sartine, and you know how much I appreciate your work. Today, however, I would like to ask you a favor that would mean more to me than anything you have done for me heretofore, although it involves a matter that is of a rather private nature." He cleared his throat and took another sip of his drink. Then he said, "I would like you to get a divorce."

"Pardon me?" said Sartine, completely caught off guard.

Malesherbes merely nodded.

"Pardon, monsieur, but as far as my marital status, I see no reason to make any changes."

"I am aware," said Malesherbes with a strained smile, "that the notion must surprise you; I also openly admit that I have neither the legal right nor the means to force you to take such a step. But I ask you to consider our relationship of many years—and to accept my assurance that if you should accommodate my request, it would prove advantageous to you."

He gazed at Sartine, but the latter did not flinch under the searching glance of his superior, although his hand holding the glass was trembling so much that he was afraid of spilling its contents.

"To make myself perfectly clear," Malesherbes went on, "the extent of my gratitude would correspond to the enormity of the favor that I am asking of you."

As if to reinforce his words, he took a pinch of snuff.

Sartine knew this gesture. "As you know," he said hesitantly, "I have lived apart from my wife for years. Nevertheless, your question catches me entirely unprepared. . . . A divorce is a very serious matter—"

"As is the life of a young person," Malesherbes interrupted him. "To put it briefly: I need your consent to adopt Dorval."

"You want to adopt my wife's son?" Sartine asked, astonished for the second time, and set down his glass. "Why in Heaven's name would you want to do that?"

"I would like to give the boy a future. A future that corresponds to his talents."

"Please don't think me dim-witted, but to be frank, I . . . still don't understand . . . I have personally never even considered such an idea. . . . And besides, a divorce, how can you suggest such a thing?" In his distress only the words of the Bible came to him: "What God hath joined together, let no man put asunder."

"Indeed, so it is written," Malesherbes confirmed. "But fortunately, for each of its well-founded rules the Catholic Church has an equally well-founded exception." He took a document from his writing table and handed it to Sartine. "Here, I have had everything prepared."

In total confusion Sartine took the page, but he was unable to read the few lines that seemed to dance before his eyes. Naturally he knew that Sophie had been the mistress of his superior for over a year; every time he thought about it, this knowledge bored deeper and more painfully into his soul. But what reason could Malesherbes have for taking the son of Diderot into his family? Diderot was an enemy of the state, Dorval a bastard, a changeling—certainly Malesherbes couldn't ignore that! Was it possible that love could blind a man to such a degree? Sartine gazed at the sheet of paper in his hand, saw the letters, the words, the sentences that now seemed to leap toward him, as if mocking him. He felt a stab of pain in his heart as he grasped their meaning; all the misery that Sophie had inflicted on him overwhelmed him anew. And now her lover was demanding that he publicly admit his humiliation, the worst humiliation a man could endure in life.

"But Dorval is my son," he said, all at once making a decision.

Malesherbes gave a dismissive wave. "Don't bother lying, I already know the truth."

"I have no idea what you're insinuating," Sartine replied firmly. "But whatever it is—I refuse to agree to the divorce."

"You are defying my express wishes?"

"Precisely!"

"You certainly have nerve. . . . I hadn't expected this, after all that I've done for you." Malesherbes's expression suddenly turned hard. "Then I have no choice but to change my request to an order. I demand your signature, Sartine. Immediately!"

"I won't even consider it."

"I repeat: That's an order!"

"It makes no difference to me!"

"You're refusing to obey me?"

"My conscience is clear. In all my years of service I have never once committed any sort of infraction. I'm not sure whether you could say the same about yourself."

"What are you getting at?"

"With your 'Memorandum Concerning Freedom of the Press' you have left behind a trail that could be very dangerous for you."

"Are you threatening me?"

"In that pamphlet you set the freedom of thought above the freedom of the state to defend itself against its enemies," replied Sartine. "For that, any other author would be sentenced to several years' imprisonment, if not to death."

"That may be," said Malesherbes with a shrug, "but you forget who I am."

"Not at all," said Sartine, aroused by this show of arrogance. "It's merely a question of how long you will continue to enjoy the advantages of your present status. I have information that points to serious abuse of your position. Witnesses have testified that you personally circumvented Diderot's arrest by warning him of the raid; some say that you even helped him to remove incriminating material. Such an act would constitute high treason."

Sartine had delivered the threat based on nothing more than a suspicion he had derived from rumors and conjectures, but from the expression on his superior's face he knew that he had hit the bull's-eye. Would the powerful man now realize that this was no buffoon standing before him?

"You loathsome little spy," said Malesherbes, and his gray eyes expressed profound contempt. "Get out of my house at once!"

"By your leave," said Sartine, taking his tricorn, which a lackey handed to him.

As the door opened he let his gaze sweep over the room one last time. No, he didn't belong in this world. Malesherbes had already turned his back on him and was leafing through some papers.

Sartine swallowed as if he had a frog in his throat. The arrogance exhibited by this man, who had foiled the success of his investigations, exposed him to ridicule, and now shown him nothing but indifference in this house, was more degrading than any insult, no matter how vicious. This gesture made it clear to Sartine who he was and where he stood. He would never be allowed to go against the wishes of his wife's lover, no matter what Malesherbes did to him. On the contrary—he, Antoine Sartine, would now be sacrificed as a tiny cog in the great wheel of power, just as he had feared long ago. He would lose everything that he had worked for in the past twenty years: his career, his future, his life. Even the lackey who held the door of the salon open for him expressed nothing but contempt, as if Sartine were a beggar who had wandered in by mistake.

All of a sudden Sartine felt as impotent as on so many sleepless nights when he had lain next to Sophie, plagued by doubts and incapable of touching her.

Without thinking about what he was saying, he once more directed his words to Malesherbes. The man could take away his honor, but not his pride.

"By the way, before I go, I'd like to pass on one more greeting." He paused before he went on. "From Abbé Morel. Of Beaulieu."

87

"He really consented to the divorce?"

The scent of ambergris, mixed with the keratinous smell of burnt hair, filled the air in the boudoir of La Pompadour as a hairdresser worked on the mistress of the king using comb, curling iron, and the talent displayed by his fingers.

"A messenger brought me the news this morning," Sophie replied. She was standing behind the hairdresser's stool with a letter in her hand. "Monsieur de Malesherbes sent it to me."

La Pompadour was listening with only half an ear. Her attention was directed at her likeness in the mirror and the beautification process, which was laboriously progressing. There were a good hundred curlers in her hair; the hairdresser freed strand after strand from the spiny implements and then worked them with a hot iron before dusting the hair with vast quantities of powder.

"Isn't it absurd?" she asked over her shoulder. "The amount of flour used to cover up my hair's natural color could feed a whole family. And then because of all the white, I need to put on even more rouge."

"Don't blame us!" replied the hairdresser, who was constantly dancing around her. "The milliners are the real villains. Women in Paris spend more on their spangled trash than they do for food and drink. What a misfortune for the husband who has to pay for everything! Some even go broke because of it! All because more and more bourgeois ladies imagine that they must have for themselves what even a marquise or a countess can hardly afford."

As the hairdresser prattled on, La Pompadour kept directing him with small comments and gestures. She was wearing so much makeup to conceal the deep, dark sadness in her face and her soul that she looked like a doll. At court it was rumored that she was suffering from consumption and that her days as Louis's favorite were numbered. Everyone knew that Demoiselle Ronan, the daughter of a lawyer from Grenoble, was contesting her place in the king's heart. This time it wasn't merely a matter of one of the many adventures in the Parc-des-cerfs, which had always left La Pompadour's status undamaged because the newest concubine failed to stir the heart of the king; this time real love was at stake. Demoiselle Ronan had the longest black hair that anyone had ever seen—so long that she could wrap it like a veil around her naked, lascivious body when she stretched out with Oriental languor on her chaise longue before Louis's covetous glances. But these charms alone were not what made the new woman of his heart so dangerous; she had something that had been denied to the marquise in all these years: She had a son whom the king of France had recognized as his own.

"Satisfied, madame?" asked the hairdresser, taking a step back in order to observe his work, spreading the fingers of his raised hands like scissors.

"Your art helps as little as the donkey's milk that I drink—but be that as it may." La Pompadour cast one last look in the mirror and then turned to Sophie. "Is that the letter you told me about?"

She took the letter from Sophie's hand and scanned the few lines.

"The usual ritual," she said when she had finished reading. "The only reason that the church accepts as valid grounds for ending a marriage. I only hope," she added with a weary smile, handing the letter back to Sophie, "that the reason given is not the truth."

Sophie felt the blood rise to her face.

"What's the matter with you? You seem suddenly quite confused." La Pompadour frowned. "Does that mean that . . . ?"

She didn't need to finish her sentence to realize that her careless remark was indeed the bitter truth. With a toss of her head she dismissed the hairdresser.

"So you never consummated your marriage?" she asked after the man had rolled his cart out of the room.

Sophie shook her head. "Sartine never touched me, not even once."

The furrows on La Pompadour's brow grew even deeper. "When a man neglects seizing pleasure from such a pretty woman as you, there can be only one reason."

"Sartine said that he didn't want to force himself on me. In his opinion only love counted. I never did understand him."

"You poor child," said La Pompadour. "I know what you must have gone through. My first husband, Monsieur d'Étiolles, surrounds himself even today with whole crowds of pretty actresses and *grisettes,* but in reality . . . But since then I've learned that love is nothing but a fantasy. It depends entirely on the imagination."

"What does imagination have to do with love?"

"The connection has been scientifically proven." La Pompadour reached for a copy of the *Encyclopedia* on her dressing table and opened it.

"Haven't you read the article on erection? No? Then listen to this: 'This term refers to the condition of the male organ in which it does not hang down, but holds itself upright because the erectile tissue of which it is composed is filled with blood and thus stiffens. This state is a result of the power of imagination, which is stimulated by the idea or the actual sight of the objects which arouse the desire for venery. In this manner the blood that flows from the arteries into the cavities or cells is at the same time prevented from flowing back through the veins . . .'"

As La Pompadour read aloud, Sophie suddenly understood the secret of her marriage. She had never seen nor touched Sartine's member—it had never become erect in her presence, even at night when they lay side by side in bed, neither of them able to sleep. Her husband was incapable of consummating the marriage—that was the truth concealed behind their strange relationship, the reason he had never touched her in all the years they had lived together. All at once she realized that Sartine had done her a great wrong.

"What do you think was his price, Sophie?"

The question forced her out of her reverie. La Pompadour had put the *Encyclopedia* aside and was looking at her.

"Price? I don't know what you're talking about . . ."

The bluish black eyes of her patroness shone as if with fever.

"There must be a good reason why Sartine agreed to the divorce," said La Pompadour. "Believe me, when a man admits to such an inadequacy with his signature, he must have been paid a very high price indeed."

88

❧ ❧

"I offer you my wholehearted congratulations, Monsieur *de* Sartine. It is an extraordinary pleasure to see you in this setting. If ever a man deserved this appointment, it is you."

"I thank you, *mon père.* I only hope that you will find me worthy of my position in the future as well."

The two men shook hands. Father Radominsky was the first visitor Sartine received in his new office, after the chancellor of the government had named him the police prefect of Paris—at the suggestion of Malesherbes's son. Subsequently King Louis had set aside from his private coffers the 250,000 *livres* that the acquisition of the highest state position in the police had cost, at the same time elevating the new lieutenant general to the nobility, so that Sartine was now able to sign his reports and decisions as "Antoine *de* Sartine." He had always known that anyone who served the state with the proper zeal could go far. Yet he had now gone farther than he had ever dreamed possible. The time of powerlessness was past.

"Your appointment is the sign that I have been waiting two years to see," said Radominsky. "God is finally on our side again! Nevertheless we must not relax our vigilance, because the enemy never sleeps. As you know, the first illustrated volume of the *Encyclopedia* is now being delivered to subscribers. The enterprise continues! I received my copy yesterday."

"I got mine a week ago."

Sartine tapped on the just-printed illustrated volume lying on his desk. Radominsky opened up the book and began leafing through it.

"What a splendid work," the priest muttered. "As splendid as if it came straight out of the Devil's workshop."

The sight of the illustrations also wrung from Sartine a covert admiration. The book depicted all the wonders of the world. Whether loom or block and tackle, the bridle for a horse or a cross-section of the human skull: The pictures showed the objects engraved on the page in such detail that they seemed to be truly before his eyes. It took a great effort of will for Sartine to tear his eyes away.

"I have information," he said, "that the Russian tsarina, Catherine, has offered the editor permission to complete the *Encyclopedia* in either Petersburg or Riga."

"The proposal is a provocation of France," replied Radominsky, still engrossed in looking at the pictures. "The intent is to give the impression that philosophy is persecuted in Paris, while the Scythians encourage it."

"Diderot turned down the offer, referring to the copyright in the manuscripts held by the publisher. He supposedly replied that he would rather become a martyr to the truth than flee abroad. He owes that much to his reputation as a philosopher."

Radominsky looked up from the book. "Do you seriously believe that's the real reason?"

Sartine shook his head.

"Of course not," the priest agreed. "Diderot feels safe in Paris, and that's why he wants to stay here."

The two men gazed at each other. Sartine knew what Radominsky meant. The plan of the Jansenists was fully under way. The Jesuit order, the vanguard of the faith and of the holy state, had been stripped of its power—because of uprisings at a couple of mission stations in faraway South America. Sartine was quite familiar with the facts: In August the parliament had reached the decision, with 890 votes to 112, that the Society of Jesus was contradicting natural law and should be exiled from the kingdom as an enemy of the French state. The possessions of the order had been confiscated, and the priests were given only eight days to clear out their houses, discard their vestments, and sever all ties with their superiors. At the same time Madame de Pompadour had instituted proceedings against the Jesuits for continuing to deny her Communion despite their claim that they harbored only feelings of gratitude and the purest affection for the king. In order to avoid the impression that they sought to unleash a new religious war in France by showing any sort of partisanship for the order, Pope Clemens had decreed that the general commander of the Society of Jesus be thrown into Castel Sant-Angelo. Subsequently, Radominsky had felt compelled to renounce Ignatius of Loyola officially—it was his only chance to remain in office as the queen's father confessor. Sartine admired how calm and composed the priest was when he bowed to his fate, though without giving up the holy struggle.

"How harmless these pictures seem," said Radominsky, as he continued to leaf through the book. "This is only part of their ploy. Malesherbes permits them to be printed and thus tacitly tolerates the continuation of the *Encyclopedia*. It's only a matter of time until the next volumes appear, with new heresies and incitements to rebellion."

"Unfortunately I can't argue with you," said Sartine. "As long as the chief censor is personally protecting the philosophers, it will be very difficult to undertake any action against them. Malesherbes has just seen to it that Rousseau was able to elude my people, although there was a warrant to arrest him because of his latest novel."

"You mean *Émile*?" Radominsky grimaced in disgust. "The song of praise for that magnificent animal! The denial of evil! As if human beings were by nature good!"

"From the pen of a man who put his children in the foundlings' home! And the censor offers protection to such riffraff."

"Malesherbes must go." Radominsky slammed the book shut and stood up. "Until then there will be no peace. But how are we to drive this Judas from power?" He stepped over to the window and looked out. "We have nothing to use against him. As the son of the chancellor and the confidant of La Pompadour he's untouchable."

Sartine let these last words hover in the air for a while before he replied.

"Not entirely," he said.

"I beg your pardon?"

Radominsky spun around and gave the police prefect an astonished look. Sartine had leaned back and was stroking his sideburns.

"I just might have an idea. . . ."

89

Unlike the "greater" postal service, the "minor" post circulated solely within the city, as well as between the city and the court at Versailles. From early to late their messengers were under way daily, delivering thousands of letters. Paris was a world unto itself. Letters saved a lot of time, obviated the necessity for many visits, and prevented making a trip for nothing. Appointments were agreed on in this way, and business deals arranged. But the "minor" post was important not only to the everyday convenience of the populace of Paris, but also to the exchange of hope and despair, of love and jealousy, pride and hatred. And occasionally a small, unobtrusive letter could fundamentally change the life of a person.

It was on an early morning when Sophie received such a missive. One of Madame de Pompadour's lackeys brought it to her apartment, as she was still occupied with her toilette. She was just brushing out her red hair, and Dorval was reading to her from a magnificently bound book that his stepfather had given him for his tenth birthday: the *Persian Letters* of Montesquieu.

Sophie was about to put the letter aside when she recognized the seal of the City of Paris. Well, what could this be? The meticulous, rigid handwriting filled her with trepidation. She sent Dorval out to milk the donkey mare and then broke the seal.

Re: The case of "Madeleine Volland"

Madame,
The aforementioned case, adjudicated in the year 1740 by the District Court of Roanne, was investigated by me at the request of a private individual nine years after the conclusion of the trial. The subject of the investigation, which was conducted in the parish of Beaulieu, the

residence and birthplace of said Madeleine Volland, were the background and motives of the proceedings, which resulted in the conviction and concomitant execution of the accused.

Circumstances concerning our relationship did not allow me at that time to inform you of the outcome of my investigation. Since these circumstances in the meantime have lost their relevance, and I no longer feel obligated by the official regulations that have hitherto curbed my tongue, I am able today to offer a correction: The church archive of Beaulieu was not, as I claimed at the time, destroyed in a conflagration; rather, I enjoyed free access to the records and fully examined the documents of the trial in the case of Madeleine Volland. I have read and verified all the germane materials and am consequently in a position to identify definitely and unequivocally the man who, with his accusation and in particular with his testimony before the court, decisively influenced the proceedings, resulting in the subsequent denouement . . .

When Sophie read the name, she grabbed at her throat in shock. The carved angel felt smooth and cold as death as she read the end of the letter. Her body was trembling all over when her eyes fell on the signature affixed by the sender:

Antoine de Sartine, Prefect of Police, Paris.

90

It was already late in the evening when Sophie appeared at Malesherbes's house on Rue Vivienne. She found him in his office by the window. He was so immersed in watching the darkness descend that he didn't notice her arrival.

"So pensive, monsieur?" she said, setting down on his desk the large sack that she had brought along from Versailles. "Why would the favorite of the favorite feel a need to brood?"

"Once again I am reminded of how well you know me," replied Malesherbes with a smile. He left the window to come and greet her.

"If I have seen through you," she said, reaching out her hand to him, "may I then inquire about the object of your scrutiny? As far as I can see, the sky is overcast. So it couldn't have been the stars."

"Unfortunately I must again admit that you are right," he said gravely. "I was just wondering whether the appointment of Sartine may have been a mistake."

"Do you harbor doubts about your decision? Last week you were heaping the highest praise on the new prefect. How am I to take this sudden change of opinion?"

"I saw Sartine the day before yesterday in Notre-Dame. Father Radominsky was holding the mass. And I had the impression that the lieutenant general actually believed in God."

"What is there to criticize about that?"

"Normally nothing. But I'm not sure whether this also applies for a police officer. Someone who is overly sure of his God usually takes little consideration of his fellow man. It's only one step from religious zeal to barbarism."

Sophie frowned. "Do you have reason to fear a police officer? I've never seen you so pessimistic."

"You're right, my dear—what use are such gloomy thoughts? Sartine's appointment is worth Dorval's happiness, especially if it means the happiness of his mother. But have you brought something? For me?"

"Indeed, monsieur. Open it."

"A present? For no reason? How charming," he said, opening the sack. Suddenly his face stiffened and his voice faltered. "What . . . what a surprise . . ."

He held the present in his hand: a broad-brimmed black hat adorned with a red plume.

"What's wrong, Monsieur? Don't you like it?"

"No, no . . . of course I do," Malesherbes stammered as he held out the hat without looking at it. "But perhaps . . . how should I say it? . . . Isn't it a bit old-fashioned?"

"Who cares about fashion? Fashion changes, but faces do not—the main thing is that it suits you. What are you waiting for? Why don't you try it on?" As he still hesitated, she took the hat from his hands and set it on his head.

For a second she closed her eyes and took a deep breath before she opened them again. Then she looked at him. Under the black brim Malesherbes's face seemed as pale as chalk. It was as if a ghost stood before her, surfacing from the depths of time. She could feel her throat tightening. "Oh my God," she whispered.

Malesherbes didn't move. His face seemed turned to stone: Evidently he too realized what her gift meant. From his gray eyes shone the irrevocable despair that comes only from a person's own actions. Moving as slowly as in a dream, he removed the hat and dropped it to the floor.

"I always feared this would happen someday," he said, his voice toneless. "Dread of this moment has haunted me every minute we have spent together. And yet I always hoped that the chalice would pass me by. Who . . . who betrayed my secret to you? Sartine?"

Sophie nodded, scarcely able to speak. Her whole past, which had lain dormant these many years, had been revived, made manifest in this man. Even more painful than the memories were the realizations: That's why Malesherbes had so often given her such strange looks, as if he were searching her face for something he couldn't quite define, as if seeking some sort of clue; that's why he cared for her son, as if he wanted to compensate Dorval for something that fate had withheld from the boy; that's why he had cried at Damiens's execution. She now understood the reason for his sympathy, his understanding, his participation in every-thing that burdened and tormented her.

Sophie saw the truth in his eyes. No, there was no longer any doubt. She had shared a bed with the man who had her mother's death on his conscience.

"Why?" she whispered. "Why?"

"I loved Madeleine . . . I wanted to give her my whole life, place at her feet everything that I owned and possessed . . ."

"And that's why my mother had to die?"

"She turned me away . . . She didn't reciprocate my feelings. She ridi-culed me, told me to go to Hell . . . I was out of my mind . . ."

"What did you say before the court?"

"I . . . I claimed that she had poisoned me, with an herbal potion . . . I was so young, I saw only the rejection, the damage to my honor as a man."

He fell silent, helpless and ashamed, looking at the floor, as his words burst like bubbles rising up from the bottom of a brackish black pond to the surface, only to dissolve into putrid nothingness. When he glanced up again, he gave her a beseeching look, as if only she could release him from despair.

"You abused the superstitious nature of humanity, took advantage of people's uncertainty and laws, all in order to send my mother to the stake?" said Sophie. "Just because she hurt your feelings, your pride, your vanity—"

Her voice failed her. He looked so wretched, it was unbearable. Her whole body was rigid—she could feel the tension in every fiber. Sud-denly she felt as sick as on the day of her First Communion. She almost thought she would vomit.

She had only one more question, although she already knew the answer. But she had to hear it from him.

"Is that why you kept helping me?"

Malesherbes nodded. "Yes, that's why—and because I . . ."

"Because you what?"

He lowered his eyes again. "It's impossible for me to say the word. Not here and not now."

Sophie had an idea what he meant. All at once she switched from the formal *vous* to the familiar *tu*. "And is that why you warned Diderot?" she asked, although she could hardly utter the words because she was so filled with loathing and revulsion. "Is that why you protected the *Ency-clopedia*?"

"How I have longed to hear *tu* coming from your lips," he whispered. "Yet when you use this word, it has become my death sentence."

"Why did you do it?" she insisted. "Because of a guilty conscience? Because of remorse? To repent for your crime?"

He looked at her. His face was contorted with humiliation and shame when he finally spoke. "I was trying to correct fate. But . . . it was a terrible mistake. No one can correct fate. . . . Destiny is stronger."

For a long time she gazed at him, speechless as she confronted the abyss that had opened up before her. She wanted to say something more, but the words failed her.

He tried to smile as he reached out his hand to her. His face was now merely a grimace punctuated with two gray eyes from which all life had vanished.

How she had respected this man. How grateful she had been to him. But now that she knew the truth, she felt only a desire to spit in his face. Why didn't she do it? Without another word she turned around and left the room.

The marble corridor was deserted. Only a night bird gone astray fluttered through the air; in the light from the chandelier, it kept flying into a windowpane, over and over.

To Sophie the long corridor seemed as empty and cold as the days that remained in her life.

91

On October 5 in the year 1763, Chrétien de Malesherbes visited his father, the chancellor of the kingdom of France, in order to submit his resignation as director of the Royal Library and chief censor of the land.

In a voice that precluded all contradiction he explained, "I cannot foresee continuing to carry out my duties in an adequate manner. I beg you to release me from my obligations."

"Is your decision founded on the fact that I have fallen out of favor with the king?" asked his father, for it was said that Louis intended to replace him in the near future.

"It naturally made my decision easier, monsieur, but it was not the cause."

"Well, I too will resign my office before they force me out. His Majesty no longer listens to my advice, so my time is up. A new world is emerging that is beyond my comprehension. But I fear that it will take cruel revenge on the old one."

"Of that there is no doubt," replied Malesherbes. "I'm equally afraid that the resistance offered by the old world will be no less cruel."

The resignation of the two statesmen went almost unnoticed by the court at Versailles, overshadowed by an event that in the past few months had descended like black crepe over the royal palace. Madame de Pompadour, the woman who had enjoyed the favor of the king for longer than any previous mistress, who had offered him support and advice regarding the wielding of his God-given powers as well as regarding his most private interests—this woman now lay dying. Even in her youth, when she still bore the name Jeanne-Antoinette Poisson, she had from time to time coughed up blood, just as she did later on during her marriage to Monsieur d'Étiolles. She had always recovered from these attacks on her body and her happiness, because she was not yet ready to leave the colorful splendor of life. But this time she could feel with unerring instinct that she was headed toward the end. Despite the donkey's-milk cure, the only remedy that seemed to help a little bit, the constant feverish tension she had withstood at court for so many years, day after day, hour after hour, had so overtaxed her frail body that she no longer possessed any means of resistance. Debilitated by countless colds, bouts of fever, and cupping cures, additionally weakened by a considerable number of miscarriages, her once so wondrous figure was now emaciated to the bone. She had no bosom left, and her formerly flawless complexion, which the portrait by the court painter La Tour had once shown to such advantage, as if her beauty could never fade, had long since turned yellow beneath all the powder and rouge. Her skin had withered like a leaf that had fallen prematurely from a dry twig and was then carried away on the wind.

Louis visited his former favorite almost every day, standing for a few minutes at her sickbed. Out of gratitude for the innumerable services she had rendered, he had granted her permission to die in the royal palace, even though protocol dictated that only princes and princesses were allowed such a privilege—an official honor for the *amie du roi* that had never before been granted to the mistress of any French king. In her old library they had prepared a bed for her. Books were her last refuge. Throughout her life they had helped her to perfect her education and had served as weapons against her many rivals and foes. Books had given her advice and guidance in matters of war as well as in matters of love; they had always provided her with the right words, informed her of the necessary facts about present and past events, and enabled her to speak without embarrassment about painting and philosophy, the art of the dance and the art of politics. Books had given her everything that she had ever needed. Now they were helping her to depart from this life.

As the bouts of fever overtook her in rapid succession, she was tormented by one question: Had she reached her goal of securing a place in history? That had been her primary endeavor ever since the moment that fate had elevated her to her high position. Behind the carefree mask, she had always dreamed of having her name connected with brilliant victories, conquered cities, and subjugated provinces—with all the glories of France. What had happened to those dreams? A few victories could be cited against countless defeats, above all her defeats as a woman. She felt vanquished, like the French generals and soldiers who after seven years of grueling battles against the Prussians and British had laid down their arms in exhaustion, so as to conclude a dubious peace with their foes. No, La Pompadour harbored no illusions. It was doubtless only out of mercy that the king still favored her. Perhaps he feared an act of desperation if he left her now.

And yet another matter occupied her thoughts in the few hours that were left to her. What would happen after she was gone? While Louis sought consolation and oblivion in the arms of the beautiful Demoiselle Ronan—full of bitterness, the marquise could smell the perfume of her rival on the king's clothing when he visited her bedside—La Pompadour's opponents were taking advantage of her infirmity to bring their troops into position at court. The old chancellor and his son had hardly resigned when their adversaries began snatching up all the important positions for themselves. With the support of the parliament as well as the archbishop of Paris, they had made the state councillor Maupéou their leader—the man who had forced into law the death penalty for all printed publications that incited revolt against the church or the state.

But one change caused the dying marquise the greatest worry; it had to do with the future fate of her beloved books. Because, only a few days after he took office as the new chancellor of the kingdom, Maupeou had named a new man as supervisor of the book trade and chief censor of the land—a man who seemed more dangerous to her than any other conceivable candidate: Antoine de Sartine.

92

In the meantime Sophie never left the sickbed of La Pompadour. The marquise's cough grew worse from day to day, the fever seemed to keep rising incessantly, and she was plagued constantly by severe attacks of choking. Dr. Quesnay, the patient's longtime personal physician, could scarcely hide his apprehension, while Sophie was busy day and night trying to ease her suffering. She carried out the instructions of the succession of doctors that Dr. Quesnay brought in as consultants in ever greater numbers; she gave the patient donkey's milk and orange blossom water to drink; she held her during the coughing fits; and she brought down the fever with damp poultices and compresses applied to her calves.

Then all of a sudden, three weeks after the marquise had retreated to the royal palace to die, an astounding improvement in her condition occurred. It was an utter miracle. The fever dropped, the coughing ceased almost completely, and one morning she even got out of bed to take her breakfast reclining on her chaise longue.

La Pompadour's gaze was clear, her voice firm, as she asked Sophie to sit down on a chair beside her.

"What will you do when I'm no longer here?"

"What kind of question is that?" replied Sophie in shock. "You shouldn't talk like that, madame. Just wait—it won't be two weeks before you're well again, and we'll take a coach ride in the Bois de Boulogne."

"I know how much you care for me, Sophie," said La Pompadour, taking her hand. "But let's not fool ourselves. This is merely the last burst of energy in my life. Let's make good use of the time for as long as it lasts." She gave Sophie an affectionate look. "So what will you do afterward? Tell me, I want to know. Will you leave the court?"

Sophie could feel that she owed her friend an answer. But she could manage no more than a mute nod.

La Pompadour didn't need words to understand her. "And Monsieur de Malesherbes? Will you take revenge on him?"

Sophie shook her head. "No. Revenge is not the solution—there is no solution. What he did is so monstrous . . . I think only God can pronounce judgment over him."

"You're right," La Pompadour agreed. "Life is too short to waste it on things we can't change. That's why we must use all our powers to devote ourselves to tasks over which we still have an influence. Tasks and people." She squeezed Sophie's hand. "Don't you think you ought to go back to Diderot? Your heart will always belong to him, I can feel it—even if you don't want to admit as much."

Sophie avoided her searching eyes. Staring at the bookshelves and the walls, she said softly, "Twice I have tried to love, and twice I have foundered."

"Don't you want to try it a third time? Don't make the same mistake I did. I gave up too early."

Sophie let her eyes wander over the morocco leather bindings on the shelves. Concealed behind the spines of the books decorated with coats of arms were multitudes of stories whose contents and denouements she would never know. Did one story more or less make any difference?

"I no longer believe in love," she said bitterly. "When people claim to have lost their heart, it's usually only their wits that have vanished. Sometimes love seems to me an emotional disturbance that people try to cure with marriage."

"That may be true of ninety percent of all cases, and here at the court of Versailles maybe even a hundred percent. But is it also true of you?" La Pompadour waited until Sophie turned to face her. "For so many years," she went on, "I tried to deny love. Because I was afraid of losing, through love, what always seemed most important to me: To have power—over myself and over others. But what is power compared with love? Love is the soul of life, the beginning and ending of everything that we do. That's why it's the only thing that increases when we give it. Closing my eyes to it was perhaps the biggest mistake of my life."

"It's not just faith that I lack, madame, I also lack power. To me, love feels like a knife stabbing at my soul."

Both women were silent for a while.

Then La Pompadour said, "Perhaps it is as you say, Sophie. Perhaps we have the power to love only once in our lives, and it has to be the first time; later we console ourselves over this great loss with small infatuations. Yes, perhaps it is even the mark of true love that it is consumed like a burning bush. But does that mean only ashes will be left in the end?"

Sophie had no answer to this question.

La Pompadour said, "If you can't go back to Diderot, at least help him complete his work."

"Why?" Sophie asked. "Whenever I try to help him everything just gets worse."

"Nevertheless, you must try, even if you don't believe in it. You owe that to the love that you once felt for him—"

A coughing fit interrupted her.

"You must stop talking!" insisted Sophie, filled with concern. "Please. This is too strenuous for you."

"It's already past," said La Pompadour though she was struggling for breath; each word she spoke seemed to cause her pain. And yet she continued, in a tremulous, almost inaudible voice. "You must promise me this, Sophie—it is your duty to help Diderot. His enemies have seized all the power in this country. When I die, there will be no one left to protect him and the *Encyclopedia* from their attacks." She raised her hand so that Sophie would not interrupt. "Until now there were strict laws, but their enforcement was always lax. With Maupeou as chancellor, enforcing the laws will become just as strict as the legislation itself. One unclear article, one wrong word is all it will take, and the *Encyclopedia* will be forever condemned. They will arrest Diderot and take him to Vincennes, or even to the scaffold."

"Do you believe they are capable of such a crime?"

"Don't you?" La Pompadour asked in return. "The new chancellor was already my enemy when I was still a beautiful woman. And Sartine will use every opportunity to take revenge for the humiliations in his life. Have you forgotten your letter? He will prove even more dangerous in the future. As prefect of police and chief of the censorship authority he is one of the most powerful men in Paris."

She sank onto her pillows in exhaustion and closed her eyes.

"What about the king?" Sophie asked. "Can we expect no help from him?"

La Pompadour smiled as if recollecting a beautiful dream. "Louis is a charming man, but he has no backbone. He's like a child; he always needs someone who cares about him and makes him happy. No, he won't help anyone."

Through the window Sophie saw that twilight was spreading between the trees and bushes. The shadows were so long that they seemed to encompass the whole park.

"I'm afraid," she whispered.

"So am I, Sophie . . . So am I . . ."

Somebody opened the door softly. An abbé came in, a thin, bony man who greeted them with a solemn nod of his head. He was carrying a communion chalice and a prayer book.

"That surprises you, doesn't it?" said La Pompadour with a smile. "Père Sacy has already agreed to hear my confession. Even at the risk of losing his position. Well, I fear it will be a rather long conversation."

"Then I'll leave you alone now," said Sophie and stood up. She bent down over the sick woman to kiss her. But La Pompadour turned away.

"No . . . it's too dangerous. You could be infected. But I thank you— for everything." She took Sophie's hands once again and gazed at her. Her eyes were glittering as if with fever again. "And don't forget, you must help Diderot. You're the only one who can protect him. Him and the *Encyclopedia* . . . But go now, please, I have a lot to tell Père Sacy— more than I would like." She was speaking so softly now that Sophie could scarcely catch the words. "He insists on reconciling me with God. And I don't even know if I'd like to be in Heaven. I'm afraid I'd find only a few people there I know."

One last smile—then she let go of Sophie's hands and turned her head to the wall.

93

On Palm Sunday in the year 1764, on April 15 around seven o'clock in the evening, the marquise de Pompadour, born Jeanne-Antoinette Poisson, divorced from Monsieur d'Étiolles, and after a restless and strenuous life took her last breath at the age of only forty-three in the royal palace at Versailles. She had been conceived in sin; she died of sorrow and consumption.

It was as if a great music box, whose soul and drive had been the Marquise, had now stopped. The golden gondolas on the canal that connected Versailles to the pleasure palace of La Celle bobbed idly at their moorings, as if they would never again be used for a pleasure party. Reflected in the still water were the pink and yellow blossoms drooping on the rosebushes. All laughter had ceased, and the Chinese lanterns in the colonnades seemed extinguished forever. Even the birds perched in the conical topiary trees along the canal had stopped chirping, and the fleecy little clouds in the blue spring sky stretching like a theater backdrop above the meerschaum-white pleasure palace did not move, as if time itself had stopped.

It was said that the king saw the funeral procession taking the mortal remains of La Pompadour to Paris, where she would be interred in the chapel of the Capuchins on Place Vendôme. He had uttered only a few cool, heartless words for the woman who for so many years had made him forget the dreariness of his life. He had never loved her, he said, and had tolerated her presence merely so he would not be forced to have her killed. And she was hardly in her grave before everyone stopped asking about her altogether, as if she had never existed. "That's the way the world is," remarked the queen, Maria Leszczynska, with some satisfaction. "It's truly not worth loving."

On the evening after the funeral, Sophie lay awake for hours, unable to sleep or formulate a clear thought. Her apartment in La Celle, which she by order of the majordomo would be allowed to keep for another month, was so empty that she seemed to hear the silence roaring in her ears. She had lost her best friend—the only female friend she'd ever had. Until the end the marquise had done everything she could to help her; even on her deathbed she had been concerned about Sophie's welfare. And that made the final admonition with which La Pompadour had parted from her seem all the more urgent. It was said at court that her heart was incapable of stirring, and yet she, of all people, had attempted to give Sophie back her belief in love, reminding her of the obligations that she had to Diderot. She could still hear La Pompadour's words echoing over and over: "One unclear article, one wrong word is all it will take . . . and they will arrest Diderot and take him to Vincennes, or even to the scaffold."

Sometime during the night Sophie gave up trying to sleep. She got out of bed, lit a candle, and drank a glass of water. She wanted to read something, anything, until morning finally came. Softly, so she wouldn't wake Dorval, she went into her little reading room. The candlestick in her hand, she went over to the shelf—and then her eyes fell on the narrow spine of a book that was wedged in between two big folios. It was a copy of *The Indiscreet Jewels*, bound in red silk. Diderot had given it to her during the brief time they lived together. Without thinking, she reached for the book, which she had not held in her hands in years.

Did she really want to read it? She had the same feeling as long, long ago in the garret room above the Procope, when she touched the lid of her forbidden little treasure chest, irresistibly drawn to the precious contents and at the same time full of anxiety. She opened the book to the last chapter, and her eyes instantly found the lines for which her heart was yearning, a message from another world that had long since faded away and yet had not stopped speaking to her.

"Far from you, Mongagul, what will become of me?" She read the words that the ring of the sorcerer coaxed from Mirzoza's jewel. "True until into the night of the grave, I would have also sought you there; and if love and constancy in the realm of the dead should be rewarded, dear prince, I would have found you. Oh! Without you the magnificent palace would have been for me merely a miserable hut . . ." Sophie tasted salt on her lips. With the back of her hand she wiped her cheeks, wet with tears. She closed the book and went over to the window. Outside the first light of dawn was rising in the sky; like threatening figures the trees and bushes of the park seemed to emerge from the nighttime shadows. No, she could no longer go back to Diderot; her love for him had been washed away. But was that reason enough to leave him to his fate?

Indecision and an irrefutable feeling of guilt weighed heavily on her soul. She herself had caused Malesherbes to resign, there was no doubt of that. But had she not put Diderot and his work in even greater jeopardy by doing so, since they were already in peril? She had to warn Diderot of his predicament; he had no inkling of what was brewing in Versailles. But would such a warning achieve anything? Sophie didn't think so. She knew Diderot: The greater the danger, the more obstinately he reacted. Even when Malesherbes had personally advised him to leave Paris, because he was at risk of being arrested after Damiens's execution and the tightening of the laws, he had refused, as stubborn as a mule—he hadn't even visited his deathly ill father in Langres, so as not to give the appearance of admitting guilt.

Sophie put the book back on the shelf. No, it made no sense to go to Diderot, and even if she did, he might not let her in. But what then could she do for him? She wasn't sure; she knew only that she couldn't simply sit by and do nothing. He was running straight toward the sword of the new chief censor; he was writing and distributing texts that would give Sartine a good reason to destroy his life and his work. There was no question that Sartine would do so. Madame de Pompadour had opened her eyes.

The very next day Sophie continued to rack her brain for a solution but without success. The labyrinth of her life seemed more confusing than ever, an inescapable maze, and the question of how she could protect Diderot from himself still haunted her as she dissolved her household at court and moved with Dorval into a small house at the edge of Paris. Two weeks after her friend's funeral, even as she attended the reading of the will to which the marquise's lawyer had invited her, Sophie's thoughts were always with Diderot.

94

The chancellery was located in Faubourg Saint-Honoré. In the large, oak-paneled room a few dozen people had already gathered. Most of them knew Sophie: a couple of fawning courtiers, a few lady's maids and valets; the chief steward, the porter, and the cellarer; as well as nameless coachmen, bearers, and gardeners; cooks, officers, and the riding master; wardrobe mistresses, milliners, and chambermaids; as well as Dr. Quesnay, naturally, and Monsieur Poisson, the younger brother of the deceased. He was now known as Monsieur de Marigny and bore the title of marquis, but nothing had changed about his manner. On the contrary: Instead of enhancing his self-assurance, the new title had increased his shyness to almost grotesque proportions—at court the most malicious satirical verses were making the rounds. Unlike most of those present, who with undisguised avarice listened to the lawyer as they waited impatiently for their turn to come, the marquis listened to the remarks quietly, his hands clasped in front of his plump paunch—a guileless man fully intending to comply with the last wishes of his sister.

"In the name of the Father, the Son, and the Holy Spirit! I, Jeanne-Antoinette Poisson, Marquise de Pompadour, former wife of Charles-Guillaume Le Normant d'Étiolles and legally divorced as to property, have composed and recorded this my last will and testament, which I desire to be carried out to its full extent. I commend my soul to God, as I pray that He will have mercy on me and forgive me my sins, in the hope of finding favor in His righteousness through the precious blood of Jesus Christ, my Savior, and through the grace of the Holy Virgin as well as all the saints in Paradise . . ."

In a nasal voice the lawyer described the assets, page by page, sentence by sentence, sounding as monotonous and boring as a priest reading the mass for the thousandth time. Sophie looked around: As familiar as the faces were to her, they already seemed foreign, although less than two weeks had passed since she had left the court. Suddenly she heard her own name.

"I bequeath to Sophie Volland, in gratitude for the affection she has displayed to my person, a pension of six thousand *livres*; to my physician, Dr. Quesnay, four thousand *livres*; Monsieur Lefèvre, my riding master, one thousand, two hundred *livres* . . ."

Sophie took a deep breath. With this pension, she knew, she would be free of all material cares for the rest of her life. She could pay the rent on her little house, and Dorval would never lack for anything. A good thing that the adoption had not gone through before Malesherbes's secret had been discovered. . . . The envious eyes directed at her for a moment soon moved on, fixing on each person in turn whom La Pompadour had mentioned in her will. Finally all eyes were staring at a single person who under the onslaught of attention turned bright red in the face from sheer embarrassment.

"As far as the rest of my property and possessions are concerned, of whatever nature they may be and wherever they may be located, then I give and bestow them to Abel-François Poisson, Marquis de Marigny, my brother, whom I do hereby make and appoint my universal successor . . ."

There followed innumerable supplementary statements with which La Pompadour bequeathed even the most inconspicuous items from the vast estate she had amassed over the course of her lifetime, each inheritance mentioned by name. Even her pets—a parrot, a dog, and a howler monkey—were listed individually; to the laughter of those present they were awarded to the natural scientist Buffon. Even more agitation was prompted by a detailed codicil with which the deceased revoked or corrected, respectively, the previously listed provisions. In a few moments the room was transformed into an Oriental bazaar. There was a great commotion of shouts and protestations as everyone ranted at the lawyer, who kept declaring that he was only announcing the desires of the deceased and bore absolutely no responsibility for the contents of the will.

In embarrassment Sophie cast down her eyes. What a disgusting spectacle! The parties fell upon each other like a horde of Armenian street vendors, quoting different versions of the will, arguing, presenting old and new versions apparently any way they liked. They deciphered and corrected as if there were no official interpretation for how the last will of the deceased was to be understood, as if the valid truth were nothing more than the last scribbled word from her hand. Sophie only hoped that the shameful scene would soon end. She was no longer listening as she toyed nervously with her bracelet, trying to divert her thoughts to other matters, to future concerns for setting up her household. Suddenly she had the feeling that her dead friend wished to speak to her. Although it seemed impossible and total nonsense, and contrary to all reason and experience, she heard the familiar voice say: "And what if someone were to treat the *Encyclopedia* in precisely the same way?"

The voice sounded so clear and distinct, as if the marquise were right there in the room. Involuntarily Sophie looked all around. What did her friend want to tell her? What did the *Encyclopedia* have to do with the reading of the will? But then it was as though scales fell from her eyes. The haggling all around her was the key: What people took to be the truth was always merely provisional; each truth set the stage for the next one. And this realization applied not only to someone's last will and testament, it applied to every bequest of the will, everything left to other people . . . The thought took Sophie's breath away, so unusual, so daring, so utterly insane did it seem to her. And yet—could that be the solution? A way out of the labyrinth in order to save Diderot and his work?

She closed her eyes and saw the smiling face of La Pompadour. Her friend seemed to be winking at her from the other side.

Without waiting for the arguments to be settled, Sophie left the room and set off. Finally she knew what she had to do.

95

❧ ☙

Land ho!

Like a captain on the bridge, Le Bréton bellowed his commands to the workers, while the whole publishing house groaned and creaked like a ship on the high seas. He urged on every man, checking the quality of the proofs, the coverage of the printing ink, the flawlessness of the paper, handing out here a word of praise and there a criticism; he pitched right in if another hand was needed on the press, so that the *Encyclopedia* would come safe to harbor. No more mistakes must occur; no one was as critical as the paying customer. It was a wonder that the subscribers weren't up in arms after all the broken promises over twenty years with regard to the price and scope of the enterprise. Eight folios of text and two of illustrations had been mentioned in the announcement prospectus, for a total of 280 *livres*. In the meantime the work had expanded to seventeen volumes of text and eleven of illustrations, which had cost each of the 4,250 subscribers 984 *livres*.

Yes, the *Encyclopedia* had become the enterprise of his lifetime.— The court almanac, which Le Bréton as the first-ranked book printer of the king still published annually, was merely a slice of bread and butter compared to this endeavor. Since most of the authors of the *Encyclopedia* had written their contributions for no honorarium, the profits amounted to more than three million *livres*. Who could have predicted that? In the beginning the plan had been only to translate a simple English lexicon into French—until Diderot had come up with his wonderful idea to dare something entirely new. Le Bréton had been forced to oust the original editor under contract in order to make room for this gloriously successful venture.

The investment had truly been worth it. Le Bréton was now a rich and powerful man, respected by cabinet ministers and feared by competitors. Long ago he had abandoned his modest sedan chair to ride through the city in his own coach-and-four to see to his business dealings. With an air of satisfaction he took the gold watch, which he had recently bought for a small fortune at the Quai de l'Horloge, from his vest pocket and snapped the lid open. In a couple of minutes he had to leave. The last text volumes were almost done. He wanted to look at a barn in Massy, in the neighborhood of his country home, which had been offered to him at a favorable rent. There, beyond the gates of the city, he could store the volumes that were already finished until distribution could finally be carried out without risk to the enterprise.

Could he manage to arrive back at his house on time that evening? He had promised his wife that he would. She had her heart set on going to the opera with him to hear an eight-year-old wonder boy from Vienna, who apparently could play piano better than any grown-up—Mozart was his name. Le Bréton had just snapped the lid of his watch shut when suddenly an unfamiliar woman stood before him, dressed in silk with a mantilla over her shoulders, a real lady. He gave her a querulous look.

"May I help you?" He had hardly spoken those four words when he recognized her. The red hair and all those freckles could belong to only one woman. "Madame Sophie? But of course. This is indeed a surprise!"

"I have come to present a proposal to you, Monsieur Le Bréton," she replied. "Do you have a moment?"

"Certainly, but perhaps we should go somewhere not quite as noisy. If you would please follow me?"

He led her from the clamorous print shop up the stairs to the salon of his private residence. It was the most elegant room in the house, and in the midst of hundreds of knickknacks of sinfully expensive Sèvres porcelain stood a real grand piano. It was the pride of the whole family, although none of them could play it. Le Bréton offered Sophie a seat on the chaise longue directly facing the splendid black-lacquered piano, so that it was impossible for her to ignore it.

"So, what is on your heart?" he asked, sinking into a easy chair. "You wanted to present a proposal?"

To his disappointment Sophie seemed not even to notice the piano, nor the satin-clad Moor who came in holding a tray—his wife had hired him a month before as a servant in order to impress a friend who owned three greyhounds, three Siamese cats, and a budgerigar. The Moor bowed again and again as he served the steaming chocolate, but Sophie began to harangue Le Bréton as fervently as an untalented author who wanted to persuade him to publish a manuscript. She told him of the death of La

Pompadour, of the new cabinet ministers, and of the laws that were now going to be put into effect. Why was she telling him all this? Le Bréton read *Le Mercure* every morning and kept up with events. Was she trying to make an impression on him with her knowledge of the goings-on at court? That didn't seem plausible—he knew and admired Sophie as a woman who made little fuss about herself. Could she have changed so much?

Then she suddenly began talking about the *Encyclopedia*. She asked detailed questions about the state of things and wanted to know how many text volumes were still to come. Above all she was interested in hearing how far along the printing had proceeded. Le Bréton frowned. Why was she so interested? She and Diderot had been separated for years. She had nothing more to do with the whole matter!

When she finally mentioned the reason for her visit, he clapped his hands to his head.

"I could never accept responsibility for that. Diderot would kill me!"

"He doesn't have to know about it," she replied as calmly as if she had asked him for a mundane favor. "As publisher you have the final responsibility for the enterprise. You mustn't risk jeopardizing more than twenty years of work at the end." And when he said nothing, she added, "Or do you want to lose all of this? The lovely porcelain, the magnificent grand piano?"

Le Bréton took out a handkerchief and wiped from his brow the sweat that was beading up in great drops. How uncomfortable this otherwise so pleasant room had suddenly become. He huffed and puffed, panted and wheezed as he squirmed on his chair without reaching a decision. What this woman was saying was indeed undeniable, and moreover she was right a thousand times over; alas, she did not know whereof she spoke when she mentioned the great danger that threatened them all. The solution that she proposed was damned clever, but how the Devil did she imagine her audacious plan could be realized? The most commonplace, devious, and shabby of censors would consider himself too good to take on such a task.

"Well, Monsieur Le Bréton?"

Full of worry he looked around. He had put the labors of a lifetime into all this luxury and magnificence. Would he have to give it all up in the future?

Le Bréton heaved one last sigh and turned back to his guest.

"And who, if you please," he asked, "should carry out such a manipulation?"

96

Saint-Cloud was a small, tranquil place in the southwest of Paris that was famous for its park and its rippling waters. Nets had been stretched from one bank of the Seine to the other to strain the water of any debris before it poured forth into the lakes and ponds, which fed countless fountains. Driven by the currents from the capital, a motley array of the strangest objects were caught in these nets, often of considerable use to the men guarding the installation. But the nets were also the reason those unfortunate Parisians who jumped into the Seine in order to depart this life were seldom granted the happiness of having the vast ocean as their grave. If there was no ice on the river, their last journey ended between the banks at Saint-Cloud, where their bodies would eventually be found. At this spot, only a stone's throw from the great river, Sophie had moved into her new home.

"Why don't we live at the king's palace anymore?"

"How often are you going to ask me that, Dorval? Because Madame de Pompadour died. But I think it's almost time for bed. It's already dark outside."

"Why doesn't Monsieur de Malesherbes come to visit us anymore? Am I no longer his son?"

Sophie looked into Dorval's distraught face. Ever since they had moved into their house in Saint-Cloud, he had changed almost beyond recognition. He didn't care about the donkey mare that Sophie ensured was brought here for him; he didn't play with the children in the neighborhood, and he showed no desire to read. He seemed to be suffering the distress of a prince who had been driven out of his fairy-tale castle. But Sophie didn't have time to explain yet again the reason they'd moved. She was expecting an important visitor.

"I know we had a splendid life in Versailles," she said. "But that's over now. Life at court was false and illusory."

"If it was so splendid there, how can it have been false?" asked Dorval, annoyed. Suddenly his blue eyes lit up. "Or do you mean we're going back to my real father?"

A knock on the front door saved Sophie the trouble of answering. "Now march! It's bedtime." After she tucked Dorval into bed, she went downstairs to answer the door.

Outside in the dark the publisher Le Bréton was waiting. Behind him in the courtyard, illuminated by the pale light of the moon, stood an overloaded horse cart. The driver climbed down from the box and unlashed the tarpaulin covering the freight.

"Bring everything into the house!" shouted Le Bréton over his shoulder. "I'm sorry it's so late," he said to Sophie. "The city gate was already closed, and I had to bribe a customs official to let me through."

As soon as the freight was unloaded, the publisher headed back to Paris—the customs officer would not wait for him past midnight. Sophie stood at the window and watched the cart rumble away until she could see only the lantern hanging from the back. As the flickering glow grew smaller and finally vanished behind a hill, she pulled the curtains closed. It was high time to begin her work.

The manuscripts and galleys were stacked up in dozens of piles on the floor, all sorted alphabetically. Sophie picked up one bundle, placed it on the writing desk, and leafed through the articles, signed by an array of different authors. The essays dealt with temptation, transport, tuberculosis . . . Once more Sophie was astounded that so much prodigious knowledge had been collected in this book. Many texts she recognized from earlier; she had edited a couple of them years before, and even written a few herself. Most of them, however, bore the abbreviation for Jaucourt. The *chevalier* had written more articles than any of the other authors, even more than Diderot.

Sophie grasped a random bundle from the stack. It was a long article for the entry on tolerance. Her hand trembled as she turned to the first page. If she actually did what she was about to do, she would not only ruin Diderot's work but his love for her as well. Yet not even this concern could dissuade her. She had no choice; it was the only way out.

It took a few seconds before she could bring herself to begin her painful task. She knew what she had to do. The procedure had been discussed in detail with Le Bréton. He had brought her only those contributions that Diderot had already read and had signed off on, thus releasing them for typesetting or printing. With strained attentiveness she began to read:

How sad it is to have to prove to people a truth that is so clear that their failure to recognize it must indicate a complete loss of all natural instincts! But since in our century there are still people who close their eyes to the evidence and close their hearts to humanity, how can we possibly submit to cowardly silence in our work?

Line by line, paragraph by paragraph, page by page Sophie read the text. When she reached the end she took the quill from the inkwell, and with a sigh she crossed out one word that could put the author in danger, then a second and a third. Cautiously she recast the sentences, checking everything that seemed to her too bold or otherwise liable to incite contradiction or persecution, even if the words spoke to her from the soul:

No! Wherever intolerance rules, it will arm people against one another. If the Christians refuse to tolerate those who refute their ideas, then those peoples will rightly ally themselves against the Christians. What reproach should we then take with regard to a prince in Asia if he hangs the first missionary that we send to him?

This paragraph alone would be enough to consign the author to the Bastille and the work to the bonfire. Sophie corrected and altered, rearranging the arguments so that they lost some of their sting; in other places she added supplementary phrases to undercut the tone and eliminate provocation. She changed blatant assertions to hidden insinuations and turned staunch theses into hesitant questions. Sometimes she was forced to delete entire sequences of sentences. The passages that fell victim to her editing grew ever longer; sometimes she would even cross out several paragraphs in a row. Tears rolled down her cheeks. She had to destroy the perfection of the work, eradicate words of truth and reason forever so as to preserve the whole from annihilation. The mutilation of the texts caused her physical pain—it was like ripping her own heart from her breast. But she had no other option to save the work; she was like a surgeon who had to amputate a limb from a patient who had developed gangrene, in order to save the patient's life. A compromise was better than sacrificing everything. The *Encyclopedia* was just the beginning; others would take the next steps. It was Sophie's task to make this beginning possible. Life always involved bowing to fate and adapting the ideal to the given circumstances—perfection was not attainable in this world. There was perfection only in pure thought, in mathematics and philosophy, and perhaps also in art. And in love?

Sophie got up and looked out at the clear, starry night. No matter how many other reasons there were to justify her destructive work—could love justify it to her? In doing what she was doing, wasn't she placing the *Encyclopedia* above love? As Diderot had once done before she left him? As if Heaven could give her an answer, she gazed at the firmament. How she envied the stars in the sky! Calm and unwavering they followed their paths, day after day, month after month, year after year, as if there could be no mistake.

She wiped away her tears and went back to her desk. She had sacrificed her love on the altar of perfection; she must not repeat this blunder with the *Encyclopedia*. And so she continued her cruel work, this murderous, unbelievable, infamous operation, in order to save the life and work of the man; this appalling task was the only way she could prove her love for him. Later, as she had agreed with Le Bréton, they would burn the galleys as well as the manuscripts, one original after the other, as the printing of the work progressed. Sophie's alterations would thus be made irrevocable.

Now and then she heard faint noises from her son's room. Each time she gave a start, conscious of her guilt like a criminal who fears being discovered. Outside in the dark, illuminated by the moon and stars, the black currents of the Seine streamed past, catching in the nets of Saint-Cloud the detritus of the great city.

97

"It's finished, Le Bréton! We've actually done it!"

"I know, I know, Diderot. But that's no reason to sit back and do nothing. We still have more than enough to keep us busy."

"Just a minute. I simply want to enjoy it . . ."

Diderot couldn't get enough of looking at the sight. Up to the smoke-blackened ceiling of the print shop towered the fresh sheets of the *Encyclopedia*, which Le Bréton's men were now loading stack by stack onto a wagon that stood ready at the rear entrance. On this day they had finally completed the seventeenth and last volume of text. There were thousands of contributions stacked here, all the wisdom of the world, written and edited, typeset and printed, encompassing almost twenty years of effort and danger, accomplished under the watchful eyes of the government, and in spite of the opposition of both the police and the clerics. Although Diderot didn't believe in miracles, this was definitely one that even he couldn't deny.

"We've beaten them *all*, even the Jesuits! Who would ever have thought it possible?"

Together with Le Bréton he was preparing for the transport of the printed sheets "abroad," although they were actually only going to the village of Massy. There the pages would be bound, with a statement that the books had been printed in another country—they had decided on Neuchâtel in Switzerland—after which they would be officially "imported" to France. Diderot was as happy as a thief to outsmart the censorship authorities in this way. The moment that he could hand over to his son and daughter the finished work was now so fast approaching that he could almost touch it.

"Onward! Why are you standing around? Hurry!"

As Le Bréton exhorted the workers to greater haste, Diderot reached for one of the sheets. He wanted to touch the finished text, take it in with all his senses, as if he had to make sure one more time that he wasn't dreaming. How lovely the paper felt, how magnificently it smelled of printing ink. No, his dream had become reality. The new bible for the new times—he had created it, and now he held it in his hands.

"Surely you don't want to start reading now!" shouted Le Bréton. "You'll have plenty of time for that later, when you're an old man. We have to get everything out of here as fast as possible. I have no wish to be caught at the last minute."

"Just one quick look in farewell, before the sheets vanish on the wagon. They're my children, after all!"

He looked up an article at random under the letter *S*. "Saracens"—one of more than five thousand articles that he had written over the years.

"When I imagine that this book is soon going to conquer the world . . ."

"Precisely!" replied Le Bréton. "Think of your immortality. But make sure that you live to see it! As long as the sheets are still here, we're sitting on a powder keg."

Diderot refused to be put off; his enjoyment of the finished work was simply too great. Full of pride he read the lines, which stood out so distinctly, black against the white background, words meant for eternity. Ostensibly they merely reflected the distant past, but actually they were intended to judge the government and the church quite harshly: "Mohammed was so convinced of the incompatibility of philosophy and religion that he decreed the death penalty for anyone who devoted himself to the free arts: the same prejudice had plagued all ages and all peoples who had tried to dispute reason."

Diderot shook his head. A shame that he had chosen the past-perfect tense here—the present tense would have been better, in order to clarify the relationship to the present day. Oh well, considering the haste with which he had penned the text, occasional incidents of carelessness were bound to slip through. Greedily he read on, immersing himself in his ideas and ignoring the minor flaw.

Suddenly he stopped short. What had he written there?

"All right, that's enough now," said Le Bréton, trying to take the sheet out of his hand. "We have no time to lose!"

"Then leave me in peace!"

Diderot refused to let go of the text. "Most of the inhabitants of

Arabia," he read aloud, "were Christians. They practiced medicine, a science that was equally useful for the princes as for the priests, for the heretic as well as for the strict believer. The Christians achieved importance through the trade that they conducted, so that the Saracens showed them the greatest respect and admiration because of the natural superiority of the Christians' enlightenment compared with their own ignorance . . ." Diderot frowned. Had he presented the Christians in the Middle East in such a favorable light? That sounded like a fairy tale from the *Thousand and One Nights*. What had happened to his criticism?

"Good God! How long are you going to—" Le Bréton didn't finish his sentence. As Diderot looked at the distraught face of the publisher, all at once a suspicion rose up in him, a fearsome, dreadful, utterly monstrous suspicion.

No!

It couldn't be!

It was impossible!

Once more he scanned the lines, feverish with agitation, from the beginning to the end. He had not only written the article, but edited it and read the proofs; he knew it backward and forward. But the further he read, the more his suspicion grew: What he was reading here was not what he had written. This article resembled his text as little as the bastard that a faithless strumpet might try to pass off on her cuckolded husband as his own flesh and blood.

In total bewilderment he looked at Le Bréton. The publisher was as white as crème fraiche.

"Now don't get excited!" wheezed the walrus. "I can explain everything."

98

It was nighttime on Rue de la Harpe. The printing presses were quiet, the workers were gone. Only on the top floor, in the editorial office below the mansard roof, were lights still burning. The dark publishing house echoed with the sound of two voices coming from this room.

"You've stuck a dagger in my heart! Twenty years of my life wasted, all for naught!"

"What a gross exaggeration! They're mere trifles, tiny details—"

"How many weeks, how many months has this deception been going on? After we defeated all our enemies, you stab me in the back—my own publisher! Has anyone ever heard of such a heinous act?"

"Go home and sleep. Get some rest. You're totally exhausted from work."

"You have distorted and mutilated and castrated my work!"

"Only for your own protection. Believe me. You'll thank me someday."

"Don't make me laugh! You were afraid of a new ban. You were thinking only of your own profit, and you acted out of the basest greed. You barbarian! You vandal! You—" Diderot was at a loss for words. What were the terrors of the barbarians, the ravages of the Vandals compared to this violation? Le Bréton had deceived him in the worst possible fashion. He alone had the opportunity to revise the manuscripts and galleys one more time before they went to press. And how he had abused this opportunity! This man who shared his interest in the success of the enterprise had dealt him a greater blow than all their enemies put together over two decades.

After Diderot had discovered the distortion of his article on the Saracens, he looked at one sheet after another. His article on Spinoza? Practically nothing was left of it—not a word that you had to touch God in order to understand Him, only a couple of harmless sentences about natural science. His article on the hegemony of the sultans? Every allusion to the hegemony of the king had been deleted—even his name had been removed, and the author of the article had been changed to Anonymous, as if he'd been taken out of circulation.

Diderot had believed he had defeated the censorship, but what was the censorship of the government compared to the censorship practiced by his own publisher? Le Bréton had sinned not only against him, but against all the authors of the last ten volumes. His axe had spared no one. Many articles were scarcely recognizable. Contributions from Voltaire, Marmontel, Turgot—the ideas of the greatest philosophers of the century had been adulterated by an underhanded scoundrel whose cowardice was exceeded only by his narrow-mindedness.

"The authors wrote their contributions without demanding an honorarium. And this is the way you thank them?"

"What? No honorarium? What about the twenty-five hundred *livres* that I paid you each year? What were you living on that whole time?"

"D'Holbach, Quesnay, Rousseau—they never saw a *sou*."

"So does that give them the right to ruin me?"

"You ruined yourself! The whole book is rubbish! The loss is nothing compared to the money you embezzled from the project. The subscribers paid for the work out of confidence in my good name, and now they receive from you this mutilated torso!"

"Don't worry about the customers. They prefer ten times over to receive a torso for their money rather than no book at all!"

"The journalists desire nothing more than to hurt us badly. They will spread rumors all over Paris, in the provinces, even abroad, that the *Encyclopedia* is nothing but a pile of tasteless rubbish. They will drag us through the muck with this book, they will mock and ridicule us. And they will accuse us all of treason. The most shameful treason that the world has ever known. You have succeeded in stripping the book of its appeal and value. As punishment you will lose everything, your honor and your fortune."

Le Bréton held up his fat white hand. Diderot broke off his harangue and gazed at him. The publisher squeezed his eyes shut so that between the bulges of fat they became no more than two slits. He was guilt personified.

"What shall I do, Diderot? Make me a reasonable proposal, and we can talk about it."

For an instant Diderot felt hopeful. "Do you still have the originals?" he asked. "The manuscripts and galleys with the proofreading? Using those I could undo the changes. It would require a great effort, but . . ."

He didn't finish his sentence because Le Bréton was shaking his head. "I'm sorry, but there are no originals left. They've all been burned."

"Then . . . then do whatever you like!" said Diderot. "I don't give a damn. I wash my hands of the whole affair."

Before Le Bréton could reply, Diderot had left the editorial office and stamped down the stairs, leaving the publishing house once and for all—deceived, humiliated, destroyed.

Outside it was as dark as on the first day of Creation.

99

In the year 1765, almost two decades after Denis Diderot at Café Procope had won over the publisher Le Bréton for his lunatic project, the crucial moment had finally come for the work of dozens of authors as well as an army of typesetters and printers. The last ten volumes of the *Encyclopedia*, sewn in paperback and bundled, were ready to be delivered.

Everything went according to plan, like a commando action organized by the general staff. In order to keep the fuss to a minimum, Le Bréton had decided to put all ten volumes on the market simultaneously. Whether in Paris or Bordeaux, Toulouse or Rennes, the delivery took place so swiftly and smoothly that neither the church nor the police seemed to get wind of the action. The greatest publishing feat had been accomplished. It was the most lavish book venture in the history of humankind since the invention of the printing press, and it occurred without further interference by the authorities, at least for the present. The *Encyclopedia* was now in the hands of its readers.

While the philosophers in the coffeehouses and garret rooms of Paris celebrated Diderot as the savior of the lexicon, Sophie, who had received one copy of each of the completed text volumes from Le Bréton, was plagued by doubts. "Printed in Neuchâtel," she read as she opened one volume, "at the workshop of Samuel Fauche & Compagnie." With the help of this book people would learn to shape their lives on earth to achieve the highest good: Happiness. And what could be more essential than that?

Haunted by doubts, her only consolation was the sight of Dorval, who immersed himself in the work of his father with all the enthusiasm of his thirteen years. He couldn't know that the texts he read were as false as the notice of the place of publication and the name of the printer—they contained only a distant echo of the messages that Diderot and his comrades-in-arms had originally intended.

"Is my father famous now?" asked Dorval.

Sophie was about to answer when a postman appeared at her open kitchen window to give her a letter. She recognized the handwriting at first glance.

Madame,

After all that has transpired between you and me in the past, I hardly dare write to you. However, since I know how dear the Encyclopedia is to your heart, I find myself today, in spite of everything, forced to break my silence.

Something unimaginable has happened: Le Bréton is in the Bastille; he was arrested as he personally delivered twenty copies of the new text volumes to subscribers at Versailles, right before the eyes of the king, so to speak. As if that were not enough, a rumor is circulating that Diderot was the one who reported him to the police—the editor betraying his own publisher! One might almost surmise that he sought to destroy his own work. What could have driven him to such madness?

Very affectionately yours, I remain
Your Chrétien de Malesherbes

Sophie bit her lip. She knew the answer to Malesherbes's question— and this knowledge nearly robbed her of all reason.

100

It is said that Paris is Paradise for women, Purgatory for men, and Hell for horses. Sartine could confirm this last as his coach jolted and bumped along on the way from his new, luxurious home in Montparnasse to the Jesuit church of Saint-Paul-Saint-Louis. Father Radominsky had summoned him so he could deliver an important message, and Sartine felt too obligated to this man to refuse a meeting, though he was up to his ears in work.

Whenever he passed through this part of the city in his coach, Sartine asked himself when the magistrate would devote the proper attention to the dangers lurking beneath the streets and squares. The reason for the countless potholes in the uneven surface was the haphazard exploitation of the underground quarries beneath Paris, which had been worked for centuries without the slightest safety precautions. By now the excavations had assumed alarming proportions, and even a cursory study of the foundation upon which entire quarters of the city rested would provoke anxiety and fear. Sartine had inspected with his own eyes the abandoned quarry that lay beneath the cellar of the astronomical observatory. Ceilings partially caved in, subsidence full of cracks and holes, pits as big as craters, pillars that threatened to collapse under the load above them, two-story stone quarries whose columns seemed capable only of shoring up each other. And the Parisians ate and drank, worked and slept in the buildings that rested atop this crumbling foundation without giving a thought to the danger.

Sartine glanced at his gold pocket watch. Why did Radominsky want to speak to him? Did the priest perhaps see an opportunity to exploit the strife among the Encyclopedists and further the cause of the church and state? Sartine knew that the rumors about Diderot and his publisher were nonsense. Diderot had betrayed no one—Le Bréton had been caught because the police had done their duty and kept their eyes open. Sartine was occupied by quite a different riddle: Why hadn't Diderot defended his work? Why had he accepted the mutilation of the *Encyclopedia* without vigorous protest? Diderot had even voiced his support for Le Bréton and contributed to the effort that eventually secured the publisher's release. Why the devil had he done that? Could it be that he knew the whole truth? A typesetter from the print shop, who had been providing Sartine with information from Rue de la Harpe for years, had told him about the manipulation of the *Encyclopedia*—and how it had all come about. But the prefect of police decided to keep this knowledge to himself for the time being. It was nobody's business but his and Diderot's.

The bells of Saint-Paul-Saint-Louis were just calling the faithful to evening mass when his coach reached the Jesuit church.

"Was there no way to prevent the release of Le Bréton?" asked Radominsky after they had greeted each other in the library.

Sartine shook his head. "My hands were tied; the chancellor gave me explicit instructions. Obviously the government is weary of the whole affair. Monsieur de Maupeou remarked as much."

"This is how people express their gratitude . . . So the text volumes have been delivered to the subscribers?"

"Unfortunately, *mon père,* all of them. If you'd like the figures, I had a survey prepared." Sartine pulled out his notebook. "Bordeaux, three hundred fifty-six copies; Toulouse, four hundred fifty-one; Rennes, two hundred eighteen—"

"Enough!" the Jesuit interrupted him. "It pains me too much to hear it."

"All the same, we have ascertained that the articles with the worst heresies have been cleaned up. I have checked the texts; in comparison with the early volumes I would call them downright harmless."

"I have also studied them." Radominsky grimaced. "'I know thy works, that thou art neither cold nor hot; I would thou wert cold or hot,' saith the Lord. 'So then because thou art lukewarm, and neither cold nor hot, I will spew thee out of My mouth.'"

"Pardon me?" Sartine asked in annoyance.

"If I have an enemy, I want to be proud of him. The articles in the last ten volumes, in comparison to the earlier ones, seem as though a castrated Diderot were guiding the pen. I hear," the priest said, changing the subject, "that Le Bréton has made a fortune."

"Indeed, they say three million *livres*. With that money he bought the house where Monsieur de Jaucourt once lived on Rue de Mâcon—his last. The *chevalier* was completely ruined financially because of the *Encyclopedia*. Le Bréton will soon be moving into the house with his family."

Radominsky nodded. "Tell me, Monsieur de Sartine, and please give me an honest answer: Which side won the victory? The Word of God or human presumption? Or," he added full of bitterness, "did Mammon triumph in the end, as the Devil wants to make us believe in the illusion of earthly reality? That would be hard to tolerate."

Sartine hesitated. "I too do not know the answer, *mon père,*" he said at last. "But if I may express my personal impressions, your question disconcerts me. It sounds—how shall I put it?—almost like a farewell."

"What an instinct for people you have," said Radominsky with a melancholy smile. "Yes, I have resigned from my position as father confessor to the queen. The resistance at court to my personage was too great since the king has now officially dissolved the Society of Jesus. I shall obey the order of my general to take with me nothing and to conceal nothing that belongs to the order, so as to prove myself through great patience as a servant of God."

Sartine took a deep breath. So that was the message Radominsky had summoned him to hear. "Do you really want to give up the fight?" he asked. "I understand that the present situation deeply wounds and offends you—no one has offered greater service to the kingdom than you. But there are encouraging signs that the wind is shifting. Almost all the bishops in the land are supporting your order, and Pope Clemens has issued a bull that expressly upholds the rights of the Society of Jesus."

"And the parliament immediately forbade the bull for Paris and all of France. No, Monsieur de Sartine, I have been on this earth too long to believe in miracles any longer. They gave me a choice: Either I swear an oath of total submission, or else I must leave my post." Radominsky raised his hands. "I have done what I could; I even renounced the founder of my order so as not to give up the fight. But now it's enough. God's will be done! I am tired, an old man with strength only for prayer."

A young abbé came in to light the candles in the library. Through the open door a sweetish smell streamed into the room from the neighboring sacristy. Did it come from a body lying in state, or was it the incense for the Sacrifice of the Mass, which was just being celebrated in the church? Sartine looked at Radominsky sitting motionless at his desk, his elbows resting on the arms of his chair, his fingertips templed before his face. For twenty years he had admired this man and simultaneously feared him. It was like losing a father.

"Where will you go, Reverend Father? To Rome?"

Radominsky shook his head. "I would like to see the Black Madonna in my home country once again. A cloister not far from Kraków will take me in. There I can wait in the company of my brothers in the faith until God in His goodness calls me to Him from this world. And you, monsieur? What are your plans?"

Sartine did not reply at once. There was still a task he had to complete. Should he reveal to the father the truth about his intentions? No, now he was his own master—he was no longer accountable to anyone.

"I will not give up the fight," was all he said. "I will keep trying to serve my king and my church insofar as I am able with my modest powers."

101

A night of wild dissipation lay behind Diderot, filled with wine and tobacco and love. He hadn't slept even an hour when he crossed the Pont Neuf that morning, squinting into the sun so dazzlingly bright, as if it wanted to rob him of his eyesight. The new lieutenant general of the Paris police and chief of the censorship authority of France, Antoine de Sartine, had summoned him for a talk at eleven o'clock. He had no choice but to comply, dressed in his sweat-stained and stinking clothes.

Diderot was so dazed that he felt the cries of the street vendors as sharp stabs in his ears. The hammering of the tinkers echoed as if the bells of Notre-Dame were tolling inside his skull, the filing of the smiths scraped and grated on his brain, and the coaches rolling by awoke in him the wish that the paving stones might be covered with padding to muffle the intolerably loud rattling of the iron-clad wheels. He had spent the entire night with the whores at the Palais Royal, who roamed about like cats through the arcade after darkness fell. They were the only creatures whose behavior matched exactly who they were, and if they were tainted with nearly all the human vices, at least they lacked the shabbiest of the lot: hypocrisy.

Diderot's stomach was growling so loudly that he stopped at a food stall at the end of the bridge. For weeks now he had been plagued by a voracious appetite that was worse than his wife's when she was pregnant. He couldn't walk past a vendor's stall without having something to eat. Ravenous and at the same time disgusted, he let his gaze wander over the items displayed. The food that ended up here had been spat on by the kitchen boys in the great houses of the nobility and spurned even by the lackeys. On tarnished plates remnants of food grew moldy in the sun; a bishop or a president of the court may have already had these victuals halfway into his mouth before he changed his mind: gnawed chicken legs, dried-up slices of roast, spoiled fish. Although it made him want to throw up, Diderot bought a portion of the repulsive stuff for three *sous*. The vendor hurried to scrape it off the plates. His hunger was stronger than his loathing; he felt only hunger, was nothing but hunger, and with his bare fingers he stuffed the cold, greasy leftovers into his mouth, as if that would fill up the gaping emptiness that had opened up inside him.

By the time he arrived at the Palais de Justice he was about to vomit. A sentry instructed him to wait outside the room of the lieutenant general. Reluctantly Diderot took a seat. As he looked around to see whether there was any water to drink, he recalled that he had sat here once before, many, many years ago. What hopes had imbued him then—hopes that no arrest, no threat, no danger however great could have shattered . . . What was he doing here now? He had nothing more to do with all this.

The door was slightly ajar, and he could see Sartine at his desk, wearing a gold-braided uniform. A secretary approached him, bowing obsequiously to whisper in his ear. A dozen office clerks waited humbly and patiently for him to make decisions, with a couple of strokes of his pen, regarding the petitions that were heaped up on his desk. Diderot had to belch. This man, he knew, had been pursuing him for years with a calm and systematic hatred. What did he have up his sleeve now, wishing to extract revenge one more time?

"Believe me, Monsieur Diderot," said Sartine when they were seated facing each other a few minutes later, "in my lifetime I would rather have had you as a friend than an enemy. We are both men of science. We believe in reason, know no prejudices, and despise any form of superstition."

"And yet worlds separate us, Your Grace," replied Diderot, more out of habit than conviction. "Because it is my job to write books, and yours to burn them."

"Isn't it better to burn a book if there is a risk that its content could cause the whole country to be ignited and go up in flames?" Sartine asked. "I do only what I consider my duty. Even though I possess neither the virtues nor the talents that I must have to deserve your respect—you cannot fault a man who has spent his best years defending the state against revolt."

"You're not defending the state, you're defending a tyrant."

Sartine measured Diderot with a disparaging expression. "The worst tyrant," he said, "is dissipation, because this tyrant lives inside of men.

I know whereof I speak; in my younger years I saw the victims of vice languishing in their hovels. My work took me to all their stations, into brothels where they get their start, and also to the Hôpital Bicêtre, where all of them end up, their faces full of suppurating boils, condemned to perish or more often to disintegrate into scraps of flesh, while their souls and their minds continue to exist in the midst of the most atrocious rot. But what's the matter, Monsieur Diderot? Would you like a drink of water?"

Without waiting for a reply, Sartine picked up the carafe that stood on his desk and poured Diderot some water. He emptied the glass in one draft, in big, greedy gulps like a man dying of thirst. Afterward he felt a little stronger.

"I know a much worse tyrant," Diderot then said. "This tyrant is like a wild animal that has dipped his tongue in human blood and now can no longer leave it alone. I know that this animal lacks nourishment and therefore preys upon the philosophers. I know that it has fixed its eyes on me, and that perhaps I will be the first to be devoured. Wherever resistance stirs, the defenders of truth cast blame on the unrest, simply because we philosophers take the liberty to point out the stupidity of it. What sort of a country are we living in? An honest man can lose his fortune and his honor within twenty-four hours because there are no laws; he can lose his freedom because the rulers are full of suspicion, and he can lose his life because they count the life of a citizen for nothing and seek to fend off contempt through actions of terror. Yes, they carry their heinous motives so far as to assert that they will keep all harm from France merely by burning books."

Sartine was staring at him so intently that Diderot stopped talking.

"Did you lend your support for the release of your publisher Le Bréton?" asked the police prefect. "Are those actually the reasons?"

Diderot suddenly had a nasty taste in his mouth, and he didn't know whether it came from the leftover food he had eaten, which he kept belching up, or from his own words, which seemed to him as foul and rotten as the food, because he was merely spewing out ruminations without believing in them.

"Is that why you summoned me here, to ask me that?" he replied uncertainly.

"Well, I would have understood completely if you had left your publisher in the lurch. Yes, I even would have found it understandable if you had reported him to the police. I hear that Le Bréton pulled the wool over your eyes in a rather wicked way."

"Because he relieved your censors of their work?" Diderot crossed his arms. "I'm sorry, Your Honor, but there I must disappoint you. I'm a philosopher, not a turncoat. Besides, in my youth I learned that once you start a project, you finish it."

"Really?" said Sartine full of astonishment. "You don't have the slightest idea."

"Idea of what?" Diderot asked impatiently.

"Of the truth," replied the prefect of police, and a subtle smile played over his lips. "The truth for which you supposedly carried the banner. But are you also capable of handling the truth when it concerns your own work?"

Sartine's expression now seemed a trace more obliging, and Diderot realized with a start that the moment of reckoning had come. All at once his jacket was too tight, and the rough woolen stockings scratched his calves so that he could hardly stand it. Only now did he notice that his clothes were sticking to his body with sweat.

"If you are a friend of the truth, Monsieur Diderot," said Sartine, "wouldn't you like to know who is actually to blame for altering the *Encyclopedia*?"

102
❧ ❧

Rockets shot into the night sky with a whoosh, exploding in crackling multicolored bursts of fire to the ooohs and aaahs of the assembled multitudes. It was Johannes Night, the eve of the summer solstice, on the Place de Grève, the site of the weekly markets and the monthly executions of those sentenced to death by parliament. Every year on June 24, the city of Paris put on a fireworks display to celebrate the beginning of summer.

The popping of the firecrackers could be heard all the way to Rue Taranne, and the flashing fireworks glinted off the windowpanes and illuminated the mansard as Diderot cleared away once and for all the cardboard cartons containing his notes and excerpts, drafts and completed manuscripts, that had formed the basis for the *Encyclopedia* over the past two decades. He didn't want to keep anything that might remind him of that enterprise.

He stood before the wreckage of his life: The heavy artillery of reason, the armada of philosophy, the siege engine of enlightenment—his life's work was nothing but a mutilated torso. He had sacrificed his dreams for the truth, in the hope of one day becoming the Lucretius, the Pliny of the new era. Dozens of unwritten dramas and novels and pamphlets had never been allowed to see the light of day because he had devoted all his efforts to the service of this one great work. He had felt himself called to touch the souls of humanity, but he had renounced this calling, putting aside his most magnificent ideas as well as his personal ambitions, in order to change the world through a single book that would collect all the knowledge of humanity in one place—he had vowed on his father's grave to take on this task. It had been his goal to draw up the map to paradise on earth. What was left of it? Even as he fought to drive out superstition from the minds of men, he himself had been duped, his work ruined, the truth distorted, the knowledge of the world castrated. By the hand of a woman whom he had loved more than any other person before or since . . .

Outside a bolt of lightning flashed through the night, followed by a clap of thunder. On the table lay a letter that Diderot had written to Sophie when he still believed that Le Bréton was the perpetrator of the betrayal:

Is that not a story to drive one mad? During four long years he had practiced his perfidy. He would get up at night, his actions akin to setting fire to his own bookshop, and that seemed to him delightful. He creeps around me with his fat and ponderous figure; he sits down, stands up, sits back down, wants to speak, is silent. Ah, what I would give if this slaughter of our work had never occurred . . .

Diderot took the sheet of paper and crumpled it in his hand. He had written the letter without sending it off, like so many other letters, wanting only to be close to Sophie in his thoughts. But what was the reality? He had poured out his heart to the very person who had his entire misfortune on her conscience. Le Bréton was merely her accomplice, a rotten little profiteer who had betrayed Diderot to ensure his own profits—a corrupt man. But Sophie? The disappointment that she had caused him was beyond measure, worse than any despair. She had dealt him a mortal blow, robbed him of all life. Because her betrayal had pushed him into an emptiness from which there was no escape: the emptiness of his soul.

Why? For what purpose?

Suddenly he was overcome by a voracious hunger, as if he hadn't seen a piece of bread in days. Should he go to the Place de Grève? There the people's feast was under way, to which the city councillors invited everyone on Johannes Night. The thought of the event made his mouth water: raised platforms from which smoked tongue, blood sausage, and rolls were thrown to the crowd, while from open spigots white and red wine poured out, which the people collected in jugs and pails.

Diderot stepped to the window and looked out into the darkness, lit up now and then with the flash of fireworks. If he hurried he could get to the Île Saint-Louis in time. But did he really want to do that? The feast at the Place de Grève was in truth a disgusting spectacle; for one night the magistrate endeavored to compensate the people for all the injustice that had been done to them over the past year. On the same site where they had slaughtered Robert Damiens like a beast, the portrait of the monarch in all his splendor could be seen on this night. Baseness and misery were the table companions at this appalling banquet. In the hands of the shameless distributors the rolls and sausages became like stones hurled from a slingshot, and anyone who valued his life was sent running. Those who pressed forward to get some of the gushing wine had to fear being knocked to the ground and trampled, while tattered musicians surrounded by stinking pans of pitch made their fiddles screech under the strokes of their stiff bows. The rabble hopped and cried and howled and stamped to the music, as happy as if they were in Paradise.

Is this what he had worked for his whole life? What bold dreams he had once given breath, and what a pitiful end they had come to. . . .

A new burst of fireworks, bigger than all the previous ones, exploded with a loud boom in the sky. For a second Paris seemed ripped from the darkness, and the alleys, the streets, the squares divulged their secrets in the flashes of the artificial lightning. Diderot nodded. Yes, life was like that, just like this night: an infinite sea of darkness, only here and there illuminated by the spasms of a flickering light.

Was such a life to be tolerated? As he sought the answer, a strange idea came to him, a small, wild idea that might perhaps inspire a novel: the story of a man who denies his own freedom and becomes fixated on the notion that everything he does is divinely predestined. Because only through such fatalism can he endure his life—his life and his freedom.

Diderot was headed straight for his writing table to jot down this idea, when there was a knock at the door.

103

In the doorway stood Malesherbes.

"May I come in?"

"If you'll excuse the mess, please do. I'm just clearing things out. What brings you here to see me?"

The former director of the Royal Library and chief censor closed the door behind him and waited for Diderot to offer him a chair. When that did not happen, he said, "Madame Sophie is about to leave Paris. I thought you ought to know."

Diderot shrugged. "What does that matter to me?"

"If you'll permit me to speak openly?"

"As you like."

Malesherbes put a hand on Diderot's arm and looked him in the eye. "Sophie loves you. No one knows this better than I. She respected me, regarded me highly, perhaps even liked me—but her love was reserved only for you. You shouldn't let her go!"

Diderot pulled his arm away. "A woman," he said with cold contempt, "is like a richly set table. But there is a great difference between looking at her before the meal and afterward."

"I can understand your cynicism. I am also familiar with the pain of separation. But don't forget: You have a son together. Dorval admires and adores you above everyone else in the world."

"Did someone send you here to tell me this? Then please tell me why my son has been kept from me all these years." Diderot shook his head. "No, I never want to see that woman again."

Malesherbes hesitated. "I know," he said, "it's not my place to demand an explanation from you. But I can neither understand nor approve of your conduct."

Diderot turned to the window so that the other man would not see his face. As the last of the rockets burst in the black sky, he said, "You always supported the *Encyclopedia,* and a few times even risked your job and your position to save it from destruction. So you have the right to know the truth."

"And what is the truth?" Malesherbes asked softly as Diderot faltered.

"Sophie destroyed the *Encyclopedia.* Without my knowledge she censored hundreds of articles behind my back, distorting them so much that they are unrecognizable. The work of years and decades was ruined."

"Impossible! Who told you such a thing?"

"Monsieur de Sartine, your successor. And he assured me that his information was reliable. Yes, she destroyed my life's work," Diderot repeated, "with the presumption and capriciousness of a despot. She betrayed me in a cowardly manner and persuaded my publisher to help her commit this act of betrayal. She abandoned me to suffer contempt, derision, and ruin. Thank God I'm old enough to know that such a crime seldom goes unpunished. That's the only consolation I have."

There was a pause. Diderot could hear his visitor taking deep breaths, as if he couldn't believe this could be true; silence filled the room like a noxious gas.

Finally Malesherbes asked, "And why do you think she did it?"

"To hurt me and to take revenge, to annihilate me—how do I know?" Diderot turned around. "But why are you asking me about motives? Can there be any reason in the world that would justify such a scandalous deed?"

Malesherbes was silent again; obviously he had no ready answer. He looked old and gray, much older than he actually was—so much had the news upset his composure. He seemed to be cogitating; almost imperceptibly he wagged his big heavy head with the carelessly coiffed wig as he kept brushing flecks of tobacco from the lapels of his brown coat.

What was going through his mind?

Diderot had never been able to figure out this man. He was the son and protégé of the former chancellor and at the same time a philosopher, state councillor to the king but nevertheless an enlightened spirit. He had banned the *Encyclopedia* and then held his hand protectively over it, officially prohibiting the printing of the text volumes and yet tolerating their completion. He seemed to contain within himself all the contradictions from which this ailing regime suffered. And now this man who had lived with Sophie for such a long time had come here to reconcile the two of them.

"I believe," said Malesherbes after a long while, "there is hardly a soul who wishes more ardently for a free press in this country than I; perhaps it is the tragedy of my life that it was precisely my task to subject thoughts and ideas written in our language to censorship. But I did learn one thing during the years that I held this regrettable office: If there must be censorship, no matter what the reason, it is best that it be exercised by an opponent of censorship."

"Why are you telling me this?" asked Diderot. "I can't see how these thoughts concern me. I'm going to resign from the editorship of the *Encyclopedia*. But all this is hardly an answer to my question."

"Don't you understand? Sophie didn't destroy your work, she saved it! Without her intervention the *Encyclopedia* would have been banned forever. It would have been put on the Index and burned. Sophie prevented that from happening. For that she sacrificed her love—the highest price a person can pay!"

"I didn't ask her to do this," replied Diderot. "And the present state of the *Encyclopedia* arouses only contempt in me. It would have been better if the work had never been published. And you talk to me of love!"

"Yes, monsieur, because the truth needs love—as love needs the truth! The two belong together. Or would you throw out the baby with the bathwater?"

"What bathwater?"

"Let me explain." Malesherbes took a deep breath before he went on. "Assume that Pythagoras had formulated even more theorems than those we know today—would the ones we have lose their validity because the others did not survive? Or assume further, that there was a fifth Gospel that was destroyed many centuries ago—is that any reason for us to burn the whole Bible today? And finally, assume that the inventor of the wheel had at the same time devised a way to drive it forward without the use of physical force—would we then have to destroy the wheel because we no longer possess the complete invention?" Malesherbes shook his head. "No, Monsieur Diderot. You must not give up! You should thank Sophie for preserving your work from total destruction, and continue on with it, as best you can. Even when we strive for perfection, life is nothing more than an attempt to achieve it through a series of greater or smaller imperfections. There is still much to do; the illustrated volumes await you!"

"You can talk as much as you like, Monsieur de Malesherbes," said Diderot, "but my decision remains firm. I want nothing more to do with this dreadful affair."

"You have accomplished such great work," his visitor insisted, "more than any other philosopher of our time—more than Voltaire and Rousseau. You have taken stock of human ideas, made an inventory of the human spirit. You have trimmed the tree of knowledge according to what is possible for humanity, you have toppled metaphysics from its pedestal and set philosophy in its place, and you were the first to recognize that the natural sciences and the mechanical arts will supplant mathematics and logic. Moreover, you have not only gathered the knowledge necessary for improving the world, but with the *Encyclopedia* you have drawn up a plan for its practical realization. You have opened up a new era, monsieur! Would you now stop halfway or even turn back?"

Diderot closed his eyes. He was tired, exhausted, empty.

"No," he said then, looking at his visitor. "I'm not chasing fame by continuing an enterprise that for me means only more torment. I have already suffered too much—and am still suffering. I do not wish to subject myself to more torture. And as far as that woman is concerned, of whom you never tire of speaking," he continued as Malesherbes made a move to interject, "all my senses cringe at the thought of seeing her ever again."

"This woman loves you! More than you can ever imagine! She has dedicated her life to your work."

"She has annihilated my work," Diderot countered, "now and for all time." He paused, then added, "She might just as well have murdered my son."

Malesherbes gazed at him, his gray eyes full of horror. Diderot returned his gaze firmly and undeterred.

They stood facing each other like this for a long while. Then Malesherbes turned and departed.

104

Malesherbes had scarcely gone out the door before Diderot began shaking all over. Until the last second of the visit he had fought to control himself, but now his powers failed him. All manner of contradictory thoughts, memories, and feelings had been stirred up inside him, fighting with one another, and raging as if his soul were a battlefield on which the demons of his life had been unleashed to wage war. He couldn't stand being in this room another minute! Unshaven, with no coat or wig or tricorn, he stumbled down the stairs and out into the open to escape the demons.

The Place de Grève was still hellishly chaotic. The fireworks were over, but sausages and rolls were still being tossed from the platforms that had been set up all around the torchlit square. Blind with desire in the flickering light, the people were madly trying to grab something else that they hoped would bring them a scrap of happiness, at least for this one night. They came to blows under the pipes from which the last dregs of the wine poured out, with more liquid flowing onto the pavement than into the tankards that were everywhere lifted into the air. Suddenly a few gold pieces were tossed from a window. In a mad frenzy, their faces smeared with blood and muck, the crowd fell upon the coins, women and men knocking one another to the ground, ready to break the next person's legs to get hold of one.

Diderot turned away in disgust. He hurried off at a run toward the Seine, and a few minutes later crossed the river, following some dark impulse toward he knew not what goal. In the smoky light from the streetlamps he saw the last of the roaming whores. They dared only point to the entrances of their tenements, out of fear they'd be arrested by the night brigades who chased after them with their pole lanterns after midnight. The only women safe from the guard were those in the Palais

Royal. That sinful paradise, which kept its doors open until two in the morning to allay the desires of lonely men, was the property of the Duc d'Orléans, and the police had as little access as the soldiers of the guard. Diderot let his gaze scan the area. Under the arcades there were so many beautiful women on view that even a man condemned to death could spend hours here without yearning for freedom. But tonight the magic was gone. Diderot didn't feel the slightest desire to speak to any of the secretive creatures who smiled at him from the shadows, and it was still hours before the night watchmen would take out their keys to lock the city gates. Diderot's inner restlessness drove him onward.

His stomach was growling. Where could he find something to eat at this hour? The market halls were the only places in Paris that never slept. Thousands of voices resounded inside, with no time to pause or sleep, and in the taverns between the stalls the brandy flowed. Diderot ordered a glass and a portion of cold beef with parsley. The liquor had been diluted with water but spiced heavily with cloves, and the beef tasted like mutton. As he drank and ate and waited for weariness to overcome him, he watched the loaded carts as they arrived from the villages and suburbs in a seemingly endless stream to deliver their freight. After the vegetable farmers came the fishmongers, and after the fishmongers the poultry and egg dealers, and after them finally the grocers of the city, for this was where all the markets in Paris obtained their wares.

As the lanterns began to fade, Diderot paid and stood up. Outside a new day was breaking, a fresh breeze wafted over from the river, and the flower and fruit halls were filled with such a lavish abundance and splendor, as though summer itself had emptied its cornucopia here. The fruits were piled up in mountains on the display tables, and the scent of roses and stocks, of herbs and spices, filled the air.

But the demons gave Diderot no rest. Where else could he possibly exorcize them?

105

An hour later Diderot found himself back at Café Procope. He hadn't entered the place in years. On this early morning there were barely a dozen customers sitting at the heavy oak tables under the smoke-blackened ceiling beams. Most of them were hidden behind a newspaper or quietly drinking a cup of coffee to wake up.

His eyes burning with fatigue, Diderot stared at the table where he was sitting. A faded date that someone had carved with a knife in the dark wood leaped out at him: October 18, 1747. He was actually seated at the same place where he had won over Le Bréton with his great plan. The publisher had carved the date after they had agreed with a hand-shake. Le Bréton had then ordered champagne because he had a feeling this was the deal of his lifetime. In contrast with d'Alembert, who had seen only the dangers—as timid as a little girl he had gazed at them with his brown eyes. At the memory of the thin, unprepossessing man Diderot was filled with regret. They hadn't seen each other in years. It was said that d'Alembert was ill and lived under the guardianship of an old maid named Julie de l'Espinasse, who held him captive in her residence, smothering him with motherly care and sugar water. The man had such a great spirit, yet such a weak character . . . Should he go to visit him? At any rate, d'Alembert had been accepted into the Académie, while this recognition had so far been denied to Diderot.

"Your order, monsieur?"

Diderot looked up. A very young waitress, not even twenty years old, stood before him. Diderot stared at her as if she were an apparition. This was exactly the way Sophie had once stood. He had tried to fend off this memory for so many hours, tried with all his might to suppress it the whole night long, as he had restlessly wandered through the streets. Here it overtook him. Where was Sophie now? Still in Paris or already traveling? He had seen her once as she had stepped out of her house onto the street, in the suburb of Saint-Cloud not far from the spot where the nets were stretched between the banks, across the Seine to catch the flotsam. He had bribed a police informer to find out her address, in the hopes of seeing his son. But the sight of her had pained him so much that he had never repeated the attempt.

"*Pardon,* monsieur, your order?" asked the waitress again.

"Bring me anything," replied Diderot. "It doesn't matter, anything you like."

"Anything? I'm sorry, we don't have that."

"All right then, a cup of hot chocolate."

"Gladly, monsieur." The girl was radiant, and she was still radiant when she returned a few minutes later, setting the steaming beverage on his table. As Diderot raised the cup to his lips, the waitress said, "If all my customers knew the good that chocolate can do, they would never order anything else. A cup costs only six *sous,* and it's the most pleasant and least expensive way to retain your strength until evening."

Diderot set down the cup and looked at her full of amazement. Her words sounded oddly familiar, as if he had heard them before . . . Heard? No! He had said them himself, he remembered now, said them and written them: a few unremarkable words among millions and millions he had either said or written sometime in his life.

"Most certainly," he replied, annoyed. "Chocolate is the best drink of all. But tell me, where did you hear this?"

"Every reasonable person knows this," she replied with a laugh. "Chocolate not only tastes good, but is satisfying all day long if it's correctly prepared. And the proper way to do it is described in a big learned book. The café owner read the passage aloud to us waitresses, so that we would remember it. And he was right; it's something really useful to know. If a customer asks me what he should drink, I always have an answer ready. But what is it?" she asked as Diderot suddenly got up, laid six *sous* on the table, and headed for the door. "Did I say something wrong?"

106

A coach with four powerful Belgian horses in harness stood waiting in front of the small house in the suburb of Saint-Cloud. Two pale, stocky porters, with necks so short and thick that their heads seemed to grow directly out of their shoulders, had been carrying out furniture and other household items since early morning: Beds, chairs, cabinets, tables, mirrors, chests, and crates in which crockery, books, and kitchen utensils were stowed. Propping one hand on a cane, they shouldered weights under which an ox would have collapsed, and yet they steered their loads so adroitly and skillfully down stairs and through doors, as if they were carrying goose-down pillows.

Sophie stood in the living room of her emptied house and looked around one last time. In half an hour the post coach would arrive. Two years she had lived here; so much time had passed since the death of the marquise de Pompadour.

Had it been a good time?

There was no sense in thinking about that—her decision was final. She wanted to leave Paris forever. Diderot had betrayed Le Bréton—the editor had caused the arrest of his publisher, as if he wanted to destroy his own work—and she bore the blame for this insanity. No, it made no sense to stay here any longer. She would go back to her village, to Beaulieu, and finally face her past after twenty-five years.

At that thought her heart skipped a beat, and she raised her hand to touch the amulet at her throat. It had been a long time since she had worn this chain—the only memento that bound her to her first home.

Should she have left her village without knowing the truth? Maybe it had been a mistake to come to Paris; maybe her whole life was nothing more than a flight from the darkness of her past.

On the windowsill lay a book. Sophie had placed it there herself the

night before, in order to pack it last before setting off on the long journey. It was bound in red silk, and the middle of the cover had been worn
almost transparent by long use: the adventures of the great Sultan Mongagul and his Princess Mirzoza . . .

It was only a single short passage that she wanted to read again, hardly
more than two dozen words, and yet they meant the world to her. Sophie
hesitated and for a long while couldn't decide, because she knew that those
few words could reach into her very soul. But then she plucked up her
courage and opened the book. It was part of her farewell to the great city.

"The tender woman is the one who gives her love without her jewel
ever speaking, or whose jewel always stirs only in favor of the one man
who encompasses all her love . . ."

Letter by letter, syllable by syllable, word by word, Sophie read the
unremarkable lines as though deciphering the hieroglyphs of her destiny.
What would have happened if she had read this one sentence at the right
time? Diderot had written it for her alone, almost against his will; he had
confessed that to her once, and yet in these words he had portrayed her
truth, the truth of her love.

Wearily she closed her eyes: Why had everything turned out the way
it had? Alas, she knew only too well: Because she had lacked the courage
to believe in her love, or the courage to dare experience happiness with
Diderot, or the courage to enter the wonderful paradise that had stood
open and free before her. She feared becoming like her mother, feared
ending up as she had. Now her jewel was forever silenced, because she
would never again see the man for whom it stirred.

Hurried footsteps woke her from her reverie.

"What's bothering you, Mama?" said Dorval, whose voice had grown
so deep over the past few months that he almost sounded like a man.
"The coach will be here soon."

"You're right," she said, placing the book in a chest that stood ready
for transport. "But what's that heavy crate you're lugging? Shouldn't you
let the men carry it?"

"No, no. It's not going on the wagon. I'm taking it in the coach."

"But why?" She looked at him. "Tell me, what have you hidden in
there?"

Dorval blushed, his childish embarrassment in sharp contrast to his
manly voice and the dark fuzz on his upper lip. "Nothing bad, Mama,
only my favorite book."

"The *Encyclopedia?*"

"Yes, the text volumes. I'm afraid they might get lost on the way. What if the cart tipped over and the books landed in a ditch? Or if there were a robbery and they were stolen?"

"Are they worth that much to you?" Sophie had to smile. "Very well then, as far as I'm concerned you can bring them along in the coach. But don't strain yourself!"

Like a soldier Dorval was still guarding his crate in the empty room when Sophie a little later left the house; she wanted to go down to the river one last time before she got into the post coach.

On the riverbank she experienced the deep, regular rushing of the Seine like an embrace. Time itself seemed to be flowing through her. Yes, she would miss the river, Sophie thought as she gazed into the green waters, the river and all the memories associated with it. . . . How bright and clear and clean the water was here; in many spots you could see all the way to the bottom, and it smelled so fresh and fragrant that it was hard to believe how much flotsam from the big city the waters carried, all the vast amounts of garbage and trash that were caught in the nets of Saint-Cloud, the whole chaotic, incidental detritus of life. . . .

Suddenly Sophie had the feeling that someone was watching her. Involuntarily she turned around.

107

"You?"

Before her stood Diderot. He looked at her with his bright blue eyes, an uncertain smile on his lips.

"The porters told me that I could find you here," he said.

"You were looking for me?"

He nodded. "Why do you want to leave?"

She thought a moment before answering.

"I simply don't think I belong in Paris. Ever since I've been here, I've just made one mistake after another. I kept heading in one direction even though I didn't want to go that way, but I just couldn't stop; I felt as if I were in a labyrinth. And if I tried to do something right, everything simply got worse." She paused. "That's why I'm leaving. Maybe it's not too late."

Diderot shook his head. "You didn't do anything wrong, Sophie. I admit that I cursed and hated and scorned you when I found out what you had done, but—"

"Then you know all about it?" she asked in shock. "That it was me and not Le Bréton?"

"Sartine told me."

"But if you knew, why in Heaven's name did you turn him in?"

"Le Bréton? Turn him in?" Diderot shook his head. "You think I'm capable of such a betrayal?"

Ashamed, Sophie lowered her eyes. "Nevertheless," she said after a while, "what I did to you was a terrible mistake, the biggest mistake I've ever made. But please believe me, I thought it was a way to help you . . ."

"Shhh," he said, placing a finger on her lips.

"Are you going to order me to be quiet again?"

For a moment the gesture made her furious, but then she looked at him. His small head with the gray shock of hair moved on his broad shoulders like a weathercock on a church steeple, and on his upper lip was a trace of foam, like a thin mustache.

"You don't have to explain anything to me," he said. "I know why you did it. A waitress at the Procope just explained it to me."

"A waitress at the Procope?"

"Do you think you're the only smart girl who ever worked there?" he asked with a grin. Then he turned serious. "It was only a trifle, and she probably thought nothing of it. But that was precisely what opened my eyes. I had ordered hot chocolate, and when she brought me the cup she extolled the advantages of chocolate, quoting my own words from the *Encyclopedia*. Can you imagine what that means to me?"

Sophie held her breath as Diderot continued.

"She stood before me, just as you did back then, and her eyes shone with enthusiasm as she recited what she had learned, although it was only about a cup of chocolate. Then I suddenly realized that anything we do to fight misery and ignorance and poverty, no matter how imperfect it may be, is still better than doing nothing at all."

Sophie swallowed hard. "So you really do understand," she whispered, "why I—"

"Yes," he said. "You didn't betray me or the *Encyclopedia*. On the contrary, you made sure that it would continue to exist. I would be a traitor myself if I gave up now." He reached out his hand to her. "Please don't leave! I need you. Together we can finish what we started."

"How . . . how can you even suggest such a possibility?" she stammered, completely bewildered. "Everything I own is already loaded up, all my household goods—my furniture, my books, my crockery."

"Don't worry about that. I'll help you unload everything."

He smiled at her. She was so surprised that she didn't know what to say. She had already made up her mind; a few minutes ago everything had seemed so clear and simple. Was she now supposed to stay here? What had gotten into him? Did he think she loved him? She knew that love was a sickness that pierced the soul like a knife, and when someone lost her heart, she really only lost her reason. She knew this better than any other person in the world; it was something she had known and thought and felt and said for a long time. . . . Was it suddenly not supposed to be true? Merely because he looked at her with those bright blue eyes of his?

Again she met his gaze, and at the same instant such a huge swarm of midges attacked her that her whole body began to tingle.

"Please don't look at me like that!" she said, her mouth suddenly dry; yet at the same time she hoped that he would never stop looking at her that way.

"Stay here, Sophie, stay in Paris!" He faltered, then he said, "Yes, please stay—with me."

He lifted her chin so that she was forced to look at him. His expression was completely serious now. All her thoughts stopped; she wasn't thinking about the next day or the journey, about Beaulieu or Paris. There was no more past and no more future—there was only this moment, only these eyes that seemed to shine like two stars.

As suddenly as it had come, the tingling stopped, the millions and millions of midges left her, and her confusion gave way to a clear and steadfast calm.

Without a word she took his hand.

It was like redemption. When she felt the firm grasp with which he held her hand, softly, very softly, a long-forgotten yearning stirred inside her for the first time in many years; everything was urging her to touch this man. She threw her arms around his neck and together they sank into a long, deep kiss, both of them enveloped by the eternal rushing of the river, which seemed to hold all the time in the world in this one moment.

As their lips parted, they could hear in the distance the horn of a postilion.

"Don't listen to it!" he said. "Or are you still waiting for a coach?"

"No, Denis," said Sophie. "But if I stay, it must be under one condition."

"And what is that?"

"That you promise me to go to the barber regularly, great Mongagul." She took a tip of his sleeve and wiped away the traces of foam that still adorned his upper lip like a thin mustache. "Or do people in your fairytale land still not shave?"

With a tender smile he shook his head. "Then you've decided?"

"Come," she said, "let's go inside. I want to introduce you to your son."

INTERIM

The Sacred Mount

1772

"Credo in unum Deum. Patrem omnipotentem, factorem coeli et terrae . . ."

In the monastery of Jasna Góra, far from Paris, far from the world, the bells of the small basilica called the monks to vespers, the hour-long evening prayers. Only Father Radominsky remained in his cell. For the past six years he'd been a guest at the "Bright Mount" in Częstochowa, Poland, not far from Kraków. Bowed by the burden of age and a much-tested life, he knelt before the Cross of the Savior to end the day in prayer, as he did every evening, alone in a conversation with God, his Lord.

". . . visibilium omnium et invisibilium. Et in unum Dominum Jesum Christum . . ."

The cell lacked any adornments: It had a bed, a table, a chair, and on the wall a cross and a bookcase. This was all he needed for the salvation of his soul. He had returned to his homeland for good, to the Black Madonna of Częstochowa. Half a century ago he had sworn an oath before that painting to dedicate his life as a soldier of the Society of Jesus to God and the Catholic Church. Now that he had once again been allowed to kiss that painting with the miraculous powers, he was waiting only to die, when it was God's will.

". . . Et exspecto resurrectionem mortuorum. Et vitam ventura saeculi . . ."

In the distance he could hear the faint booming of the guns. No, even this fortress of God was not immune to the attacks of the world; the Russian army had already reached the foot of the cloister walls. But what import did such a threat have in the face of eternity? The sacred mount had already survived many attacks; it was the Holy Virgin Mary and not its solid stonework that had always protected it. She was the sole true queen of Christianity. With Her help the cloister would withstand yet another assault.

There was a knock on the door.

"Dominus vobiscum!"

"Et cum spiritu tuo!"

A young monk, the gatekeeper of the cloister, entered the cell. He was carrying a big, heavy package. As soon as Radominsky saw it, he put an end to his devotions.

"From Paris?"

"Yes, Reverend Father."

"Very good, set it on the table."

When the gatekeeper left the cell, Radominsky rose from his kneeling position. With gout-ridden fingers he untied the cord. He could hardly wait to hold the contents in his hands.

"Come, Holy Spirit," he whispered as he loosened the knot, reciting the devotion in Latin, "send from Heaven the radiance of Your light . . ."

Impatiently he tore off the wrapping. It was a book, bound in the finest Morocco leather: The eleventh and final illustrated volume of the *Encyclopedia*. He had received every volume of the great work; Sartine had sent them one after another over all these years since Radominsky had left Paris. Besides the *Summa Theologica* of Thomas Aquinas, the *Encyclopedia* was his only reading material in this holy seclusion.

"Perfect consoler, sweet guest of the soul, sweet coolness . . ."

So now the work was completed. Radominsky nodded. Diderot, his eternal foe, had continued the work undeterred despite the countless animosities and adversities to which he had been subjected; he had given up personal glory and had published nothing else—no dramas, no novels, no treatises—so as to devote his whole life to this one great task. Yes, Radominsky had always known it, ever since he had first met this man in the prison at Vincennes: They were very much alike, even though they had been at war with each other for an entire lifetime.

"Thou art repose in labor, refreshment in the heat, consolation through the tears . . ."

Radominsky opened the heavy book: "Printed by André-François Le Bréton, Royally appointed book printer to the King, Paris, Rue de la Harpe, 1772." He scrutinized the frontispiece. What hadn't he done to prevent this work from being published? He had employed all his powers, all his intellectual gifts and all his energies which the Lord had bestowed on him to put an end to the *Encyclopedia*. No effort had been too great for him, no peril too menacing—he had even committed a sin by repudiating the founder of his order, and risked his own salvation in order to serve the just cause. But God had decided otherwise. Why?

"O most blessed Light, fill the hearts of Thy believers . . ."

Radominsky shook his head. Had his efforts failed because of pride, because of his sin of *superbia* against the Holy Spirit, just as his Jesuit brothers in the faith had also failed? He had an inkling that humility was perhaps the only virtue that had never found a place in his heart, and therefore he must fear that the curse of Saint Francesco di Borgia would also be leveled against him. But Radominsky did not believe that this was the true cause of his defeat. A suspicion had been lodged in his chest for years, like an evil black serpent spraying its poison into his soul, the poison of doubt. Yes, Father Radominsky doubted—both God and himself. If it was God's will that this book should exist, if the Almighty had guided the gigantic ship of the *Encyclopedia* through all the storms of the times until it reached safe harbor almost unscathed, if thousands upon thousands of people were now able to read the teachings of the philosophers, the new order of things, which refuted metaphysics and religion in order to explain everything that happened on earth, from beginning to end, solely based on reason and experience—then, yes then, he, the Jesuit Radominsky, had misunderstood the signs. He had confused the cause and effect of God's will with human action, because it was not men but God Himself in His inscrutable ways Who had wanted this book to be created and had generated this triumph of knowledge over revelation.

"Without Thee we mortals are meaningless and empty, nothing is innocent . . ."

Radominsky licked a fingertip and began to page through the illustrated volume. Overwhelmed by its magnificence, he studied the pictures. It was as if in this book the entire creation of God were appearing before him in all its glory and magnitude. He saw deserts and oceans, animals and plants, people and their works. He saw how the progeny of Adam raised themselves up from the dust, how they tilled their fields and harvested their crops, how they made tools, wheels and plows and scythes, how they built houses and cities, churches and palaces, how they opened up the bodies of animals and human beings, invented all manner of equipment and machines, explored infinity with telescopes and used microscopes to examine tiny life-forms that no eye could see unaided; and how they split apart the aspects of life and then recombined them, in an eternal striving to subjugate the earth. The illustrations were of such perfection that it was easy to forget that they were merely depictions of true reality.

"Cleanse Thou the foul, quench the thirsty, heal the wounded . . ."

Only with effort could Radominsky bring himself to take his eyes off the book, which duplicated Creation in a manner as splendid as it was obscene. Then he closed the folio. But his thoughts found no rest. What was the secret concealed behind this work, the real and true reason Almighty God had wanted to include it in the great plan of Providence? With a sigh, Radominsky stroked the leather of the binding, slowly and tenderly, the way a lover caresses one last time a beautiful woman who refuses him her secret.

"Soften the hardened, warm the chilled, guide the lost . . ."

Radominsky looked out the open window. The view did his soul good. How beautiful and glorious God had made the world! The rumbling of the artillery had ceased, as if the war had yielded to the afternoon sunshine that had dipped the land in its golden light, like the light of eternal grace. The ripe grain in the fields billowed softly in the breeze; the air was filled with the humming of myriad creatures once more raising their voices before they sank into the great sleep of night. Radominsky was suddenly overcome by the feeling of humility that had always eluded him in the long years of his service to God; it was as though his senses opened for a brief moment to receive the message. Everything on earth that passed away, died in the service of life, subsumed in the progress of creation, which renewed itself over and over, striving toward its own perfection.

"Give to Thy faithful, who believe in Thee, the holy sevenfold gift . . ."

The thought struck Radominsky with such force that he had to gnash his teeth. Was this the secret behind the *Encyclopedia,* the reason this book had cast its spell over him from the beginning like the sinful beauty of a naked female body? The realization pained him like a thorny barb in his flesh, and in his heart he rebelled against it the way the Savior in the garden of Gethsemane had rebelled against the will of the Divine Father, in the desperate hope that this chalice would pass him by. Yet he understood the message of the Lord. He, Radominsky, soldier in the Society of Jesus, had not been able to stop the *Encyclopedia,* because the striving of humanity for knowledge and truth could not be suppressed. The growth of the spirit was an essential part of Creation; it was planned like the growth of the body, of the plants and animals and people—every living thing that God had created.

"Give the deserved reward for our virtue, give a healthy end, give eternal bliss!"

Radominsky lifted the book and stood up. Had his life been in vain? The question weighed like lead upon his shoulders; he was scarcely able to take the few steps to the bookshelf, as in the distance one last cannon boomed. The priest registered the sound with bitter satisfaction. No, the fight was not yet lost. What he had taken part in was only one battle, but the war would go on as long as human beings walked the earth. The eternal struggle between good and evil would not be decided until Judgment Day.

"Amen! Hallelujah!"

Radominsky made the sign of the Cross, then he set the folio on the bookshelf next to the other volumes; spine against spine they stood resplendent in his cell: the most important book of humanity since the Bible, the Book of Books.

What a wonderful, what a devilish work . . .

Where would it carry humanity?

EPILOGUE

The Scaffold

1794 / YEAR II

108

A new era had dawned. The storm of the revolution had passed over France, five long years of rage and fury that shook the land to its foundations. Not a stone was left atop another until the kingdom—whose rulers had believed themselves safe for centuries because of the grace of God, and who had then forfeited it all in a matter of a few decades in Heaven and on earth—came to an end in the flames of rebellion. It was like the blood-red setting sun after a summer day that had lasted too long. The whole edifice of power, decayed and foul, rotten from foundation to roof, collapsed forever, incapable of enduring even one blink of an eye longer against the violent storm of rebellion that had seized the people.

Yes, the great kraken had found the power to raise itself from its marshy bed and renew both its head and limbs. The French people had deposed their king and stormed the Bastille, which was the infamous prison of the old regime and the symbol of tyrannical cruelty; behind those thick, cold walls countless victims had met an atrocious end, nameless and without benefit of law. The families of the nobility, abandoning the oaths of fealty that their forefathers had made to the rulers of France, left the country in droves in order to save their necks and their property from the wrath of their former drudges and lackeys. The third estate took power. The national assembly, which now passed the laws, eliminated the class privileges of feudalism and replaced them with innate, inviolable, and inalienable human rights, which henceforth would protect the freedom and well-being of the citizens against the despotism of the state. The privileges connected to the ownership of land were abolished, the payment of the religious tithe was also repealed as well as hereditary nobility, and the assets of the church were confiscated and made the property of the people.

Had the golden age of reason arrived? The era when justice would prevail and neighbor would love neighbor? The paradise on earth in which human beings would no longer behave like wolves to other human beings, but everyone would be friends and brothers?

Beware the beast that uses reason to satisfy its desires! The new regime in the land had licked blood and did not want to settle for half the power. When the king attempted to leave the country like innumerable dukes and counts before him, a second wave of agitation arose that was even more violent than the first. The people were goaded on by the leaders of the revolutionary Paris Commune, in which all the hate and rage that had been bottled up during the times of bondage now rose up to be the primary power in the state. Storming the Bastille, they also attacked the royal gardens of the Tuileries. Louis XVI, having long ago been stripped of his omnipotence, was divested of his last powers and titles and taken into custody together with his family; as "Citizen Louis Capet" he was sentenced to death for treason and executed.

The republic was proclaimed, and to signal that the old times would never return, the National Assembly abolished the old calendar and introduced a new measurement of weeks, months, and years. This new calendar started at the elimination of the monarchy on September 22, 1792. Weeks were now divided into ten days, days into ten hours, and like the months they were all given new names. But while time passed as it always had done, only the names of the days, weeks, and months changed on the calendar pages; the murder and slaughter among people continued as it had since the world began. As though there had never been a revolutionary shift of power, the bloodbath at the Champs de Mars, in which hundreds of opponents of the king had once perished, was followed by the even bloodier September massacres, in which thousands of royalists lost their lives. And the atrocities of the Ancien Régime were followed by the reign of terror of the Jacobins, those merciless sons of the Enlightenment. Taking revenge for injustices hundreds of years old, they executed anyone who dared speak out against them and the new laws—with the sole difference that now the murders and massacres no longer were done in the name of Almighty God, but in the name of Liberty, Equality, and Fraternity.

109

❦ ❧

"Allons enfants de la patrie, le jour de gloire est arrivé . . ."

It was the third of Floréal of the Year II, or April 22, 1794, by the old calendar. A horde of schoolchildren crossed Sophie's path as she left Café Procope, where she had drunk a cup of chocolate to fortify herself for the difficult walk she had to make on this sunny spring morning. She was singing the "Marseillaise," the song of the Revolution, the strains of which had accompanied the killing of so many people. Was that why the people had learned to read and write?

Sophie too had sung the song of the Revolution, during the march of the women of Paris to Versailles in 1789, the year of the great famine. Thousands of mothers had set off on the road to the royal court, and more crowds joined in from every quarter and every suburb in order to force King Louis to supply the city with enough flour so that the bakers could bake bread again and the children would no longer have to starve. What wonderful hopes people had harbored back then . . .

And now? Marching two abreast like little soldiers, the schoolchildren entered the square by the Old Comédie, where a scaffold had been erected—there was one in every section of the city, to cope with all the executions that the new regime of the Jacobins demanded. The teachers visited the gruesome places with their pupils in order to show them an example of the blessings of the Revolution. For the condemned were no longer burned at the stake or drawn and quartered as under the old regime. Instead they were transported from life to death in a practical, scientific manner, beheaded with the help of an ingenious mechanism that a philanthropic doctor named Guillotin had invented.

The blood from the executions of the day before still stained the guillotine blade. Sophie saw how the schoolchildren were instructed by their teacher to climb up on the scaffold to take a close look, one by one, at the place of execution. Sophie herself had never had the chance to go to a real school—Abbé Morel's Communion preparation had been the only schooling she'd ever received, more than fifty years before. Now every child in France had the opportunity to learn to read and write. What a tremendous step forward. What appalling barbarity . . .

Sophie turned her eyes away from the children. Her goal was the prison of Port Libre in the suburb of Saint-Jacques, not far from the former Jansenist cloister of Port Royal, where more than six hundred prisoners had been interned as enemies of the Republic, waiting for trial or death. Despite her sixty-five years, Sophie had decided to make the journey on foot. One of the prisoners had asked to see her so he might speak with her one last time before his execution. At the thought of seeing him again her heart grew so heavy that she would have preferred to turn around and go back. But that was not possible. Even though she had decided a long time ago never to see this man again, she could not refuse his last wish.

Why had he called her to come and see him? What did he want from her?

Near the church of Saint-Germain-des-Prés Sophie left the boulevard and headed south via Rue de Rennes. Regardless of the Revolution, everyday life in the big city had hardly changed. In earlier times Paris had been named Lutetia, the city of mud—a name that Sophie thought was still justified. No matter how careful you were, nothing would protect you from the splashing of muck, filth, and excrement that was flung about everywhere by the brooms of the street sweepers and the coaches rattling past; many Parisians even claimed that the shoeshine boys were the most important servants in the entire city. Powdered and groomed women lifted their skirts to cross the streets so as not to dirty their hems; their companions walked on tiptoe next to them, trying not to get stains on their white half-stockings. Lemonade sellers made their way with their trays through the throng to the booths of the pastry bakers, sausage makers, and meat roasters, and the street vendors with their loud, shrill cries extolled to housewives and cooks their fish and meat, vegetables and fruit, trying to drown out the cacophony of the street musicians who produced a deafening noise on almost every street corner. No, the Parisians had changed as little as their city. They wanted only to live, love, and be happy—never mind who was ruling them at the moment.

After walking for three hours Sophie reached her destination. Before the gate of the prison two guards blocked her way.

"Halt! Your name?"

"Citizen Volland."

Sophie showed them a permit that Dorval had acquired for her. Her son was an influential man in the city; the Jacobins had appointed him commissioner of training and education.

"One moment, citizen."

The older of the two soldiers vanished into the building with her papers, while the younger one kept a watchful eye on her. To escape his scrutiny Sophie moved aside a few steps and gazed into the window of a nearby booklender.

In the fully stuffed shop window she discovered—among dog-eared novels and tattered dramas, philosophical treatises, almost untouched theological works, and countless scientific discourses—a complete set of the *Encyclopedia*: seventeen text volumes and eleven illustrated ones. The maroon linen covers were spotted and stained, worn out by people thirsting for knowledge; for years they had rented these volumes and looked things up, dipping again and again into the inexhaustible wealth of human knowledge.

Sophie heaved a deep sigh. How this book had changed her life. How this book had changed the world. And now the man who had made it possible, without whom it never would have been published, sat in a prison cell waiting for her. For her and for death—a sentence handed down by other, younger men who were, ironically enough, his spiritual sons.

"Citizen Volland?"

Sophie turned around. In the prison doorway stood the older guard, waving her permit to motion her forward.

"The prisoner is ready!"

110

When Sophie entered the cell, an unfamiliar old man stood before her. She looked at him with annoyance. Had they led her to the wrong prisoner? In her confusion she almost turned around, but then she saw a smile in his gray eyes.

"Thank you for coming."

She gave a start when she heard his voice. "Monsieur de Malesherbes?"

It took a while before she recognized his face behind the old, wizened features. All at once her heart started pounding. They hadn't seen each other in a quarter of a century, ever since the day he had confessed to her how he had betrayed her mother.

"I had hoped," he said softly, "you would wear your amulet."

"The angel?" she asked, astonished. "You always used to say you didn't like it."

"Yes, I know. But perhaps it would have brought me some luck on my last journey."

"Luck?"

Malesherbes hesitated. Then he said, "I know this sort of amulet from my hometown. They are made from the bones of those who have been executed. I wanted to ask you for the talisman as a last gift to take with me to the grave. For my salvation, and . . ." he added haltingly, "to free you from it."

Sophie didn't understand what he meant by that. Sartine had given her the pendant; he brought it home from Beaulieu, after he had searched through the church archives. But when she saw the boundless sadness in Malesherbes's eyes, a thought came to her like a cold breath of evening, and she suddenly felt chilled. Was the amulet, the only memento she possessed of her village, this talisman she had worn at her throat for half a lifetime, possibly . . . ? The idea was so intolerable that she forced herself to push it away. The past was so long ago. And the present posed so many questions.

"Why did they convict you?" she asked. "Because you defended the king before the revolutionary tribunal?"

"The court found that I had conspired against the liberty of the French people. But does it even matter?"

"You—a conspirator against liberty?" Sophie shook her head. "As long as I've known you, you have fought for the cause of liberty—for liberty and for enlightenment. Don't these people know that?"

Malesherbes shrugged his shoulders. "They are blinded, Sophie. By their hatred and by their principles, which may cause even more damage than their hatred. They are filled with the idea of justice, but they pursue this justice with the same fanaticism that the Jesuits showed in their fight for the divine grace of the king. They know only the logic of the mind, and they act solely from calculated reason. They have no love."

Sophie nodded. She had said almost the same words to her son, who defended the rule of the Jacobins as a cruel but indispensable necessity for progress.

"Sometimes," she whispered, "I get the feeling that the world is darker than ever."

"No, you mustn't speak that way," said Malesherbes. "The tiniest spark of enlightenment always shines brighter than the dark moon of superstition. Don't forget that we're still at the very beginning, and after us, many more people will come. Enlightenment cannot be achieved with a single effort of will, and no matter how strong that effort might be, it is a Sisyphean task, a task that is constantly renewed, and each generation will have to keep working at it in their own way. The *Encyclopedia* opened up a gigantic portal for humanity, and now it's up to humanity to step through it. But to do that, people have to learn to follow not only their reason, but also their hearts."

Sophie looked out through the bars on the window. In the crown of an apple tree on a freshly blossomed twig a sparrow perched, preening its feathers so assiduously that it didn't notice the cat slinking toward it. Sophie turned back to Malesherbes.

"Do you think that such a time will ever come?"

"Who knows?" he replied. "Perhaps I'm mistaken and my dream is only an empty illusion, the nattering of a senile old man. Nevertheless, I hold on to it because faith and hope and love count no less than understanding and experience and reason. Because people have a will to live only as long as they believe in a better future, full of hope and love. And that's the most important thing."

"You can say that?" asked Sophie. "On the day of your execution?"

He gave her a sad smile. "I am now seventy-two years old," he said, "old enough to endure justice. Even when it takes detours and goes astray in its attempt to be validated. I deserve death and I'm ready to die. Not because I defended the king or might be a conspirator, but because I—"

He fell silent. Sophie looked at him. She also understood without words what he was trying to tell her. Yes, now she knew why he had called her to come here.

As if he had guessed her thoughts, he pronounced the one, all-important question: "Can you forgive me, Sophie?"

She cast down her eyes. Although she'd been expecting that question, she couldn't give him an answer. No matter how long ago the events of the past, the wounds that he had caused still pained her soul. So many other questions were connected to this one question . . . How would her life have turned out if her mother had been allowed to live? Perhaps she would never have had this feeling of anxiety that had haunted her all her life, the fear of love, the fear of books . . . Maybe she would have lived for years and decades by Diderot's side, as the happiest woman in the world. Would she have? Really? Maybe she never would have met Diderot if it wasn't for Malesherbes, maybe she would never have left her village. Maybe, maybe, maybe.

Without consciously deciding what to say, Sophie began to speak. The words simply came of their own accord.

"When Diderot died ten years ago," she said softly, "they dissected his body—at his request. Even after death he wanted to contribute to increasing knowledge about the nature of human beings and the riddle of existence. Above all, the doctors were interested in his brain, which had stored such an incredible amount of knowledge and had produced so many ideas. They wanted to study the type and manner of his thinking, but their expectations were not fulfilled. It turned out that it wasn't his brain that exhibited special characteristics, but his heart; it was about two-thirds larger than that of a normal person."

Malesherbes listened to her without a word, his steady gaze filled with an uneasy sense of hope. When she finished speaking he closed his tired eyes. Then he bent over her hand to kiss it.

He remained in that position for a long while, a moment frozen in eternity.

When he straightened up, his eyes were shining with tears.

"Thank you," he said quietly but in a firm voice. "Now I have found my peace and can finally die."

Without another word he turned and looked out the window. Sophie understood that this was farewell. Despite his age his posture was erect as he stood there, dressed as before in a brown coat of simple material, the plait of his three-knot wig carelessly hanging down his back.

"You shall have the amulet," she whispered. "I will give it to you for your journey."

Then she left the cell.

When she stepped outside she encountered bright sunshine. Before the portal Dorval was waiting. Her son had come to fetch her. His wife was expecting a baby, and Sophie had promised to assist with the birth.

She took his arm, and as a drum roll sounded in the distance they walked to the coach that stood waiting for them on the square.

The labor pains had already started, so they had to hurry.

Acknowledgments

"Gratitude," Diderot wrote in the *Encyclopedia*, "is a burden, and every burden wants to be shaken off." Here the master is mistaken, thank God! For me it is not an uncomfortable burden, but a welcome pleasure to thank everyone who contributed to the genesis of this novel, including in particular:

Roman Hocke. He made sure that I did not lose myself in the seas of historical possibilities or stray from the course of my story.

Serpil Prange. For her clear insight into so many things, from which I am always learning.

Hans Jörg Hämmerling. His insistence on advancing the human condition has (I hope) brought me a few millimeters forward.

Christina Spittel. Not only for her research, which spared me from many an embarrassment, but also for her comments, as impertinent as they were intelligent.

Stephan Triller. Through our frequent phone conversations he has helped me with almost all my books. Offering advice from *A* to *Z*, but above all from *K* to *K*.

Brigitte Dörr. She kept reminding me of Paris. And thus brought me back to my theme with the unerring tenacity of a will-o'-the-wisp.

Helmut Henkensiefken. For his creative imagination and his constant readiness to start over at "zero."

What would an author be without his publishing house? Last but not least I would like to thank the management and colleagues of Droemer Verlag, who have given me the best support that any author could wish for. Susanne Klein, Klaus Kluge, Beate Kuckertz, Herbert Neumaier, Christian Tesch, and Hans-Peter Übleis—they made my story into a book.

Fiction and Truth

There was a mysterious woman in Diderot's life: Sophie Volland. For decades she lived at his side, and yet we do not know who she really was or how close her relationship was with him. All we know is what is contained in the letters that Diderot wrote to her—and it is only because of a last will and testament written in her own hand that we know she was a real person.

In the character of a female philosopher I have attempted to give this woman an identity and a history. It is my way of gaining access to the world of the *Encyclopedia* and of presenting a narrative showing the great intellectual drama of the eighteenth century: the demands of the Enlightenment for a happiness to be found inside each individual, which required rebelling against theological dogma and rejecting the notion of a paradise after death. The following events that are mentioned in the novel have been confirmed through my research.

1745: In this year the last trials against witches, sorcerers, and magicians are held in France. The laws enacted during the reign of Louis XIV are still valid, stating that any attempted murder using poison is identical to magic, since both made use of the same potions. February—At a masked ball Madame de Pompadour ensnares King Louis XV. As a result, two factions are formed at court in Versailles: on one side a circle of enlightened individuals surrounding the new favorite of the monarch, and on the other side a party of devotees supporting Queen Maria Leszczynska and her Polish father confessor Radominsky.

1746: Royal printing privilege is granted for the *Encyclopedia*; the original plan of the consortium of printers under the leadership of Le Bréton, the royally appointed book printer to the king, is an expanded translation of Chambers's *Cyclopaedia* from English.

1747: Diderot writes *The Indiscreet Jewels,* motivated by the demands of his mistress Madame de Puisieux; Le Bréton persuades Diderot and d'Alembert to become the editors of the *Encyclopedia;* the project develops into an independent enterprise. April 30—Renewal of the printing privilege. October 18—End of editors' contract.

1748: In January *The Indiscreet Jewels* is published; commencement of work on the *Encyclopedia;* the editors convince well-known philosophers and scientists to contribute articles; the Paris police begin systematic surveillance of suspicious literati and their activities; by 1753 there are dossiers on around five hundred authors.

1749: Diderot's "Letter Concerning the Blind" appears anonymously. July 24—Diderot is arrested; interrogation and transfer to Vincennes; the publishers cease payments to their editors, and Diderot has to ask his father to support his family. August 13—Diderot signs a written confession and vows good behavior in the future. September—Rousseau visits Diderot in prison, and they discuss the prize-winning essays of the Académie Dijon. November 3—Diderot is released from custody; he breaks off his relationship with Madame de Puisieux.

1750: Rousseau introduces Diderot to Grimm and d'Holbach; General State Councillor Malesherbes, son of Chancellor Lamoignon, becomes director of the Royal Library and chief of the censorship authority. November—the advance prospectus of the *Encyclopedia* appears, provoking the first counterattacks by the Jesuits.

1751: June 24—Release of Volume I. Editorial highlights: the preface and the Tree of Knowledge. Delivery begins on June 28; enthusiastic reception by the public; intensified attacks by the Jesuits; Diderot makes Jaucourt a fellow author and co-worker.

1752: January 1—Release of Volume II; scandal about the article "Certitude" by the theologian de Prades; the "de Prades case" turns into the "*Encyclopedia* case"; Diderot asks the mistress of the king, Madame de Pompadour, for help, but his plea is in vain. January 29—Public condemnation of the *Encyclopedia* by the archbishop of Paris. February 7—Volumes I and II are banned, and the publication of all further volumes is prohibited. February 25—Malesherbes warns Diderot of a house search that he has ordered, and helps him remove incriminating material; d'Alembert considers for the first time quitting his co-editorship; de Prades flees with the aid of Voltaire to Prussia; rumors circulate that Diderot also wants to flee the country; an attempt is made by the Jesuits of Trévoux to take over the *Encyclopedia*. The gunpowder anecdote: Madame de Pompadour convinces King Louis of the usefulness of the *Encyclopedia*. April—The government allows the publishers and editors to continue the project; the *Encyclopedia* henceforth appears under tightened censorship conditions, without the royal approval of the king, but with his tacit permission. Result of the scandal: sudden fame of the *Encyclopedia* all over France and Europe, and the number of subscribers climbs dramatically; Diderot is nominated for membership in the Royal Society and d'Alembert in the Académie Française.

1753: February—Diderot is rejected by the Royal Society; birth of his daughter, Angélique. November 15—Volume III of the *Encyclopedia* is published.

1754: De Prades publicly recants his "errors." October 14—Volume IV of the *Encyclopedia* is published in an edition of 3,000; Diderot negotiates a new, improved contract with Le Bréton; his family moves from Rue de l'Estrapade to Rue Taranne, where Diderot will live and work for the next thirty years; the Jesuits create the journal *L'année littéraire*, the main task of which is to combat the *Encyclopedia*. November 30—d'Alembert is admitted into the Académie Française.

1755: First attested meeting between Diderot and Sophie Volland; Voltaire settles in Geneva; enraged reactions of his rival Rousseau, who believes his home city to be lost because of Voltaire's presence; Volume V of the *Encyclopedia* with Diderot's article "Encyclopédie" is published. November—The court painter La Tour finishes his portrait of Madame de Pompadour, which shows the mistress of the king holding Volume IV of the *Encyclopedia*.

1756: Outbreak of the Seven Years' War; elevation of Madame de Pompadour to *femme d'honneur* of the queen; first visible signs of her physical deterioration as well as the start of her insidious loss of power; d'Alembert continues to distance himself from the *Encyclopedia*.

1757: January 5—The former lackey Robert Damiens attempts an assassination of the king; the assailant is mentioned in association with the *Encyclopedia*; the government increases its pressure on Malesherbes to proceed against the philosophers. February—Diderot's drama *The Natural Son* appears. March 7—Voltaire asks d'Alembert to complete the *Encyclopedia* in Switzerland. March 28—Damiens's execution staged as a great spectacle to deter other potential enemies of the state. April 16 to August 27—Tightening of the laws with threat of the death penalty for any inflammatory writings as a result of the attack on the king; many authors refuse any further association with the *Encyclopedia*. October 15—Première of *The Cacouacs*, a satire about the philosophers. October to December—"Trials and tribulations" at the country manor house La Chevrette—Rousseau has a falling-out with Diderot. November—Volume VII of the *Encyclopedia* with d'Alembert's article "Geneva" appears.

1758: Attacks in France and from abroad against d'Alembert's article "Geneva," with Rousseau as its sharpest critic. January—D'Alembert resigns co-editorship of the *Encyclopedia*, and Diderot is now the sole editor; Voltaire demands that Diderot return his manuscripts. December—Helvétius's essay "On the Spirit" appears, and church and state react with furious attacks; Diderot is assumed to be the co-author of the essay, and the *Encyclopedia* thus comes under attack.

1759: January 23—"On the Spirit" and the *Encyclopedia* are simultaneously condemned by the parliament. March 4—The *Encyclopedia* is put on the Index by the Vatican; Malesherbes officially revokes permission for publication and advises Diderot to flee Paris; Diderot refuses to leave the capital, and then experiences depression and anxiety upon being arrested. Crisis meeting of the editor and publisher: final break with d'Alembert. June 3—Diderot's father dies in Langres. July 21—Malesherbes's "compromise of Solomon": the censor grants permission for a *collection of one thousand plates about the sciences, the free arts, and* *technology* to be printed, a camouflage designation for the illustrated volumes of the *Encyclopedia*. Condition for the permission to print: the publishers must pay a penalty of seventy-two *livres* to each subscriber as damages for the forbidden text volumes. July 25—Diderot travels to Langres to settle his father's estate; decides in the future no longer to publish any of his own writings that might jeopardize the *Encyclopedia*. A sigh of relief on his return to Paris: the subscribers settle for the illustrated volumes as compensation for the text volumes. September 3—All Catholics are forbidden to read the *Encyclopedia* by order of the pope and under threat of excommunication; on the same day, nine Jesuits are sentenced to death because of an attack on King Joseph I. September 8—Confirmation of the printing privilege for the illustrated volumes; Diderot continues working in secret as sole editor with a reduced staff on the remaining ten text volumes. November 24—The king grants Antoine Sartine a noble title and also offers personal financial support to make him police prefect of Paris; the first verified letters of Diderot to Sophie Volland.

1760: March—Violent attacks by the devotees; the Comédie Française becomes a new battleground with the performance of Palissot's satire *The Philosophers*. July—Voltaire's counterattack with *Les Écossaises,* a satire about the Jesuits; Voltaire's attempt to make Diderot a member of the Académie only further strengthens resistance to the *Encyclopedia*.

1761: Work continues on the text volumes thanks to the tireless collaboration of Jaucourt; Le Bréton begins toning down hundreds of contributions to the *Encyclopedia* behind Diderot's back. The plan of the publisher and his editor: to print the remaining text volumes at a fictitious location "abroad," and then re-import them to Paris.

1762: Delivery of the first illustrated volumes to subscribers. August—The parliament dissolves the Jesuit Order because of unrest at the Central American mission stations. Invitation from Tsarina Catherine II to complete the *Encyclopedia* in Russia; Diderot declines with reference to the publisher's copyright.

1763: Chancellor Lamoignon falls out of favor, and his son Malesherbes resigns; rapid physical deterioration of Madame de Pompadour; Sartine is promoted to chief of the censorship authority; end of the Seven Years' War.

1764: April 15—Madame de Pompadour dies at Versailles. November 12— Diderot discovers that his publisher Le Bréton has censored the last ten volumes of the *Encyclopedia* on his own authority; Diderot confronts the ruins of his life, succumbing to depression and gluttony.

1765: Completion of the last text volumes amid conflicting emotions; all the work is now being done by Jaucourt, who at his own expense hires a half dozen writers and consequently has to sell his house; Diderot begins work on *Jacques the Fatalist*; the last ten volumes printed in Paris are warehoused in a suburb of the capital.

1766: Simultaneous delivery of the last ten text volumes of the *Encyclopedia*. End result: Diderot is full of contempt for his own work, Jaucourt is ruined, and the booksellers make fantastic profits. April—Le Bréton is turned in and arrested and taken to the Bastille; Diderot intervenes on behalf of the publisher and Le Bréton is released; Diderot is celebrated as the savior of the *Encyclopedia*, while Le Bréton buys Jaucourt's last house. Diderot's bitter realization: He has sacrificed his whole life as well as all his unwritten masterpieces for a flawed *Encyclopedia*.

1767: Diderot is admitted to the Petersburg Academy of Arts and invited by Tsarina Catherine to Russia; Diderot rents a room in Sèvres where he can spend time away from his family.

1768: The publisher Panckoucke acquires the rights to all future editions of the *Encyclopedia*; Panckoucke offers Diderot the job of supervising a new edition; Diderot declines the offer so that he can complete the editing of the illustrated volumes.

1769: *D'Alembert's Dream* is published, Diderot's literary-philosophical reconciliation with his former comrade-in-arms.

1772: Delivery of the last illustrated volume of the *Encyclopedia* to subscribers.

1784: July 31—Diderot dies of heart failure, and according to his wishes his body is dissected; according to the autopsy report, his heart is two-thirds larger than that of a normal person.

1789: The year of the Revolution: the storming of the Bastille, the hunger march of the women of Paris to Versailles, gradual degradation of the king's power, abolition of class privileges, Declaration of the Rights of Man, and establishment of the National Assembly.

1793: Malesherbes defends King Louis XVI before the Revolutionary Tribunal against the charge of treason.

1794: Malesherbes is sentenced to death for "conspiracy against the liberty of the French people" and executed on April 22.